BY IAN RANKIN

Ian Rankin

writing as Jack Harvey

Bleeding Hearts

ORION

An Orion paperback
First published in Great Britain by Headline in 1994
This paperback edition published in 2001 by
Orion Books Ltd,
Orion House, 5 Upper St Martin's Lane, London WC2H 9EA

A CIP catalogue record for this book is available from the British Library.

ISBN: 0 75284 332 X

Typeset by Deltatype Ltd, Birkenhead, Merseyside

Printed and bound in Great Britain by
Clays Ltd, St Ives plc

For Elliott and Fawn

Part One

1

She had just over three hours to live, and I was sipping grapefruit juice and tonic in the hotel bar.

'You know what it's like these days,' I said, 'only the toughest are making it. No room for bleeding hearts.'

My companion was a businessman himself. He too had survived the highs and lows of the 80s, and he nodded as vigorously as the whisky in him would allow.

'Bleeding hearts,' he said, 'are for the operating table, not for business.'

'I'll drink to that,' I said, though of course in my line of work bleeding hearts *are* the business.

Gerry had asked me a little while ago what I did for a living, and I'd told him export-import, then asked what he did. See, I slipped up once; I manufactured a career for myself only to find the guy I was drinking with was in the same line of work. Not good. These days I'm better, much cagier, and I don't drink on the day of a hit. Not a drop. Not any more. Word was, I was slipping. Bullshit naturally, but sometimes rumours are difficult to throw off. It's not as though I could put an ad in the newspapers. But I knew a few good clean hits would give the lie to this particular little slander.

Then again, today's hit was no prize: it had been handed to me, a gift. I knew where she'd be and what she'd be doing. I didn't just know what she looked like, I knew pretty well what she'd be wearing. I knew a whole lot about her. I wasn't going to have to work for this one, but prospective future employers wouldn't know that. All they'd see was the score sheet. Well, I'd take all the easy targets going.

'So what do you buy and sell, Mark?' Gerry asked.

I was Mark Wesley. I was English. Gerry was English too, but as international businessmen we spoke to one another in mid-Atlantic: the lingua franca of the deal. We were jealous of our American cousins, but would never admit it.

'Whatever it takes, Gerry,' I said.

'I'm into that.' Gerry toasted me with whisky. It was 3 pm local time. The whiskies were six quid a hit, not much more than my own soft drink. I've drunk in hotel bars all over the western world, and this one looked like all of them. Dimly lit even in daytime, the same bottles behind the polished bar, the same liveried barman pouring from them. I find the sameness comforting. I hate to go to a strange place, somewhere where you can't find any focus, anything recognisable to grab on to. I hated Egypt: even the Coke signs were written in Arabic, and all the numerals were wrong, plus everyone was wearing the wrong clothes. I hate Third World countries; I won't do hits there unless the money is particularly interesting. I like to be somewhere with clean hospitals and facilities, dry sheets on the bed, English-speaking smiles.

'Well, Gerry,' I said, 'been nice talking to you.'

'Same here, Mark.' He opened his wallet and eased out a business card. 'Here, just in case.'

I studied it. Gerald Flitch, Marketing Strategist. There was a company name, phone, fax and carphone number, and an address in Liverpool. I put the card in my pocket, then patted my jacket.

'Sorry, I can't swap. No cards on me just now.'

'That's all right.'

'But the drinks are on me.'

'Well, I don't know—'

'My pleasure, Gerry.' The barman handed me the bill, and I signed my name and room number. 'After all,' I said, 'you never know when I might need a favour.'

4

Gerry nodded. 'You need friends in business. A face you can trust.'

'It's true, Gerry, it's all about trust in our game.'

Obviously, as you can see, I was in philosophical mood.

Back up in my room, I put out the Do Not Disturb sign, locked the door, and wedged a chair under the handle. The bed had already been made, the bathroom towels changed, but you couldn't be too careful. A maid might look in anyway. There was never much of a pause between them knocking at your door and them unlocking it.

I took the suitcase from the bottom of the wardrobe and laid it on the bed, then checked the little Sellotape seal I'd left on it. The seal was still intact. I broke it with my thumbnail and unlocked the suitcase. I lifted out some shirts and T-shirts until I came to the dark blue raincoat. This I lifted out and laid on the bed. I then pulled on my kid-leather driving-gloves before going any further. With these on, I unfolded the coat. Inside, wrapped in polythene, was my rifle.

It's impossible to be too careful, and no matter how careful you are you leave traces. I try to keep up with advances in forensic science, and I know all of us leave traces wherever we are: fibres, hairs, a fingerprint, a smear of grease from a finger or arm. These days, they can match you from the DNA in a single hair. That's why the rifle was wrapped in polythene: it left fewer traces than cloth.

The gun was beautiful. I'd cleaned it carefully in Max's workshop, then checked it for identifiers and other distinguishing marks. Max does a good job of taking off serial numbers, but I always like to be sure. I'd spent some time with the rifle, getting to know it, its weight and its few foibles. I'd practised over several days, making sure I got rid of all the spent bullets and cartridge cases, just so the gun couldn't be traced back to them. Every gun leaves particular and unique marks on a bullet. I didn't believe that at first either, but apparently it's true.

The ammo was a problem. I didn't really want to tamper with it. Each cartridge case carries a head stamp, which identifies it. I'd tried filing off the head stamps from a few cartridges, and they didn't seem to make any difference to the accuracy of my shooting. But on the day, *nothing* could go wrong. So I asked Max and he said the bullets could be traced back to a consignment which had accompanied the British Army units to Kuwait during the Gulf War. (I didn't ask how Max had got hold of them; probably the same source as the rifle itself.) See, some snipers like to make their own ammo. That way they know they can trust it. But I'm not skilled that way, and I don't think it matters anyway. Max sometimes made up ammo for me, but his eyes weren't so great these days.

The ammo was .338 Lapua Magnum. It was full metal-jacket: military stuff usually is, since it fulfils the Geneva Convention's requirements for the most 'humane' type of bullet.

Well, I'm no animal, I wasn't about to contravene the Geneva Convention.

Max had actually been able to offer a choice of weapons. That's why I use him. He asks few questions and has excellent facilities. That he lives in the middle of nowhere is a bonus, since I can practise all day without disturbing anyone. Then there's his daughter Belinda, who would be bonus enough in herself. I always take her a present if I've been away somewhere. Not that I'd . . . you know, not with Max about. He's very protective of her, and she of him. They remind me of Beauty and the Beast. Bel's got short fair hair, eyes slightly slanted like a cat's, and a long straight nose. Her face looks like it's been polished. Max on the other hand has been battling cancer for years. He's lost about a quarter of his face, I suppose, and keeps his right side, from below the eye to just above the lips, covered with a white plastic prosthesis. Sometimes Bel calls him the Phantom of the Opera. He takes it from her. He wouldn't take it from anyone else.

I think that's why he's always pleased to see me. It's not just that I have cash on me and something I want, but he doesn't see many people. Or rather, he doesn't let many people see him. He spends all day in his workshop, cleaning, filing, and polishing his guns. And he spends a lot of his nights there, too.

He had a Remington 700, pre-fitted with a Redfield telescopic sight. The US Marines use this military version of the 'Varmint' as sniper rifles. I'd used one before, and had nothing against it. More interesting though was a Sterling Sniper Rifle. Most people I'd met thought only cars were made in Dagenham, but that's where the Sterling was crafted. It was user-friendly, down to the cheek-rest and the grooved receiver. You could fit it with any mounting-plate you wanted, to accommodate any telescope or night-sight. I admit, it was tempting.

There were others, too. Max didn't have them, but he knew where he could get them: an L39A1, the ugly Mauser SP66, a Fusil Modele 1 Type A. I decided I wanted British; call me sentimental. And finally Max handed over the gun we'd both known I'd opt for: a Model PM.

The manufacturers, Accuracy International, call it the PM. I don't know what the letters stand for, maybe Post-Mortem. But the British Army know it as Sniper Rifle L96A1. A mouthful, you'll agree, which is why Max and I stick to calling it the PM. There are several versions, and Max was offering the Super Magnum (hence the .338 Lapua Magnum ammo). The gun itself is not what you'd call a beauty, and as I unwrapped it in my hotel room it looked even less lovely, since I'd covered its camouflage with some camouflage of my own.

The PM is olive green in colour, fine if you are hiding in the trees, but not so inconspicuous when surrounded by the grey concrete of a city street. So in Max's workshop I'd wound some grey adhesive tape around it, wearing my gloves all the time so as not to leave prints on the tape. As a result, the PM now looked like the ballistic equivalent of the Invisible Man, all bandaged except for the bits I needed left open to access. It was a neat job of binding; the wrapping around the stainless-steel barrel alone had taken a couple of hours.

The PM is a long rifle, its barrel nearly four inches longer than the Remington. It's also heavy, to say that it's mostly plastic, albeit high-impact plastic: double the weight of the Remington, and over four pounds heavier than the Sterling. I didn't mind though, it wasn't as if I'd be carrying it through the jungle. I made it even longer by fitting a flash hider of my own construction. (Max smiled with half of his face as he watched me. Like me, he is an admirer of beauty and craft, and the best you could say of my finished product was that it worked.)

All the guns Max had offered me were bolt-action, all were 7.62mm, and all had barrels with four grooves and a right-hand twist. They differed in styles and muzzle velocity, in length and weight, but they shared one common characteristic. They were all lethal.

In the end, I decided I didn't require the integral bipod: the angle I'd be shooting from, it would hinder rather than help. So I took that off, minimally reducing the weight. Although the PM accepts a 10-round box, I knew I'd have two bullets at most, preferably only one. With bolt-action rifles, you sometimes didn't have time for a second shot. While you were working the bolt, your quarry was scuttling to safety.

I picked the gun up at last, and stood in my bedroom staring into the full-length mirror on the wardrobe door. The curtains were closed, so I was able to do this. I'd already fitted the telescopic sight. Ah, Max had made things *so* difficult. He could give me a Redfield, a Parker-Hale, the Zeiss Diavari ZA . . . even the old No. 32 sniping telescope.

But the PM wasn't geared up for these, so instead of fussing and having to make my own special sight-mounting plate, I opted for a Schmidt and Bender 6×42 telescopic sight, all the time telling myself I was maybe, for once, going to too much trouble.

I was ready to pick off a flea from a cat's whisker at 600 yards, when all I had to do was hit a human target, out in the open, at something like a tenth of that. What was I doing buying all this lavish craft and expertise when something bashed together in China would achieve the same objective? Max had an answer.

'You like quality, you like style.'

True, Max, true. If my targets were suddenly to depart this world, I wanted them to have the best send-off I could give them. I checked my watch, then double-checked with the clock-radio.

She had just over two hours to live.

2

Everything was waiting for Eleanor Ricks.

She'd woken that morning after a drugged sleep, knowing yet another day was waiting out there, ready to bite her. Breakfast and her husband Freddy were waiting in the kitchen, as was Mrs Elfman. When Eleanor and Freddy were both working, Mrs Elfman came in and got breakfast ready, then cleaned everything away and tidied the rooms. When they weren't working, she did the cleaning but no cooking. Freddy insisted that one or other of them *had* to be capable of preparing cereal or sausage and eggs and a pot of coffee, so long as their minds weren't on work. Funny, usually Eleanor ended up cooking if Mrs Elfman wasn't around, even if she'd to go to work while Freddy was 'resting'. Today, however, was a work day for both of them.

Freddy Ricks was an actor, of consequence (albeit in TV sitcoms) in the early 80s but now squeezing a living from 'character' parts and not many of them. He'd tried some stage acting but didn't like it, and had wasted a good deal of their joint savings by spending fruitless time in Hollywood, trying to call up favours from producers and directors who'd moved on from British TV. Today, he was starring in a commercial for breakfast cereal. It would be head and shoulders only, and he'd be wearing a yellow oilskin sou'wester and a puzzled expression. He had two lines to say, but they'd dub another actor's voice on later. Freddy couldn't understand why his own voice wasn't good enough for them. It had, as he pointed out, been quite good enough for the 12 million viewers who'd tuned in to *Stand By Your Man* every week of its runs in 1983–4.

He sat at the table munching cornflakes and reading his preferred tabloid. He looked furious, but then these days he always looked furious. The radio sat on the draining board, volume turned down low because Freddy didn't like it. But Mrs Elfman liked it, and she angled her head towards the transistor, trying to catch the words, while at the same time washing last night's dishes.

'Morning, Mrs E.'

'Morning, Mrs Ricks, how did you sleep?'

'Like a log, thanks.'

'All right for some,' Freddy muttered from behind his cereal spoon. Eleanor ignored him, and so did Mrs Elfman. Eleanor poured herself a mug of black coffee.

'Want some breakfast, Mrs Ricks?'

'No thanks.'

'It's the most important meal of the day.'

'I'm still full from last night.' This was a lie, but what else could she say: if I eat a single morsel I'm liable to be throwing up all morning? Mrs Elfman would think she was joking.

'Is Archie up?'

'Who knows?' growled Freddy.

Archie was their son, seventeen years old and the 'computer player' in a pop group. Eleanor had never heard of anyone 'playing' the computer as a musical instrument, until Archie had shown her. Now his band were making their second record, their first having been a success in local clubs. She went to the bottom of the stairs and called him. There was no answer.

'He's like bloody Dracula,' complained Freddy. 'Never seen in daylight hours.' Mrs Elfman threw him a nasty look, and Eleanor went through to her study.

Eleanor Ricks was a freelance investigative journalist who had somehow managed to make a name for herself without recourse to the usual 'investigations' of pop stars, media celebrities, and royalty. But then one day she'd found that magazines wanted to send round journalists to profile *her*, and she'd started to rethink her career. So now, after years of newspaper and magazine articles, she was finally going into television – just, it seemed, as Freddy was moving out of it. Poor Freddy: she gave him a moment's thought, then started work.

Today she was interviewing Molly Prendergast, the Secretary of State for Social Security. They were meeting at a central hotel. They wouldn't be talking about anything concerning the Department of Social Security, or Molly Prendergast's position there, or even her standing in her own political party. It was much more personal, which was why they were meeting in a hotel rather than at the Department's offices.

It was Eleanor's idea. She reckoned she'd get more out of Molly Prendergast on neutral ground. She didn't want to hear a politician talking; she wanted to hear a mother . . .

She went through her notes again, her list of questions, press clippings, video footage. She spoke with her researchers and assistant by phone. This was an initial interview, not intended for broadcast. Eleanor would take a tape recording, but just for her own use. There wouldn't be any cameras or technicians there, just two women having a chat and a drink. Then, if Prendergast looked useful to the project, there'd be a request for a proper on-screen interview, asking the same or similar questions again. Eleanor knew that the Molly Prendergast she got today would not be the one she'd get at a later date. On screen, the politician would be much more cautious, more guarded. But Eleanor would use her anyway: Prendergast was a name, and this story needed a name to get it some publicity. Or so Joe kept telling her.

The batteries for her tape recorder had been charging up overnight. She checked them, taping her voice then winding it back to listen. The recorder, though small, had a stereo microphone built into it and a tiny but powerful external speaker. She would take three C90 tapes with her, though it was expected to be an hour-long interview. Well, it might overrun, or a tape might snap. What was she thinking of? It wouldn't overrun. Two C90s would do it. But she'd best take a lot of batteries.

She rewound the video compilation and studied it again, then went to her computer and tweaked some of her questions, deleting one and adding two new ones. She printed off this new sheet and read it over one more time. Then she faxed it to her producer, who phoned back with the okay.

'You're sure?' Eleanor asked.

'I'm sure. Look, don't worry about this, Lainie.' She hated him calling her 'Lainie'. One day, she'd tell him to his face ... No, that wasn't true, was it? It was a small price to pay for Joe Draper's backing. Joe was an excellent producer, if, like so many of his television colleagues, a bit of a prima donna. He'd earned his money doing a cop drama series and a couple of sitcoms (one of them with Freddy playing the errant next-door neighbour), then had set up his own production company, which specialised in documentaries and docu-dramas. These were good days for independent producers, so long as you knew your market and had a few contacts in the TV broadcasting companies. Joe had plenty of friends: his weekend coke parties at his home in Wiltshire were *very* popular. He'd invited her along a couple of times, but had neglected to invite Freddy.

'You forget, Joe, I'm new to this, I can't be laid back like you.' Okay, so she was fishing for a compliment, and of course, Joe knew it.

'Lainie, you're the best. Just do what you're best at. Talk to her, open her up, then sit back and look interested. That's it. You know, like you were a . . .' Here it came, another of Joe's tortured similes. 'A lion tamer. You go in there, crack your whip, and when she starts to do the trick, you can relax and take the applause.'

'You really think it's that simple, Joe?'

'No, it's hard work. But the secret is, don't make it *look* like hard work. It should be smooth like the baize on a snooker table, so smooth she doesn't know she's been potted till she's falling into the pocket.' He laughed then, and she laughed with him, amazed at herself. 'Look, Lainie, this is going to be good TV, I can feel it. You've got a great idea, and you're going about it the right way: human interest. It's been a winning formula since TV had nappies on. Now go to it!'

She smiled tiredly. 'All right, Joe, I will.' Then she put down the phone.

Satisfied, Eleanor phoned for a bike messenger. She wrote a covering note, put it with a copy of the questions into a large manila envelope, and wrote Prendergast's name and her home address on the front of it. When the bike arrived she hesitated before letting him take the envelope. Then she closed the door and exhaled. She thought she might throw up, but didn't. That was it. Those were the questions she'd be running with. There was little else to do until five o'clock but panic and take a few pills and try on clothes. Maybe she'd go out for a little while to calm herself down, walk to Regent's Park and along the perimeter of the Zoo. The fresh air and the grass and trees, the children playing and running or staring through the fence at the animals, these things usually calmed her. Even the jets overhead could have an effect. But it was fifty-fifty. Half the time, after they calmed her she had to sit on a park bench and cry. She'd bawl and hide her face in her coat, and couldn't explain to anyone why she was doing it.

She couldn't explain, but she knew all the same. She was doing it because she was scared.

In the end she stayed home. She was soaking in the bath when the phone rang. Mrs Elfman had already gone home, having once more informed Eleanor that she would not touch Archie's room until he'd sorted the worst of it out for himself. Freddy had left for his sou'wester cereal slot, not even saying goodbye or wishing her luck. She knew he wouldn't be home again. He'd stop in one of his many pubs to talk to other embittered men. It would be seven or eight before he came back here. As for Archie, well, she hadn't seen him in days anyway.

She'd let the phone ring for a while – what could be so important? – but then realised it might be Molly Prendergast querying or nixing one of the new questions. Eleanor reached up and unhooked the receiver from the extension-set on the wall above the bath. It had seemed mad at the time, a phone in the bathroom, but it came in useful more often than they'd thought.

'Hello?'

'Eleanor?'

'Geoffrey, is that you?'

'Who else?'

'You always seem to catch me in the bath.'

'Lucky me. Can we talk?'

'What about?'

'I think you know.'

Geoffrey Johns was Eleanor's solicitor, and had been for fifteen years. Occasionally, her journalism had landed her with an injunction, a libel suit or a court appearance. She knew Geoffrey very well indeed. She could imagine him seated in his grandfather's chair in his grandfather's office (also at one time his father's office). The office was stuffy and gloomy, the chair uncomfortable, but Geoffrey wouldn't make any changes. He even used a bakelite telephone, with a little drawer in the base for a notepad. The phone was a reproduction and had cost him a small fortune.

'Humour me,' she said, lying back further in the water. A telephone engineer had told her she couldn't electrocute herself, even if the receiver fell in the water. Not enough volts or something. All she'd feel was a tingle. He'd leered as he'd said it. Just a tingle.

'I think you know,' Geoffrey Johns repeated, drawling the

15

words out beyond their natural limits. Eleanor had a feeling he spoke so slowly because he charged by the hour. When she didn't say anything he sighed loudly. 'Are you doing anything today?'

'Nothing much. I've an interview this afternoon.'

'I thought we might meet.'

'I don't think that's necessary.'

'No?' Another silence, another pause. 'Look, Eleanor—'

'Geoffrey, is there something you want to say?'

'I . . . no, I suppose not.'

'Look, Geoffrey, you're one of the dearest people I know.' She halted. It was an old joke between them.

'My rates are actually very reasonable,' he supplied, sounding mollified. 'What about next week? I'll buy you lunch.'

She ran the sponge between her breasts and then over them. 'That sounds heavenly.'

'Do you want to fix a date now?'

'You know what I'm like, Geoffrey, I'd only end up changing it. Let's wait.'

'Fine. Well, as the Americans say, have a nice day.'

'It's gone two, Geoffrey, the best of the day's already over.'

'Don't remind me,' said Geoffrey Johns.

She reached up to replace the receiver in its cradle, and wondered if Geoffrey would try charging her for the call. She wouldn't put it past him. She lay in the bath a little longer, until there was just enough hot water left in the tap to let her shower off. She ran her fingers through her hair, enjoying the sensation, then towelled briskly and set off naked to the bedroom for her clothes.

She'd had her yellow and blue dress cleaned specially, and was glad the day was sunny. The dress worked best in sunlight.

16

3

I took a cab from the hotel.

My destination was only a ten-minute walk away, but I knew I'd be less conspicuous in a taxi. London cab-drivers aren't, in my experience, the all-knowing and inquisitive individuals they're often made out to be. They nod at you when you tell them your destination, and that's about it. Of course, mine had one comment ready as I got into his cab.

'What you got there then, a bazooka or something?'

'Photographic equipment,' I answered, though he showed no interest. I had manoeuvred the long metal box into the back of the cab, where, angled between the top corner of the rear window and the bottom front corner of the door diametrically opposite, it afforded me scant space for myself. It was longer than it needed to be; but it was also the shortest adequate box I could find.

It was silver in colour, with three clasp-locks and a black carrying-handle. I'd bought it in a specialist shop for photographers. It was used for carrying around rolls of precious background paper. The shop assistant had tried to sell me some graduated sheets – they were on special offer – but I'd declined. I didn't mind the box being too big. It did anything but announce that there was a gun inside.

In the movies, the local assassin tends to carry a small attaché case. His rifle will be inside, broken down into stock, fore-end and barrel. He simply clips the parts together and attaches his telescopic sight. Of course, in real life even if you get hold of such a weapon, it would not be anything like as accurate as a solid one-piece construction. Normally, I'd carry my rifle hanging from a special pouch inside my raincoat, but the PM was just too long and too heavy. So instead of walking, I was taking a taxi to the office.

I'd been watching the weather for a couple of hours, and had even phoned from the hotel for the latest Met Office report. Clear, but without bright sunshine. In other words, perfect conditions, the sun being a sniper's worst enemy. I was chewing gum and doing some breathing exercises, though I doubted they'd be effective in my present cramped condition. But it was only a few minutes until the driver was pulling into the kerb and dropping me outside the office block.

This was a Saturday, remember, and though I was in central London my destination wasn't one of the main thoroughfares. So the street was quiet. Cars and taxis waited for the lights to change further down the road, but the shops were doing slow business and all the offices were closed. The shops were at street level, the usual mix of ceramics studios, small art galleries, shoe shops, and travel agents. I paid the driver and eased the carrying-case out on to the pavement. I stood there until he'd driven off. Across the street were more shops with offices above, and the Craigmead Hotel. It was one of those old understated hotels with overstated room rates. I knew this because I'd toyed with staying there before opting for a much safer choice.

The building I was standing outside was a typical central London office complex, with four steps up to an imposing front door, and a façade which in some parts of the city would hide a huge family home broken up into flats. Indeed, the building next-door had been converted to flats on all but its ground and first floors. My chosen site, however, was currently being gutted and reshaped to offer, as the billboard outside put it, Luxury Office Accommodation for the 21st Century.

I'd been along here yesterday and the day before, and again earlier today. During the week, the place was busy with workmen, but this being Saturday the main door was locked tight, and there was no sign of life inside. That's why I'd chosen it over the flats next door, which offered the easier target but would probably be in use at weekends. I walked up to the main door and worked the lock. It was a simple Yale, not even permanently fixed. The real locks would come later on in the renovation. Meantime, there being little inside worth pinching, the contractors hadn't bothered with a quality lock.

They hadn't got round to installing the alarm system yet either: another reason for my choice. Wires led out of the front wall into fresh air. Later, they'd be hooked up to the alarm and a casing put over the whole. But for now security was not the main concern.

I'm not the world's greatest locksmith, but any housing-estate teenager could have been into the place in seconds. I walked into the entrance hall, taking my carrying-case with me, and closed the door behind me. I stood there for a minute listening to the silence. I could smell drying plaster and wet paint, planed wood and varnish. The downstairs looked like a building site. There were planks and panels of Gyproc and bags of cement and plaster and rolls of insulation. Some of the floorboards had been lifted to allow access to wiring ducts, but I didn't see any fresh rolls of electrical cable: the stuff was probably too valuable to be left lying around. The electrical contractor would take it away with him every night in his van and bring it back again next day. I knew a few electricians; they're careful that way.

There were also no power-tools lying around, and very few tools of any description. I guessed they'd be locked away somewhere inside the building. There was a telephone on the floor, one of those old slimline models with the angular receiver resting over the dial. It was chipped and dotted with paint, but more surprisingly was attached to a phone-point on the wall. I lifted the receiver, and heard the familiar tone. I suppose it made sense: this was going to be a long job; there'd have to be some means of communication between the gang and their base. I put back the receiver and stood up.

Since I hadn't been in the place before, I knew I had to get to know it quickly. I left the case in the reception area and headed upstairs. Some doors had been fitted, but none were locked, except one to a storage area. I presumed that was where the tools were kept.

I found the office I needed on the second floor.

The first floor was too close to ground level. There was always the chance of some pedestrian glancing up, though they so seldom did. The third floor, on the other hand, made the angle a little too difficult. I might have accepted its challenge, but I knew I needed a good hit. No time for games today, it had to be fast and mundane. Well, not *too* mundane. There was always my calling card.

My chosen office was as chaotic as any other part of the building. They were fitting a false ceiling, from which fell power points, probably for use with desktop computers. The ceiling they were putting up, a grid of white plastic strips, would be hiding the real ceiling, which was ornately corniced with an even more ornate central ceiling-rose, presumably at one time surrounding the room's main light fitting, a chandelier perhaps. Well, they're fucking up old buildings everywhere, aren't they?

I checked my exits: there was only the front door. It looked like they were working on a fire exit to the rear of the building, but meantime they'd left all their ladders and scaffolding there, effectively barricading the door. So when I left, I'd have to leave through the front door. But that didn't worry me. I've found that just as attack is the best form of defence, so boldness can be the best form of disguise. It's the person slinking away who looks suspicious, not the one walking towards you. Besides, attention was going to be elsewhere, wasn't it?

The window was fine. There was some ineffective double glazing, which could be slid open, and behind which lay the original sash-window. I unscrewed the window lock and tried opening it. The pulleys stuck for a moment, their ropes crusted with white paint, and then they gave with an audible squeak and the window lifted an inch. With more effort, I opened it a second and then a third inch. This wasn't ideal. It meant the telescopic sight would be pointing through the glass, while the muzzle would be stuck into fresh air. But I'd carried out an assassination before under near-identical conditions. To be honest, I could probably have forced the window open a bit further, but I think I was looking for just a *little* challenge.

I peered out. No one was looking back at me. I couldn't see anyone in the shops over the road, and no one staring from the hotel windows further along. In fact, some of the shops looked like they were closing for the day. My watch said 5.25. Yes, some of them, most of them, would close at 5.30. The tourists and visitors at the Craigmead Hotel wouldn't be in their rooms, they'd still be out enjoying the summer weather. By six o'clock, the street would be dead. I only had to wait.

I brought the case upstairs and opened it. I couldn't find a chair, but there was a wooden crate which I upended. It seemed strong enough, so I placed it by the window and sat on it. The PM lay on the floor in front of me, along with two bullets. I sat there thinking about cartridges. You wouldn't think something so small and so fixed in its purpose could be quite so complex. Straight or bottleneck? Belted, rimmed, semi-rimmed, rimless or rebated? Centre-fire or rim-fire? Then there was the primer compound. I knew that Max mixed his own compound using lead styphnate, antimony sulphide and barium nitrate, but in a ratio he kept to himself. I picked up one of the bullets by its base and tip. What, I wondered, is it like to be shot? I knew the answer in forensic terms. I knew the kinds of entrance and exit wounds left by different guns at different ranges and using different ammunition. I had to know this sort of thing, so I could determine each individual hit. Some snipers go for the head shot; some of them call it a 'JFK'. Not me.

I go for the heart.

What else did I think about in that room, as the traffic moved past like the dull soothing roll of waves on a shore? I didn't think about anything else. I emptied my mind. I could have been in a trance, had anyone seen me. I let my shoulders slump, my head fall forward, my jaw muscles relax. I kept my fingers spread wide, not clenched. And with my eyes slightly out of focus, I watched the second hand go round on my watch. Finally I came out of it, and found myself wondering what I would order for dinner. Some dark meat in a sauce rich enough to merit a good red wine. It was five minutes to six. I picked up the PM, undid the bolt, pushed home the first bullet, and slid the bolt forward. Then I took a small homemade cushion from my jacket pocket and placed it between my shoulder and the stock of the rifle. I had to be careful of the recoil.

This was a dangerous time. If anyone saw me now, they wouldn't just see a man at a window, they'd see the barrel of a gun, a black telescopic sight, and a sniper taking aim. But the few pedestrians were too busy to look up. They were hurrying home, or to some restaurant appointment. They carried bags of shopping. They kept their eyes to the treacherous London paving slabs. If a cracked slab didn't get you, then the dog shit might. Besides, they couldn't look straight ahead; that was to invite a stranger's stare, an unwanted meeting of eyes.

The sight was beautiful, it was as if I was standing a few feet from the hotel steps. There was a central revolving door, and ordinary push-pull doors to either side. Most people going into or coming out of the hotel seemed to use the ordinary doors. I wondered which one she would use. It was six now, dead on the hour. I blinked slowly, keeping my eyes clear. One minute past six. Then two minutes past. I took deep breaths, releasing them slowly. I'd taken my eye away from the telescope. I could see the hotel entrance well enough without it. Now a car was drawing up outside the hotel. There was a liveried chauffeur in the front. He made no effort to get out and open the back doors. The man and woman got out by themselves. He looked like a diplomat; the car carried a diplomatic plate below its radiator grille. They walked up the three carpeted steps to the revolving door. And now two women were coming out.

Two women.

I put my eye to the telescopic sight. Yes. I pulled the gun in tight against my cushioned shoulder, adjusted my hands a fraction, and put my finger on the trigger. The two women were smiling, talking. The diplomat and his wife had moved past them. Now the women were craning their necks, looking for taxis. Another car drew up and one of the women pointed towards it. She started down a step, and her companion followed. The sun appeared from behind a cloud, highlighting the yellow and blue design on her dress. I squeezed the trigger.

Straight away, I pulled the gun in from the window. I knew the hit had been good. She'd fallen backwards as if pushed hard in the chest. The other woman didn't realise for a moment what had happened. She was probably thinking, fainting fit or heart attack. But now she'd seen the blood and she was looking around, then crawling down the steps on her hands and knees, taking cover behind the diplomat's car. The driver was out of the car and looking around. He'd pulled a pistol from inside his jacket and was screaming at the diplomat to get indoors. The driver in the other car seemed to have ducked down in his seat.

And now there were sirens. You were always hearing sirens in central London – ambulances, fire engines. But these were police cars and they were screaming to a stop outside the hotel. I stood up and moved away from the window. It was impossible, they couldn't be here so quickly.

I took another look. Some of the police were armed, and they were making for the block next to this one, the block with all the flats in it. Passers-by were being ordered to take cover, the woman was yelling and crying from the cover of the car, the armed chauffeur was crouching over the lifeless body. He put his hands up when the police took aim at him, and started to explain who he was. It might take them a little while to believe him.

I knew I had seconds to get out. They'd turn their attention to this building next. I put the gun back in its box along with the unused bullet, closed the box, and left it there. Normally I'd take the gun away with me and break it up, then dispose of it. Max never wanted my guns back, and I couldn't blame him. But I knew I couldn't risk walking out with that carrying-case.

As I walked downstairs, the idea came to me. There was a hospital just a few blocks away. I picked up the telephone and dialled 999, then asked for an ambulance.

'I'm a severe haemophiliac, and I've just had a terrible accident. I think there's haemorrhaging to the head.' I gave them the address, then put the phone down and went in search of a brick. There were some just inside the front door. I picked one up and smashed it into my forehead, making sure the edge of the brick made the initial contact. I touched my forehead with the palm of my hand. There was blood.

And then from outside came the sound of a muffled explosion: my calling card.

I'd planted the device in the morning. It was at the bottom of a dustbin in an alley behind some restaurants. The alley was about five hundred yards from the Craigmead Hotel. It was a small bomb, just big enough to make a noise. The alley was a dead end, so I doubted anyone would be hurt. Its purpose was to deflect attention while I walked away from the scene. I knew it would still deflect attention, but I doubted I'd be able to walk away without being spotted by the police.

Now there was another siren, not a police car but an ambulance. God bless them, the emergency services know that when a haemophiliac phones them up, it has to be priority. I unlocked the main door and looked out. Sure enough, the ambulance had drawn up outside. One of the ambulancemen was opening the back door, the other was climbing out from the driver's side.

Together they pulled a stretcher from the back of the ambulance, manoeuvred it on to the pavement, and wheeled it towards the front door. Someone, a policeman probably, called out to them and asked what they were doing.

'Emergency!' one of them called back.

I held the door open for them. I had a hand to my bloody forehead, and an embarrassed smile on my face.

'Tripped and fell,' I said.

'Not surprised with all this rubbish lying around.'

'I was working upstairs.'

I let them put me on to the stretcher. I thought it would look better for the audience.

'Do you have your card?' one of them asked.

'It's in my wallet at home.'

'You're supposed always to carry it. What's your factor level?'

'One per cent.'

They were putting me in the ambulance now. The armed police were still in the apartment block. People were looking towards the source of the explosion from a few moments before.

'What the hell's happened here?' one ambulanceman asked the other.

'Christ knows.' The second ambulanceman tore open a packet and brought out a compress, which he pressed to my forehead. He placed my hand on it. 'Here, you know the drill. Plenty of pressure.'

The driver closed the ambulance doors from the outside,

leaving me with his colleague. Nobody stopped us as we left the scene. I was sitting up, thinking I wasn't safe yet.

'Is this your card?' The ambulanceman had picked something off the floor. He started reading it. 'Gerald Flitch, Marketing Strategist.'

'My business card. It must have fallen out of my pocket.' I held out my hand and he gave me back the card. 'The company I'm working for, they're supposed to be moving into the new office next week.'

'It's an old card then, the Liverpool address?'

'Yes,' I said, 'our old offices.'

'Are you factor eight or nine, Mr Flitch?'

'Factor eight,' I told him.

'We've got a good Haematology Department, you'll be all right.'

'Thank you.'

'To tell you the truth, you'd have been as quick walking there.'

Yes, we were already bumping through the hospital gates and up to the Emergency entrance. This was about as far as I could take the charade. I knew that behind the compress the bleeding was already stopping. They took me into Emergency and gave a nurse my details. She went off to call someone from Haematology, and the ambulancemen went back to their vehicle. I sat for a few moments in the empty reception area, then got up and headed for the door. The ambulance was still there, but there was no sign of the ambulancemen. They'd probably gone for a cup of tea and a cigarette. I walked down the slope to the hospital's main entrance, and deposited the compress in a waste-bin. There were two public telephones on the wall, and I called my hotel.

'Can I speak to Mr Wesley, please? Room 203.'

'Sorry,' said the receptionist after a moment, 'I'm getting no reply.'

'Can I leave a message? It's very important. Tell Mr

Wesley there's been a change of plans, he has to be in Liverpool tonight. This is Mr Snipes from Head Office.'

'Is there a number where he can contact you, Mr Snipes?' I gave her a fictitious phone number prefixed with the Liverpool code, then put down the phone. There was a lot of police activity on the streets as I walked back to my hotel.

The thing was, the police would find the PM, and then they'd want to speak to the man who'd been taken away in the ambulance. The nurse in Emergency could tell them I'd given the name Gerald Flitch, and the ambulanceman could add that my business card had carried a Liverpool address. From all of which, they could track down either Flitch's Liverpool home or his employers and be told he was on a trip to London, staying at the Allington Hotel.

Which would bring them to me.

The Allington's automatic doors hissed open, and I walked up to the reception desk.

'Any idea what's going on? There are police all over the place?'

The receptionist hadn't looked up yet. 'I heard a bang earlier on,' she said. 'I don't know what it's about though.'

'Any messages for me? Wesley, Room 203.'

Now she looked up. 'Goodness, Mr Wesley, what happened to you?'

I touched my forehead. 'Tripped and fell. Bloody London pavements.'

'Dear me. I think we've got some plasters.'

'I've some in my room, thanks.' I paused. 'No messages then?'

'Yes, there's a message, came not ten minutes ago.' She handed it to me, and I read it.

'Shit,' I said in exasperation, letting my shoulders slump for the second time that day. 'Can you make my bill up, please? Looks like I'll be checking out.'

I couldn't risk taking a cab straight from the Allington to

another hotel – the cabbie would be able to tell police my destination – so I walked about a bit, lugging my suitcase with me. It was lighter than before, about fourteen pounds lighter, and too big for the purpose. Having used nearly all my cash settling my bill, I drew two hundred out of a cash machine. The first two hotels I tried were both full, but the third had a small single room with a shower but no bath. The hotel sold souvenirs to guests, including a large holdall with the hotel name emblazoned front and back. I bought one and took it upstairs with me. Later that evening, I took my now empty suitcase to King's Cross. Luggage lockers are hard to find in central London, so I deposited the case in the left luggage room at King's Cross station. Seeing the size of the case, the man behind the desk braced himself before attempting to lift it, then was caught off-balance by how light it was.

I took another cab back to my hotel and settled down to watch the news. But I couldn't concentrate. They seemed to think I'd hit the wrong person. They thought I was after the diplomat. Well, that would help muddy the water, I didn't mind that at all. Then they mentioned that police had taken away a large box from a building across from the hotel. They showed the alley where my little device had gone off. The metal bin looked like torn wrapping. Nobody had been injured, though two kitchen assistants in a Chinese restaurant had been treated for shock and cuts from flying glass.

They did not, of course, speculate as to how police had arrived on the scene so quickly. But I was thinking about it. I was tumbling it in my mind, and not coming up with any clever answers.

Tomorrow, there'd be time for thinking tomorrow. I was exhausted. I didn't feel like meat and wine any more. I felt like sleep.

4

There was little love lost between Freddy Ricks and Geoffrey Johns, despite which, the solicitor was not surprised to receive Freddy's call.

Freddy was half cut, as per usual, and sounded dazed.

'Have you heard?'

'Yes,' Geoffrey Johns said, 'I've heard.' He was seated in his living room, a glass of Armagnac trembling beside him on the arm of the sofa.

'Jesus Christ,' wailed Freddy Ricks, 'she's been *shot!*'

'Freddy, I'm . . . I'm so sorry.' Geoffrey Johns took a sip of burning liquid. 'Does Archie know?'

'Archie?' It took Freddy an understandable moment to recognise the name of his son. 'I haven't seen him. I had to go down to the . . . they wanted me to identify her. Then they had to ask me some questions.'

'Is that why you're phoning?'

'What? No, no . . . well, yes, in a way. I mean, there are things I have to do, and there are about fifty reporters at the garden gate, and . . . well, Geoffrey, I know we've had our differences, but you *are* our solicitor.'

'I understand, Freddy. I'll be straight over.'

In Vine Street police station, Chief Inspector Bob Broome was deciding what to say to the press. They were clamouring around the entrance to the gloomy station. Even on sunny days, Vine Street, a high narrow conduit between Regent Street and Piccadilly, got little light, though it managed to get all the available traffic fumes and grime. Broome reckoned the station had affected him. He thought

29

he could remember days when he used to be cheerful. His last smile had been a couple of days ago, his last full-throated laugh several months back. Nobody bothered trying to tell him jokes any more. The prisoners in the cells were a more obliging target.

'So what've we got, Dave?'

Detective Inspector Dave Edmond sat opposite Broome. He had a reputation as a dour bugger, too. People seeing them together usually gave the pair a wide berth, like you would a plague ship. While Broome was tall and thin with an undertaker's pallor, Edmond was round and tanned. He'd just returned from a fortnight in Spain, spent guzzling San Miguel on some beach.

'Well, sir,' he said, 'we're still taking statements. The gun's down at the lab. We've got technicians in the office building, but they won't be able to report before tomorrow.'

There was a knock at the door and a WPC came in with a couple of faxes for Broome. He laid them to one side and watched her leave, then turned back to Edmond. His every action was slow and considered, like he was on tranquillisers, but Edmond for one knew the boss was just being careful.

'What about the gun?'

'Sergeant Wills is the pop-pop guru,' Edmond said, 'so I've sent him to take a look at it. He probably knows more than any of the eggheads in the Ballistics section. From the description I gave him, he said it sounds military.'

'Let's not muck about, Dave, it's the Demolition Man again. You can spot his m.o. a mile away.'

Edmond nodded. 'Unless it's a copycat.'

'What are the chances?'

Edmond shrugged. 'A hundred to one?'

'And the rest. What about the phone call, did we take a recording?'

Edmond shook his head. 'The officer who took the call has

typed out what he remembers of the conversation.' He handed over a single sheet of paper.

The door opened again. It was a DC this time, smiling apologetically as he came in with more sheets of paper for the Chief Inspector. Outside, there were sounds of frenzied activity. When the DC had gone, Broome got up, went to the door, and pulled a chair against it, jamming the back of the chair under the knob. Then he walked slowly back to his desk.

'Shame we didn't get it on tape though,' he said, picking up Edmond's sheet of paper. 'Male, English, aged between twenty and seventy-five. Yes, very useful. Call didn't sound long distance.' Broome looked up from the report. 'And all he said was that there was going to be a shooting outside the Craigmead Hotel.'

'Normally, it would be treated as a crank, but the officer got the impression this one wasn't playing games. A very educated voice, quite matter-of-fact with just enough emotion. We couldn't have got men there any quicker.'

'We could if we hadn't armed some of them first.'

'The man who called, who do you think it was?'

'I suppose it could have been the Demolition Man himself. Maybe he's gone off his trolley, wants us to catch him or play some sort of cat-and-mouse with him. Or it could be someone who spotted him, but then why not warn those people on the steps?' Broome paused. His office wasn't much bigger than an interview room; in some ways, it was even less inviting. He liked it because it made people who came here feel uncomfortable. But Dave Edmond seemed to like it too . . . 'The people on the steps, that's another thing. We've got a journalist, a Secretary of State, and some senior bod from an East European embassy.'

'So which one was the target?' Edmond asked.

'Exactly. I mean, did he get who he was going after? If not, the other two better be careful. Remember, he's shot the wrong bloody person before.'

Edmond nodded. 'It'll be out of our hands soon anyway.'

This was true: Scotland Yard and the Anti-Terrorist unit would pick over the bones. But this was Bob Broome's manor, and he wasn't about to just hand the case over and catch a good night's sleep.

'Bollocks,' he said. 'What about this other phone call, the one to the Craigmead?'

'We're talking to the receptionist again. All she knows is that a man called wanting to speak to Eleanor Ricks. Ricks was paged, but she ignored it.'

'She hadn't left?'

'No, the receptionist says she walked past the desk while her name was being put out over the loudspeakers.'

'Was the Secretary of State with her?'

'Yes. But she says she didn't hear anything.'

'So maybe Eleanor Ricks didn't hear anything either?'

'Maybe.'

'But if she'd taken the call . . .'

'Molly Prendergast would have walked out of the hotel alone.'

'And we'd have a clearer idea who the intended target was.' Broome sighed.

'So what's our next step, Bob?'

Broome checked his watch. 'For one thing, I've a transatlantic call to make. For another, there's the media to deal with. Then I'll want to see those buggers at the hospital.'

'They're being brought in.'

'Good. Nice of them to help him escape, wasn't it?'

'Think he might've had an accomplice?'

'I think,' said Bob Broome, getting to his feet, 'he might've just lost one of his nine lives.'

'That phone call, sir.'

'Oh, right.' Broome sat down again. Someone was trying the door, but the chair was holding. He picked up the phone. He knew one man who'd want to know the Demolition Man was back in London. 'I want to place a call to the United States,' he said into the receiver.

5

Hoffer hated flying, especially these days when business class was out of the question. He hated being cooped up like a factory chicken. He was strictly a free-range cockerel. The crew didn't like it if you strayed too far for too long. They were always getting in the way, squeezing these damned tin trolleys down aisles just wide enough for them. Those aisles, they weren't even wide enough for *him*. You were supposed to stay in your seat to make the trolley-pushers' jobs easier. Screw them, he was the customer.

There were other problems too. His nose got all blocked up on long-haul flights, and his ears bothered him. He'd yawn like a whale on a plankton hunt and swallow like he was choking down a lump of concrete, but his head got more and more like a pressure cooker no matter what he did. He waited till the better-looking stewardess came along and asked her with a pained smile if she had any tips. Maybe there were tablets these days for this sort of thing. But she came back to his seat with two plastic drinks cups and said he should clamp them over his ears.

'What is this, a joke? I'm supposed to wear these things all the way to London?'

He crunched the plastic cups in his beefy fists and got up to use the bathroom. There was a guy four rows back who kept laughing at the in-flight movie, some Steve Martin vehicle which had left the factory without wheels or any gas in its tank. The guy looked like he'd have laughed at Nuremberg.

The bathroom: now there was another problem. A Japanese coffin would have been roomier. It took him a while to get everything set out: mirror, penknife, stash. They'd been sticky about the knife at airport security, until he explained that he was a New York private detective, not a Palestinian terrorist, and that the knife was a present for his cousin in London.

'Since when,' he'd argued finally, 'did you get *fat* terrorists? Come to that, when did you last see a pocket-knife terrorist? I'd be better armed with the in-flight knife and fork.'

So they'd let him through.

He took a wrinkled dollar bill from his pocket and rolled it up. Well, it was either that or a straw from the in-flight drinks, and those straws were so narrow you could hardly suck anything up. He'd read somewhere that eighty percent of all the twenty-dollar bills in circulation bore traces of cocaine. Yeah, but he was a dollar sort of guy. Even rolled up, however, the dollar was crumpled. He considered doing a two-and-two, placing the powder on his pinky and snorting it, but you wasted a lot that way. Besides, he was shaking so much, he doubted he'd get any of the coke near his nose.

He'd laid out a couple of lines. It wasn't great coke, but it was good enough. He remembered the days of great coke, stuff that would burn to white ash on the end of a cigarette. These days, the stuff was reconstituted Colombia-Miami shit, not the beautiful Peruvian blow of yore. If you tried testing it on a cigarette tip, it turned black and smelt like a Jamaican party. He knew this stuff was going to burn his nose. He saw his face in the mirror above the sink. He saw the lines around his mouth and under his eyes, coke lines. Then he turned back to the business at hand and took a good hit.

He wiped what was left off the mirror with his thumb and rubbed it over his gums. It was sour for a second before the freeze arrived. Okay, so he'd powdered his nose. He doubted it would put wheels on the movie, but maybe he'd find something else to laugh at. You never could tell.

Hoffer ran his own detective agency these days, though he managed to employ just two other tecs and a secretary. He'd started in a sleazy rental above a peep show off Times Square, reckoning that was how private eyes operated in the movies. But he soon saw that clients were put off by the location, so he took over a cleaner set of offices in Soho. The only problem was, they were up three flights of stairs, and there was no elevator. So Hoffer tended to work from home, using his phone and fax. He had one tec working for him; he'd only met the guy twice, both times in a McDonald's. But the clients were happier now that Hoffer Private Investigations was above a chi-chi splatter gallery selling canvases that looked like someone had been hacked to death on them and then the post mortem carried out. The cheapest painting in the shop covered half a wall and would set the buyer back $12,000. Hoffer knew the gallery would last about another six months. He saw them carry paintings in, but he never saw one leave. Still, at least Hoffer had clients. There'd been a while when he'd been able to trade on his name alone, back when the media exposure had been good. But stories died quickly, and for a while the name Hoffer wasn't enough.

$12,000 would buy about eight weeks of Hoffer agency time, not including expenses. Robert Walkins had promised to deposit exactly that sum in the agency's bank account when Hoffer had spoken to him by phone. It was funny, speaking to the man again. After all, Walkins had been Hoffer's first client. In some ways, he was Hoffer's *only* client, the only one that mattered.

The Demolition Man was in action again, and Hoffer badly wanted to be part of the action. He didn't just want it, he *needed* it. He had salaries and taxes to pay, the rent on his apartment, overheads, and money for his favourite drugs. He needed the Demolition Man. More crucially, he needed the publicity. When he'd started out for himself, he'd hired a publicity consultant before he'd hired an accountant. When he'd learned enough from the publicist, he'd kicked her out. She had a great body, but for what she was costing him he could *buy* a great body, and it wouldn't just talk or cross its legs either.

When he'd got the call from London, he'd been able to pack his bags in about thirty minutes. But first he'd called to get a ticket on the first available flight, and then he'd called Robert Walkins.

'Mr Walkins? This is Leo Hoffer.' On the force, they'd all called him Lenny, but since he'd left the force and recreated himself, he'd decided on Leo. The Lion. So what if he was actually Capricorn?

'Mr Hoffer, I take it there's news?' Walkins always sounded like he'd just found you taking a leak on his carpet.

'He's in London.' Hoffer paused. 'London, England.'

'I didn't think you meant London, Alabama.'

'Well, he's there.'

'And you're going to follow him?'

'Unless you don't want me to?'

'You know our agreement, Mr Hoffer. Of course I want you to follow him. I want him caught.'

'Yes, sir.'

'I'll transfer some funds. How much will you need?'

'Say, twelve thou?' Hoffer held his breath. Walkins hadn't been tight with money, not so far, though he'd nixed Hoffer travelling club class.

'Very well. Good luck, Mr Hoffer.'

'Thank you, sir.'

Then he'd packed. It didn't take long because he didn't own a lot of clothes. He checked with Moira at the office that she'd be able to control things for a week or so. She told him to bring her back a souvenir, 'something royal'.

'What about a pain in the ass?' he'd suggested.

He finished packing and called for a cab. He didn't have any notes to take with him. All the notes he needed were firmly lodged inside his head. He wondered if he should take a book with him for the journey, but dismissed the notion. There were no books in the apartment anyway, and he could always buy a couple of magazines at the airport. As a final measure, he stuck his penknife in his carry-on luggage, and his mirror and stash in his inside jacket pocket. The knife, of thick sharp steel, was purposely ornate and expensive: that way people believed him when he said it was a gift for his cousin. It was French, a Laguiole, with mahogany handle and a serpent motif. In emergencies, it also had a corkscrew. But the real quality of the thing was its blade.

He knew the cab was on its way, which left him only a few minutes to make his final decision. Should he carry a gun? In the wardrobe in his bedroom he had a pump-action over-under shotgun and a couple of unmarked semi-automatic pistols. He kept the serious stuff elsewhere. Ideally, he'd go get something serious. But he didn't have time. So he grabbed the Smith & Wesson 459, its holster and some ammo from the wardrobe. He packed it in his suitcase, wrapped in his only sweater. The door buzzer sounded just as he was closing his case.

At London Heathrow, he phoned a hotel he'd used before just off Piccadilly Circus and managed to get a room. The receptionist wanted to tell him all about how the hotels were quiet for the time of year, there just weren't the tourists around that there used to be . . . Hoffer put the phone down on her. It wasn't just that he felt like shit. He couldn't understand what she was saying either.

He knew he could claim for a cab, so schlepped his stuff down to the Underground and took a train into town. It wasn't much better than New York. Three young toughs were working the carriages, asking for money from the newly-arrived travellers. Hoffer hadn't taken the Smith & Wesson out of his case yet, which was good news for the beggars. London, he decided, was definitely on its way down the pan. Even the centre of town looked like it had been turned over by a gang. Everything had been torn up or sprayed on. Last time he'd been in London, there had been more punks around, but there'd been more life to the place too, and fewer street people.

The train journey took forever. His body knew that it was five hours earlier than everyone around him thought it was. His feet were swollen, and sitting in the train brought on another bout of ear pressure. Plastic cups, for Christ's sake.

But the receptionist smiled and was sympathetic. He told her if she really felt sorry for him he had a litre of Scotch in his bag and she knew his room number. She still managed to smile, but she had to force it. Then he got to his room and remembered all the very worst things about England. Namely, the beds and the plumbing. His bed was way too narrow. They had wider beds in the concentration camps. When he phoned reception, he was told all the beds in the single rooms were the same size, and if he wanted a double bed he'd need to pay for a double room. So then he'd to take the elevator back down to reception, get a new room, and take the elevator back up. This room was a little better, not much. He switched the TV on and went into the bathroom to run a bath. The bath looked like a child might have fun in it, but an adult would have problems, and the taps were having prostate trouble if the dribble issuing from them was anything to go by. There wasn't even a proper glass by the sink, just another plastic tumbler. He unscrewed the top from his Johnny Walker Red Label and poured generously. He was about to add water from the cold tap, but thought better of it, so he drank the Scotch neat and watched the water finally cover the bottom of the bath.

He toasted the mirror. 'Welcome to England,' he said.

He'd arranged to meet Bob Broome in the hotel bar.

They knew one another from a conference they'd attended in Toronto when both had been Drugs Squad officers. That was going back some time, but then they'd met again when Hoffer had been in London last trip, just over a year ago. He'd been tracking the Demolition Man then, too.

'You mean Walkins is still paying you?' Broome sounded awed.

'I'm not on a retainer or anything,' Hoffer said. 'But when we hear anything new on the D-Man, I know I can follow it up and Walkins will pay.'

Bob Broome shook his head. 'I still can't believe you got here so quickly.'

'No ties, Bob, that's the secret.' Hoffer looked around the bar. 'This place stinks, let's go for a walk.' He saw Broome look at him, laughed and patted his jacket. 'It's okay, Bob, I'm not armed.' Broome looked relieved.

It was Sunday evening and the streets were quiet. They walked into Soho and found a pub seedy enough for Hoffer's tastes, where they ordered bitter and found a corner table.

'So, Bob, what've you got?'

Broome placed his pint glass carefully on a beermat, checking its base was equidistant from all four edges. 'There was a shooting yesterday evening at six o'clock, outside a hotel near the US Embassy. A minute or two after the shooting, a bomb exploded in a rubbish bin nearby. We had an anonymous call warning us, so we sent men over there. We arrived just too late, but in time to start a search for the assassin. But he'd been a bit too clever. We went for the building directly in front of the hotel, and he'd been holed up in the office block next-door. He must have seen us coming. He called for an ambulance, gave them some story about being seriously ill, and they whisked him away to hospital from right under our noses.'

Hoffer shook his head. 'But you've got a description?'

'Oh, yes, a good description, always supposing he wasn't wearing a wig and coloured contact lenses.'

'He left the weapon behind?'

Broome nodded. 'An L96A1 Sniper Rifle.'

'Never heard of it.'

'It's British, a serious piece of goods. He'd tweaked it, added a flash hider and some camouflage tape. The telescopic sight on it was worth what I take home in a month.'

'Nobody ever said the D-Man came cheap. Speaking of which . . . ?'

'We don't even know who his target was. There were four people on the steps: a diplomat and his wife, the Secretary of State for the DSS, and the journalist.'

'How far was he away from the hotel?'

'Seventy, eighty yards.'

'Unlikely he missed his target.'

'He's missed before.'

'Yeah, but that was a fluke. He must've been after the reporter.'

'We're keeping an open mind. The diplomat seems sure he was the intended victim.'

'Well, *you* have to keep an open mind, I don't. In fact, I'm famous for my *closed* mind.' Hoffer finished his drink. 'Want another?' Broome shook his head. 'I need to see anything you've got, Bob.'

'That's not so easy, Leo. I'd have to clear it with my—'

'By the way, something for your kids.' Hoffer took an envelope from his pocket and slid it across the table. 'How are they anyway?'

'They're fine, thanks.' Broome looked in the envelope. He was looking at £500.

'Don't try to refuse it, Bob, I had a hell of a job cashing cheques at the hotel. I think they charged me the same again for the privilege, plus they had an exchange rate you wouldn't accept from a shark. Put it in your pocket. It's for your kids.'

'I'm sure they'll be thankful,' Broome said, tucking the envelope in his inside pocket.

'They're nice kids. What're their names again?'

'Whatever you want them to be,' said the childless Broome.

'So can you get me the info?'

'I can do some photocopying. You'll have it first thing in the morning.'

Hoffer nodded. 'Meantime, talk to me, get me interested. Tell me about the deceased.'

'Her name is Eleanor Ricks, 39, freelance journalist. She covered the Falklands War and some of the early fighting in ex-Yugoslavia.'

'So she wasn't just puffing fluff?'

'No, and lately she'd made the move into television. Yesterday she had a meeting with Molly Prendergast, that's the DSS Minister.'

'What was the meeting about? No, wait, same again?' Hoffer went to the bar and ordered two more pints. He never had to wait long at bars; they were one place where his size lent him a certain authority. It didn't matter if he wasn't wearing great clothes, or hadn't shaved in a while, he had weight and he had standing.

That was one reason he did a lot of his work in bars.

He brought the drinks back. He'd added a double whisky to go with his beer.

'You want one?' But Broome shook his head. Hoffer drank an inch from the beer, then poured in the whisky. He took two cigarettes from one of his packs of duty free, lit them and handed one to Broome.

'Sorry,' he apologised, 'bad habit.' It wasn't everyone who wanted him sucking on their cigarette before they got it. 'You were telling me about Molly Prendergast.'

'It was an interview, something to do with Ricks's latest project, the one for TV. It's an investigation of religious cults.'

'And this MP has something to do with them?'

'Only indirectly. Her daughter was involved in one for a

42

while. Prendergast and her husband had to fight like mad to get her back. In the end, they virtually had to kidnap her.'

'And that's what Ricks wanted to talk about?'

'According to Mrs Prendergast.'

'You don't sound too sure.'

'I've no reason to suppose she'd lie. Besides, her story is backed up by the programme's producer.'

'What's his name?' Hoffer had taken a notebook and pen from his pocket.

'Joe Draper. One strange thing, somebody called the hotel. They asked for Eleanor Ricks and said it was urgent. She was paged, but she didn't take the call. Not many people knew she was going to be there. Draper's one of the few.'

'Which TV company is it?'

'It's a small independent production company. I think it's just called Draper Films or Draper Vision, something like that.'

'You work too hard, Bob, you know that? I mean, you're a seven-day man, am I right? Of course I'm right. You've got to rest your brain some time.'

'It's not easy.'

'But if you don't rest your brain, you start forgetting things, like whether it's Draper Films or Draper Vision. I mean, little things, Bob, but little things can be the important things. You're a cop, you know that.'

Broome didn't look happy at this little lecture. In fact, he finished his drink and said he had to be going. Hoffer didn't stop him. But he didn't hang around the pub either. It reminded him of a few bad Irish bars he knew in and around the other Soho. He headed across Shaftesbury Avenue and into Leicester Square, looking for interesting drugs or interesting whores. But even Leicester Square was quiet. Nobody worked a patch these days. It was all done by mobile phone. The telephone kiosks were full of whores' business cards. He perused them, like he was in a gallery, but didn't find anything new or exciting. He doubted there was anything new under the sun, though apparently they were doing mind-boggling things with computers these days.

There were some kids begging from their doorway beds, so he asked them if they knew where he could find some blow, then remembered that over here 'blow' could mean boo. They didn't know anyway. They hardly knew their own damned names. He went on to Charing Cross Road and found a taxi to take him to Hampstead.

This was where the D-Man had carried out his other London hit, at an office on the High Street. As usual, he'd kept his distance. He'd fired from a building across the street, the bullet smashing through a window before entering and leaving the heart of an Indian businessman who'd been implicated in a finance scam involving several governments and private companies.

The D-Man always kept his distance, which interested Hoffer. Often, it would be simpler just to walk up to the victim and use a pistol. But the D-Man used sniper rifles and kept his distance. These facts told Hoffer a lot. They told him that the D-Man was a real pro, not just some hoodlum. He was skilled, a marksman. He gave himself a challenge with every hit. But he was also squeamish the way hoodlums seldom were. He didn't like to get too close to the gore. He kept well away from the pain. A single shot to the heart: it was a marksman's skill all right, hitting dead centre every time.

He'd planted a bomb in Hampstead too, though he hadn't needed one. The police had thought they were dealing with an IRA device, until they linked it to the assassination. Then Hoffer had come along and he'd been able to tell them quite a lot about the Demolition Man. Few people knew as much as Hoffer did about the D-Man.

But Hoffer didn't know nearly enough.

He took another cab back to the hotel, and got the driver to give him half a dozen blank receipts, tipping him generously as reward. He'd fill the receipts in himself and hand them to his client as proof of expenses.

'Anything else you want, guv?' said the driver. 'An escort? Bit of grass? You name it.'

Nostrils twitching, Hoffer leaned forward in his seat.

'Get me interested,' he said.

6

Mark Wesley was dead.

It was a shame, since it meant I'd have to close a couple of bank accounts and get rid of a bunch of expensive counterfeit identity cards and an even more expensive counterfeit passport with some beautifully crafted visas in it.

More drastic still, it was the only other identity I had in the UK, which meant that from now on I'd have to be me. I could always arrange to create another identity, but it took time and money.

I'd spent a long time not being me. It would take a while to get used to the name again: Michael Weston. The first thing I did was rent a car and get out of London. I rented from one of the big companies, and told them it might be a one-way rental. They explained that one-way rentals are more expensive, but since I was guaranteeing it with a credit card they didn't seem to mind.

It was a nice car, a red Escort XR3i with only 600 miles on the clock. I drove to a shopping complex just off the North Circular Road and bought, amongst other things, a hat. Then I headed north. I didn't phone ahead. I didn't want Max expecting me.

I'd spent a lot of time thinking, and I kept coming up with the same answer: someone had tipped off the police, someone who had wanted me caught. There were only two possibilities: Max, or my employer. I never like to know who I'm working for, just as I never like to know anything about the person I'm being paid to kill. I don't want to be involved, I just want the money. The work I get comes from a variety of middlemen: a couple in the USA, one in Germany, one in

Hong Kong, and Max in England. It was Max who'd contacted me with the job I'd just done. He was the only other person apart from my employer who knew the details of the job.

Like I say, I'd given it a lot of thought, and still it came down to Max or my employer. This still left the question of why. Why would Max want me arrested? Was the money suddenly not enough to salve his conscience? He could get out any time he wanted to, but maybe he didn't realise that. If he wanted out, but thought I wouldn't like such an idea, maybe he also thought I'd want to kill him. Was he just getting his retaliation in first?

Then there was my employer. Maybe he or she had got cold feet at the very last, and phoned for the cops. This seemed the more likely answer, though there was one other consideration: what if the whole thing had been a trap from the start? I was sure I could come up with other theories, but they all led in the same direction: I was going to have to talk to Max. Then maybe I'd have to find out who my employer was, and ask them a few questions, too.

It bothered me. I hate to get involved. I hate to know. But this time there might be no other way. I might have to find out *why* I'd been paid to assassinate Eleanor Ricks. I'd seen the papers and the news. It was in my favour that the authorities were baffled. They still didn't know who my target had been. But I knew, right down to her name and the details of her dress. The diplomat had been there by pure chance, though not the politician. Whoever had known Eleanor Ricks would be coming out of the hotel at six knew her very well. So they almost certainly also knew the politician would be with her. Was I scaring off the politician? Was I sending a message?

Maybe you begin to see why I don't like getting involved.

I didn't rush my journey. I wanted my arrival to surprise Max. If I turned up straight away, he would probably be less surprised. But I broke my journey quite near him in

Yorkshire, so I could walk in on him early the following morning. Max was a careful man, but he didn't go armed to the breakfast table. He was also surrounded by fields and hills. No one would hear a shot, no one would hear a burial.

No one except Belinda.

I booked into a small hotel, wearing my cap at the reception desk. Then I went out and had a haircut, quite a severe one.

'You sure about this?' the barber asked.

'I'm sure,' I said. 'It's for the summer. Gets too hot otherwise.'

'True enough,' he said, picking up the scissors.

I wore the cap again on my way back to my room, then washed my hair and used some of the dye I'd bought on it, turning it from dark brown to inky black. I looked at my eyebrows too, but reckoned I could get away with not dyeing them. The cropped hair didn't take long to dry. The cut on my forehead was healing quickly, though there was still bruising around the scab.

I unpacked my bag. I'd bought some new clothes at the shopping centre and ditched the ones I'd worn for the hit. This wasn't a special precaution: I always wear cheap clothes on a hit, then discard them afterwards. If you've used a gun, forensic scientists will find traces of the primer compound on your hands and clothes. Incredible, isn't it? When I tell Max these things, he doesn't believe me. He says they make it all up to scare people off using guns. Maybe he's got a point. In the bag I also had my standby, a .357 Magnum, not bought from Max this time but from a friend in France. It was a Colt copy, and not a very good one. On the firing range, it seemed to want to aim everywhere but at the bull. Its saving grace was that, like all revolvers, it scared people. That was its job. I didn't think it would scare Max; nevertheless, I wanted him to know I was armed.

There wasn't much else in the bag except for a manila envelope, a few bottles of fine white powder, some larger

48

bottles of sterilised water, and a couple of packs of disposable syringes. I always kept them in the bag, ever since a hotel maid had spotted them in my bathroom and informed the manager that I was dealing heroin from my room. Poor girl, she'd been so embarrassed afterwards. But I'd left her a tip anyway.

I lay on my bed for a while, running one finger through what was left of my hair and stroking the cat with the other. The cat belonged to the hotel. I'd seen it in the lobby on arrival and made a clicking noise to attract it.

'Don't bother,' the receptionist had said. 'Geronimo's very timid.'

Maybe, but I have a way with animals. Geronimo had padded meekly to my room unsummoned, and had miaowed at the door until I let him in, after which he'd twined himself round my legs a few times, then rubbed his jaw along my proffered knuckles, leaving his scent on me. I didn't have anything for him to eat, but he forgave me. So we lay, the pair of us, our eyes closed, somewhere between thought and nothingness, until I went down to the bar for some supper.

Back in my room, having drunk an indifferent half-bottle of Montrachet, I opened the manila envelope. This contained all the details of the hit, everything my employer had wanted me to know about Eleanor Ricks. I'm not a forensic scientist or a descendant of Sherlock Holmes, but I could tell the stapled sheets of paper had been word processed. The print quality was good, and the printing itself nice and regular. The paper was heavy and had a watermark. There was no handwriting anywhere; even the envelope had been typed. All it said was 'Private & Confidential'.

I read through the information again, searching for clues to my employer's identity. There was a photo of the target, too. It was a head and shoulders shot. She was smiling, her head tipped to one side so the hair fell and rested on her shoulder. It looked to me like a professional job, a publicity shot. For a start, it was black and white, and how many

49

people use monochrome film these days? Plus it was obviously posed, definitely not a snapshot.

Who would have access to publicity shots? The photographer of course, plus the model. The model's employers, and probably members of her immediate family . . . plus fans, the housekeeper, and anyone who happened to snatch one off a desk. I wasn't exactly narrowing things down.

I've said I don't like knowing about my targets, but my employer this time had sent me a lot of information, much of it extraneous. The amount of background they knew, they had to be close to the target. I mean, this wasn't the sort of stuff you could glean from press cuttings alone. They had to have known her pretty damned well. Either that or they'd been extremely thorough in their research.

None of which explained how they'd known the sorts of colours she'd be wearing on the day. I was back to family and the people she worked with. I had the idea I was going to have to go back to London and do some digging . . . but that would all depend on what Max had to say.

I settled my bill that night, since in the morning I intended starting off before breakfast. But the manageress wouldn't hear of this, and was up at six to cook me bacon and scrambled eggs and boil some tea. She even sat with me as I ate, though I'd have preferred to be alone.

'Long drive ahead of you?'

'Not really. Just a busy day.'

'I know all about that, sweetie.'

I smiled, but doubted this. As I left, Geronimo came out to the car with me, but then caught the scent of something better and trotted away. There was a heavy dew on the car, and the morning was raw, with cloud low and thick in the valleys and the roads wet. But the XR3i started at the first turn of the ignition. I had the .357 on the passenger seat, covered with the local freesheet which I'd picked up in the bar last night. As I drove off, I knew I had a long walk ahead.

Max's house sat in nine acres of moorland, the monotony broken only by the dry-stone dykes which divided the land into unused enclosures. The dykes had been built to give local employment during the hardest years of the 1920s. They were never intended to be put to any use. Max used those nearest his house as firing ranges, and had converted a long Dutch-style barn into an indoor range. The rest of the farm buildings had either been knocked down or left to fall in their own good time. Piles of rocks dotted what had been the farmyard. Max had graded them into large, middling and small, for no good reason that I could see. But then he was always methodical, even with debris.

I stopped the car about a mile from the house and left it on the grass verge, then climbed over one of the walls and started walking. The grass was wet underfoot, and I wished I'd bought some boots. But better this than driving up to the house. You could hear a car from hundreds of yards away. Though I could see the house, I knew the kitchen faced on to the interior farmyard, not out over the moors. I counted fewer than a dozen trees in the whole expanse, and wondered how Bel could live here.

I'd pushed the Magnum into my trouser waistband, but the ground was so uneven I transferred it to my jacket pocket. I kept a hand on it as I walked. I'd noticed in the car that brown spots of rust were appearing on the barrel. That was the problem with a cheap gun, it wasn't worth the maintenance.

Halfway across the first field, I stopped dead. I didn't know if I was ready for this. It was a long time since I'd used a handgun, even as a means of threat. Besides, if Max didn't have anything to do with it, I had a favour to ask of him . . . and of Bel.

Max no longer kept a dog. He thought animals belonged in the wild. There were no pets at all on the farm, though

Bel was soppy about cats and dogs and horses. Everything was quiet as I clambered over the last wall on to the track. If Max kept to his regular schedule, he'd be in the kitchen just now, probably eating something macrobiotic. He was on a weird diet which he swore was keeping the cancer at bay. I walked around the side of the house and peered round the wall. The farmyard was silent. I could see Max's Volvo estate parked in the barn, and behind it one of the human-shaped targets belonging to the indoor range. I took the Magnum from my pocket and walked to the kitchen door, turning the handle.

The kitchen had been gutted and redone about a year ago. It was all gleaming white tile and white units. Kept fanatically clean, it reminded me more of a hospital lab than a kitchen. And at its centre, seated at a foldaway table, was Max. He was already dressed and had strapped his mask across his maimed cheek and jaw. He was trying to eat something brown and sludgy with a teaspoon, and listening to the 'Today' programme on Radio Four.

'I wondered when you'd get here,' he said, not looking up. He had one hand on his bowl, the other holding his spoon. He was showing me both hands so I wouldn't get nervous. I wasn't aiming the gun. It was hanging almost casually from my hand. 'Want some breakfast?'

'You don't sound surprised to see me, Max.'

Now he looked up at me. 'That's some serious haircut, boy. Of course I'm not surprised. I heard what happened. They said the police were on the scene just too late to stop the shooting. I knew what you'd think.'

'What would I think, Max?' I leaned against the sink, keeping my distance.

'Do you want some breakfast?'

'I've had some, thanks.'

'Tea?'

'All right.' He got up to fetch a mug from the rack. 'You haven't answered my question.'

'That's because it's a stupid question. I was waiting for you to come up with a cleverer one.' He shuffled back to the table with the mug. 'Sit down, why don't you? And put away that bloody awful revolver. It embarrasses me having to look at it. Bloody cheap Asian copy, you'd probably miss me even at six feet. How far out of alignment is it?'

'About half an inch at twenty yards.'

Max wrinkled his nose. 'And it's rusting. If you tried popping me with that, I'd more likely die of shame than anything.'

I smiled, but didn't put the gun away. Max sighed.

'If not for me, then for Bel.'

'Where is she?'

'Sound asleep in her bed, lazy sow. Here, do you want this tea?'

I took the mug from the table and placed it on the draining board, leaning against the sink again.

'So,' said Max, 'someone knew you were doing the hit, and they tipped off the police. Stands to reason it must have been me or whoever was paying you in the first place.' I nodded. He looked up at me again. 'Well, it wasn't me. I don't blame you for being cagey, but it wasn't. So all I can do is tell you how the job came about. A man phoned me, a greaseball called Scotty Shattuck. Do you know him?' I shook my head. 'He was regular Army, but got a fright or something in the Falklands. Collected a few ears as souvenirs, and when the Army found out they dumped him back into society. He's tried his hand at mercenary work since, trained some of the fighters in Sarajevo. He doesn't have much of a rep, spends more time bouncing for night clubs than doing short-arms practice.'

'Where does he live?'

'Don't rush me, Mark. Shattuck said he had a client who was interested in having a job done. What he meant was someone had slipped him a few quid to find an assassin.'

'Why didn't he just take the job himself?'

'Maybe he pitched for it but the client knew his rep. Anyway, I said I'd need a few details, and we met in Leeds. He handed over a sealed envelope, giving me the gen I gave to you when I phoned you.'

'How much did he know about the hit?'

Max shrugged. 'The envelopes weren't tampered with, but he could always have torn open the original envelopes, read the gen for himself, and put it in a fresh envelope after.'

'Would he be curious enough to do that?'

'I don't know, maybe. Shattuck would like to play with the big boys. He seemed to think I was some sort of pimp with a stable of snipers, asked if I'd give him a trial. I told him to behave. And he did behave, too, except when payment time came.'

'Yes?'

'At our final meet, again in Leeds, he handed over the case. The final details were there, but the cash was short. Two hundred short. He said it was his cut. I told him that was fine by me, but the person the money was going to wouldn't be pleased. I asked him if two hundred was worth having to look over his shoulder the rest of his life and not go near windows.'

I grinned. 'What did he say?'

'He didn't say anything, he just sort of twitched and sweated. Then he took the money out of his pocket and handed it over.' Talking was thirsty work for Max. He had a straw in his mug of tea and took a long suck on it.

'So where can I find him, Max?'

'I don't know.'

'Come on, you must know.'

'I never needed to know. It was always him that contacted me.'

I raised the gun ever so slightly. 'Max,' I said. I didn't bother saying anything else. I was too busy looking at the kitchen doorway, the one leading to the hall and the rest of the house. Bel was standing there. She was wearing a short nightdress, showing very nice legs.

She was also pointing a shotgun at me.

'I know how to use it, Mark. Put away the gun.'

I didn't move. 'Let's get one thing straight,' I said. 'If you're going to be working for me, my name's not Mark Wesley any more. It's Michael Weston.'

Max leapt from his chair.

'Jesus, Bel! That's a Churchill *Premier*!' He ran to the doorway and took the shotgun from her. 'Do you know how much one of these is worth?'

'About ten grand,' she said.

'Ten grand is right. Less if it's been fired.' He broke open the barrels to show that Bel hadn't bothered loading the thing. I put my Magnum down on the draining board.

'Look,' said Max, 'let's all calm down. I'll tell you what I can about Shattuck, Mark.'

'Michael.'

'Okay, Michael. I'll tell you what I can. But let's sit down. All this Gunfight at the OK Corral stuff makes me nervous, especially in the kitchen. Do you know how long it took me to do this tiling?'

So Max put the kettle on and we sat down. Bel gave me a lopsided smile, and I winked back at her.

'Black suits you,' she said, meaning my hair. 'Even if that haircut does make you look like a copper.' She touched my foot with her own under the table. We'd played this game before, enjoying the fact of having a secret from Max. I tried to remember that only a few minutes ago, she'd been aiming a shotgun at me, albeit unloaded. Bel had the face of a sixth-form schoolgirl, but I knew there was much more to her than that.

'Sorry,' I said, 'I haven't brought you a souvenir this trip.'

She attempted a pout. 'I'm hurt.'

I put my hand in my pocket and pulled out the hat I'd bought. 'Unless you want this.'

She took it from me and looked at it. 'Gee, thanks,' she said, her voice heavy with irony. 'I'll keep it under my pillow.'

Max was massaging his jaw. Usually he didn't say much, understandably. He'd said more in the past twenty minutes than he would over the course of a normal day.

'What was that about me working for you?' Bel asked, folding her arms.

'More properly, working *with* me.' I was looking at Max as I spoke. 'I'm going to have to go back to London, there are questions I need to ask. I'd look less conspicuous with a partner. Plus maybe there are some people I can't talk to myself. But Bel could talk to them.'

'No,' Max said.

'I pay well, and I'd look after her. I'd play it straight. First sign of danger, I zoom back up here with her.'

'What am I, a ventriloquist's dummy?' Bel had risen from the table and was standing with hands on hips. 'Why not ask me yourself? You sound like you're asking to borrow a car or a bike, not a person.'

'Sorry, Bel.'

'You're not going,' said Max.

'I haven't said anything yet!' she protested, slapping the table with her hand. 'I want to hear about it first.'

So I told her. There was no point leaving anything out. Bel wasn't stupid, she certainly wasn't naïve. She'd have rooted out a lie. It isn't easy telling someone what you do for a living, not if you're not proud of your work. I'd never minded Max knowing, but Bel . . . Bel was a slightly different proposition. Of course, she'd known all along. I mean, I was hardly coming to the farm, buying guns, firing them, customising them, I was hardly doing any of this as a weekend hobby. Still, her cheeks reddened as I told my story. Then a third round of tea was organised in silence, with the radio switched off now. Bel poured cereal for herself and started to eat. She'd swallowed two spoonfuls before she said anything.

'I want to go.'

Max started to protest.

'A few days, Max,' I broke in, 'that's all. Look, I need help this time. Who else can I turn to?'

'I can think of a dozen people better qualified than Bel, and always keen to make money.'

'Well, thanks very much,' she said. 'Nice to know you have such a high opinion of me.'

'I just don't want you—'

She took his hand and squeezed it. 'I know, I know. But Michael needs help. Are we supposed to turn our backs? Pretend we've never known him? Who else *do* we know?'

It hit me then for the first time. They lived out here in the wilds through necessity not choice. You couldn't run a gun shop like Max's in the middle of a town. But out here they were also lonely, cut off from the world. There were twice-weekly runs into the village or the nearest large town, but those hardly constituted a social life. It wasn't Max, it was Bel. She was twenty-two. She'd sacrificed a lot to move out here. I saw why Max was scared: he wasn't scared she'd get hurt, he was scared she'd get to like it. He was scared she'd leave for good.

'A few days, Max,' I repeated. 'Then I'll bring Bel back.'

He didn't say anything, just blinked his watery eyes and looked down at the table where his hands lay, nicked and scarred from metal-shop accidents. Bel touched his shoulder.

'I'll go pack a few things.' She gave me another smile and ran from the room. Only now did I wonder why she was so keen to go with me.

We were awkward after she'd gone. I rinsed out the mugs at the sink, and heard Max's chair scrape on the floor as he stood up. He came to the draining board and picked up the revolver.

'Do you need anything?' he asked.

'Maybe a pistol.'

'I think I've got something better than a pistol. Not cheap though.'

'Money's no object this time, Max.'

'Mark . . . Sorry, I mean Michael. Funny, I'd just got used to calling you Mark.'

'I'll be another name soon enough.'

'Michael, I know you'll take care of her. But I wouldn't like . . . I mean, I don't want . . .'

'This is strictly business, Max. Separate rooms, I promise. And besides, Bel can look after herself. She's had a good teacher.'

'Don't patronise me,' he said with a smile, putting down the Magnum and reaching for a dishtowel.

7

'You're not a reporter, are you?'

It was first thing Monday morning and Hoffer wasn't in the mood. The ambulance was parked in a special unloading bay directly outside Casualty, and the ambulanceman was in the back, tidying and checking.

Hoffer stood outside, one hand resting on the vehicle's back door. He had a sudden image of himself slamming the ambulanceman's head repeatedly against it.

'I've told you, I'm a private investigator.'

'Only I told the police everything I know, and then the bleeding newspapers start hassling me.'

'Look, Mr Hughes, I've shown you my ID.'

'Yeah, anyone can fake an identity card.'

This was true, but Hoffer wasn't in a mood for discussion. He had a head like a St Patrick's Day parade in Boston. Plus his ears still weren't back to normal. Every time he breathed in through his nose, it was like he was going to suck his eardrums into his throat.

'Talk to me and I'll go away,' he said. That usually worked. Hughes turned and studied him.

'You don't look like a reporter.'

Hoffer nodded at this wisdom.

'You look like a cardiac arrest waiting to happen.'

Hoffer stopped nodding and started a serious scowl.

'All right, sorry about that. So, what do you want me to tell you?'

'I've seen the transcript of your police interview, Mr Hughes. Basically, I'd just like to ask a few follow-up questions, maybe rephrase a couple of questions you've already been asked.'

'Well, hurry up, I'm on duty.'

Hoffer refrained from pointing out that they could have started a good five minutes ago. Instead he asked about the phony patient's accent.

'Very smooth,' said Hughes. 'Polite, quiet, educated.'

'But definitely English?'

'Oh, yes.'

'Not American? Sometimes the two can sound more similar than you'd think.'

'This was English. I couldn't tell you which county though. He wasn't a Yank, I'm sure of that.'

'Canadian possibly?' Hughes shook his head. 'Okay then, you've given a fairly good description of him, what he was wearing, his height, hair colour and so on. Do you think his hair might have been dyed?'

'How am I supposed to know?'

'Sometimes a dye job doesn't look quite right.'

'Yeah? We must meet a different class of women.'

Hoffer tried to laugh. The door handle felt good in his hand. He kept looking at Hughes's head. 'And it couldn't have been a toupee?'

'You mean an Irish?' Hoffer didn't understand. 'Irish jig, wig. No, I'm sure his hair was his own.'

'Mm-hm.' Hoffer had already spoken to the nurse in Emergency, the one who'd taken the man's details and then gone to call a haematologist. She'd been as much help as codeine in a guillotine basket. He rubbed his forehead. 'He told you he was a haemophiliac.'

'He *was* a haemophiliac.'

'You sure?'

'Either that or he has one in the family. Or maybe he just went through medical school.'

'He knew that much about it?'

'He knew about factor levels, he knew haemophiliacs are

60

supposed to carry a special card with them, he knew they get to call the emergency number and order an ambulance if they hurt themselves. He knew a lot.'

'He couldn't just have been guessing?'

Hughes shook his head. 'I'm telling you, he *knew*.'

'Who's your haematologist here?'

'I don't know, I just act as chauffeur.'

'That's being a bit harsh on yourself.'

Hughes's look told Hoffer flattery wasn't going to work. 'What about the business card, it fell out of his pocket?'

'Yes. He said it was his, but the police tell me it wasn't. They had me take a look at Gerald Flitch, I mean the real Gerald Flitch. It wasn't him.'

'Mm, I want a word with him myself.'

The Casualty doors crashed open as the ambulance driver pulled a wheelchair out and down the ramp. Hughes jumped out of the ambulance. There was a woman in the wheelchair so ancient and still she looked like she'd been stuffed.

'Here we are again, Mrs Bridewell,' Hughes yelled at her, as they prepared to hoist her into the ambulance. 'Soon have you home.'

'Is it worth the trip?' Hoffer muttered to himself. He turned away from the ambulance, but Hughes called to him. The driver was already getting into his seat and starting the engine. Hughes had an arm on the back door, ready to close it.

'I meant it about the cardiac. You really should lose some weight. We could do our backs in rolling you on to the stretcher.'

'You're all heart, pal!' Hoffer called, but he called it to a slammed door as the ambulance revved away. He walked back up the hill to Emergency. The same nurse he'd spoken to was still there. She didn't look like she'd been pining.

'Just one more thing,' Hoffer said, raising a crooked index finger. 'Who do I speak to about haemophilia?'

'It means love of blood, literally.'

Dr Jacobs was a small man with one of those English-actor voices that make American women wet their drawers. It was like Jeremy Irons was behind the scenes somewhere and Jacobs was his dummy. He also had the hairiest arms Hoffer had seen outside a zoo, and he only had ten minutes to spare. He was explaining what the word haemophilia meant.

'That's very interesting,' said Hoffer. 'But see, the man we're dealing with here, he's a hired killer, a gunman. He also uses explosives. Does that sound like a suitable occupation for a haemophiliac?'

'No, it doesn't. Well, that's to say, not for a *severe* haemophiliac. You see, there are three broad levels of haemophilia. You can be severe, moderate, or mild. Most registered haemophiliacs in the UK are severe – that is, they show less than two percent factor activity.'

'What's factor activity?'

'Haemophiliacs, Mr Hoffer, suffer from a clotting deficiency in the blood. Clotting is a complex event, involving thirteen different factors. If one thing happens, then another happens, and we get a knock-on effect. When all thirteen things have happened, we get blood clotting. But haemophiliacs lack one of the factors, so the knock-on can't happen and clotting can't take place. Most haemophiliacs suffer from a factor eight deficiency, some from a factor nine deficiency. There are a few even rarer conditions, but those are the main two. Factor eight deficiency is termed Haemophilia A, and factor nine Haemophilia B. Are you with me so far?'

'Reading you like braille.'

Dr Jacobs leaned back in his black leather chair. He had a small cluttered office, all textbooks and test results and piles of unanswered mail. His white coat was hanging up behind the door, and there were a lot of framed certificates on the walls. His arms were folded so he could run his hands over his monkey arms. Hair sprouted from the collar of his shirt. Naked, Hoffer bet you could use him as a fireside rug.

'Severe haemophiliacs,' the doctor said, 'make up over a third of all haemophilia cases. They can suffer spontaneous internal bleeds, usually into soft tissues, joints and muscles. As children, they're advised to stay away from contact sports. We try to make them get a good education, so they can get desk jobs rather than manual ones.'

'They don't go into the armed forces then?'

Dr Jacobs smiled. 'The armed forces and the police won't recruit from haemophiliacs.'

Hoffer frowned. If there was one thing he'd been sure of, it was that the D-Man had been either a soldier or a cop. 'No exceptions?'

'None.'

'Not even if they've got the milder form?'

Jacobs shook his head. 'Something wrong?' he said.

Hoffer had been tugging at his ears. 'Flying does things to my ears,' he said. 'Say, can you help? Maybe take a look?'

'I'm a haematologist, Mr Hoffer, not ENT.'

'But you can prescribe drugs, right? Some painkillers maybe?'

'Consult a GP, Mr Hoffer.'

'I can pay.'

'I'm sure you can. Did you catch your cold on the plane?'

'Huh?' Hoffer sniffed so much these days, he was hardly aware of it. He blew his nose and reminded himself to buy more paper handkerchiefs. Damned nose was always itchy too. 'It's this lousy weather,' he said.

The doctor looked surprised and glanced out of his window. It was another beautiful day outside. He looked back at Hoffer.

'The police have already asked me about this assassin. It seems from what I hear that he does possess some knowledge of haemophilia, but as I told them, I just can't visualise a severe haemophiliac being an assassin. He told the ambulanceman that he was one per cent. I think he was lying. I mean . . . well, this is guesswork.'

'No, go on.' Hoffer stuck his shred of handkerchief back in his pocket.

'Well, it seems to me that these weapons he uses, they would have a recoil.'

'Believe it.'

'You see, any recoil might start a severe haemophiliac bleeding. It wouldn't be long before he'd start to suffer problems with his shoulder. After which he wouldn't make much of a marksman at all.'

'What about a moderate sufferer?'

'Even with a moderate sufferer, there would be dangers. No, if this man suffers from haemophilia, then he is a mild case.'

'But he'd still know about the disease, right?'

'Oh, yes. But he'd also be able to injure himself without needing medical aid afterwards. Simple pressure on the cut would be enough to stop it.'

Hoffer chewed this over. 'Would he be registered?'

'Almost certainly.'

'I don't suppose those records . . . ?'

Jacobs was shaking his head. 'If the police wish to apply to see them, then of course there might be a chance, especially if it's a case of catching a murderer.'

'Yes, of course. Dr Jacobs, how many mild sufferers are there?'

'In the UK?' Hoffer nodded. 'About fifteen hundred.'

'Out of how many?'

'Roughly six and a half thousand.'

'And how many of those fifteen hundred can we discount?'

'What?'

'You know, how many are kids, how many are pensioners, how many are women? It's got to bring the number down.'

64

Jacobs was smiling. 'I have some pamphlets here you should read, Mr Hoffer.' He opened a desk drawer, hunting for them.

'What? Did I say something funny?'

'No, it's just that haemophilia affects only men. It's passed on from the mother, not the father, but it is only passed on to the sons.'

Hoffer read the pamphlets as he sat in the bar of the Allington Hotel.

He found it all unbelievable. How could a mother do that to her son? Unbelievable. The women in the family could carry the disease, but they almost never suffered from it. And if they passed it on to their daughters, the daughters could fight it. It was all down to chromosomes. A boy got his mother's X and his father's Y, while a girl got two X chromosomes, one from each parent. The bad genetic information was all in the X chromosome. A man with haemophilia passed his bad X to his daughter, but the good X she got from her mother cancelled the bad X out. So she became a carrier but not a sufferer. Each female had two X chromosomes, while males had an X and a Y. So boys had a fifty-fifty chance of getting the bad X passed on to them from their mothers. And they couldn't override it because they didn't have another good X chromosome, they had a lousy Y which wasn't any use in the battle.

There was other stuff, all about Queen Victoria and the Russian royal family and Rasputin. Queen Victoria had been a carrier. There didn't have to be a history of haemophilia in the family either, the thing could just spontaneously occur. And a mild haemophiliac might never know they had the disease till it came time for a surgical operation or tooth extraction. The more Hoffer read, the more he wondered about going for a blood test. He had always bruised easily, and one time he'd been spitting blood for days after a visit to his dentist. Maybe he was a haemophiliac. He wouldn't put anything past his mother.

He wasn't sure what difference it made, knowing the D-Man was probably a sufferer. It could just be that his family had a history of haemophilia; he could just be an interested onlooker. Hoffer wasn't going to be given access to any records, and even if he did get the records, what would he do with them? Talk to every single sufferer? Drag them here and let Gerry Flitch take a look at them?

Ah, speaking of whom . . .

'Mr Flitch?'

'Yes.'

Hoffer offered his hand. 'Leo Hoffer, can I buy you a drink?'

'Thank you, yes.'

Hoffer snapped his fingers, and the barman nodded. The first time Hoffer had done it, the barman had given him a stare so icy you could have mixed it into a martini. But then Hoffer had given him a big tip, and so now the barman was his friend. Hoffer was sitting in a squidgy armchair in a dark corner of the bar. Flitch pulled over a chair and sat down opposite him. He flicked his hair back into place.

'This has all been . . . I don't know,' he began, unasked. 'It's not every day you find out you've had drinks bought for you by an international terrorist.'

'Not a terrorist, Gerry, just a hired gun. Do you mind if I call you Gerry?'

'Not at all . . . Leo.'

'There you go. Now, what'll it be?' The barman was standing ready.

'Whisky, please.'

'Ice, sir?'

'And bring some water, too, please.'

'Certainly, sir.'

Hoffer handed his empty glass to the barman. 'And I'll have the same again, Tom.'

'My pleasure, Mr Hoffer.'

Gerry Flitch looked suitably impressed, which had been the plan all along. Hoffer gathered up his haemophilia pamphlets and stuck them down the side of the chair. It was a great chair, plenty big enough and damned comfortable. He wondered if he could buy it from the hotel, maybe ship it back.

'You said you're a private detective, Leo.'

'That's right, Gerry.'

'And the police tell me you're very well known.'

'In the States, maybe.' Good. As suggested, Flitch had called Bob Broome to check Hoffer's credentials. 'So tell me about Saturday, Gerry. No rush, I just want to listen.'

Tom the barman arrived with their drinks, and Hoffer gave him another tip. 'Let us have some nuts or something, Tom, huh?'

'Surely, Mr Hoffer.'

The nuts and crisps arrived in small glass bowls. Hoffer helped himself to a fistful. He'd had a mellowing-out joint half an hour ago, and was now hungry.

'Well,' said Flitch, 'what is there to tell? I was drinking at the bar, sitting on one of those stools there. This guy came in for a drink, and sat a couple of stools away. He was drinking some soft drink, grapefruit and lemonade I think.'

'It was tonic, not lemonade. We know that from his bar tab.'

Flitch nodded. 'Yes, tonic, that's right. Anyway, we got talking.'

'Who started?'

'I think I did.'

'And did this guy, did he speak sort of grudgingly?'

'No, not at all, he seemed very pleasant. You wouldn't think he had murder on his mind.'

'Maybe he didn't. These guys have a way of blocking it out when they want to. So what did you talk about?'

Flitch shrugged. 'Just general stuff. He told me he was in

import-export, I told him I was a marketing strategist. I even gave him my card.' He shook his head. 'What a mistake *that* was. Next thing I know, armed police are at the door of my room.'

'You're the biggest break we've had, Gerry. It was the Demolition Man who made the mistake, accepting your card.'

'Yes, but now he knows who I am, who I work for, where I live. And here I am talking to you.'

'But he won't know you've talked to us until he's arrested. Besides, he's not stupid. He won't come near you.'

'He won't have to come near me though, will he? From what I've heard, a few hundred yards would be close enough.' Flitch finished his drink. Hoffer knew the man was nervous, but he suspected Flitch was a heavy drinker anyway. The guy was young, late-twenties, but he had a face that was hardening prematurely, losing its good looks and gaining jowls. Only a big man, a man like Hoffer himself, could carry jowls and not look like a drunk. Flitch was a drunk in the making, and the pattern was just about complete.

'Tell me something, Gerry, you ever do coke?'

Flitch's eyes widened. 'I take it you don't mean the soft drink?'

'I do not.'

Flitch shrugged. 'I might've done a little at parties.' He narrowed his eyes. 'Why?'

Hoffer sat forward. 'Know where I could get some?'

Flitch smiled. 'In Liverpool I could help you, but not down here.'

Hoffer sat back again and nodded slowly, then craned his neck. 'Another round here, Tom.' Flitch didn't say no. Hoffer rubbed a hand across his nose. 'So what else did you talk about? Family? Background? That's what businessmen talk about in strange bars, isn't it?'

'Not us, it never became personal. We talked about how

easy things had seemed in the mid-80s, then how tough they'd become, and how tough they still were. He said something like, "There's no room for bleeding hearts in our line of work".' Flitch shivered at the memory.

'The guy's got a sense of humour,' Hoffer remarked. Tom arrived with the drinks. 'Gerry, I'm not going to ask you what this guy looked like. You've already given the cops a good description, and he'll have changed his appearance by now anyway. I'm going to ask for something more difficult.' Hoffer sat forwards. 'I want your impressions of him as a man. Just close your eyes, think back on that day, fix it in your mind, and then say anything you want to say. No need to feel embarrassed, the bar's empty. Go on, close your eyes.' Flitch closed them. 'That's right. Now, to get you warmed up, I'll ask a few questions about him, okay?'

'Okay.' Flitch's eyelids fluttered like young butterflies.

'Tell me about his movements, were they stiff or fluid? How did he pick up his glass? Did you see him walk?'

Gerry Flitch thought for a moment and then started to speak.

Afterwards, Hoffer washed his face and hands in the men's room and looked at himself in the mirror. He felt tired. He'd have to phone Walkins tonight with a preliminary report. There'd be plenty to tell him. Walkins was greedy for information about the Demolition Man. It was like he wanted to build up a good enough picture so he could then tear it to shreds. Hoffer couldn't really figure Walkins out. There were no photographs of his daughter in Walkins' house, though there were plenty of his wife, who'd died of lung cancer. The man was loaded, a fortune made in politics. When he was a senator, Walkins had tucked the money away, probably most of it legit. You didn't have to be crooked in politics to make a small fortune. But when he'd left politics, Walkins must have done something to turn his small fortune into a large one, large enough to pay for Hoffer's obsession and still leave plenty over.

He thought about doing a couple of lines. They'd keep him awake and alert. But he had one more job to do yet, and besides, he was perilously close to the end of his stash. He left the men's room and sweet-talked the receptionist, who let him take a look at Room 203. The police had given it a good going over. There was still fingerprint powder on the dressing table, wardrobe and television. But it looked like 'Mark Wesley' had spent some time before checking out engaged in a bit of dusting. He'd left a couple of dry bath-towels on the floor of his room, and why else would they be there if he hadn't been using them as dusters? However, the police reckoned they had half a palm print from the inside of the door, and an index finger from the courtesy kettle. They could not, of course, be sure whose prints they were. They might belong to a maid or a visitor or a previous occupant. They'd only know when they arrested Mark Wesley, or whatever he was calling himself now. They'd also dusted the ambulance, but Wesley had been helped in and helped out. He hadn't touched a thing.

The room didn't tell Hoffer anything. Gerry Flitch hadn't told him much either. He was building up his own picture of the D-Man, but didn't know where that would get him. He was no psychologist, no specialist in profiling. He had a friend at the FBI who might make more sense of it all. He went back to reception and found that the receptionist had his print-out and photocopies all ready. He handed her the promised twenty. He'd already been given the information by Bob Broome, but he wanted to check that Broome was playing straight with him. The information was all here. He'd used a credit card to reserve his room, but had paid cash when he checked out. The police had run tests and serial number checks on all the cash taken by the hotel on Saturday. The potential big break, though, was the credit card. The home address Mark Wesley had given to the hotel was false, but the credit card had turned out to be genuine.

It had taken a while to wring the information out of the credit card company, but now they knew all the lies Wesley had told them: occupation, date of birth, mother's maiden name . . . Well, maybe it was all a fabrication, but maybe there were a few half-truths and little slips in there. It would all be checked out. The credit card company sent its statements to an address in St John's Wood, and that's where Hoffer was headed, as soon as his chauffeur arrived.

Broome arrived only five minutes late, so Hoffer forgave him.

'Had a productive morning?' Broome asked, as his passenger got in.

'I think so, what about you?'

'Ticking over.'

On the way to St John's Wood, Hoffer told Broome some of what he'd found out about haemophilia.

'If we could get a list of registered haemophiliacs, I bet we could narrow it down pretty fast.'

'Maybe. I'll see what I can do. It could be a dead end.'

'Hey, we won't know till we've got our noses pressed against the wall, will we?'

'I suppose not. But maybe we can take a short cut. We're just passing Lord's, by the way.'

'Lord who?'

'Just Lord's. It's the home of cricket.'

'A sports field, huh? Cricket's the one that's like baseball, only easier?' Broome gave him a dark look. 'Just kidding. But did you ever watch a game of baseball? Greatest game on earth.'

'That must be why so many countries play it.'

They arrived at a block of flats and parked in the residents' only parking area. When they got to the right door, Broome made to ring the bell, then noticed Hoffer slip the Smith & Wesson out from his waistband.

'Christ, Leo!'

'Hey, our man may be in there.'

'It's a mail service, that's all. An accommodation address. Remember, they're expecting us, so put that gun away.'

Reluctantly, Hoffer tucked the pistol back into his waistband and buttoned his jacket. Broome rang the doorbell and waited. The door opened.

'Mr Greene?'

'Chief Inspector Broome?'

'That's right, sir.' Broome showed his ID. 'May we come in?'

'Of course.'

They were led down a short dimly-lit hall and into a living room. It was a ground-floor flat, as small as any Hoffer had been in. One bedroom and a bathroom, but the kitchen was part of the living room. It was well-finished though, if you liked your home decorated according to fashion rather than personal preference. Everything had that just-bought-from-Habitat look.

Desmond Greene was in his 40s, wiry and slack-jawed with hands that moved too much and eyes that wouldn't meet yours. When he talked, he looked like he was lecturing the pale yellow wallpaper. Hoffer marked him straight away as gay, not that that meant anything. Often Hoffer met men he was sure were gay, only later to be introduced to their pneumatic wives. Not that that meant anything either.

Broome had made a point of not introducing Hoffer. It wasn't exactly Metropolitan Police policy to drag New York private eyes around with you on a case. Maybe Broome was hoping Hoffer would keep his mouth shut.

'How long you been running this set-up, Mr Greene?' Hoffer asked.

Greene's fingers glided down his face like a skin-cream commercial. 'Four and a half years, that's quite a long time in this business.'

'And how do potential clients find you?'

'Oh, I advertise.'

'Locally?'

A wry smile. '*Expensively*. I run regular advertisements in magazines.'

'Which magazines?'

'My Lord, you *are* curious.'

Hoffer tried out his own wry smile. 'Only when I'm hunting a cold-blooded killer and someone's standing in my way.'

Greene looked giddy, and Bob Broome took over. Hoffer didn't mind, he reckoned he'd scared Greene into telling the truth and plenty of it. He didn't even mind the way Broome looked at him, like Hoffer had just asked a boy scout to slip his hand into his trouser pocket and meet Uncle Squidgy.

'How long have you been handling mail for Mr Wesley?'

'You understand, Chief Inspector,' Greene said, recovering slightly, 'the purpose of a mailing address is confidentiality?'

'Yes, sir, I understand. But as I told you over the phone, this is a multiple murder inquiry. If you do not cooperate, you'll be charged with obstruction.'

'After which we'll take your chintzy flat apart,' added Hoffer.

'Gracious,' said Greene, having a relapse. 'Oh, goodness me.'

'Hoffer,' said Broome quietly, 'go and put the kettle on. Maybe Mr Greene would like some tea.'

What am I, the fucking maid service? Hoffer got up and went to the kitchenette. He was behind Greene now, and Greene knew it. He sat forward in his chair, as though fearing a knife between the shoulder blades. Hoffer smiled, thinking how Greene would react to the feel of a cold gun muzzle at the back of his neck.

'So,' Broome was saying, 'are you willing to assist us, sir?'

'Well, of course I am. It's not my job to hide murderers.'

'Maybe if you told me a little of the service you offer Mr Wesley?'

73

'It's the same as my other customers. There are forty-odd of them. I receive mail, and they can contact me by telephone to find out what's arrived, or they can have the mail forwarded to them monthly. I also operate a call-answering and forwarding service, but Mr Wesley didn't require that.'

'How much mail does he receive?'

'Almost none at all. Bills and bank statements.'

'And does he have the stuff forwarded?'

'No, he collects it in person.'

'How often?'

'Infrequently. Like I say, it's just bank statements and bills.'

'What sort of bills?'

'Credit cards, I'd guess. Well, he doesn't need a credit card statement to pay off the account, does he? A simple cheque and note with his account number would do it.'

'That's true. He never has the stuff forwarded to him?'

'Once he did, to a hotel in Paris.'

'Do you remember the name of the hotel?'

Greene shook his head. 'I'm sorry, it was well over a year ago.'

'Maybe two years ago?' Hoffer added.

Greene half-turned to him. 'Could be.'

Hoffer looked to Broome. 'That Dutchman, the heroin pusher. The D-Man took him out in Paris a couple of years back.'

Broome nodded. The kettle came to the boil and Hoffer picked it up, then thought better of it.

'Does anyone *really* want tea? Me, I could murder a drink.'

'I've some gin,' Greene said. 'Or a few cans of lager.'

'It's your party, Des,' Hoffer said with a grin.

So Broome and Hoffer had a can of lager each, and Greene sat with a gin and tonic. He loosened up a little after that. The lager was fine, even though a couple of months past its sell by.

'Okay,' said Broome, 'so mail gets sent here and Wesley phones up and you tell him what's arrived?'

Greene nodded, stirring his drink with a finger and then sucking the tip.

'Does he ever get you to open mail and read it to him?'

Greene smacked his lips. 'Never.'

'And he's never received anything other than bills?'

Hoffer interrupted. 'No fat brown envelopes full of banknotes? No large flat packages with photos and details of his next hit?'

Greene quivered the length of his body.

'Can you give us a description of him?' Broome asked, ignoring Hoffer. The description Greene gave was that of the man Gerry Flitch had given his card to.

'Well, that's about all for now, Mr Greene,' said Broome. He placed his empty can on the carpet.

'But there's one other thing,' said Greene.

'What's that?'

'Aren't you going to ask if there's any mail waiting for him?'

'Well, is there?'

Greene broke into a huge wrinkle-faced grin. 'Yes!' he squealed. 'There is!'

But having got both men excited, he now seemed to want to stall. It was a crime, after all, to open someone else's mail without their express permission. So Broome had to write a note to the effect that he was taking away the letter, and that he was authorised to do so. Greene read it through.

'Can you write that I'm exonerated from all guilt or possible legal action?'

Broome scribbled some words to that effect, then signed and dated the note. Greene studied it again. Hoffer was close behind him, breathing hard.

'Fine,' said Greene, folding the note but leaving it on the breakfast bar. He went off to fetch the letter. When he was out of the room, Hoffer tore a fresh sheet of paper from the writing pad, folded it, and put it down on the breakfast bar, then lifted Broome's note and scrunched it into a ball before dropping it into his pocket. He winked at Broome. Greene came back into the room. He was waving a single, slim envelope.

'Looks like a bank statement,' he said.

It was a bank statement.

The bank was closed when they got to it, but the staff were still on the premises, balancing the day's books. The manager, Mr Arthur, ushered them into his utilitarian office.

'I can't do anything tonight,' he said. 'It's too late to get anyone at head office. You realise that there are channels that must be gone through, authorisations, and even then a really thorough check could take some considerable time.'

'I appreciate all of that, sir,' said Bob Broome, 'but the sooner we can get the ball rolling, the sooner we'll be near the goal. This man has murdered over half a dozen individuals, two of them in this country.'

'Yes, I do understand, and tomorrow morning we'll do everything we can, as quickly as we can, it just can't be done tonight.'

They were in the Piccadilly branch of one of the clearing banks. It was, naturally, a busy branch, perfect for someone like the Demolition Man, who needed to be anonymous.

'If we could just talk about his account for a few minutes, sir,' Broome said. The manager glanced at his wall clock and sighed.

'Very well then,' he said.

Broome produced the bank statement. There wasn't much to it. It referred to the previous month, and showed a balance of £1,500 on the 1st, with cheque and cashpoint withdrawals through the month totalling £900, leaving a closing credit balance of £600. Arthur typed in the account number on his computer.

'Mm,' he said, studying the screen, 'since that statement was drawn up, he's withdrawn another £500.'

'In other words,' said Hoffer, 'he's all but emptied the account?'

'Yes, Friday, Saturday and Sunday. He withdrew money on each day.'

Hoffer turned to Broome. 'He's shedding Mark Wesley.' He turned to the bank manager. 'Mr Arthur, I think you'll find that account stays dormant from now on.'

'Can we find out where he took the cash from?' Broome asked.

Arthur studied the screen again. 'Central London,' he said.

'What about old cheques?' Hoffer asked. 'Do you hold on to them?'

'Yes, for a while at least.'

'So we could look at his returned cheques?'

Arthur nodded. 'After I've had authorisation.'

Broome looked at Hoffer. 'What are you thinking?'

'He has to pay people, Bob. Maybe he doesn't always have the cash on him.'

'You think he pays for his guns and explosives *by cheque?*'

Hoffer held his hands up, palms towards Broome. 'Hey, maybe not, but we need to check. Could be there's something he's paid for, or *someone* he's paid for, that can lead us right to him. He'll be underground now, busy making himself a new identity. All we have to go on is the old one. I say we dig as far as we can.' He turned to Arthur, who was looking dazzled by this exchange. 'We need old cheques, old statements, and we need to know the site of every auto-teller he's used. There could be a pattern that'll tell us where he's based.'

'Auto-teller?' said Arthur.

'Cash machine,' explained Broome.

8

I sat in my hotel room, counting out my money.

I had $4,500 in cash, money I'd been keeping safe at Max's farm. I had another $5,000 in cash in a safe deposit box in Knightsbridge, and $25,000 cash in another safe deposit box at the same location. I reckoned I'd be all right for a while. I'd all but emptied the Mark Wesley bank account, and had disposed of his credit cards. I still had my Michael Weston account and credit cards, and no matter how far the police probed into 'Mark Wesley', I couldn't see them getting close to Michael Weston.

The hotel I was in had asked for a credit card as guarantee, but I'd paid upfront instead. I put some of the money back in my holdall, and put some in my pocket, leaving a couple of thousand still on the bed. I had more money in New York, and some in Zurich, but I definitely wouldn't need to touch that.

I rolled up the final two thou and stuck it in the toe of one of my spare shoes, then put the shoes back in the closet. I'd had to take everything out of the holdall. The stiff cardboard base was loose, and I'd slipped the money under it. There was a soft knock at the door. I unlocked it and let in Bel.

'How's your room?' I asked.

'All right.' She'd taken a shower. Her hair was damp, her face buffed. She was wearing jeans and a T-shirt. We were in a new hotel, the Rimmington. It wasn't central, but I didn't mind. I knew returning to London so soon was dangerous. I didn't want to be anywhere near the Craigmead or the Allington. So we were in a much smaller hotel just off Marylebone Road, handy, as the receptionist said, for

Madame Tussaud's, the Planetarium, and Regent's Park. We were supposed to be on holiday from Nottingham, so we looked interested as she told us this. Actually, Bel had more than *looked* interested.

'There won't be much time for sightseeing,' I warned her now.

'Don't worry,' she snapped back, 'I'm here to work. What's that?' She was pointing to my 'works'. They were lying on the bed, syringes and all. I started loading them back into the holdall.

'Are you on drugs?'

'No, I just ... sometimes I need an injection. I'm a haemophiliac.'

'That means you bleed a lot?'

'It means when I bleed, sometimes it won't stop without help.'

'An injection?' I nodded. 'But you're all right?'

I smiled at her. 'I'm fine.' She decided she'd take my word for it.

'So where are you taking me for dinner?'

'How about a burger?'

'We had burgers for lunch.'

This was true. We'd stopped at a motorway service area, where the burgers had looked the most appetising display. Bel deserved better, especially on her first night in London. That makes her sound naïve, a country bumpkin, which she wasn't. But she hadn't been to London in five years, hadn't been out of Yorkshire for the best part of a year. I wondered if I'd been right to bring her. How much of a liability might she become? I still didn't think there'd be any real danger, except of arrest.

'Well, you decide: Italian? Indian? Chinese? French? Thai? London can accommodate most tastes.'

She flopped down on my bed and assumed a thoughtful pose.

'So long as it's between here and Tottenham,' I added,

'but then you can find most things between here and Tottenham.'

I was all for taking a cab to Tottenham, but Bel wanted to ride on the tube. We'd dropped the XR3i back at its shop, and I'd settled for it in cash. There was no point hanging on to it; I thought we'd be in London for a few days. One thing about Bel, she surely did look like a tourist, wide-eyed and unafraid and ready to meet a stranger's eyes, even to smile and start a conversation. Yes, you could tell she was new in town. I couldn't help but be a bit more worldly, even though I was a tourist too. We got off the tube at Seven Sisters and ate at a Caribbean restaurant, where Bel had to have a second helping of the planter's punch and was nearly sick as a result. She didn't eat much though, apart from the dirty rice and johnny cakes. The fish was too salty for her, the meat too rich.

There was an evening paper in the restaurant, and I flicked through it until I found the latest on the Ricks assassination. The diplomat from the Craigmead was caus-ing a stink, talking about lax security and an MI5 plot against him. According to his version, MI5 and some country neighbouring his own were in cahoots.

'Keep muddying the water, pal,' I told his grainy photograph. There was a more interesting snippet further down the page, added almost as an afterthought. It talked about a 'mystery call' to the Craigmead Hotel, a summons Eleanor Ricks had ignored. It intrigued me. Had my paymaster got cold feet and tried to warn her? And being unable to reach her, had he then phoned the police instead? I'd heard stories about employers changing their minds. I wouldn't mind if they did, so long as they weren't looking for a refund. If they wanted their money back, well, that was a different proposition entirely.

We walked up the long High Road, looking into a few of the less salubrious pubs. I'd already explained to Bel who I was looking for, and she seemed glad of the fresh air and exercise. The traffic was blocked all the way up the High Road to Monument Way, and all the way down Monument Way too. We stopped in at the Volley, but there was no one there I knew. I always had to be careful in Tottenham. There were people I might meet here who might assume I was either after something or being nosy. For example, sometimes I bought plastic explosives and detonators from a couple of Irishmen who lived here. They weren't really supposed to sell the stuff on, and they were always nervous.

Then there was Harry Capaldi, alias Harry Carry, alias Andy Capp, alias Harry the Cap. It was true he sometimes wore a cap. It was true, too, that he was always nervous. And if Harry got the fright and went into hiding, I wouldn't be very happy. So I was being careful not to ask for him in any of the bars. I didn't want word getting to him before I did. Somewhere in the middle of the Dowsett Estate, Bel started complaining about her feet.

'We'll take a rest soon,' I said. I led her back to the High Road and the first pub we went into, she sat down at a table. So I asked what she was drinking.

'Coke.' I nodded and went to the bar.

'A coke, please, and a half of bitter.' While the barmaid poured our drinks, I examined the row of optics. I'd been close to ordering a brandy. Close, but not that close. Harry the Cap wasn't in the bar. Maybe he stayed home on a Monday night. I didn't want to go calling on him. I knew he owned a couple of guns, and the people in the flat upstairs from him were dealers. It would only take one shot, and the whole building might turn into *Apocalypse Now*. I took the drinks back to our table. Bel had taken off her shoes and was rubbing her feet. The men at the bar were so starved of novelty that they were watching her like she wasn't about to stop at the shoes. When she took her jacket off I thought one of them was about to fall off his stool.

'New shoes,' Bel said. 'I knew I shouldn't have brought them.'

'And they say townies are soft.'

She glared, then smiled. 'Cheers,' she said, lifting her glass. She crunched on a piece of ice and looked around the bar. 'So this is the big bad city? How do we find your friend?'

'We keep looking. You'd be surprised how many pubs there are between here and White Hart Lane.'

'And we go into every one of them?'

'That's the idea.'

'Couldn't you just phone him instead?'

'He's not on the phone.'

'Then I suppose we keep walking.' She took another drink.

'Speaking of phoning, have you called Max?'

'Give me a break, I only left him this morning.'

'He'll be worried.'

'No, he won't. He'll be watching reruns of *Dad's Army* and laughing his head off.'

I tried to visualise this, but failed.

'Look, Michael, do you mind me saying something?'

'What?'

'Well, we're supposed to be together, right? As in a couple. Look at you, you look more like my minder.'

I looked down at myself.

'I mean,' Bel went on, 'you're sitting too far away from me for a start. It's like you're afraid I'll bite. And the way you're sitting, you're not comfortable, you're not enjoying yourself. You're like a flick knife about to open.'

'Thanks,' I said. I slid closer to her on the bench-seat.

'Better, but still not great,' she said. 'Relax your shoulders and your legs.'

'You seem to know a bit about acting.'

'I watch a lot of daytime TV. There, that's better.' We were now touching shoulders and thighs. I finished my drink.

'Right, we better get going.'

'What?'

'Like I say, Bel, a lot of pubs still to go.'

She sighed and slipped her shoes back on. The men at the bar turned their attention to the television. Someone by a riverbank was gutting a fish.

We were in a pub on Scotland Green, the one people use after they've signed on at the dole office across the road. It was always busy, and was all angles and nooks. It might be small, but that didn't mean you couldn't hide in it. Harry the Cap was hiding round the corner beside the fruit machines. He was seated on a high stool, wearing a paisley-patterned shirt intended for someone three decades younger, jeans ditto, and his cap. It struck me I should have brought him the one I'd bought; he'd have appreciated it more than Bel.

He wasn't playing the machines, and in fact was staring at the cigarette dispenser.

'Hello there, Harry,' I said. He stared at me without recognition, then laughed himself into a coughing fit. Three gold chains jangled around his neck as he coughed. There were more gold bands on his wrists and fingers, plus a gold Rolex on his right wrist.

'Dear God,' he said at last, 'that nearly killed me.' He wiped his eyes. 'Did you beat him up afterwards?'

'Who?'

'The blind fella who gave you that haircut. It's diabolical. I won't even tell you what I think of the colour.'

'Why not take out an ad?'

'Sorry, son.' He lowered his voice and cleared his throat. 'Do I need an invite or are you going to introduce me?'

'Sorry, Harry, this is Belinda. Belinda, Harry.'

'What're you drinking, girl?'

She looked to me first and I nodded. 'Coke, please.'

'Needs your permission, does she? And you'll be wanting a double brandy, I take it?'

'Not tonight, Harry. A half of bitter's fine.'

83

He shook his head. 'My hearing must be going.'

'Let me get these,' I said. 'Are you still TJ?'

'That I am.' Bel looked puzzled, so he spelt it out. 'Tomato juice. I can't drink any more, it makes my hands shake.'

She nodded, understanding everything. I got the drinks in while Harry tried his usual chat-up lines. I needn't have worried; Harry was okay. He was stone cold sober and he wasn't dodging police or warrant-servers or his ex-wife's solicitors. He was fine.

When I got back, Bel was playing one of the bandits.

'She's had four quid out of it already,' Harry said.

'And how much has she put back?'

Harry nodded sagely. 'They always put it back.'

Bel didn't even look at us. 'Who's "they"?' she said. 'Women in general, or the women you know in general? I mean, there's bound to be a difference.'

Harry wrinkled his nose. 'You see,' he said in a stage whisper, 'things haven't been the same since women's lib. When my Carlotta burnt her bra, I knew that was the end. Cheers.'

'Cheers.' I sipped my beer and managed to catch Bel's eye. She gave me a wink. 'Harry,' I said, 'we need something.'

'We?'

'Bel and me.'

'What do you need? A wedding licence?'

'No, something that'll get us through a few doors, something with authority stamped on it.'

'Such as?'

'I was hoping you'd have a few ideas.'

He rubbed his unshaved jaw. 'Yes, I could maybe do you something. When would you need it?'

'Tonight.'

His eyes widened. 'Jesus, Mark, you've given me tough ones before, but this . . .'

'Could you do it though?'

'I wasn't expecting to work tonight . . .' From which I

knew two things: one, that he *could* do it; and two, that he was wondering how much he could charge.

'It would be cash?' he said. I nodded. 'It's cash I like, you know that.'

'I know that.'

'Jesus, tonight. I don't know . . .'

'How much, Harry?'

He took off his cap and scratched his head, forgetting for a moment his psoriasis. Huge flakes of skin floated on to his shoulders. 'Well now, Mark, you know my prices are never unreasonable.'

'The difference is, Harry, this time *I'm* not getting paid.'

'Well, that may make a difference to you, Mark, it doesn't make a difference to *me*. I charge what's fair.'

'So tell me what's fair.'

'Five hundred.'

'What do I get for five hundred?'

'Two identity cards.'

'That's not much to show.'

He shrugged. 'At short notice, it's the best I can offer.'

'How long would it take?'

'A couple of hours.'

'All right.'

'You've the money on you?' I nodded, and he shook his head. 'Running around Tottenham with five hundred on him, and I bet he's not even carrying a knife.'

Behind us, the bandit began coughing up another win for Bel.

'This is definitely your lucky night,' said Harry the Cap.

'Make yourselves at home.'

It wasn't easy in Harry the Cap's first-floor flat. For one thing, what chairs there were were piled high with old newspapers and magazines. For another, half the already cramped living room was taken up with a rough approximation of a photographer's studio. A white bedsheet had been

85

pinned to the wall to provide a backdrop, and there was a solitary bruised flash-lamp hanging from a tripod. Harry gave the back of the lamp a thump.

'Hope the bulb's not gone, bleeding things cost a packet.' The bulb flashed once, then came on and stayed on. 'Lovely,' said Harry. There was a plain wooden dining-chair which seemed to be the tomcat's regular perch, but Harry tipped the reluctant beast on to the floor and placed the chair in front of the bedsheet, angling the lamp so that it hit an imaginary spot just above the back of the chair. 'Lovely,' he said again.

Then he started tinkering with his pride and joy. It was a special camera which in the one unit could take a photo (slightly smaller than passport size), develop it on to an ID card, and then laminate the card. Harry patted the machine. 'Bought it from a firm that went bust. They used to do identity cards for students.'

Bel was standing in front of a mirror, combing her hair into place. The mirror was large and old and hexagonal, and in its centre was a posed photograph of a bride and groom with their best man and bridesmaid.

'Your parents?' Bel asked.

'Nah, picked it up down Brick Lane. A lot of people make your mistake. Sometimes I don't own up.'

'Where's that music coming from?'

'Upstairs, some black kids.'

The constant bass was like a queasy heartbeat. It seemed to envelop the flat.

'Can't you complain?' said Bel. Harry laughed and shook his head.

'Right,' he said, 'I'll just get the cards typed up.'

He had an old manual typewriter, the sort they'd thrown from offices on to the street in the 70s. It was solidly built, but the keys needed realigning. Or maybe they just needed a clean.

'You'll never notice once the machine's reduced it.'

This, I knew from previous experience, was true. Once the card had been filled in, it was placed inside the unit, a suitcase-sized object attached to the camera, and a reduced-size copy was made, only now with photograph in place. Normally, I didn't bother too much. People seldom really scrutinised an ID card of any make or variety. If they saw that the photo was you, they were satisfied. But this time was different.

'Remember, Harry, some of the people I'll be dealing with might just give my ID more than a cursory glance. Don't go making any typing errors.'

'Do me a favour, I did a secretarial course at night school. Seventy words a minute.'

'I didn't know there were seventy two-letter words.'

I left him to get on with it. Bel flicked a final hair into place and turned to me. She offered me the comb, but I shook my head. I looked in the mirror and saw a hard-looking bloke staring back. He had cropped black hair and a professional scowl. He looked just like a policeman.

'Which area do you want?' Harry asked from the typewriter.

'Better make it Central.'

'Central,' he acknowledged. 'Good, I know how to spell that.'

A good forger's art, of course, does not lie in making up the fake ID. Anyone can fake an ID. The forger's art lies in having to hand authentic or authentic-looking blank ID forms. Harry would never tell anyone where his blanks came from, or even if they were the genuine article. I reckoned he'd got his hands on a real ID form a while back, and had a friendly printer run up a few hundred. There were other things he could do, like put an official stamp on something. Those he made himself, and they were beautiful. He'd done a US visa for me once that was incredibly lifelike. Only, without me knowing, he'd made it a *student* visa. The questions at Immigration had almost given me away. Next time I'd seen Harry, I'd been able to get a fake passport at a reduced rate.

'I'll need both your signatures,' he said. He'd switched on an anglepoise lamp and put on a pair of John Lennon-style NHS glasses, the kind you hate to have to wear as a kid, but often crave as an adult. I'd never needed glasses. People said it was a sign of having lived a pure life.

I was using the name Michael West on my ID, while Bel was Bel Harris. She said she'd rather stick with her own Christian name. They say that the best lies have a nugget of truth in them, and these names were just different enough from our real names that they wouldn't help the police. I'd sometimes called myself Michael West in the USA, but never before in England. Bel was having enough trouble as it was remembering my name was now Michael and not Mark. She didn't need another name to confuse her.

'Right, sweetheart,' said Harry, 'if you'll sit on that chair . . .'

Bel turned to me. 'Is he talking to you?'

'I think he means you.'

'Oh dear,' said Harry, 'I forgot for a moment there. Women's lib, eh? Don't mind me, love, just sit down anyway.'

Bel eventually sat down, and Harry stuck the ID form he'd just typed into the suitcase-machine.

'Don't smile or frown,' he told Bel, 'just look natural. That's about as natural as a performing seal. Better, better.' There was a flash, and Harry stood up straight. 'Lovely. Takes about half a minute. Sit yourself down, Mark.'

We changed places.

'By the way, Harry, you'd better take a few extra shots of me. I want you to set up a whole new identity.'

'That takes time, Mark.'

'I know. What shall we say, four days?'

'Make it five. What do you need: passport, driving licence, National Insurance number?'

'They'll do for a start.'

'We're talking serious money.'

'I know. I'll give you two hundred on account.'

'Now, just think bland thoughts. Mushy peas, liquor, the Spurs midfield. Look at him, he's a natural.'

There was a flash, then Harry switched to his everyday SLR camera and plugged it into the flash-lamp. He fired off a few more shots, asking me questions while he did.

'What name?'

'How about Michael Whitney?'

'Date of birth?'

'Same as mine. No, make it a month earlier. Place of birth: London. You can make the rest of it up as you like.'

'I will then.'

When he peeled the paper from my card and handed it to me, the clear plastic laminate was still warm. Behind the plastic, I wore that same policeman's scowl. Bel wasn't happy with her card. She reckoned she looked like a frightened animal. I studied her card but had to disagree.

'Look on the bright side, Bel. At least it'll give them a laugh when they arrest us. Harry, have you got any of those—'

But he was already coming back into the room, waving two small black leather wallets.

'Put them in here,' he said. 'You can fill the spare pockets with anything you like.' He crumpled one in his hand. 'Give them a bit of a seeing to first though, otherwise they look like they've just come from the sweatshop. He smiled at me. 'No extra charge.'

Which was my cue to hand over the cash.

We took a mini-cab from the office at the corner of Harry the Cap's road. Our driver didn't even know where Marylebone was, and mention of Baker Street and Regent's Park didn't ring any of his rusted bells. So I gave him some directions, and kept giving them all the way back to the hotel. He radioed his office to see how much he should charge.

'Depends whether they look loaded or not,' said the crackly voice. The driver looked at me in his rearview, and I shook my head at him. I gave him the money, but no tip, seeing how I'd have been better driving myself and letting him sit in the back.

I'd got him to drop us a couple of streets from the hotel. If anyone got to Harry the Cap, they might ask questions at the cab office, and the cab office wouldn't forget a fare from Tottenham to Marylebone Road. I didn't want anyone coming any closer to me than that. And yes, I *did* have someone specific in mind.

'Hang on,' said Bel, 'I want a pizza.' So we went to a takeaway and stood with the delivery riders while Bel's deep-pan medium seafood was constructed. Then it was back to the hotel. I took her to her room. She lifted the pizza box to my nose.

'You want to help me with this?'

Which was, however innocent its intention, an invitation to her bedroom, where we'd have to sit on the bed to eat.

'Not hungry, thanks,' I said. But I'd paused too long.

'I won't tell my dad.' She was smiling. 'Shouldn't we talk anyway? Go through the plan for tomorrow?'

She had a point. 'Over breakfast,' I said.

'Cold pizza maybe?'

'Don't be disgusting.'

I went to my room and called Max. He'd been sitting right by the phone.

'Everything's fine,' I said. 'I'll give you the number here, you can call Bel any time you like.'

'Thanks,' he said grudgingly. He then found a pen and some paper. I gave him the hotel number and Bel's room number. 'She'll probably be calling you herself,' I said.

'If she hasn't already forgotten me.'

'Don't be daft, Max, she talks about you all the time.' This was a lie; she hadn't mentioned her father all day until I'd brought up the subject in the pub. *I won't tell my dad.* ''Night, Max.' I put down the phone.

I'd known Bel for a few years now, and naturally sex had never . . . well, it wasn't that I didn't like her. It wasn't that we didn't flirt. It wasn't even that I was scared Max would bury me in one of his walled fields. It was mostly that I didn't, as the Americans say, 'do' sex any more. It didn't exactly go with the lifestyle. The women I met in my life I met infrequently and for necessarily short periods. If I wanted to get to know any of them, I had to construct a set of lies and half-truths. You didn't get too many ads in the lonely hearts columns from women looking to meet 'tall okay-looking assassin, 30–35, interested in ballistics, cuisine, international travel'. So I'd given up on women. I didn't even use hotel whores often, though I liked to buy them drinks and listen to their own constructed stories.

Speaking of which, I knew I had one more call to make. It had taken me a while to get round to it. I picked up the receiver and pressed the digits from memory. I have a good memory for numbers. The call was answered.

'Allington Hotel, can I help you?'

'Yes, I'd like to speak to a Mr Leo Hoffer, please.'

'Hoffer? One moment, please.' A clack of computer keys. 'I'm sorry, sir, we don't appear to have a guest with that name.'

'I'm sure he's staying there,' I persisted. 'He was there today, or maybe he's booking in tomorrow?'

'Hold on, please.' She muffled the phone with her hand and asked a colleague. The colleague took the receiver from her.

'Hello, sir? I think there must be a misunderstanding. Mr Hoffer did visit the hotel earlier today, but he isn't a guest here.'

'Damn,' I said. 'I must have got a crossed line. You don't happen to know where he's staying, do you?'

'I'm sorry, sir. At least you know Mr Hoffer's in town.'

'Yes, that's true. At least I know that. You've been very helpful.' I put down the phone. After a minute or two, I allowed myself a small smile. It was good to know Leo was here. Where he was, the circus would surely follow, by which I mean the media circus he seemed always to attract . . . and to covet. I always knew when Leo was on my trail, no matter how far behind.

I only had to pick up a paper and let the interviewer tell me about it.

I'd seen Leo on TV in the States. Frankly, I wasn't flattered. They say it's nice to feel wanted, but Leo looked like the one who should be in the slammer.

There was a soft knock at my door. Two short, one long: our agreed signal. I sighed, got off the bed, and unlocked the door.

'Got anything for indigestion?' Bel said.

'Okay,' I said, letting her in, 'let's go through tomorrow.'

And we did. I had us stand in front of the mirror and showed Bel how to act like a police officer, how to stand, how to speak, what to say. She smiled too much at first, so we got rid of that. And she had a natural slouch, the result, so she said, of always being taller than her girl friends and trying to bring herself down to their level.

After an hour, she got bored and started making mistakes again.

'Listen,' I said. 'We'll get one or two shots at this. After that it'd be too risky. The police are bound to find out there are impostors going around. So we've got to make the most of it, understood?' I waited till she nodded. 'Remember, these IDs weren't cheap. Now, look at yourself in the mirror, you're slouching again.'

She straightened up.

'Better.' I was standing close behind her. 'Now do one last thing for me.' She turned to me.

'What?'

92

'Go phone your father.'

She narrowed her eyes. 'Yes, boss,' she said.

I locked the door after her.

9

The hardest work Hoffer had done so far in London was find a dealer who didn't think he was an undercover cop or the vigilante father of some teenage addict.

There was crack around, but not much actual cocaine. The stuff he'd ended up buying was far from premium grade, probably five parts lidocaine and three parts baking soda, but there was no way he was going to start doing crack or free-basing, he'd seen too much hurt result from those particular by-ways. He'd been a New York street cop when crack first hit town. In a matter of months the drug had swamped the housing schemes. Earlier in the 80s he'd been friends with another cop who'd started free-basing. That cop had gone downhill like a well-oiled skateboard, careering all the way.

Hoffer had got into drugs the same way. He spent his days busting pushers and users, living so close to drugs that it was like the fucking things were whispering to him, even in his sleep. One day he'd confiscated some bottles of rock cocaine, only he'd handed them in one short. He soon found that there was an underclass of police officer that used a lot of drugs. Some of them just took drugs off one pusher and resold to another, keeping a little back along the way. Others had deep habits and pinhole eyes, real smack heads. You were in a privileged position, being a cop. You didn't have to look far or try hard to score a baggie of white shit, and you so seldom had to pay. But free-basing, that was a nightmare. Someone had tried to introduce him to it, recycling their smoke into a balloon and offering him the used smoke. Hoffer had never enjoyed the more social aspects of drug use, and drew the damned line at breathing somebody else's high.

So here he was in London, doing what he did.

He added a couple of hundred milligrams of speed to his purchase, and to offset the speed asked about quaaludes or 'bennies', but ended up with Librium and a bit more boo.

'Packing heat,' he said to himself afterwards. Soho had still failed to provide a night's fun, so he'd prowled the West End, sitting in a fag bar for quarter of an hour before realising his mistake, and finally locating a hooker who wouldn't accompany him to his hotel, but could provide relief in her own quarters. Hoffer couldn't agree to this; he'd gone to a hooker's greasy bedroom before, only to have her pimp try to roll him. So they made do with a back-alley blow job, for which she charged a twenty. That put her on £240 an hour, which was decent money. It was even more than Robert Walkins was paying.

In the morning he had a shower, the bath being too narrow for anything like a soak, put on a sober blue suit, and went to see his bank manager.

Mr Arthur looked like *he* was the one begging a loan for his daughter's life-saving surgery.

'Events will take their course, Mr Hopper.'

'That's Hoffer.'

'Of course, Hoffer.' Arthur gave a smile like a toad at mating time. 'But it's a bit early yet to expect any results, as I say.'

'Say whatever you like, shithead, but listen to this.' Hoffer leaned forward in his cramped chair. 'I don't have to play by any rules, so if you want to be able to leave your office every lunchtime and evening without having to check both ways for baseball bats, I suggest you give events a kick along the course they're taking.'

'Now look here—'

'I *am* looking, and all I see is something I try not to tread in on the sidewalk. And I don't mean manholes. Now get hassling head office for all you're worth, and meantime let me see what you've got here behind the scenes.'

Arthur's top lip was glistening with sudden perspiration. He looked like he'd lost about twenty pounds in stature.

'I've got an appointment at eleven.'

'Cancel it.'

'Look, you can't just—'

'I thought I already was.' Hoffer stood up, keeping his hands in his pockets. With his elbows jutting from his sides, he knew he looked like something from the jungle. Arthur would have clambered up the cheese-plant in the corner if he'd had any motive power. 'Now go fetch me the files.'

He sat down again, trying to look comfortable. The bank manager sat there for a few moments, just to show he wasn't intimidated. Hoffer allowed this with a shrug. They both knew the truth. Mr Arthur got up slowly, his hands gripping the edge of the desk. Then he walked out of the office.

He came back with a couple of files and some sheets of photocopier paper. 'This is all I can find just now. Most of our records get sent to head office eventually.'

'Tell them you want them back here pronto. What about the check on Wesley's current account transactions?'

'It's being carried out. We have to go through all the old cheques. They're not kept in neat little piles.'

Hoffer reached out a hand for the files. There was a knock at the manager's door.

'Ignore it,' said Hoffer.

'I certainly shan't.' Arthur walked briskly to the door and pulled it open. 'This is the man, officers.'

Hoffer turned his head lazily. At the door stood two uniformed policemen. So Arthur hadn't just been seeking out the files. Hoffer peeked at them anyway. They contained only blank sheets of typing paper.

'You sonofabitch,' he said. The policemen then asked him

96

to accompany them, and he rose from his chair. 'Certainly,' he said. 'No problem here,' he assured them.

But all the time he had eyes only for Mr Arthur.

'Never again! Do you hear?'

Hoffer heard. He was bored of hearing it. Bob Broome didn't seem to have any other words in his vocabulary.

'Can we turn the record over, Bob?'

Broome slapped his desk. 'It's not funny, Hoffer. It's not a game. You can't go around threatening bank managers. Jesus Christ, they run the country.'

'That's your problem then. Still, it could be worse.' Broome waited for an explanation. 'At least Arthur didn't look Jewish.'

Broome collapsed on to his chair. 'You're slime, Hoffer.'

Hoffer didn't need that. 'Yeah, I'm slime, but I'm slime that *pays*. So what does that make you?'

'Hold on a second.'

'No, shut up and listen. Remember, I've been a cop, I know what it's like. You try to look busy, but most of the time you're treading water waiting for somebody to come tell you who it is you're looking for. I can't do that any more. I don't have that luxury. What I've got is a head and a pair of fists, and if you don't like that, then just keep out of my way.'

'I just saved you from a barrow-load of manure.'

'And I thank you for that, but I've walked away from shit before without needing a pitchfork up my ass.'

Broome shook his head sadly. 'I don't want you around, Hoffer.'

'Tough titty.'

'I mean it. I don't want you anywhere near.'

'I can handle that, Chief Inspector.' Hoffer stood up. 'But remember, *you're* the one who called me, *you're* the one who took my money.' Hoffer walked out of the office. He didn't bother closing the door.

On his way out of Vine Street, he saw DI Dave Edmond going in. They knew one another through Broome.

'Hey ... Dave, right?' said Hoffer, the bright smiling American.

'That's right,' said Edmond.

'Are you busy?'

'Well, I was just ...'

'I thought maybe I could buy you a drink?'

Edmond licked his lips. It had been a whole eleven hours since he'd last touched a drop. 'Well, that's very kind.'

Hoffer put a hand on his shoulder. 'Ulterior motive, Dave. I've got a couple of questions, and Bob thought maybe you wouldn't mind ...'

'What sort of questions?' Edmond was already being steered back the way he'd come.

'Oh, just background stuff. You know, ballistics, scene of crime, that sort of thing. And anything you have on the deceased.'

Edmond had said that if they were going to talk about guns, maybe he should invite Barney along. Sergeant Barney Wills was the station's arms aficionado. So they took Barney with them to the pub.

It was another of those 'olde worlde' interiors which bored Hoffer stupid. In America, a bar looked like a bar, a place where you went to drink. He couldn't see the point of horse brasses and framed prints of clipper ships and shelves of books. Yes, *books*, like people might suddenly mistake the place for a library and decide to have a drink anyway while they were there.

It was all a joke too, hardly any of it authentic. The prints were fresh and framed in plastic, the books bought by the yard. Often he despaired of the English. They were too easy to con. Edmond and Barney were perfect material for a *real* con artist, perfect because they thought they were putting one over on *him*. He was just a loud Yank with money to spend and a lot of daft notions. They'd play him along, laughing at him, taking his drinks, and they'd tell him a few stories along the way.

Hoffer didn't mind this game. He knew who was screwing who. If the scene had been a porn movie, the two policemen would have had their cheeks bared in submission.

Barney told him what the lab had discovered about the sniper rifle. Namely that it had indeed fired the fatal shot, and that it was a specialist weapon, in use in the armed forces but not in general circulation. Arms weren't easy to come by in Britain anyway, though recently the crack dealers hadn't been having any problems. The Army and the Royal Marines used the L96A1, but civilian target shooters wouldn't use one.

'It was a Super Magnum,' Barney said, between gulps of Scotch. '.338 Lapua Magnum ammunition. Christ knows where he got it.'

'There must be a few bent gun dealers around,' Hoffer suggested.

'Yes, but even they wouldn't deal in an L96. I mean, half of them wouldn't even know how to begin getting hold of one. This thing fires a thousand yards, who needs that? And the sight he had on it, this was quality gear, must've cost a fortune.'

'Someone must've been paying a fortune,' Edmond added.

'Question is, who?' Hoffer got in another round. 'I've looked into assassins, guys, I mean the whole tribe of them. Leaving out the one-off crazies who go blast their local burger joint with an Uzi, they tend to come from a military background. Makes sense, right? I mean, that's where they get the training, that's where they first taste what a gun can do.'

Both men nodded, too busy drinking to interrupt.

'But this guy is a haemophiliac, or at least we think he is, and the doctors assure me the military won't accept haemophiliacs.' Hoffer's own words hit him: *military background*. Maybe he was on to something. He thought about it for a minute. Edmond and Barney didn't seem to notice. They started up a conversation about some cricket match. Eventually Hoffer drifted back to the real world. It was the tap of empty glass on wooden table that did it. Not that his companions were hinting or anything.

'This'll have to be the last round, guys. We're all busy people.' So he got them in again, and decided the balance was all wrong. He was shelling out, and not getting back much of a dividend.

'So, Barney, what about these gun dealers? The bent ones, I mean. Are they on a list or anything? I'd appreciate a look-see.' What else could Barney do but nod and say he'd see what he could do? Hoffer turned to Edmond.

'Now, Dave, you were going to tell me about Eleanor Ricks ...'

The Army camp wasn't such a bitch to find after all.

Hoffer had been expecting a hellhole in the middle of nowhere, but this was just north of London, on the edge of a commuter town and slap next-door to a housing estate.

When he'd spoken to the camp by telephone, they'd said he could take a mainline train up there, it only took half an hour. So that's what he did. The people were kidding themselves if they thought they lived in the 'country'. They weren't living *in* anything, they were living *on* something, and that something was borrowed time. London was snapping at their shoelaces. They worked there, earned their living there, and London wanted something back in return. It wanted *them*.

They tried to look prosperous and talk differently, but they were pale, almost ill-looking, and their cars only made traffic jams. Hoffer, who had considered taking a cab all the way, was relieved he'd gone by train. The roads he saw were crammed. Someone mentioned a nineteen-mile tailback on the M25. They called the road an 'orbital'. You could orbit the globe in less time. The train wasn't quite perfect though. It had been late leaving London, and it hadn't been cleaned or aired since depositing its rush-hour cattle in London. It smelt bad and there was trash on the floor.

The cab Hoffer took from the station didn't smell much better, and there was only slightly more room in the back than in a British Rail seat. He stuffed his legs in a diagonal and made do like that. He got the cab to drop him at the camp entrance. He was surprised to see armed guards on the gate. One nodded him in the direction of the gatehouse.

'What's the problem, chief?' Hoffer asked, as the guard on the gatehouse phoned him in.

'Terrorists,' the guard said. 'We're on constant alert.'

'I thought they'd stopped bothering you guys, started bothering the rest of us instead?'

'You never know.'

Armed with this philosophical nugget, Hoffer was pointed in the direction of the office he wanted.

He was met halfway by a young soldier whose face looked to have been pressed the same time as his shirt and pants.

'Mr Hoffer? The Major's expecting you.'

'It's good of him to see me at short notice.' Hoffer almost had to jog to keep up with the man. Somewhere along the route, Hoffer was supposed to catch the guy's name, but he was too busy catching his own breath. He was led into a building and told to take a seat. He was glad to. He tried focusing his eyes on the recruiting posters and glossy brochures. You'd think you were booking a holiday for yourself rather than a bruising career. The soldiers in the brochures looked tough and honest and Christian. You just knew democracy and the free world would be safe in their hands, even if you were dropping them into a country where they couldn't speak the language and the distant hills were full of mortar and Mullahs.

Hoffer caught himself whistling 'God Bless America' and checked it just in time.

A door opened along the hall. 'Mr Hoffer?'

Hoffer walked along the hall to meet the Major. His name was Major Drysdale, and he had a cool dry handshake, a bit like a Baptist minister's. 'Come in, please.'

'I was telling your . . . ah, I was saying I appreciate you seeing me like this.'

'Well, your call was intriguing. It's not every day I get to meet a New York detective. Speaking of which, there are certain formalities . . . Could I see your identification?'

Hoffer reached into his pocket and produced his detective's ID, which had been unfortunately mislaid at the time of his resignation from the force. It came in useful sometimes. People in authority would often prefer to speak to a real police officer than a shamus. Hoffer reckoned this was one of those times. Drysdale took down a few details from the ID before handing back the wallet. That worried Hoffer, but not much. He might go on to an Army file, but he doubted they'd go so far as to phone his supposed employers in the States. He kept reading about military cutbacks, and phone calls cost money.

'So,' said Major Drysdale, 'what can I do for you, Detective Hoffer?'

It was a small plain office, lacking any trace of personality. Drysdale might have just moved in, which would explain it. But Hoffer thought the man looked comfortable here, like he'd sat in the office for years. He wasn't much more than PR, a public face for the Army. The camp's real muscle was elsewhere. But Hoffer didn't need muscle, he just needed a few questions answered. He needed a friendly ear. He was on his best behaviour and in his best suit, but Drysdale still treated him with just a trace of amusement, like he'd never seen such a specimen before.

As to the Major himself, he was tall and skinny with arms you could have snapped with a Chinese restaurant's crab-crackers. He had short fair hair and blue eyes out of a Nazi youth league, and a moustache which could have been drawn on his face with ballpoint. He wasn't young any more, but still carried acne around his shirt collar. Could be he was allergic to the starch.

'Well, Major,' Hoffer said, 'like I said on the telephone, it's a medical question, and a vague one at that, but it's in connection with a series of murders, assassinations to be more accurate, and as such we would appreciate any help the Army can give.'

'And you're working in tandem with Scotland Yard?'

'Oh, absolutely. I have their full backing.'

'Could you give me a contact name there?' Drysdale poised his pen above his notepad.

'Sure. Uh, Chief Inspector Broome. That's B-r-o-o-m-e. He's the man to talk to. He's based at Vine Street in central London.'

'Not Scotland Yard?'

'Well, they're working together on this.'

'Orange, isn't it?'

'Sir?'

'Vine Street.' Hoffer still didn't get it. 'On the Monopoly board.'

Hoffer grinned, chuckled even, and shook his head in wonder at the joke.

'Do you have a phone number for the Chief Inspector?'

'Oh, yessir, sure.' Goddamned Army. Hoffer gave Major Drysdale the number. His skin was crawling, and he had to force himself not to scratch all over. He wished he hadn't taken some speed before setting out.

'Maybe before we start,' Drysdale was saying now, not stonewalling exactly, just following procedure, 'you could tell me a little about the inquiry itself. Oh, tea by the way?'

'Yes, please.'

Drysdale picked up his phone and ordered tea and 'some

biccies'. Then he sat back and waited for Hoffer to tell him all about the D-Man.

It took a while, but eventually, two cups of strong brown tea later, Hoffer got to the point he'd wanted to start with. Drysdale had asked questions about everything from the assassin's first error to the sniper rifle he'd used in London. And he'd kept on scribbling notes, though Hoffer wanted to say it was none of his goddamned business, tear the pad from him, and chew it up with his teeth. He was sweating now, and blamed tannin poisoning. His throat was coated with felt.

'So you see,' he said, 'if the man we're looking for hasn't exactly been *in* the Army, well, maybe he's been or still is connected to it in some way. The most obvious connection I can think of is family.'

'You mean a brother or sister?'

'No, sir, I mean his father. I think it would have to be his father, someone who might have instilled in him a . . . relationship with weapons.'

'We don't normally allow children to train with live ammo, Detective Hoffer.'

'That's not exactly what I'm saying, sir. I mean, I'm sure the Army's probity is above . . . uh, whatever. But say this man was good with firearms, well, wouldn't he want to pass that knowledge and interest on to his son?'

'Even if the son could never join the Army?'

'The kid could've been a teenager before anyone found out he was a haemophiliac. Mild sufferers, sometimes they don't find out till they're grown up. It takes an operation or something before anyone notices they have trouble getting their blood to clot.'

'This is all very interesting,' said Drysdale, flicking through his copious notes, 'but I don't see where it gets us.'

'I'll tell you, sir. It gets us a kid who's diagnosed haemophiliac by an Army doctor, sometime in the past, maybe between twenty and thirty years ago. You must have records.'

Drysdale laughed. 'We may have records, but do you know what you're asking? We'd have to check every Army base here and abroad, every medical centre. Even supposing they held records from so long ago. Even supposing the child was treated by an Army doctor. I mean, he might easily have gone to a civilian doctor. Putting aside all this, he would have taken his records with him.'

'What?'

'When you change doctors, your new doctor requests from your old doctor all your medical notes. You don't keep them yourself, your doctor keeps them. Your *present* doctor.'

'Are you sure? Maybe if I spoke to someone from your medical—'

'I really don't think that's necessary.'

Hoffer considered his options. He could whack the guy. He could wheedle. He could offer some cash. He didn't think any of these would work, so he decided to be disappointed instead.

'I'm real sorry you can't find it in yourself to help, Major. You know how many innocent people this man has murdered? You know he'll keep on doing it till he's caught? I mean, he's not going to give it up and move jobs. I can't see him waiting tables at IHOP or somewhere.'

Drysdale smiled again. 'Look, I know what you're saying. I appreciate that you—'

Hoffer got to his feet. 'No, sir, with all due respect I don't think you do know. I won't waste any more of your time.' He turned to the door.

'Wait a minute.' Hoffer waited. He turned his head. Drysdale was standing too now. 'Look, maybe I can initiate a few general inquiries.'

Hoffer turned back into the room. 'That would be great, sir.'

'I can't make any promises, you understand.'

'Absolutely. We're all just trying to do what we can.'

Drysdale nodded. 'Well, I'll see what I can do.'

'I really appreciate that, sir.' Hoffer took Drysdale's hand. 'I'm sure I speak for us all.'

Drysdale smiled a little sheepishly. Then he said he'd get someone to escort the detective back to the gate.

'I'll be in touch,' said Hoffer.

While he waited back in the reception area for his 'escort' to appear, he spotted a drinking fountain and flew towards it, filling his mouth with water, gargling, spitting it back, and finally swallowing a few mouthfuls.

'How can they drink that stuff?' he asked himself as he wiped his mouth.

'It's only water,' his escort said from behind him.

'I meant the goddamned tea,' said Hoffer.

10

I knocked again.

'Come on,' I said, 'let's get busy. We're not tourists any more.'

Not that Bel had seen many of the sights of London, unless 'sights' was broad enough to encompass Tottenham and a couple of low-class restaurants. I listened at her door until I could hear her getting out of bed.

'I'll meet you downstairs,' she called.

I went back to my room and tried phoning again. This time I got through. I was calling someone at British Telecom. His name was Allan and he didn't come cheap.

'It's me,' I said. 'Have they started tapping your line yet?'

'No, just everybody else's. I can give you the latest royal dirt if you like.'

He didn't sound like he was joking. 'No thanks,' I said. 'I'm after a couple of numbers.'

'I take it you mean unlisted, or you'd be calling Directory Enquiries.'

'I've checked, they're unlisted. The first is a woman called Eleanor Ricks.'

'The one who got shot?'

'Could be.'

'You've got to be careful, man. Sometimes Scotland Yard or MI5 stick keywords into the system. If you say the word and they catch it, they record your whole conversation.'

Allan was always trying to impress me – or scare me, I didn't know which – with this sort of comment.

'Her husband may be the subscriber,' I carried on. 'He's

called Frederick Ricks. According to the tabloids, they live in Camden. I'll need their address, too.'

'Got it.' He paused. 'You said a couple of names?'

'Joe Draper, he heads a TV production company. He's got a house in Wiltshire, the phone number there would be useful, plus any address for him in town, apart from his office. His office is in the book.'

I could hear Allan writing the information down. I gave silent blessing to the British media, who had provided me with the information I had.

'I see inflation's in the news again,' he said at last.

'Not another hike, Allan. You're pricing yourself out of the game.'

'As a special offer to regular subscribers, the increase has been held to ten percent for one month only.'

'Generous to a fault. Same address?'

'Who can afford to move?'

'Tens and twenties all right?'

'Sure.'

'Oh, one more name . . .'

'Now who's pushing it?'

'Call it my free gift. Scotty Shattuck.' I spelt it for him. 'Somewhere in London probably, always supposing he's got a phone.'

'Right, I'll do my best. Later today, okay?'

'I'll stick your fee in the post. If I'm not here, leave the details with reception. Here's the number.'

I gave it to him and terminated the call. Downstairs, Bel was already seated in the small dining room, pouring cereal from a one-portion pack.

'I see you're not one of these women who takes forever to dress.' I sat down beside her.

'Know a lot about that, do you?'

'What do you mean?'

'Oh, nothing.' She poured milk and started to eat. I knew what she meant. She meant she was good-looking and I hadn't made a pass at her, so what did that make me? She was wearing trousers and a blue blouse and jacket. They were the plainest items in her luggage. I tried to see her as a police officer. I couldn't. But then I'd be the one doing the talking; I'd be the one they'd be looking at. And examining myself in the mirror this morning, I'd seen a hard-nosed copper staring back at me. He looked like he wanted to take me outside.

'Aren't you eating?' Bel asked.

'I never eat much in the morning. I'll just have some coffee.'

'You will if anyone turns up to serve you. I haven't seen a soul since I came in. The stuff's all on that sideboard, but there's no coffee.'

I went to the sideboard to take a look. A thermos flask turned out to contain hot water, and there was a jar of instant coffee in one of the cupboards.

'Yum yum,' said Bel.

The coffee tasted the way thermos coffee always tastes. It reminded me of sports fields, of games watched with my father, the two of us sheltering beneath a tartan travelling-rug or umbrellas and hoods, depending on the weather. There'd be coffee and sandwiches at half-time. Thermos coffee.

'So the schedule for today,' said Bel, scraping up the last of the cereal, 'is a visit to Testosterone City, yes?' I nodded. 'And I provide the decoration while you ask your questions?' I nodded again. 'Are you quite sure you need my expensive skills, Michael? I mean, performing monkeys come cheap these days.' Then she touched the back of my hand. 'Only teasing. Drink your coffee and let's get out of here. This dining room's like something out of a horror film. I keep thinking all the other guests and staff have been murdered in their beds.' She started to laugh, but stopped abruptly, and her look was somewhere between embarrassment and fear. I knew exactly what had struck her: that there was only one murderer around here.

I didn't know where to find Scotty Shattuck, but wasn't prepared to sit around the hotel waiting for Allan to get back to me. So we got a taxi on Marylebone Road and headed for Oxford Street, where, above a shop selling what can be best described as 'tat', there was a gym and health centre called Chuck's.

Max had been able to offer a good physical description of Shattuck, and it pointed to a man who did more than jog around the park to keep himself in shape.

'He's like a cross between a Welsh pit-pony and a brick shithouse,' Max had said.

There were a lot of gyms in London, a lot of places where sweaty males pushed weights, goaded by other musclebound lifters. Some of them no doubt took a few drugs to aid muscle development and performance. They were the sorts who have gaps between their upper arms and their torsos when they walk, and can't do anything to close those gaps.

A lot of gyms, but only one or two like Chuck's. Chuck's was more than a gym, it was a place to hang out, a haven for those who need to keep fit between assignments. You didn't get the grossly over-muscled at Chuck's. You got authentic hard men, men who'd been in the armed forces, or who had come out but still kept fit. Men sometimes recruited for work overseas, work they talked about in Chuck's, but seldom outside. I'd been introduced to Chuck's by an ex-Royal Marine who'd been my contact on an earlier job. He wasn't there when we walked in, but Chuck himself was.

He was about fifty, hair like steel wool, and he wore a green combat-style T-shirt, straining across his chest. The men on the machines behind him whistled appreciatively at Bel as Chuck came towards us. Bel's face reddened with anger.

'What can I do for you?'

'Are you the owner of this establishment, sir?'

He got a bored look on his face. One question had established in his mind who he was dealing with. I knew he wouldn't recognise me; I'd changed a lot since Brent Storey had brought me here.

'That's right,' he said warily.

'I'm looking for someone called Scotty.' Chuck's face stayed blank.

'As in "Beam me up?"' he hazarded. I didn't smile.

'Scotty Shattuck,' I went on. I had one hand in my pocket. I was wearing tight black leather gloves, as was Bel. We'd bought them on the way here. Her idea. They shouldn't have worked, but in fact they did make us look more like police officers. 'He works weights,' I went on. 'Little guy, but well-built. He's ex-Army.'

'Sorry,' said Chuck, ignoring all this, 'I didn't catch your name.'

'West, Detective Inspector West.'

'And this is . . . ?' He meant Bel.

'DC Harris,' she said, stony-faced. Chuck gave her a good long examination, not caring if I noticed or not. The two customers using the apparatus had stopped and were sauntering this way, rubbing their necks with towels. Another three men were squatting by the window. The noise of traffic was a low persistent growl, with vibrations from the buses shaking the mirrors on the walls.

'Well,' Chuck said at last, turning back to me, 'can't help, I'm afraid.'

'Look, we don't want any trouble. It's just that I need to talk to Mr Shattuck.'

'I don't think so.' Chuck was shaking his head, hands on his hips.

'He's not in trouble or anything, Mr . . .'

'People just call me Chuck. Know why? Because if I don't

like someone, I'm liable to chuck them out of that window over there.'

'Ever tried a policeman?'

'Funny you should say that. Just tell me what you want to talk to Scotty Shattuck about.'

'You know him then?'

'Maybe I'm just curious.' He was checking the floor between us.

'Come on,' said Bel, 'let's go.'

Chuck looked up. 'All I want to know is why you want him.'

The last time I'd been here with Brent, the atmosphere had been very different. But then I'd been with a member, with someone everyone knew. I hadn't been a policeman then either. I'd misjudged this place. It looked like Chuck had a score to settle with law and order.

'Afraid not,' I said, shaking my head. 'But I can assure you it's nothing serious.'

'No?'

The two hard men were flanking Chuck now. They knew they didn't need to say anything. Their voices would only have spoiled the picture they made.

Suddenly Bel flipped open her ID the way she must have seen actors do on the television. 'If you don't tell us where to find Mr Shattuck, you'll be hindering our inquiries. That could be construed as obstruction, sir.'

Maybe she'd been watching too much daytime TV.

Chuck smiled, first at one of his men, then at the other. He seemed to find something interesting on the tips of his shoes, and studied them, talking at the same time.

'I've nothing to say. I don't know anyone called Scotty Shattuck. End of story. Goodbye, adios, au revoir.'

I stood my ground for a moment longer, knowing I didn't believe him. We could back off, or we could try another tactic. We didn't have time to back off. Besides, if we left now, word could get back to Shattuck, causing him to disappear. There was one option left.

So I drew the gun.

It's not easy to conceal a Heckler & Koch MP5, but it's always worth the effort. It was why I'd borrowed a Barbour jacket from Max. It was roomy, and he'd sewn a pocket into it so the gun could be carried more easily. So what if I sweated in the heat?

At twenty inches long and six pounds weight, the MP5 can be carried just about anywhere without creating a stir. It only created a stir when you brought it out and pointed it at someone. I held it one-handed and pointed it directly at Chuck.

'This thing's got a fifteen-round mag,' I said, 'and I've set it on a three-round burst. You've been around, Chuck, you know what that'll do to you. You'll be lying in two pieces on the floor, and so will everybody else. Whole thing'll take just a couple of seconds.'

Chuck had taken a couple of steps back and raised his hands slightly, but otherwise seemed fairly calm under the circumstances.

'I want to know where he is,' I said. 'When you tell me, I'm going to go talk to him. That's all, just talk. But if he's not there, if someone's warned him, then I'm coming back here.'

Chuck's minders couldn't take their eyes off the gun. To be honest, I didn't think I could aim the thing properly, never mind fire it. I wasn't used to sub-machine guns, far less ones so short you could use them one-handed like a pistol. I was brandishing it for two reasons. One, I knew it would scare the shit out of everyone. Two, I didn't have time to take 'no' as the answer to any question I needed to ask.

'I didn't think you were a cop,' Chuck sneered.

'I only want to talk to him.'

'Go fuck yourself.'

The men who'd been crouching by the window had risen

to their feet. I could hear Bel breathing just half a step behind me. I should have known a pretty face wouldn't have been enough for people like Chuck. They'd gone way beyond pretty faces in their time.

He wasn't going to speak, so I waved the gun around a bit. One of his minders spoke for him, maybe for all of them.

'Scotty lives in Norwood, near Crystal Palace.'

'I need an address.'

He gave me one. 'But he hasn't been in for a while. I haven't seen him around either.'

'You think he's got a job?'

The gorilla shrugged.

'Okay,' I said, 'sorry for any inconvenience.' I started backing towards the door. Bel was already on her way. 'I'll let you get back to your weight-gain. Looks like a few of you have lost a pound or two into your underwear.' I looked at Chuck again and waved the gun a final time. 'They call it the mercenary's life-support.'

Then we were gone.

The taxi took us south of the river.

Bel said she felt drunk, with the excitement at the gym and then our brief jog to the traffic lights where a taxi was just unloading. I didn't want to talk about it, not in a taxi, so she waited till the driver dropped us off. We were standing on Church Road, a busy two-lane street of large detached houses. The area must have been posh at one time, but most of the buildings had fallen into disrepair to a lesser or greater degree. The house we were standing outside definitely fell into the category of 'greater degree'. It was a huge monstrous affair, all angles and gables and windows where you'd least expect to see them. Paint had faded and peeled from it, and some of the windows were covered with blankets for curtains, or with boards where the glass should be. The even larger house next to it had been added to and converted into a hotel. I imagined the cheapest rooms would be those to the side.

Bel wasn't looking at the house, she was looking at me, wanting me to say something.

'I wouldn't have used it,' I offered.

'Really?'

'Really.'

She broke into a nervous laugh. 'The look on their faces.' It was one of those laughs which can easily turn to sobbing. 'I was scared, Michael, and I was *behind* the bloody gun!'

An elderly lady was wheeling her shopping-trolley past us. She smiled a greeting, the way some old people do.

'Keep your voice down,' I cautioned. Bel quickly took my meaning.

'Sorry.'

'Look, Bel, I don't want to stick around London any longer than I need to. That's why I used the gun. I can't hang around being pleasant and polite and waiting for answers. I need them fast.'

She was nodding. 'Understood.' She turned at last to the house. 'God, it's ugly.'

'Let's make this short and sweet,' I said, heading for the front door.

The expansive front garden had been concreted over some time before, but weeds and grass were pushing their way through. There were huge cracks and swells in the concrete, doubtless caused by the roots of several mature trees nearby. A car sat on the concrete, covered by a black tarpaulin which itself now sported a covering of wet leaves, moss and bits of rubbish. It was sitting so low to the ground, it either had flat tyres or none at all. Past it, a dozen steps led to the front door, rotten at its base. There was an intercom next to the door, complete with buzzers for eight flats. Only three had names attached. None of them was Shattuck. I pressed one anyway. There was no reply. I pressed another, then another. Still no reply. Bel placed her hand against the door and gave it the slightest push. It swung inwards.

'Shall we?' she said.

There was a lot of mail in the entrance hall, along with litter which had blown in over time, and an untidy mouldering heap of free newssheets. Someone had left a bicycle frame against the wall. There was no sign of any wheels.

Some mail sat on an upturned cardboard box. Most of the letters were for Scotty Shattuck, some identifying his address as Flat 5. I checked the postmarks. They went back almost a week.

'Doesn't look good,' I said.

We climbed the creaking stairs, hearing no sounds from the other flats, and encountering not a soul. Flat 5 was three storeys up, near what had to be the top of the house, though the stairs kept winding. The door was cheap and newish, a wooden frame with thin panelling over it. A single Yale had been fitted. The door had no handles or nameplate. There were scrapes on the jamb near the lock.

'Looks like someone kicked the old door in.'

'Maybe he locked himself out.'

'Maybe. Since when he's had this new one fitted, but hasn't got round to adding decent locks yet.'

'That's handy,' said Bel. She pulled a small kit of tools from her pocket. 'I brought this along, thought it might be useful.'

She got to work on the Yale. It took her less than a minute to open it. Not fast, but quieter than a burst from the MP5.

'I knew there was some reason I wanted you with me,' I said.

She smiled. 'My dad taught me how to do it years ago. We only had one front-door key back then. He said this would save him having to get one cut for me.'

'That sounds like Max all right.'

Bel put away her lockpicker's kit and we entered Scotty Shattuck's flat. You could tell straight away he hadn't been there for some time. The place felt lifeless. It was a bachelor pad, sloppily decorated with nude mags, beer cans and empty containers from Indian takeaways. There was one chair, separated by a footstool from the TV and video. In the only bedroom, the bedclothes were messed up. The magazines here were a mix of middling porn and specialist titles for arms collectors and users. A few empty cartridge cases had been lined up like ornaments on the mantelpiece. Mirror tiles had been fixed to the ceiling above the bed.

'Ugh,' said Bel.

The room was dark, its walls lined with large cork tiles to which Shattuck had pinned pictures from his magazine collection. Women and guns. Sometimes he'd cut carefully around the guns and Sellotaped them on to the women so it looked like the nude models were carrying them.

'Ugh,' Bel said again.

I started opening drawers. What was I looking for? I didn't think I'd find a forwarding address, but I might find something. I'd know it when I found it.

What I found were packets of photographs. I sat on the bed and went through them. They were mostly of Scotty and his colleagues in action: firstly in what I took to be the Falklands, then later in what might have been Yugoslavia. The soldiers were fully kitted, but you could tell Scotty was regular Army in the Falklands, and mercenary by the time of Sarajevo. In the later shots, he wore camouflage greens, but no markings. His smiling colleagues looked like nice guys to do business with. They liked to wear green vests, showing off biceps and triceps and bulging chests. Actually, most of them were going to seed, showing beer guts and fat faces. They lacked that numb disciplined look you see in the regular Army.

I knew Scotty from Max's description. I knew him, too, because he was in a few photos by himself. He was dressed in civvies, and photographed at ease. These photos were taken by the sea, and on some parkland. Probably they'd been taken by a girlfriend. Scotty flexed his muscles for her, posing at his best. Bel took one look at him.

'Ugh,' she said.

He didn't look that bad. He had a long drooping moustache which Max hadn't mentioned, so had probably been shorn off. He was square-jawed and wavy-haired, his shape not quite squat, but definitely not tall enough for his girth. I stuck one of the photos in my pocket – it showed Shattuck with some girlfriend – and put the rest back in the drawer.

'Anything else?' I asked Bel, who'd been roaming.

'Nothing,' she said.

There was a squeal of braking tyres outside. No uncommon sound in London, but I went to the window and peered out anyway. A car had stopped outside the house. It was an old Jaguar with a purple paint job. The driver was still wearing his white work-out vest. He probably had his towel with him too. There was somebody else in the passenger seat, and Chuck was fuming in the back.

'Time to go,' I told Bel. She didn't hang around. I'd seen a back door on the ground floor, and just hoped we'd have time to make it that far. I took out the MP5 as we descended, but held it beneath my coat. Either Chuck and his men were so incensed at the way they'd been treated that their pride had compelled them to follow us or else they were making a rational move. If the latter, then they had to be tooled up. If the former, I'd be in for a beating anyway.

And I'd always tried to avoid contact sports.

We were in luck. They were sitting it out in the car, waiting for us to emerge. The back door was locked by means of a bolt top and bottom, easily undone. I pulled the door open and we found ourselves in a garden so overgrown it hardly justified the term. We waded through it to the side fence and clambered over into the rear car park of the hotel.

The MP5 jabbed my gut as I climbed the fence. I double-checked that its safety was still on.

From the car park, we climbed over a low brick wall on to a piece of waste ground. Past this, we found ourselves emerging from behind a public toilet on to a completely different road, busy with traffic and pedestrians. A bus had pulled up at its stop, so we jumped aboard. We didn't know where it was going, and the driver who was waiting to be paid didn't seem about to tell us, so I reached into my pocket for some coins.

'Two to the end of the line,' I told him.

Then we climbed to the top deck and took the empty back seat. A purple Jag would be easy to spot if it tried following us, but it didn't.

'I wonder how long they'll sit there?' Bel asked.

I told her I couldn't care less.

We ended up taking a train back over the Thames, and a taxi from the station to our hotel. The receptionist had a message for me, two telephone numbers and their corresponding addresses. As I'd already seen, Scotty Shattuck didn't possess a phone. But now I had addresses and numbers for the Ricks's household and Joe Draper's Barbican flat.

While Bel took a shower, I started phoning. It was probably late enough in the police inquiry for me to be asking follow-up questions. All I needed was gumption and one hell of a lot of luck. Chuck wouldn't go to the police, he wasn't the type. But I knew things were going to get increasingly dangerous the closer we got to the real police inquiry, which was why I didn't give myself time to think. If I'd thought about it, I might not have made the calls.

As it was, I stumbled at the first fence. My call to the Ricks's Camden home was intercepted by the operator, who told me all calls were being rerouted. Before I had time to argue, I was back to the ringing tone, and my call was answered by a secretary.

'Crispin, Darnforth, Jessup,' she said, as though this explained everything.

'I've just been rerouted by the operator,' I said. 'I was trying to get through to—'

'One moment, please.' She cut the connection and put me through to another secretary.

'Mr Johns's office, how can I help you, sir?'

'I was trying to reach Mr Frederick Ricks.'

'Yes, all calls to Mr Ricks are now being dealt with by this office. You understand that his wife was killed recently.' She gave the news with relish. 'And Mr Johns, as the family's solicitor, has taken on the task of dealing with all enquiries.'

'I see. Well, this is Detective Inspector West, I've just been brought into the inquiry and I wanted a few words with Mr Ricks.'

'Mr Ricks and his son have gone away for a few days. Someone on the inquiry should be able to give you the details you need.'

She was boxing me into a corner. I could either throw in the towel or box myself out again.

'Would it be possible to speak to Mr Johns?'

'I'm sure that could be arranged.'

'I meant just now.'

She ignored this. 'Three-thirty this afternoon, all right?' Then she gave me the address.

I put down the phone and thought, not for the first time, of leaving London, leaving the whole mess behind. It was madness to keep on with this. But then what was the alternative? If I didn't find out why I'd been set up and who was behind it, how could I take another job? I went down to Bel's room and she let me in. She was dressed, but wearing a towel wrapped turban-style around her head.

'So what are we up to this afternoon?' she asked.

'Doing our police act for Eleanor Ricks's solicitor.'

She took off the towel and let it fall to the floor. Already she'd become a seasoned hotel guest. Next she'd be requesting more shampoo and teabags.

'I'm enjoying this,' she said. I looked surprised. 'Really, I am. It beats staring at sheep and dry-stone dykes all day.'

'I thought you watched daytime TV.'

'It beats that, too.' She sat down on the bed and, taking my hand, guided me to sit beside her. She didn't let go of my hand.

'Have you phoned Max lately?' I asked.

'That's a low punch.'

I shrugged. 'It's the only punch I've got.'

'Good.' She leaned towards me and touched her lips to mine. I was slow responding, so she opened her eyes. 'What's wrong?'

I pulled away from her, but slowly and not too far. 'We don't seem to be getting anywhere. It's all dead ends.'

'No, Michael,' she said, 'not *quite* all dead ends.' Our next kiss lasted a lot longer. By the end of it, her hair was all but dry, and this time she pulled away first.

'Can I just say one thing, Michael?'

'What?'

'In that gymnasium . . .'

'Yes?'

'You were holding the MP5 all wrong.'

'I was?' She nodded. 'Don't tell me you've actually fired an MP5?'

She looked surprised at the question. 'Of course I have. I get to fire most of my dad's guns eventually. Want me to give you some tips?'

I blinked. 'I'm not sure.'

She laughed at the look on my face. 'You thought you were getting Little Red Riding-Hood, is that it?'

'Well, I certainly didn't think I was getting the wolf.'

This time when we kissed, we used our hands to unbutton one another's clothes . . .

11

'You weren't entirely truthful, were you, Mr Hoffer?'

The speaker was DI Dave Edmond. He was in the same pub he'd been in before with Hoffer. And as before, Hoffer was buying him a drink.

'A couple of large Scotches, please.' Hoffer turned to the policeman. 'How do you mean?'

'You didn't tell me you'd had a blow-up with my boss. He's not very pleased with you, Mr Hoffer.'

'Did you tell him we'd had a drink?' Edmond shook his head. 'What he doesn't know can't hurt him, right?'

'It can hurt me, if he ever finds out.'

'Why should he, Dave? Besides, you can look after yourself.' Hoffer sniffed and scratched his nose. The drinks arrived and he proffered a twenty. 'Keep five for yourself,' he told the barman, 'and keep these coming till the change runs out.' He then handed a whisky to Edmond, who dribbled water into it.

'Come on,' said Hoffer, 'let's sit down.'

The just-the-one-after-work commuter drinkers had departed, so there were tables free. Hoffer liked Edmond less than he liked Bob Broome, but he smiled anyway. He needed a friend in the police investigation, and if Broome could no longer be bought, others like Edmond could. Broome would return to the fold. They'd fallen out before and then made things up. But meantime Edmond would suffice.

'I like your style, Dave. You're not showy. You're the sort of guy who gets things done, who doesn't make a song and dance number out of it.' Hoffer lit a cigarette, then slid the pack towards the policeman.

'Cops are cops,' Edmond said.

'God, that's true.'

'I hear you left the force.'

Hoffer opened his arms. 'I failed the physical. I was fine once I'd caught the bad guys. I could sit on them till they 'fessed up. But I just couldn't catch them.' Hoffer laughed and shook his head. 'No, it was the Walkins case. I got obsessed with it. So much so, my chiefs decided to move me to some other investigation. I couldn't take that, so I resigned and set myself up as a private dick. Only, the only case I was interested in was the Walkins one.'

'There was something about it in the papers.'

'Hey, the media *loved* my story. They brought it flowers and chocolates. I'd given up a good career to make a life of hunting this mystery gunman. And the millionaire father of one of his victims was paying me. Are you kidding? It made great copy. Plus of course I was a fat ugly bastard, they loved that too. They like anything but *normal* in their photographs.'

Edmond laughed. Hoffer liked him even less.

'They still love me,' he went on. 'And I don't mind that. See, some people think I'm pandering to them, I mean to the press, and maybe they're right. Or maybe I'm on some ego trip. All this may be true, but consider.' He raised a finger. 'The Demolition Man knows I'm out there. He knows I'm not going away. And I really get a kick out of *that*. Maybe he's not worried, but then again maybe he is.'

'You don't think he'd take a pop at you?'

Hoffer shrugged. 'I never think about it.' He'd told this story many dozens of times, always leaving out just a few truths. Such as the fact that his employers had *requested* his resignation when they'd decided he was doing a bit too much obvious nose talc. It was Hoffer's story that he'd resigned so he could follow up the Walkins story in his own way and his own time, but really he'd been given an ultimatum. Of course, once he'd explained to a reporter that he now had only one mission in life, then he'd had to do something about it, just to show willing. And then old man Walkins had come along and offered to pay him, and the story had expanded until he was trapped. Now he had his office and his employees and his reputation. He couldn't just walk away from the D-Man, even if he wanted to.

And he often thought that he wanted to.

'So how much do you make?' Edmond asked, the way serving policemen always did, sooner or later.

'Think of a number and double it,' Hoffer said. Then he laughed. 'No, I'm a businessman, an employer, I've got overheads, salaries to pay, taxes and shit. I don't come out so far ahead.'

'Walkins must be rich though.'

'You kidding? He's loaded.'

'Is it right that his daughter was a mistake?'

Hoffer nodded. She was just about the only mistake the D-Man had ever made. He had eleven, maybe twelve clean hits to his name, plus Ellen Walkins.

'She was eighteen, standing in the doorway saying goodnight to some people after a dinner party. They were all government people, plus wives, family. She wasn't the target. They reckon the target was a congressman with very strong views about certain foreign policies. Any number of dictators and crooked governments would have paid to have him shut up. But the step was icy and the fucker slipped. The bullet had been going straight through his heart, but it hit Ellen instead. The investigation got taken off our hands pretty fast. I mean, it was too big for just the police to handle. I couldn't let them do that.'

'Why not?'

The barman had appeared with two more whiskies, plus a bottle of water, giving Hoffer time to consider the question. It was one he'd asked himself a few times. Why couldn't he just let it go?

'I don't know,' he said honestly. 'I just couldn't.' He

sniffed again and shook himself up. 'Jesus, you don't want to hear all this. *You* should be the one doing the show and tell. So what have you got?'

Edmond pulled an envelope from his jacket pocket. Inside were several folded xerox sheets. There were photocopies of bank statements and old cheques, together with a run-down of cash machines Mark Wesley had used.

'It's not complete yet,' Edmond explained. 'This is just the first tranche. I could get into a lot of trouble for this.'

'You could,' agreed Hoffer, slipping an envelope across the table. 'But this might cheer you up.'

Edmond counted the money into his pocket, crumpling the envelope into their ashtray, then sat waiting. Hoffer didn't say anything for a while.

'Guy does a lot of travelling,' he said at last, reaching for his whisky.

'We'll check the travel companies mentioned, see if they can give us details.'

'Of course you will. What about these cash withdrawals? Any pattern you can see?'

Edmond shook his head. 'Except that some of them are in Yorkshire, according to Vine Street's geography A-level. Not in cities either, in country towns.'

'Maybe he lives there?'

Edmond shrugged. 'He's bought a whack of traveller's cheques too, by the look of it. One of those cheques to Thomas Cook isn't for travel.' He pointed to the photocopy. 'See? They've written on the back what it's for, purchase of traveller's cheques.' Hoffer nodded. 'We'll see if we can take it any further. If we can get the numbers of the traveller's cheques, might be we can find where he's used them. There's just one thing . . .'

'What's that, Dave?'

'Well, all we seem to be doing is tracking *backwards* through an identity he's already shed. Where will that get us?'

'Use your head, Dave. We can't track him forwards, so what else can we do? This way, we tie down accomplices, contacts, maybe we find patterns, or even a clue to his next hit. This for example.' Hoffer was tapping a cheque.

'Ah, I was coming to that,' said Edmond.

'So,' said Hoffer, 'here's a cheque made out to someone called . . . what is that name?'

'It says H. Capaldi,' said Edmond.

'Right, so who is he?'

'He's a counterfeiter.' Now Edmond had Hoffer's full attention.

'A counterfeiter?'

Edmond nodded. 'Harry the Cap's been around for years, done some time, but when he comes out he goes back to what he's best at.'

'What does he forge?'

'Documents . . . anything you want really.'

'Where can I find him?'

Edmond licked his lips. 'About four hundred yards up the road.'

'What?'

'We've brought him to Vine Street. Bob Broome's got him in an Interview Room right this minute.'

Hoffer waited for Edmond to come back.

It took a while, and he was starving, but he daren't leave the pub and miss the policeman's return. Instead, he ate potato chips and peanuts and then, as a last resort, a toasted sandwich. It was alleged to be cheese and ham. If you'd served it up in a New York bar, your client would have returned at dead of night with a flame thrower.

After all the whisky, he took it easy and went on to beer. The stuff was like sleeping with a severe anorexic: warm and dark and almost completely flat. Barney hadn't come up with a list of bent gun dealers yet, so he'd nothing to read but Edmond's photocopies. They didn't throw up much apart from Yorkshire and this guy called Capaldi, who didn't live in Yorkshire. Hoffer guessed that the bank was for convenience only, and that the D-Man kept the bulk of his money in stashes of ready cash. The travel stuff didn't interest him, though if they found he'd been cashing traveller's cheques in Nicaragua or somewhere, that would be a different story.

Edmond shrugged as he came to the table.

'He's not saying anything. Bob tried an obstruction number on him, but Harry's been around too long for that. His story is that he met a guy in a pub and the guy needed cash.'

'And this Harry, being the trusting sort, gave the stranger £500 and accepted a cheque?'

'Well, he says he got the cheque *and* a Rolex as security.'

'Did the mystery man ever come back for his watch?'

'Harry says no. He says he flogged the watch and cashed the cheque.'

'Did Bob ask him why he hung on to the cheque so long? It took him nearly six months to cash it.'

'Bob did mention it. Harry said something about mislaying it and then finding it again.'

'This guy's wasted as a counterfeiter, he should be on the improv circuit. I know comedians in New York couldn't make up stories that fast.' He paused. 'Or that full of shit either.'

'What can we do?'

Hoffer's eyes widened. 'You mean that's it? You can't lean on him a little? What about the trusty British truncheon? You guys are purveyors of torture equipment to the world, you can get this slob to talk.'

Edmond shook his head slowly throughout.

'You're right we can lean on him, but only so far. Harry knows the score. If he doesn't want to talk, he won't.'

'Jesus.' Hoffer sat back. 'I don't believe this. All right, where is he?'

'Who?'

'Perry Mason. Who the fuck d'you think I mean? I mean Capaldi!'

'He's probably on his way home by now.'

'Where does he live?'

Edmond looked like a cricketer who suddenly finds he's walked on to a baseball diamond. 'Wait a minute,' he said.

'Tell me where the fuck he lives!' Hoffer reached around his back to scratch it. Or maybe he was tampering with the stitches on the ball.

'He lives in north London,' Edmond said. Then he gave the American the address.

Tottenham seemed a pretty sleepy place. Though it was a warm summer's night, there weren't many people on the streets. What people there were on the streets were black, which didn't bother Hoffer one bit. He didn't have a racist bone in his body. He'd take on *anyone.*

He was running up some good cab receipts for Walkins. He got a couple more blanks from his driver and gave the guy a healthy tip. The house where Harry Capaldi lived was a narrow three-storey building, its third storey no more than an attic. But from the doorbells, it had been sliced and diced into three apartments. Hoffer rang Capaldi's bell. There wasn't any answer. He looked around him. The street was quiet and dark. It was like they'd turned down the juice; the street-lamps were a puny glow most of which was obscured by insect life.

Hoffer charged the door with his shoulder. He kept low, putting his weight against the keyhole. The door gave a little, but then resisted. At the second attempt, it flew open. He walked quickly to the first floor. There was no use knocking at Capaldi's door. The guy was either in and not answering, or else not in, and the only way to answer it one way or the other was to keep on going. This time it took a good four attempts before the door gave. When it did, it brought Hoffer into a hallway smelling of cooking fat and stale beer.

'I only want to talk,' he called, pushing the door closed. 'I'm not the cops, I'm just a guy. Mr Capaldi? Hey, anyone home?'

There was a light on in the room at the end of the hall, and the sound of a TV or something. But Capaldi could have left it on when the police had come to take him to Vine Street. Or maybe he left it on all the time whatever, so nobody'd think the place was empty. Hoffer eased the Smith & Wesson out of his pocket and felt a little more comfortable.

'Mr Capaldi?' he repeated. Then he pushed the door at the hall's end. It was a cramped room, mostly due to the large piece of photographic equipment sitting in the middle of it. Edmond had mentioned this. It was for taking reduced-size photos and fixing them on ID cards and the like. As Edmond had said, you couldn't prosecute; Capaldi was legitimate owner of the equipment. And he was always too clever to let them find anything else, no fake IDs or blank forms, nothing incriminating.

There was an old dining table by the window, the sort with legs which folded beneath it and wings which folded down so it didn't take up space. Something was making a noise beneath it, a cat or dog. Hoffer crouched down and took a look, then walked forward a couple more steps to get a better fix on it. He crouched down again and pocketed the gun.

'I think,' he said, 'we'd talk more comfortably if you came out of there, Mr Capaldi.'

Capaldi came out stiffly from beneath the table. He was shaking, and had to be helped to a chair.

'Who are you?' he said. But Hoffer was busy pouring Irish whiskey into a used glass. He handed it to Capaldi.

'Drink this. Sorry if I gave you a fright.' He looked over at the table. 'You'd hardly believe a full-grown man could squeeze into there, would you?' Then he turned back to

Capaldi and grinned. 'You must've been scared shitless. Who'd you think was ringing your bell, aliens? Think I was going to suck your heart out? Nope, all I want to do is have a little talk . . . Jesus, what's wrong with your head? It's like a fucking snowstorm.'

'Who are you?' Capaldi repeated. He found his cap and placed it firmly on his head.

'Doesn't matter who I am, Mr Capaldi. What matters is, I want to know about Mark Wesley.'

'I already told the police, I only met the guy—'

'I know, in a bar. But between you, me, and the police, that's a crock of shit. Now, they can't do much but tut-tut and send you off with a warning. Me, I can do better than that.' He produced the gun again. 'I can shoot you.' Capaldi looked like someone had stuck him to the chair with superglue – head, arms, legs, the lot. 'Now, I don't want to shoot you. I don't know anything about you, it may be you're a very nice man, generous to a fault, friendly with the neighbours, all that jazz. To be frank, that doesn't mean squat to me. I still might have to shoot you, unless you start telling me what you wouldn't tell the police.'

Hoffer leaned forward and lifted the whiskey glass from Capaldi's unresisting hand. He turned the glass around to drink from the clean side, and finished the whiskey in a single gulp. Now that he was calmer, he could hear a thudding bass sound from upstairs, shaking the ceiling and walls.

'Ten seconds,' he said quietly. 'And I'm not counting aloud.'

He always believed in giving people time to consider their next move, especially when they were scared senseless. He'd been that scared himself once or twice in the past, and you really did lose your senses. You could eat, but not taste. You couldn't smell anything, except maybe your sweat. Your sense of touch was restricted to the cooling damp of your trouser legs, or the gun nuzzling your head. You certainly couldn't see straight, or hear rational arguments.

It was good to have some time to adjust.

'Nine, ten,' Hoffer said. 'Shame it has to end like this, Mr Capaldi.' He touched the gun to the counterfeiter's head.

Capaldi started to speak, sort of. It took him five or six goes to utter the single word 'Jesus', and a few more tries before he could manage 'Don't shoot me.'

'Why not?'

'What?'

'Why not?'

'Because I'm not . . . because I . . . Jesus, all I did was . . .' He came to a dry stop.

'All you did was what? Make him up a new ID? *What?*' Then Hoffer too stopped, his mouth gaping. 'You son of a bitch,' he said at last. 'You've *seen* him, haven't you? I mean recently, in the last day or two?' He glanced towards the photographic equipment, all set up with a flash-lamp and a chair for the sitter.

'He's still in town, isn't he?' Hoffer could hardly believe it. 'Why's he still here? No, wait.' He knew there were other questions to ask first, so many of them it was a matter of getting the order right. Capaldi was staring past Hoffer's shoulder. When Hoffer turned his head, he saw why. There were two big black men standing in the hall, looking in on the scene. They had their mouths open, lower lips curled.

'No problem here, guys,' Hoffer called.

But there certainly *was* a problem. They'd probably seen the busted main door, and now Capaldi's door in the same state. And whoever they thought Hoffer was, he wasn't police. Even the cops in Tottenham didn't pack a .459 with their handcuffs.

They ran for the front door, yelling out someone's name. He could hear them climbing the stairs, heading for the second floor. Hoffer looked back at Capaldi, seeking an explanation.

'They deal a bit of dope,' Capaldi said. 'They don't like strangers.'

'Oh, shit.' Hoffer started pulling Capaldi to his feet. 'You're coming with me.'

But Capaldi resisted. More than that, he was still too scared to operate his legs, and Hoffer couldn't carry him, not with dope dealers on his ass.

'We'll finish our chat later,' he promised, then ran for the door. He could hear loud voices upstairs, not just two of them but three or four or five. He started down the stairs for the front door. He could hear footsteps pounding after him. Finish it now or keep running? He wondered if they'd fire on him out on the street? If yes, then it was better to make a stand here. But some instinct told him to get his fat self outside. There were houses on one side of the street only, the other being wall and embankment leading to a railway line. He didn't know which way to run. There didn't seem an obviously busier road in either direction. So he took a left and ran.

There were more houses, then some lock-ups, and then a corner shop. The street met another one at a T-junction, and he made the junction just as four figures came cautiously out of Capaldi's building. One of them pointed at him, and another raised a pistol. It could have been anything, airgun, starting-gun, even a water pistol. Hoffer wasn't taking any chances.

As far as he could aim, he aimed over their heads, but not so far over their heads that they'd think he didn't mean business. A couple of them dove back indoors again, but the one with the pistol kept cool and fired off two shots. The first hit some harling on the wall of the corner shop, while the second went through its display window, leaving large radial fractures around the hole.

'Fuck this,' said Hoffer, letting off a couple more and not caring where they went. He turned the corner into the new road, ignoring the people who were coming to their windows and doors. They seemed to go back inside pretty damned quick, but at least they came to look, which was more than would've happened in New York. At the bottom of the street, he saw a busy well-lit road, buses passing along it. He thought he recognised it from the cab ride. He kept turning around, but no one seemed to be following him. He knew they'd probably get a car first and follow him in that. Gun-toting drug dealers were so lazy these days.

'Damn,' he said, 'I could do with some dope, too.' Maybe they'd sell him some before taking off the top of his head. He'd known dealers kill their victims by ODing them. Well, let them try that trick on him with a mountain of opalescent coke, he'd put them out of business before he died.

He'd tucked the gun into his waistband and closed his jacket. He wasn't running any more, just walking very briskly. There were sirens ahead. Yes, he'd passed a police station on the way here. He walked into a pub as the sirens approached, looked around the interior as though searching for someone, then stepped out again when the sirens had passed. There was an Indian restaurant coming up. It was curtained from the road, nobody could see in or out.

If he kept moving, someone would stop him, be it police or irate dealers. There were no cabs to be seen, and the buses didn't move fast enough to be havens. He could walk, or he could hide. And if he was going to hide, why not hide somewhere he could get a meal and a drink? He pushed open the door of the Indian place and found another door which he had to pull. The restaurant was quiet, and he got the table he asked for: in a corner, facing the door. Anyone coming into the restaurant had to close the first door before opening the second. For a second or two, they'd be trapped between the two. He'd be able to pick them off while still spooning up the sauce, like a scene out of *The Godfather*.

'Quiet tonight,' he said to the young waiter.

'It's always quiet midweek, sir.'

After the meal, he had a couple of drinks in what seemed to be an Irish bar, not a coloured face in the place. There was a sign on the door saying 'Sorry, No Travellers'. He almost hadn't gone in, but then the barman explained that it meant tinkers, gypsies, not visitors. They all had a good laugh about that.

He took a taxi back to Capaldi's flat and made the driver go straight past it. Now that he thought of it, Capaldi would be long gone. He might not come back till all the heat had died. He might never come back at all. He'd either talk to Hoffer, and the D-Man would kill him, or he'd stay quiet and Hoffer might kill him. It wasn't much of a life, was it?

'Piccadilly Circus, please,' Hoffer told the driver.

'You're the guv'nor.'

It was unfortunate they'd been interrupted. All Hoffer knew now was that the D-Man had stayed in town after the assassination, when normally he'd have taken off. Why? That was the question. What was there for him here?

The tip-off, it had to be the tip-off to the police. The assassin was mad about it, and maybe he was going to do something about it. He'd be tracking down his paymasters. He'd be seeking out whoever set him up.

'I'll be damned,' Hoffer said to himself. At this rate, even in a city of ten million people, they might end up bumping into one another by accident.

He spent the rest of the drive wondering what his opening line would be.

12

Bel and I sat waiting for our meeting with Joe Draper. His production company had a set of offices on the top floor of a building near Harrods. We'd arrived early so Bel could do some window-shopping. I offered to buy her anything she liked, but she shook her head, even when I said I'd dock it from her pay.

Actually, we hadn't stayed long in the store. She'd looked a bit disgusted with it all after a while. She'd hooked her arm through mine as we'd walked to Draper Productions.

'Relax,' she'd told me.

We'd spent last night in bed together, Bel asking questions about my life, and me deciding how to answer them. I'd deflected her for a while by talking about guns. She knew a lot about guns and ammo, but that didn't mean she liked them. They scared the hell out of her.

Now we sat in Draper's offices, pretending to be CID. We were wearing the same clothes as yesterday, down to the black leather gloves. We weren't leaving fingerprints anywhere. Bel flicked through a trade mag, while I watched Teletext. There were three monitor-sized TVs in reception, all with the sound turned down. One of them was showing a looped montage of recent Draper output. The secretary kept deflecting calls to Draper's assistant.

'I did that,' I said. Bel looked up from her magazine. Teletext was running a news page, all about how two East European countries were about to close their shared border. Tensions had been high between the neighbours since the break-up of the Soviet Union, but a recent perceived assassination attempt on a diplomat based in London had brought things to a head.

'Maybe you should do something about it,' she whispered. The whisper wasn't necessary, the secretary having put on headphones so she could start some audio-typing.

'Like what?'

'I don't know, own up or something, say the diplomat was never your target.'

'But that would mean telling them who my *real* target was. I quite like it that they're not sure.' I was smiling, but Bel wasn't.

'You could start a war, Michael.'

I stopped smiling. 'You're right. Maybe I could offer Draper the exclusive.'

She slapped me with the magazine, then went back to reading it. Teletext flipped to its News Directory. There was some story near the bottom about a shoot-out on a north London street. It was coupled with another story, some get-tough-on-drugs speech the Home Secretary had made. I didn't think it meant anything, but I got up and went over to the secretary. She stopped her tape.

'Yes?'

'Do you have a handset for the TV?' She looked disapproving. 'I don't want to change channels, I just want to check a story on Teletext.'

Without saying anything, she opened a drawer and brought out a couple of remotes.

'One of these has Teletext,' she said, restarting her tape.

'Thanks a million,' I muttered. I aimed one of the remotes and pressed three digits. Up popped the story. There was a bit about the Home Secretary first, then a slim paragraph about gunshots fired in a street in Tottenham. It was the street where Harry the Cap lived. Maybe some people believe in coincidence. I'm not one of them. I knew Hoffer was getting too damned close.

Just then Draper's door opened and a young man and

136

woman came out. They were dressed like students, but carried briefcases. The boy had a ponytail, while the girl's blonde hair was cropped short and tipped with red dye. They shook hands with Draper, then headed for the door. Draper checked something with the secretary, then came towards us.

'Sorry to keep you, Inspector West.'

'That's all right, sir, we appreciate your finding time to see us.'

He was ushering us into his office. 'The gloves are a nice touch,' he said. I didn't get it. 'I used to produce a cop show called *Shiner*, maybe you know it?'

'I used to watch it,' said Bel. Draper looked pleased.

'Only,' he said, 'the Inspector in that used to wear gloves like yours.'

'I see,' I said. Draper saw that he hadn't scored any points, and shifted in his swivel-chair.

'I'm not sure how I can help. I've already told your colleagues everything I can think of.'

'Just a few follow-up questions, sir. A fresh perspective.'

'Well, okay then.' He clasped his hands in front of him. 'Tea or coffee?'

'No, thank you, sir. This is DC Harris, by the way.'

Draper had been staring at Bel. 'We're thinking of pitching a police documentary series,' he informed her. 'Ever wanted to be on television?'

She smiled professionally. 'I don't think so, sir. Bright lights make me nervous.'

Draper laughed. 'Too much like the interrogation room, eh?' Now he turned to me. 'Shoot.'

I suppose he meant I could start asking questions.

'We'd like to know a little more about Ms Ricks, her family, colleagues, any possible enemies she may have had.'

'Well, none of her colleagues was an enemy. Lainie had a first-rate reputation. All her fellow journalists admired her. I

137

dare say a few TV people were preparing knives, but only in the figurative sense.'

'How do you mean?'

He opened his hands. 'She was going to be a star. She was a natural on TV.' He looked at Bel again. 'Know why? Because she didn't trust the medium. And that came over, that honesty, that sense that she wasn't going to put up with any manure.'

'But she hadn't actually made any programmes?'

'That's true, I'm talking about the mock-ups we do beforehand, especially with a tyro. Lainie breezed it. It was like she was walking on water. I knew when we got her on the screen, she'd start to make . . . not enemies exactly, but there'd be jealousy from other presenters, because she was going to show them how the job should be done.' He shook his head and calmed a little. 'She's a big loss.'

He sounded like he was thinking of her in financial terms.

'What about her family?' I asked. 'Did you know them?'

'Oh yes, I suppose I knew them as well as anyone can.'

'Meaning?'

Draper sighed, like he didn't gossip normally, but since we were the police how could he refuse?

'Freddy's not an easy man to like, Inspector. I mean, his star's so low it's sweeping up leaves. And that doesn't sit easy with Freddy. He still wants to act the soap star. Did you ever see him in *Stand By Your Man*? It wasn't exacting stuff. Also, it was ten years ago, something Freddy doesn't seem to realise. He sees all this "vintage" comedy being repeated on the box, and his stuff isn't there. No surprise to anyone else, believe me. Meanwhile he sees his wife breaking into TV and there I am telling her how wonderful she's going to be. You can see it's not easy for him.'

'Yes, I can imagine. Did they have arguments?'

'All the time.'

'What about?'

'Everything under the sun. You want an example?' I

nodded. 'Okay, Freddy blew their savings on a trip to Hollywood. He was out there looking for work, but all he came back with were a tan and some books of matches from expensive restaurants. Lainie was furious with him.' He paused. 'Look, there's no way Freddy would put out a contract on Lainie, that's not what I'm saying here. They had arguments, but they were never physical. They didn't even really have screaming matches. They just smouldered and wouldn't communicate for weeks on end. All I'm saying is, they did not have the perfect marriage. But then who does?'

Bel had a question. 'Did you like Ms Ricks as a person, Mr Draper?'

'Like her? I loved her. I'd've liked nothing better than . . .' He stopped and shook his head. 'I don't know.' His eyes were growing moist, but then he'd been around actors all his working life. Some tricks must have rubbed off.

'She had a son,' I nudged.

'That's right, a useless streak of sham called Archie. I say that, watch this, he'll be a millionaire at twenty-one.'

'What does he do?'

'He's in a band, programmes music samples, that sort of thing.'

'Electronics.'

'Yeah, I can't see the band doing much. I listened to their stuff as a favour, in case we could use any of it as backing to our programmes. Forget it. But Archie's a genius, in a limited sort of way. I see him moving into production, and *that's* where he'll make his pile.'

'Mr Draper, I know you've been asked this question before by my colleagues, probably by the media too, but can you think of anyone who would have wanted Eleanor Ricks dead?'

He shook his head. 'It had to be a mistake. The bastard was obviously after Prendergast or the foreigner. Got to be.'

'You sent Ms Ricks to interview Molly Prendergast?'

'No, it was Lainie's idea. I mean, she was running the whole show. It was her story right down the line, minimum input from me. She'd say she wanted to go in a certain direction, we'd talk about it, and she'd go off and do it. She was the driver, me, I was somewhere in the boot, like luggage. I hardly saw the light of day.'

'And what direction was she travelling in?'

He sighed. 'It'll probably never get made now.'

'We've spoken with Ms Ricks's solicitor, a Mr Johns. He mentioned something about religious cults?'

Draper nodded. 'Prendergast's kid was in a cult for over a year. In the end, Prendergast mounted a commando-style raid to snatch her back. This was a couple of years back, it made the news at the time. The daughter's not too bad now, it was *her* we wanted for the programme, but her mother said no, if we wanted to speak to anyone it would have to be her. Lainie set up the meeting partly to get Prendergast's story, and partly to make her change her mind. We thought once Prendergast met Lainie, she might melt a bit.'

'So it was a programme about Prendergast's daughter?'

'God, no, she was just a sentence, a phrase, in a much bigger book. No, Lainie was looking at the cult itself.'

'Which one?'

'The Disciples of Love. Sound like a band out of the 60s, don't they? You can see them opening the show at Monterey.'

'What sort of . . . tone was the documentary going to take?'

'It was basically an exposé of how the group is run. They've got one of these charismatic leaders, you know, like at Waco or the Children of God. But most sects go for your wallet before they try to snatch your soul, and the Disciples aren't like that. They take in poor people.'

'I don't see the problem.'

'Well, they won't say how they're funded. Lainie reckons it takes thousands, maybe hundreds of thousands a year to keep them operating, and their total income can't even be half that. So where does the money come from?'

'Did she try asking them?'

'They didn't so much stonewall her as put up the Great Wall of China. She got some financial wizards to do some sniffing. We got a bill from them that nearly killed us budget-wise, but they couldn't tell us anything about the Disciples.'

'Do you have anything here about the project? I mean, something I could take away with me?'

'Sure, I've got a few copies of the Bible.'

'Bible?'

He smiled again. 'That's what we work from, it's a sort of blueprint of the shape the documentary's going to take. We use it to get backers interested.' He opened a cupboard. It was full of bulging files and reams of typed paper, scripts and the like. It took him a few seconds to find what he was looking for.

'Here we go, take one each.'

The Bible was loosely bound with a cardboard cover and a thin plastic sheet protecting it. There were holes in the cover through which appeared the name of the project, Draper's and Ricks's names, and a few other details.

The project was just called *Disciples of Love*, but with a question-mark.

'I appreciate this, Mr Draper. I'll see these get back to you.'

He shrugged. 'Keep them. The whole thing's history without Eleanor Ricks.'

'One last thing, did she have any favourite colour of clothing?'

The question threw him, so I smiled reassuringly. 'We're still wondering if maybe the assassin mistook her for Mrs Prendergast.'

'I see what you mean, Lainie wearing the kind of clothes Prendergast would normally wear.' He nodded to himself.

'Well, I know one thing, she did like to empathise with her interviewees, and that could sometimes mean dressing like them. As to favourite colours . . .' He shook his head. 'The best I can come up with is bright colours, reds, blues, yellows. Primary colours.'

I nodded. I'd been told to look for yellow and blue. I stared at Draper, trying to see something behind his eyes, some inkling of guilt. But where was his motive? No, there was nothing there.

'What about Mrs Prendergast?' Bel inquired suddenly.

'What about her?' Draper asked back.

'She's a public figure, and she's tough, plus she's got an interest in the cult.' Draper still didn't get it. 'She might be persuaded to take over where Ms Ricks left off.'

Draper leapt to his feet. I thought he was going to vault the desk, but he just leaned over it towards Bel.

'Brilliant!' he shrieked. 'That's fucking brilliant!' He slapped the desk with both hands and shook his head wildly. He was somewhere in the hinterland between laughter and tears. 'That is just *so* brilliant. Why didn't I think of it?'

Bel's look towards me confirmed she thought this a tautology. Draper couldn't get us out of there quick enough, but all the time trying to be polite. He had his hand on Bel's shoulder and one on my back. He was telling her to think about fronting his documentary series.

'All right,' she said, 'I'll think about it.'

'You'd be a great loss to the force,' I told her as we left.

Outside, I headed for the first newspaper kiosk I saw, and bought up several of the dailies. I wanted more on the Tottenham shoot-out. I didn't think Harry would have said anything, but how could I be sure? Without a trip to Tottenham, the answer was, I couldn't.

I told Bel she deserved some time to herself, and managed to press £50 on her, which in Knightsbridge would just about pay for a passable lunch. Then I headed north. I knew this was one of the most stupid things I'd ever done, but I couldn't talk myself out of it. One thing I did know was that if I was going to meet Hoffer, I didn't want Bel around. No matter that she was my best form of camouflage, I'd promised she wouldn't be in danger.

Before we separated, she made me make a phone call. Afterwards, I said I'd see her back at our hotel. She kissed my cheek, and I pressed a finger to her chin. She didn't tell me to be careful, but I knew what she was thinking.

All the way to Tottenham, I found myself doing something I never ever do. I thought of the past. Not the distant past, I don't mind that, but the more recent past, and my life as an assassin. Well, what else was I going to do with my life? I'd never fancied being deskbound, but the Army weren't going to have me. As a teenager I was clever but easily bored, and I was frustrated that I couldn't play football or rugby. I did try to take part in games sometimes, but the other kids knew about me, and they wouldn't come near. They were being kind in their way, I suppose, but I couldn't see it at the time. All I saw was that I was different. I started to spend more time on the gun range, and I acquired a marketable skill.

My father had started me off, despite my mother's warnings. He was a top-class target shooter himself. He started me with air pistols and air rifles, then we moved up to real ammo, small calibre at first. Funny to think those afternoons of bonding had led me here.

Here, thinking about my victims.

I had never had much of a conscience. Like I say, everyone bleeds. But then I'd missed a target and killed an innocent girl. That was when word started to go round that I was losing it. I'd cried about that girl. I'd sat by a hotel swimming pool in the Bahamas and played it through in my head, over and over again, the New York cold, that icy step, that single slip . . .

They called me the Demolition Man, but all I'd ever really

demolished were lives. You could buy a new dustbin, new windows, you could repair walls with fresh bricks and mortar. But I'd noticed something in Draper's office, I'd noticed his pain. He'd lost someone, and the loss, for all my glibness at the time, was not merely financial. He'd lost someone he loved. He might be a hard-nosed businessman, a schemer, a ruthless capitaliser on rumour and grief. I'd seen the clips from some of his programmes; they concentrated on the tearful close-up and the hounding of interviewees. But he was human too. He could feel what his victims felt. He was feeling it now.

See, that's why I like to get away from the scene. I never go back. I don't buy the papers or anything, I don't read about myself and cut out my exploits to stick in some scrap album. I do the job and I get the hell away. I never think about it afterwards. I drown the memories in alcohol and travel.

Well, here I was stone-cold sober, and travelling towards something, not away from it. I wasn't even armed, and I knew Hoffer would be.

I got the cab to drop me on the High Road, and walked the few hundred yards to Harry's street. The front door was still waiting to be repaired. I could see where the lock had been wrenched open, but there were no signs of leverage, no marks left by a crowbar. No footprints on the door either, which meant it had been a shoulder charge.

There was noise on the stairs. A black man came down, on his way out. He glared at me.

'What happened here?' I asked. He ignored me. 'I'm a friend of Harry's.'

He gave me a look brimming with distrust. 'He ain't in, man.'

'What happened to the door?'

'Some big white fucker rammed it.' If he'd been a dog he'd have been sniffing me. 'Cop?' I shook my head. He looked around him, up and down the street. A train which had been sitting at the station started to move past us, way up the embankment. 'Some big guy, right? Kicked the door in, kicked in Harry's door. We came back and thought someone was ripping us off, right? So in we go, and this guy's got a gun out and he's standing over Harry. Harry's looking like he's going to croak, right? So we chased the fucker off.'

I whistled. He shifted his weight, looking pleased at the part he'd played in the drama.

'Is Harry all right though?'

'Dunno, man, he took off. Cops wanted to talk to him, but Harry was gone.'

'I don't blame him.'

'Yeah.'

'No point trying his door?'

'The place is picked clean. Cops didn't put a lock on it, so kids went in and ripped off everything. We had to chase them off, too.'

I nodded, though suspecting that the bulk of Harry's goods were now sitting in a pile in the flat above his.

'Thanks for helping him out,' I said.

'Hey,' he shrugged, 'what are neighbours for, right?'

Back in my room, I lay on the bed and read the *Disciples of Love?* project. Eleanor Ricks had been planning little less than an assassination of her own. The cult had its roots in the Pacific north-west of the USA, an area I knew, but its branches stretched all around the world. There were more than a dozen communes in Europe, but only one in Great Britain. Prendergast's daughter had actually belonged to a commune in south-west France, but the focus of Ricks's investigation was the British enclave on the Scottish west coast.

According to some notes added at the back of the file, she'd twice visited Scotland, but was planning a much longer visit once she'd completed what she called her 'primary research'. Only she'd never been allowed to finish that research.

The funding of the sect seemed to be the key. So long as no one would explain it, you could guess any way you liked: drugs, prostitution, blackmail, coercion. There were press cuttings in the file referring to stories about other cults, not just the Branch Davidian in Texas but the Children of God in Argentina and some Southern Baptist splinter groups in Louisiana and Alabama. As far as I could see, cults in general provided a useful service: they kept the arms dealers in business. Koresh's group in Waco had stockpiled enough weapons for Armageddon and beyond. I'd visited Texas. To buy a gun, any gun, all you needed was a state driver's licence and a form you completed yourself stating you'd never been in an asylum and you weren't a drug addict. They have about four guns in Texas for every man, woman and child. And those are the *legal* ones. I knew there were plenty of gun dealers who didn't require any ID from their buyers, just a wad of cash. I'd once bought a night-vision scope from a man with a military haircut after I got talking to him in a bar in Lubbock. I paid half the market price. It was the only good thing that happened to me in Lubbock, until I met Spike. Spike was, Max and Bel apart, the closest thing I had to a friend in the whole overpopulated world.

And Spike was crazy, gun crazy.

Bel gave her knock and came into my room. She was red-cheeked as she flopped on to the bed beside me.

'I must've walked for miles,' she said. 'How did it go?'

'I don't think we can hang around much longer.'

'Well then, that makes it easy.'

'What do you mean?'

She rolled on to her side and propped her head on one hand. 'I've just spent an hour in a cafe reading through the file.' She nodded at my copy. 'And the way I see it, the Disciples of Love are as likely suspects as anyone.'

'How would they know what clothes she'd be wearing?'

'They must have had someone watching her, otherwise they couldn't have compiled all that information they gave you. Maybe the watcher spotted that she wore similar clothes every day, or every interview she did.'

Yes, I'd thought of that myself. 'Maybe,' I said.

'Look,' said Bel, 'there's the jealous husband, the misunderstood teenage son, the producer who wanted to jump into bed with her, the lawyer who might have been just behind him in the queue.'

It was true that the solicitor, Geoffrey Johns, had professed a more than merely professional interest in Eleanor Ricks when we'd talked to him.

'So we've got a lot of possible paymasters,' I said.

'Agreed, but none as strong as the Disciples of Love. Look at what she was saying about them. I mean, from those American press clippings these aren't people to toy with.'

Bel had another point. The Disciples of Love had been in trouble in the USA after a journalist had been beaten up and another pummelled with his own camera.

'We don't know they'd go as far as assassination.'

'We don't know they wouldn't. Besides, there's my final point.'

I smiled. So far, we'd been thinking along such similar lines that I knew what was coming.

'The need to get out of London,' I said. Bel nodded agreement.

'We've got two choices,' she said. 'We either wait it out here until Shattuck comes back, since he's the only one who can tell us for sure who hired you. Or we scarper. We can always come back later, and meantime we could be doing something useful like checking on the Disciples of Love.'

'You took the words right out of my mouth,' I said. 'And I can always drop you off at Max's on the way.'

'What?' She sat up. 'What do you mean?'

'Bel, I needed you here to give me some cover. I don't need any cover in Scotland.'

'How do you know?'

'I just do. They're not combing the streets for an assassin up there.'

'But there's this man Hoffer. If he's figured things out this far, what's to stop *him* going to Scotland?'

'What if he does? Are you going to shield me from him?'

I was smiling, but she wasn't. With teeth gritted she started to thump my arms. 'You're not leaving me behind, Weston!'

'Bel, see sense, will you?'

'No, I won't.' She was still thumping me. 'I'm going with you!'

I got off the bed and rubbed my arms. Bel put a hand to her mouth.

'Oh my God,' she said, 'I forgot! Michael, are you all right?'

'I'm fine. There'll be bruises maybe, but that's all.'

'Christ, I'm sorry, I forgot all about . . .' She got off the bed and hugged me.

'Hey, not *too* hard,' I said. I was laughing, but when I looked at Bel she had tears in her eyes. 'It's okay,' I said. 'I'm a haemophiliac, not a paper bag. I won't burst.'

She smiled at last, then embraced me again.

'I'm coming with you,' she said. I kissed both her eyes, tasting salt from her lashes.

'We'll talk to Max,' I said.

13

'Come in, Mr . . . ah . . .'

'Hoffer.'

'Absolutely. Take a seat, won't you?'

Geoffrey Johns's office was everything Hoffer loathed and loved about England. It was old-fashioned, a bit dusty, and fairly reeked of centuries of history and family and tradition. There was something upright and solemn and confidential about it. You couldn't imagine Johns in red braces and Gekko-slick hair, doing billion-dollar deals on the telephone. He was more father-confessor than lawyer, and though he wasn't so old, he put on a good act of being wise, benign and endearingly fuddled. Like making Hoffer introduce himself, even though he knew damn fine who he was. Hoffer wanted to flick the man's half-moon glasses into the wastebin and slap him on the head, try to wake him up. The twentieth century was drawing to a close, and Geoffrey Johns was still working in the Dickens industry.

'Now then, Mr . . . ah . . . Hoffer.' He'd been shuffling some papers on his desk. They were little more than a stage-prop, so Hoffer bided his time, sitting down and smiling, arms folded. The solicitor looked up at him. 'Some tea perhaps? Or coffee, I believe you Americans prefer coffee.'

'We prefer, Mr Johns, to cut through all the shit and get down to business.'

Johns didn't peer through his spectacles at Hoffer, he dropped his head and peered *over* them. 'There are courtesies to be observed, Mr Hoffer. Mrs Ricks's family is still in mourning. I myself am still in a state of some shock.'

'She was a good client, huh?'

Johns wasn't slow to get the meaning. 'I regarded her as a *friend*, one I'd known for many years.'

Hoffer's attention had been attracted to the bakelite telephone. It made him smile. The solicitor misunderstood.

'Good God, man, what is there to smile about?'

'Your phone,' Hoffer said. 'It's a phony, isn't it? I mean a fake.'

'I believe it's a replica.'

'Lot of fakes about these days, Mr Johns. I'll have tea, please, milk and two lumps of sugar.'

Johns stared at him, deciding whether or not to let the brash American have his tea. Politeness won the argument. Johns buzzed his secretary and asked for a pot of tea.

'I believe,' Hoffer said, 'your principal duty lies with your clients. Would you agree, Mr Johns?'

'Of course.'

'Well, one of them's been murdered. And her family have asked you for your help. Now, way I see it, they want her killer found, *she* would want her killer found, and probably you do too.'

'Of course I do,' fussed the lawyer. 'No "probably" about it. I think they should bring back hanging for terrorists.'

'Terrorists? What makes you say that?'

'What?'

'That the assassin was a terrorist?'

'Well, who was his intended victim?'

'I've no reason to believe it wasn't Mrs Ricks.'

'Really? But the MP and the diplomat . . . ?'

Hoffer shook his head. 'The Demolition Man usually gets who he aims for.'

'Ah, but the papers say he shot the wrong person in New York. They say that's where *your* story starts.'

Hoffer accepted this. He'd been interviewed yesterday and this morning by a couple of papers and a radio station. No television yet, which was surprising. The story had a new angle with the two East European countries closing their mutual border. The Demolition Man was still news, and Hoffer always gave good copy.

'As I see it, Mr Hoffer,' Johns went on, 'my duty is to aid the official police investigation any way I can. I don't believe you form part of that investigation, therefore I'm not *obliged* to grant you an interview at all.'

'If you know anything,' Hoffer said, 'you'll know that if anyone's going to catch this man, that person is me.'

'Really? And how long have you been tracking him? Quite a while, I believe.'

Hoffer was getting to like the solicitor better all the time.

'Have you spoken to the police much?' he asked.

'Practically every day, *twice* yesterday.' Johns shook his head. 'I try to help where I can, but some of the questions . . .'

A tray of tea arrived. Hoffer gave the secretary a good look as she stood beside him and leaned over to put the tray down on the desk. Great legs, nice ass, but a face so thin and sharp you could use it as an awl.

'Thank you, Monica,' said Johns. After the secretary had gone, he started pouring milk and tea with the grace of a duchess.

'I'll let you help yourself to sugar.'

Hoffer helped himself. 'What sort of questions?' he asked casually.

'Well, the one that got me was: what colours did she like to wear? I couldn't see the point of that at all, but the officer said he had his reasons for asking.'

'Didn't tell you what those reasons were though?'

'No, he didn't. A typical policeman, I'm afraid.'

'Her favourite colours, huh?' Hoffer pondered the question himself, seeking the point behind it, while he stirred his tea. It was one of those elegant little china cups with a handle so overelaborate and undersized that he ended up with his hand around the cup itself, ignoring the handle.

Johns seemed to be having no trouble with his own handle. They probably taught tricks like that in law school.

'I should tell you, Mr Johns, that I'm working pretty closely with the London police. They know I'm on the right side. I mean, we've all got the same objective, right?'

'Yes, I understand.'

'So don't misunderstand me.' Hoffer smiled humbly. 'The press don't always paint the real picture of me. I'm not after glory or anything, I'm not some obsessed crazy guy with a mission from on high. I'm just a cop doing my job.' Sincerity was easy. 'And I'd appreciate your help.'

Johns put down his cup. 'And you shall have it, so far as I can give it.'

The telephone interrupted them. It might be a replica, but it had a nice old tinny ring which faded only slowly after Johns picked up the receiver.

'Monica, I wanted all calls held. All right, put him on. Hello, Ray, what can I do for you? No, I haven't had the news on this morning. What's that?' He looked at Hoffer and kept looking. 'That's interesting. When was this? Mm, well, I don't know what to think. No, no comment at this time. Thank you, goodbye.'

He put down the phone but left his hand on the receiver.

'That was a reporter,' he informed Hoffer. 'He says a local radio station has been contacted by someone claiming to be the assassin.'

'Some crank,' said Hoffer. 'What's he saying?'

'He says he wants the two East European countries to know he wasn't hired to assassinate the diplomat. He says he got who he was aiming at.' Johns looked very pale as he lifted his hand from the receiver. 'I think I need something stiffer than tea.'

There was a drinks cabinet beneath the window. Johns poured a dark liquid into two tiny stemmed glasses. There was about a shot's worth in the glass he handed to Hoffer, who sniffed it.

'Sherry,' said Johns, gulping his down.

Hoffer, who'd only come across the stuff in English trifle, knocked it back, rolling it around his mouth before swallowing. It was sour to start with, but quickly got mellow as it warmed his gut.

'Not bad,' he said.

'You still think this was a crank call?' asked the solicitor.

'I don't know.'

'Maybe your man has just found himself a conscience.'

'Some conscience.' Hoffer still didn't get the question about Ricks's clothes. 'The policeman you spoke to yesterday, the one who asked what Mrs Ricks normally wore, can I ask who he was? Was it Chief Inspector Broome maybe? Or DI Edmond?'

'No, neither of those, though I've spoken to them before. This was someone new to the inquiry. He apologised for asking questions I'd probably been asked before.'

'Was he on his own?'

'No, he was with another officer.'

'He didn't have brown hair, did he?'

'Black hair, cut short as I recall.'

Hoffer was beginning to wonder. Mark Wesley had got some fake ID from Harry Capaldi . . .

'Did they show you any identification?'

'Oh, yes. The man was called Wes . . . no, hold on.' Hoffer had nearly leapt from his chair, but the solicitor was fussing on his desk again, trying to find a scrap of paper or something. 'Here it is. Inspector West.'

'No first name?'

'No. His assistant was a woman, a Detective Constable Harris.'

Hoffer shook his head slowly. 'I don't know them,' he said, not convinced he was quite telling the truth.

Bob Broome wasn't thrilled to see him. Vine Street was its

usual chaos and gloom. Broome wouldn't let Hoffer past the front desk, so Hoffer waited for Broome to descend.

'I'm busy,' he said curtly, when he finally arrived.

'You'll find time for me, Bob, when you hear what I've got.'

Broome narrowed his eyes. 'I've got enough cranks around here as it is.'

'You don't think that call was a crank, do you?'

'I don't know.'

'Have you got a recording or just a transcript?'

Broome narrowed his eyes further. 'Is that all you're here for, to try pumping me about the phone call?'

Hoffer shook his head defiantly. 'Just tell me this: DI West and DC Harris, do you know them?'

'First names?' Hoffer shook his head. Broome gave it another couple of seconds. 'Never heard of them.'

'West sounds a bit like Wesley, doesn't it?'

'Come on, Hoffer, what's your story?'

'Can we go upstairs and talk about it? I feel like a victim stuck down here.'

Broome decided to give the American the benefit of his very grave doubts.

'Come on then,' he said. On the way up, they passed Barney coming down. He winked at Hoffer.

'I'll have it for you tomorrow,' he said.

'Thanks,' Hoffer said, trying to sound guilty or embarrassed as Broome gave him a long dirty look.

When they got to the office, Broome made a show of checking the time. 'You've got five minutes,' he told Hoffer. Then he sat down and looked like he was waiting for a show to begin.

'I don't pay dues to any acting union, Bob.' Hoffer sat down slowly, taking a while to get comfortable. 'I'll put it to you straight, but stop acting like you're in a sulk.'

'*Sulk?* You're going around like *you're* the Chief Inspector and I'm just some office-boy who gets in your way. I'm not sulking, Hoffer, I'm bloody furious. Now, what have you got for me?'

A Detective Constable came into the room and placed a small packet on Broome's desk. Broome ignored it, waiting for Hoffer to speak. Hoffer pointed to the packet.

'Is that the tape, Bob?' Broome didn't say anything. 'Come on, let's listen to it.'

'First tell me what you know.'

'Well, "know" is a bit strong. But there's this solicitor, Geoffrey Johns. Know what johns are in the States? Well, never mind.'

'I know Mr Johns.'

'Yes, you do. But you don't know anyone called West or Harris. West's in his mid-thirties, tall and lean, with short black hair. He's with a young woman, pretty tall with short fair hair. I'll let your guys go get more detailed descriptions from Johns and his secretary.'

'Good of you. So you think West is Wesley?'

'Yes.'

'And he's posing as a police officer?'

'With ID faked up by Capaldi.'

'Why?'

Broome had asked one of the questions Hoffer couldn't answer.

'And who's his partner?'

Now he'd asked the other. Hoffer shrugged. 'I don't know, but he was asking questions about Ricks. The important thing is, he's still in town and he's asking around. By rights he should be miles away, but he's here under our noses.' The image made Hoffer think of something. He sniffed the thought away. 'He's *here*, Bob, and the only reason I can think of why he's still around is that he's on to something.' He paused. 'I think he's going after his employer.'

'What?'

'The anonymous phone call, the one that nearly got him caught, he's after whoever made it. Stands to reason it must have been someone close to the deceased, otherwise how would he know where to find her?' He clicked his fingers. 'That's why he's asking about her clothes.'

'Her clothes?'

Hoffer's mind was racing. 'He must've been told what she'd be wearing! Christ, could that be it?'

'I'm not really getting this, Hoffer.'

Hoffer slumped back as far as he was able in his chair. 'Me neither, not all of it. Just pieces, and the pieces don't all make sense.'

Broome fingered the packet, but didn't seem in a hurry to open it. 'Hoffer,' he said, 'there was some shooting in north London last night.'

'Yeah, I read about it.'

'We've got a description of a fat man seen running away.'

'Uh-huh?'

Broome pinched the bridge of his nose. 'There's also been a mugging, except that no money was taken from the victim.' Broome looked up. 'You're supposed to ask me who the victim was.'

Hoffer blew his nose before asking. 'So who was it?'

'Mr Arthur, the bank manager.'

Hoffer threw his used tissue into the bin beside Broome's desk.

'You wouldn't know anything about it, Hoffer?'

'Give me a break, Bob. I haven't mugged anyone since I quit the NYPD. You get a description of the assailants?'

Broome was staring at Hoffer. 'He was hit from behind. He's got concussion.'

Hoffer shook his head. 'Nice guy, too. Nobody's safe these days.'

Broome sighed and rubbed his eyes. 'All right,' he said, 'let's listen to the tape.'

He had a DC bring in a portable cassette player and set it up.

'This local station must be on their toes,' said Hoffer.

'They tape all calls to the news desk, partly as a favour to us.'

'Why?'

'Because the IRA often call a local radio station to take responsibility for a bombing. That way the news gets on the air faster, plus it doesn't look like they're cooperating with us.'

'So the radio station's a kind of go-between?'

'Sort of, yes.' Broome loaded the tape and pressed Play. There was some soft hissing, which became louder until someone spoke.

'News desk, Joely speaking.'

'This is the Demolition Man, do you understand?'

'Dem . . . ? Oh yes, yes, I understand.'

'Listen then. Tell everyone I hit my intended target, got that? I wasn't after the diplomat. He just happened to be there. Understood?'

'Mm, yes.' Joely was obviously writing it all down. 'Yes, I've got that. Can I just ask—'

'No questions. If anyone thinks this is a hoax, tell them Egypt, the Cairo Hilton, twelfth of December two years ago.'

'Hello? Hello?' But the Demolition Man had put down the phone. Broome listened to the silence for a few moments, then stopped and rewound the tape.

'The original's gone to the lab boys,' he said. 'We'll see what they say.'

'Sounded like he was in a callbox, and not long distance. He's English, isn't he?'

'Sounds it. Sounded like he was trying to disguise his voice too.'

Hoffer smiled. 'You weren't taken in by the Jimmy Durante impression?'

'Maybe he's got a cold.'

'Yeah, maybe.'

Broome looked at Hoffer. 'Egypt?'

Hoffer nodded. 'Yeah, it's not one everyone knows about.

Nobody's been able to say it was the D-Man, so it never makes the papers. It was a precision hit, long-range, but he didn't leave a bomb. Either that or the bomb didn't detonate.'

'Who did he kill?'

'Some Arab millionaire with big gambling debts which he was unwisely ignoring.' Hoffer shrugged. 'The gambler was a Mr Big, didn't think anyone could touch him. He had an armoured Mercedes and four bodyguards a grenade launcher couldn't't've budged. They used to huddle round their boss when he went anywhere, like he was Muhammad Ali going into the ring. Then, pop, a bullet hits the guy smack in the heart, and they're all looking around, only they don't know where to look because there's nothing there to look at. They reckon it was a hit from six, maybe seven hundred yards.'

'You know a lot about it.'

'I've had a lot of time to look things up. I've got a file of more than sixty assassinations going back fifteen years. He could be behind any number of them.'

'Would anyone else know about it?'

'Only someone as obsessed as me.' Hoffer paused. 'It's him on the tape, I know it's him.'

'We'll see if the boffins can come up with anything.'

'Such as?'

'You'd be surprised. We've got linguistic people who might pin down his accent, even if you and I can't tell he's got one. We could get it down to a region or county.'

'Wow, I'm impressed.'

'It's slow and methodical, Hoffer, that's how we do things. We don't go shooting our mouths off and our guns off.'

'Hey, I make the jokes around here.'

'Just don't become a joke, all right?'

'Whoa, Bob, okay, you got me, I yield to your sharper wit. Now what say I get a copy of that tape?'

'What say you don't?'

'Still sore at me, huh?'

'What's Barney got for you?'

'Just a few names, gun dealers.' Hoffer shrugged. 'You're not the only one who can be slow and methodical. Gumshoes do a lot of walking, Bob, a lot of knocking on doors.'

'Just don't come knocking on mine for a while, Leo.'

'Whatever you say, Bob.' Broome had gone back to calling him Leo; it was going to be all right between them. Hoffer got slowly to his feet. 'What about Inspector West?'

'I'll have someone talk to Mr Johns, get a description circulating.' Hoffer nodded. 'Don't expect a bunch of roses, Hoffer, you just did what you're supposed to do *all* the time. If you get anything else, come back and see me.'

Hoffer fixed a sneer to his face. 'You can fucking well go whistle, Bob.' He opened the door, but turned back into the room. 'You know how to whistle, don't you?'

And then he was gone.

Hoffer sat next morning, lingering over the hotel breakfast. The hotel he was in had a restaurant which opened on to the street, and was open to the public as well as to residents. Something inside Hoffer didn't like that. Anyone could walk in off the street and sit down next to you. There was a guy sitting by the window who looked like Boris Karloff had donated to a sperm bank and Bette Davis had picked up the jar. He wore little round Gestapo-style glasses which reflected more light than there was light to reflect. He was reading a newspaper and eating scrambled eggs on toast. He gave Hoffer the creeps.

Hoffer wasn't feeling too well to start with. He didn't have earache any more, but he had a pain in his side which could be some form of cancer. Through the night he'd woken in agony with a searing pain all down one side of his back. He'd staggered into the bathroom, then out again, and was about to phone for an ambulance when he discharged a sudden belt of gas. After that he felt a bit better, so he tried again and got out another huge belch. Someone hammered on the wall for a couple of moments, but he ignored them. He just sat there bare-assed on the carpet until he could stop shaking.

Christ, he'd been scared. The adrenaline had kept him awake for another hour, and he'd no pills left to knock him out.

He put it down to nervousness. He'd called Walkins, and Walkins hadn't been too happy with Hoffer's report.

'Mr Hoffer, I wish you wouldn't sound so excited all the time.'

'Huh?'

'I don't know what you think you're doing. I mean, you call me with news of great import, and say you're getting close, and you sound so thrilled at the prospect. But Mr Hoffer, we've been here before, *several* times before, and each time you get my hopes up, the next thing I know your lead has proved false or the trail has grown cold. I want more than your hope, Mr Hoffer. I want a result. So no more acting, no more milking me for money. Just find him, and find him fast. The media would love me to tell them you've been a fake all along.'

'Hey, stop right there! I'm busting a gut here, I'm working round the clock. You think you pay me too much? You couldn't pay me *half* enough for what I go through for you.'

'For me?'

'You bet it's for you! Who else?'

'Yourself perhaps, your reputation.'

'That's a crock of shit and you know it.'

'Look, let's not get into a fight.'

'I didn't start it.' Hoffer was standing up in his room, facing the dressing-table mirror. He was hyperventilating, and trying to calm down. Walkins was thousands of miles away. He couldn't hit him, and he didn't want to hit a stand-in. He took deep slow breaths instead.

'I know you didn't, Mr Hoffer, it's just that . . . it's just we've been here before. You've sounded so close to him, so excited, so *sure*. Do you know what it's like at this end, just waiting for your next call? You can't possibly know. It's like fire under my fingernails, knives stuck between my ribs. It's . . . I can hardly move, hardly bear to do anything except wait. I'm as housebound as any invalid.'

Hoffer was about to suggest a portable phone, but didn't think flippancy was in order.

'Sir,' he said calmly, 'I'm doing what I can. I'm sorry if you feel I build up your hopes without due cause. I just thought you'd want to know how it's going.'

'I do want to know. But I'd rather just be told the sonofabitch was dead.'

'Me, too, sir, believe me.' Hoffer stared at the gun lying on his bedside cabinet. 'Me, too.'

And here he sat next morning, awaiting his order of Full English Breakfast with orange juice, toast and coffee. His waitress was a crone. She was probably in the kitchen grinding up wormwood to add to the egg-mix. He wondered if maybe she had a sister worked in the porn cinema where he'd wasted more money than time last night. There were three movies on the bill, but he'd lasted only half the first one. The stuff they were showing was as steamy as a cold cup of coffee, and the 'usherette' who'd waddled down the aisle selling ices had looked like she was wearing a fright-mask. She'd still managed to exude more sex than the pale dubbed figures on the unfocused screen. The film was called *Swedish Nymph Party*, but it started with some cars drawing up outside a mountain chalet, and the licence plates were definitely German, not Swedish. After that, Hoffer just couldn't get into the film.

London was definitely getting shabby.

A few more hungry clients wandered in off the street. There was no one about to show them to a table, so some wandered back outside while others sat down and then wondered if they'd maybe walked into Tussaud's by mistake.

'Mr Hoffer.'

'Hey, Barney, sit down.' Hoffer half rose to greet the policeman. They sat opposite one another. 'I'd ask you to share my breakfast, only I don't have any yet, and the speed they're serving you could probably come back after work and they'd be pouring the coffee.'

'I'm fine, thanks.'

'I'm glad someone is. Thanks for coming.'

'I think it suits us both. You're not exactly this month's centrefold at Vine Street.'

'Yeah, Bob really holds a grudge, huh? Just because I took him off the payroll. Speaking of which . . .' Hoffer handed over two twenties. 'This ought to cover your expenses.'

'Cheers.' Barney put the notes in his pocket and produced a folded-up piece of lined writing paper. It looked like he'd saved it from a wastebin.

'This is a class act, Barney.'

'You wouldn't have been able to read my typing, and names are names, aren't they?'

'Sure, absolutely.' Hoffer unfolded the paper gingerly and laid it on the table. It was a handwritten list of names. There were two columns, one headed 'London/South East' and the other 'Other Areas'. But there were only names, no addresses or other information.

'Maybe I pay too much,' said Hoffer.

'What's the matter?'

'This tells me less than Yellow Pages, Barney. What am I supposed to do, scour the phone book for these guys or what?'

'You said you wanted their names.'

'What did you think I would do with them? Find one I liked and name my first son after it?' The policeman looked uncomprehending. He couldn't understand why Hoffer wouldn't be pleased.

'This is all hush-hush info. I mean, on the surface these guys are clean. This isn't the sort of gen you could just get anywhere.'

'I appreciate that, really I do. I hear what you're saying. But Jesus, Barney, I expected a little more.'

Barney took the list back and studied it. 'Well, I could give you some addresses off the top of my head.'

'That would help. I'd be real grateful.' Hoffer took the list back and got a pen from his pocket. He looked around in vain for his breakfast. 'Two more minutes, I swear, then I'm going into that fucking kitchen and cooking it myself.'

A new waitress had appeared at the front of the restaurant and was handing menus to customers who'd come in, and taking the orders from others. Then Hoffer's waitress appeared with a tray full of food, but took it to another table.

'That fuck came in after me!' Hoffer hissed. 'Hey! Excuse me!' But the waitress had dived back into the kitchen.

'These first three are south London,' Barney was saying, his finger on the list. 'He lives in Clapham, that one's Catford, and the third one is Upper Norwood. Actually, Shattuck's not a dealer so much as a buyer, but he sometimes tries selling stuff on.' Hoffer was scribbling the information down. 'Now as for these others . . .'

'Hey, wait, you said addresses.'

So Barney screwed shut his eyes and concentrated like he was the last man left in the quiz show. He came up with three streets, but only one positive house number.

'They're not big streets though.'

'I am duly thankful,' Hoffer said dubiously. The waitress appeared bearing another tray, this time laying it on Hoffer's table.

'I've got to tell you, honey,' he said, 'the starving in Africa get fed faster than this.'

She was unmoved. 'We've got staff problems.'

'Right, it takes them longer than other people to fry ham. Tell them to turn the gas on next time.'

'Very droll.' She turned away with her empty tray. Hoffer attacked a small fat sausage, dipping it in the gelatinous yellow of his solitary egg.

'This is one sad-looking breakfast,' he said. It looked almost as lugubrious as Barney, and had all the charm of the guy in the Gestapo glasses, who was now having a third cup of coffee. The toast felt like they'd lifted it from a pathology lab, where it must have lain not far from the deep-frozen pats of butter.

'These others,' Barney was saying, 'the other London names, they're north of the river or a bit further out. That one's Clapton, that one's Kilburn, he's Dagenham and the last one's Watford.'

'Addresses?'

Barney shrugged. 'Then there are these ones outside London. One's near Hull, there are two in Yorkshire, a couple in Newcastle, one in Nottingham, and one in Cardiff.' He paused. 'I'm not exactly sure which one's which though, not off-hand.' He brightened and stabbed at a name. 'He's definitely Bristol though.'

'Bristol, huh? Well, thanks for your help. Thanks a heap.' He tried the coffee. By this stage of the meal, it could hold few surprises. Hoffer was suitably laconic. 'Shit,' he said. 'You know, Barney, a lot of people complain about the food in the States. They say it's beautifully presented, you know, great to look at, but that it doesn't taste of much. Either that or it's all fast food, you know, burgers and pizza, and there's no real *cuisine*. But I swear, compared to the stuff I've eaten in London, a poor boy sandwich from some mosquito-filled shack in the Everglades is as foie gras and caviar.'

He stared at Barney. Barney stared back.

'You don't much go for it then?'

Hoffer was still staring. 'Did you say Yorkshire?'

'Pardon?'

'Two of these guys live in Yorkshire?'

'Yeah, Yorkshire . . . or Lancashire, thereabouts.'

'This is important, Barney. Yorkshire? Think hard.'

'I don't know . . . I think so, yes.'

'Which ones?'

Barney could see this meant a lot to Hoffer. He shook his head like a pet pupil who's failing his mentor. 'I don't know. Wait a minute, Harrison's in Yorkshire.'

Hoffer studied the list. 'Max Harrison?' he said.

'Yes, he's Yorkshire, but I think he's retired. He got cancer or something. It rotted all his face.'

'Terrific. I'd still like an address.' Hoffer was speaking slowly and carefully.

'I can find out.'

'Then find out. It's *very* important.'

'Why Yorkshire?'

'Because the Demolition Man has spent some time there, and some money there.' Hoffer went down the list again, picking between his teeth with one of the tines of his fork. None of the names set any bells ringing. 'I need to know about the Yorkshire dealers, Barney, I need to know about them soonest, *capisce?*' Barney looked blank. 'Understood?' Now Barney nodded. 'Good man. How soon?'

'Later today, maybe not till tomorrow.'

Which meant Barney couldn't get them till tomorrow, but didn't want to admit it straight out.

'I mean,' he went on, 'I've got my real job, you know. I can't suddenly go off and do other stuff, not without a good reason.'

'Isn't my money reason enough?'

'Well, I won't say it isn't welcome.'

'A hundred if I get them today, otherwise it's another forty.'

Barney thought about haggling. He was London-born and bred, and Londoners were famed for their street wisdom, their deal-doing. But one look at the New Yorker told Barney he wasn't going to win.

'I'll do what I can,' he said, getting to his feet.

'And Barney, typed this time, huh? Bribe a secretary if you have to. Use your old charm.'

'Okay, Mr Hoffer.' Barney seemed relieved to be leaving. He sought a form of farewell, and waved one arm. 'Enjoy your breakfast.'

'Thank you, Barney,' said Hoffer, smiling a fixed smile. 'I'll certainly try.'

He stuck with the coffee and toast. After all, breakfast was included in the price of his room. The toast put up some resistance to the notion of being gnawed to bits and swallowed, but the coffee seemed to have a fine corrosive quality. So engaged was he in the battle, that Hoffer didn't notice the Karloff-Bette Davis test-tube baby leave his table and start walking back through the dining area towards the hotel proper. But he noticed when the man stopped at his table and smiled down on him.

'What am I, a circus act?' Hoffer said, spitting flecks of bread on to the man's burgundy jacket. It was one of those English-style jackets that the English seldom wore, but which were much prized by Americans.

'I couldn't help hearing you try to . . . ah, summon the waitress,' the stranger said. 'I'm American myself.'

'Well,' Hoffer said expansively, 'sit down, pardner. It's good to see another patriotic American.'

The man started to sit.

'Hey,' snapped Hoffer, 'I was being ironic.'

But the man sat down anyway. Close up, he had a thin persistent smile formed from wide, meatless lips. His face was dotted with freckles, his hair short and bleached. But his eyes were almost black, hooded with dark bags under them. He wasn't tall, but he was wide at the shoulders. Everything he did he did for a specific purpose. Now he planted his hands on the table.

'So, how're things going, Mr Hoffer?'

'I get it, another fan, huh? No autographs today, Bud, okay?'

'You seem nervous, Mr Hoffer.'

'As of right now I'm about nervous enough to bust you in the chops.'

'But you're also curious. You wonder who I am really. On the surface you affect disdain, but beneath your mind is always working.'

'And right now it's telling my fists to do the talking.'

'That would be unwise.' There were long regular spaces between the words.

'Persuade me.'

The man looked at the cold food still left on Hoffer's plate. 'The food here is appalling, isn't it? I was disappointed when you booked into this hotel. I was thinking more the Connaught or the Savoy. Have you ever eaten at the Grill Room?'

'What are you, a food critic?'

'My hobby,' the man said. 'How's your mission going?'

'Mission?'

'Locating the Demolition Man.'

'It's going swell, he's upstairs in my room watching the Disney Channel. Who are you?'

'I work for the Company.'

Hoffer laughed. 'You don't get any points for subtlety, pal. The *Company*? What makes any of my business the CIA's business?'

'You're looking for an assassin. He has murdered United States citizens. Plus, when he kills, he often kills politicians.'

'Yeah, scumbags from sweatshop republics.' Hoffer nodded. 'Maybe they're all friends of yours, huh? How come you haven't introduced yourself before?'

'Well, let's say we're *more* interested now.'

'You mean now he's almost started World War Three? Or now he's killed a journalist? Let's see some ID, pal.'

'I don't have any on me.'

'Don't tell me, you left it in your other burgundy jacket? Get out of my face.'

The man didn't look inclined to leave. 'I'm very good at reading upside down,' he said.

Hoffer didn't understand, then saw that Barney's sheet of paper was still spread open by the side of his plate. He folded it and put it away.

'Arms dealers?' the man guessed. When Hoffer didn't say anything, his smile widened. 'We know all about them, we had that information days ago.'

'Ooh, I'm impressed.'

'We even know what you told Chief Inspector Broome yesterday.'

'If you know everything, what do you want with me?'

'We want to warn you. You've managed to get close to the Demolition Man, but you need to be aware that we're close to him too. If there should come a confrontation . . . well, we need to know about you, and you need to know about us. It wouldn't help if we ended up shooting at one another while the assassin escaped.'

'If you're after him, why not just let me tag along?'

'I don't think so, Mr Hoffer.'

'You don't, huh? Know what I don't think? I don't think you're from the Company. I've met Company guys before, they're not a bit like you. You smell of something worse.'

'I can produce ID given time.'

'Yeah, somebody can run you up a fake. There used to be this nifty operator in Tottenham, only he's not at home.'

'All I'm trying to do here is be courteous.'

'Leave courtesy to the Brits. Since when have we ever been courteous?' Hoffer thought he'd placed the man. 'You're armed forces, right?'

'I was in the armed forces for a while.'

Hoffer didn't want to think what he was thinking. He was thinking Special Operations Executive. He was thinking

National Security Council. The CIA was a law unto itself, but the NSC had political clout, friends in the highest and lowest places, which made it infinitely more dangerous.

'Maybe we're beginning to see eye to eye,' the man said at last.

'Give me a name, doesn't matter if it's made up.'

'My name's Don Kline, Mr Hoffer.'

'Want to hear something funny, Don Kline? When I first saw you I thought, Gestapo-style glasses. Which is strange, because normally I'd think John Lennon. Just shows how prescient you can be sometimes, huh?'

'This doesn't get us very far, Mr Hoffer.' Kline stood up. 'Maybe you should lay off the narcotics, they seem to be affecting your judgement.'

'They couldn't affect my judgement of you. *Ciao*, baby.'

For something to do, Hoffer lit a cigarette. He didn't watch Kline leave. He couldn't even hear him make a noise on the tiled floor. Hoffer didn't know who Kline was exactly, but he knew the species. He'd never had any dealings with the species before, it was alien to him. So how come that species was suddenly interested in the D-Man? Kline hadn't answered Hoffer's question about that. Did it have to do with the journalist? What was it she'd been investigating again? Cults? Yes, religious cults. Maybe he better find out what that was all about. Wouldn't that be what the D-Man was doing? Of course it would.

He foresaw a triangular shoot-out with the D-Man and Kline. Just for a moment, he didn't know which one of them he'd be aiming at first.

His waitress was back.

'No smoking in this section.'

'You're an angel straight from heaven, do you know that?' he told her, stubbing out his cigarette underfoot. She stared at him blankly. 'I mean it, I didn't think they made them like you any more. You're gorgeous.' These words were obviously new to the waitress, who softened her pose a little. The brittle beginning of a smile formed at the corners of her mouth.

'So what are you doing this evening?' Hoffer went on, rising to his feet. 'I mean, apart from scaring small children?'

It was a low blow, but no lower than the one she gave him.

Part Two

14

We took a train from Euston to Glasgow.

I'd decided against renting a car in London. Rentals could always be checked or traced. By now, I reckoned there was a chance the police – or even Hoffer – would be finding out about DI West and DC Harris. Plus they had the evidence of my phone call to the radio station. They knew I was still around. They'd be checking things like hotels and car hire.

So I paid cash for our train fares, and paid cash to our hotel when we booked out. I even slipped the receptionist £20, and asked if she could keep a secret. I then told her that Ms Harrison and I weren't supposed to be together, so if anyone should come asking ... She nodded acceptance in the conspiracy. I added that even if she mentioned my name to anyone, I'd appreciate it if she left Bel's name out.

Bel had phoned Max and told him of her plan to go north with me. He hadn't been too thrilled, especially when she said we'd be passing him without stopping. She handed the phone to me eventually.

'Max,' I said, 'if you tell me not to take her, you know I'll accept that.'

'If she knows where you're headed and she's got it in her head to go, she'd probably only follow you anyway.'

I smiled at that. 'You know her so well.'

'I should do, she gets it all from me. No trouble so far?'

'No, but we're not a great deal further forward either.'

'You think this trip north will do the trick?'

'I don't know. There should be less danger though.'

'Well, bring her back without a scratch.'

'That's a promise. Goodbye, Max.'

I put Bel back on and went to my room to pack.

On the train, I reread all the notes on the Disciples of Love.

'You must know it by heart by now,' Bel said, between trips to the buffet. We were in first class, which was nearly empty, but she liked to go walking down the train, then return with reports of how packed the second-class carriages were.

'That's why we're in here,' I said. It's a slow haul to Glasgow, and I had plenty of time for reading. What I read didn't give me any sudden inspiration.

The Disciples of Love had been set up by an ex-college professor called Jeremiah Provost. Provost had taught at Berkeley in the 70s. Maybe he was disgruntled at not having caught the 60s, when the town and college had been renamed 'Berserkeley'. By the time he arrived at Berkeley, things were a lot tamer, despite the odd nudist parade. The town still boasted a lot of strung-out hippies and fresher-faced kids trying to rediscover a 'lost California spirit', but all these incomers did was clog the main shopping streets trying to beg or sell beads and hair-braiding.

I was getting all this from newspaper and magazine pieces. They treated Provost as a bit of a joke. While still a junior professor, he'd invited 'chosen' students to his home at weekends. He'd managed to polarise his classes into those who adored him and those who were bored by his mix of blather and mysticism. One journalist said he looked like 'Beat Poet Allen Ginsberg before the hair went white'. In photos, Provost had long frizzy dark hair, kept parted at the front, a longish black beard and thick-lensed glasses. It's hard to get kicked out of college, especially if you're a professor, but Provost managed it. His employers didn't cite aberrant behaviour, but rather managed to dig up some dirt from his past, showing he'd lied in his initial application form and at a later interview.

Provost stuck around. He was busted for peddling drugs,

but it turned out he'd only given them away, never sold them. He was fast turning into a local underground hero. His shack-style house in a quiet residential street in Berkeley became a haven for travellers, writers, musicians and artists. The outside of the house boasted a huge paste-and-wire King Kong climbing up it until the authorities dismantled it. The house itself was painted to resemble a spaceship, albeit a low-built cuboid one. Inside the house, Jeremiah Provost was slowly but surely leaving the planet Earth.

Out of this home for strays emerged the Disciples of Love. It was a small enterprise at first, paid for, as investigative journalism revealed, by a legacy on which Provost had been living. His family was old Southern money, and as the elders passed away their money and property kept passing to Provost. He sold a couple of plantation houses, one of them to a museum. And he had cash too, as aunts and uncles found he was their sole surviving heir.

An article in a Californian magazine had gone farther than most in tracing Provost back to his childhood home in Georgia. He'd always been pampered as a child, and soundly beaten too, due to a doting mother and a disciplinarian father (whose own father had financed the local Ku Klux Klan). At school he'd been brilliant but erratic, ditto at college. He'd landed a job at a small college in Oklahoma before moving to Nebraska and then California.

He found his vocation at last with the Disciples of Love. He was destined to become leader of a worldwide religious foundation, built on vague ideals which seemed to include sex, drugs and organic vegetables. The American tabloid papers concentrated on the first two of these, talking of 'bizarre initiation rites' and 'mandatory sexual relations with Provost'. There were large photos of him seated on some sort of throne, with long-haired beauties draped all around him, swooning at his feet and gazing longingly into his eyes, wondering if he'd choose them next for the mandatory sexual relations. These acolytes were always young women, always long-haired, and they all looked much the same. They wore long loose-fitting dresses and had middle-class American faces, strong-jawed and thick-eyebrowed and pampered. They were like the same batch of dolls off a production line.

None of which was my concern, except insofar as I envied Provost his chosen career. My purpose, I had to keep reminding myself, was to ask whether this man's organisation could have hired a hit-man. It seemed more likely that they'd use some suicide soldier from their own ranks. But then that would have pointed the finger of the law straight at them. The Disciples of Love were probably cleverer than that.

The Disciples really took off in 1985. Trained emissaries were sent to other states and even abroad, where they set up 'missions' and started touting for volunteers. They offered free shelter and food, plus the usual spiritual sustenance. It was quite an undertaking. One magazine article had costed it and was asking where the money came from. Apparently no new elderly relations had gone to their graves, and it couldn't just be a windfall from investments or suddenly accrued interest.

There had to be something more, and the press didn't like that it couldn't find out what. Reporters staked out the Disciples' HQ, still the old Spaceship Berkeley, until Provost decided it was time to move. He pulled up sticks and took his charabanc north, first into Oregon, and then Washington State, where they found themselves in the Olympic Peninsula, right on the edge of Olympic National Park. By promising not to develop it, Provost managed to buy a lot of land on the shores of a lake. New cabins were built to look like old ones, grassland became vegetable plots, and the Disciples got back to work, this time separated from the world by guards and dogs.

Provost was not apocalyptic. There was no sign in any of his writings or public declarations that he thought the end of the world was coming. For this reason, he didn't get into trouble with the authorities, who were kept busy enough with cults storing weaponry like squirrels burying nuts for the winter. (These reports were mostly written before the Branch Davidian exploded.) The Revenue people were always interested though. They were curious as to how the cult's level of funding was being maintained, and wanted to know if the whole thing was just an excuse for tax avoidance. But they did not find any anomalies, which might only mean Provost had employed the services of a good accountant.

Lately, everything had gone quiet on the Disciples news front. A couple of journalists, attempting to breach the HQ compound, had been intercepted and beaten, but in American eyes this was almost no offence at all. (The same eyes, remember, who were only too keen to read new revelations of the sex 'n' drug sect and its 'screwball' leader.)

All of which left me where precisely? The answer was, on a train heading north, where maybe I'd learn more from the cult's UK branch. Bel was sitting across from me, and our knees, legs and feet kept touching. She'd slipped off her shoes, and I kept touching her, apologising, then having to explain why I was apologising.

We ate in the dining car. Bel took a while to decide, then chose the cheapest main dish on the menu.

'You can have anything you like,' I told her.

'I know that,' she said, giving my hand a squeeze. We stuck to non-alcoholic drinks. She took a sip of her tonic water, then smiled again.

'What are we going to tell Dad?'

'What about?'

'About us.'

'I don't know, what do you think?'

'Well, it rather depends, doesn't it? I mean, if this is just a . . . sort of a holiday romance, we're best off saying nothing.'

'Some holiday,' I joked. 'He'd work it out for himself, no matter what we said.'

'But if it's something *more*, then we really should tell him, don't you think?'

I nodded agreement, saying nothing.

'Well?' she persisted. 'Which is it?'

'Which do you think?'

'You're infuriating.'

'Look, Bel, we've not known each other . . . I mean, not like this . . . for very long. It hasn't been what you'd call a courtship, has it?'

She grinned at the memories: producing the gun in Chuck's Gym, fleeing his men in Upper Norwood, making false documents in Tottenham, pretending to be police officers . . .

'Besides,' I said, 'the sort of work I'm in doesn't exactly make for a home life. I've no real friends, I'm not sure I'd even know how to *begin* the sort of relationship you're suggesting.'

Now she looked hurt. 'Well, that's very honest of you, Michael. Only it sounds a bit feeble, a bit like self-pity.'

My first course arrived. I ate a few mouthfuls before saying anything. Bel was looking out of the window. Either that or she was studying my reflection. It struck me that she knew so little about me. The person she'd seen so far wasn't exactly typical. It was like she'd been seeing a reflection all along.

'Once you get to know me,' I confided, 'I'm a really boring guy. I don't do much, I don't say much.'

'What are you trying to tell me? You think I'm looking for Action Man, and I'm not.' She unfolded her napkin. 'Look, forget I said anything, all right?'

'All right,' I said.

I thought about our relationship so far. There'd been some kissing and hugging, and we'd spent two nights together. We hadn't done anything though, we'd just lain together in the near-dark, comfortable and semi-clad. It wasn't that I didn't want to make love with her. I don't know what it was.

Part of me wished I'd left her behind in London, or insisted on dropping her off in Yorkshire. It was hard to concentrate with her around. I knew it was harder to take risks, too. I'd taken them in London, then regretted them afterwards. In Scotland, I wouldn't take any, not with her around. I'd be like one of those Harley Davidson riders, forced by circumstance to wear a crash helmet. But when I looked across the table at her, I was glad she was there looking back at me, no matter how sulkily. She kept my mind off Hoffer. He was in danger of becoming an obsession. He'd come close to me once before, last year, after a hit in Atlanta, not far from the World of Coca-Cola. I'd visited the museum before the hit, since my target would visit there during his stay in the city. But in the end I hit him getting out of his limo outside a block of offices. He was being fêted in the penthouse suite while he was in Atlanta. The bastard was so tough, he lived a few hours after my bullet hit home. That doesn't normally happen with a heart shot. It's the reason I don't shoot to the head: you can blast away a good portion of skull and brain and the victim can survive. Not so with a heart shot. They took him to some hospital and I waited for news of his demise. If he'd lived, that would have been two fails from three attempts and my career would not have been in good shape.

After the news of his death, I moved out of my hotel. I'd been there for days, just waiting. Across the street was an ugly windowless edifice, some kind of clothing market. 'A garment district in a box' was how a fellow drinker in the hotel bar described it. It was so grey and featureless, it made me book a ticket to Las Vegas, where I didn't spend much money but enjoyed seeing people winning it. The few winners were always easy to spot; the countless losers were more like wallpaper. Hoffer looked like a loser, which was

179

why despite his bulk he was hard to notice. But then he made a mistake. He had himself paged in the hotel casino. I'm sure he did it so people might recognise him. I recognised his name, and watched him go to the desk. Then I went to my room and packed. I could have taken him out, except no one was paying me to. Plus I'd already disposed of my armoury.

I still don't know how he tracked me. He has a bloodhound's nose, as well as a large pocket. So long as Walkins is paying him, I'll have to keep moving. Either that or kill the sonofabitch.

What sort of a life was that to share with someone?

I found out in Vegas that my victim had been a prominent businessman from Chicago, down in Atlanta for the baseball. In Chicago he'd been campaigning to clean up the city, to bring crooked businesses to light and reveal money laundering and bribery of public officials. In Vegas the saloon consensus was that the guy had to be crazy to take that lot on.

'You see a sign saying "Beware – Rattlesnakes", you don't go sticking your head under the rock. Am I right or am I right?'

The drinker was right, of course, but that didn't make me feel any better. I felt bad for a whole two hours and five cognacs, after which I didn't feel much of anything at all.

And then Hoffer had come to town, as welcome as a Bible salesman, sending me travelling again.

No, mine was definitely not a life for sharing, not even with someone like Bel.

We stuck around Glasgow long enough to rent a car. Now I was clear of London and the immediate investigation, I didn't mind. It was another Ford Escort, white this time and without the options. Driving out of the city was not the happiest hour of my life. The centre of the city was based on the American grid system, but there were flyovers and motorways and junctions with no route signs. We found ourselves heading south, and then west, when what we wanted was north. The directions the man at the rental firm had given us proved useless, so I pulled into a petrol station and bought a map book. Although we were on the road to Greenock, we could cut over a bridge at Erskine and, with any luck, join the A82 there.

We cheered when the roadsign informed us we'd found the A82, and the drive after that was beautiful. The road took us winding along the westernmost side of Loch Lomond, Bel breaking into half-remembered songs about high roads and low roads and people wearing kilts. After Loch Lomond we stopped at Crianlarich for food, then cut west on to the A85, the country wild and windswept. It had been raining on and off since we'd crossed the border, but now it became torrential, the wind driving the rain across our vision. We hit the tip of another forbidding loch, and soon reached the coast, stopping in the middle of Oban to stretch our legs and sniff out accommodation.

There were No Vacancy signs everywhere, till we asked at a pub on the road back out of town. Bel had wanted to stay near the dockside, and I told her that was fine by me, I just hoped she'd be warm enough sleeping out of doors. When she saw our two rooms at the Claymore, though, she brightened. The woman who showed us up said there'd be a 'rare' breakfast for us in the morning, which I took to mean it would be very good rather than hard to find or undercooked.

The rooms smelt of fresh paint and refurbished fittings. Bel had a view on to fields next to the pub. There were sheep in the fields and no traffic noises. It was just about perfect. The rain had even stopped.

'And I could understand every word she said,' she claimed with pride, referring to our strained conversation with the car hire man in Glasgow, and the local in Crianlarich who had tried engaging Bel in conversation about, so far as either of us could make out, trout-tickling.

We ate in the bar, and asked casually if our hostess knew where Ben Glass was.

'It's out past Diarmid's Pillar. Hillwalkers, are you?'

'Not exactly.'

She smiled. '*Beinn Ghlas* is a summit between Loch Nell and Loch Nant.'

'That doesn't sound what we're looking for. It's more of a . . . commune, a religious community.'

'You mean the New Agers? Yes, they're off that way.'

'You don't know where, though?'

She shook her head. 'How was the Scotch broth?'

'It was delicious,' Bel said. Later, we asked if we could borrow a map of the area. Most of the roads were little more than tracks. The only Ben Glass I could see was the summit.

'I don't suppose they'd be in the phone book?' Bel suggested.

'We could try Yellow Pages under cults.'

Instead, we went back into Oban itself. It was too late in the day to start our real business, so we became tourists again. The wind had eased, and there was no more than a marrow-chilling breeze as we traipsed the harbour area and the shops which had closed for the day. Bel huddled into my side, her arm through mine. She had the collar of her jacket up, and the jacket zipped as high as it would go. There were other holidaymakers around us, but they looked used to the climate.

'Let's go in here,' Bel said, picking a pub at random. I could see straight away that it was a watering-hole for locals, and that strangers, while tolerated in the season at least, couldn't expect a warming welcome. The customers spoke in an undertone, as though trying to keep the place a secret. Bel ignored the atmosphere, or lack of one, and asked for a couple of malts.

'Which malt?' the red-cheeked barman asked back.

'Talisker,' she said quickly, having just seen a bottle displayed in a shop window.

The barman narrowed one eye. 'What proof?'

That got her. She thought he must mean proof of age.

'Seventy, I think,' I said.

'And double measures,' said Bel, trying to recover. As the barman stood at his row of optics, she saw there were three grades of Talisker: seventy, eighty and one-hundred proof. She nodded at me and smiled, giving a shrug. We paid for our drinks and went to a corner table. The bar grew silent, waiting to eavesdrop. They were out of luck. The door swung in and a laughing group of teenagers stormed the place. They couldn't be much over the legal drinking age, and a few of them might even be under it. But they had confidence on their side. Suddenly the bar was lively. Someone put money in the jukebox, someone else started racking up for a game of pool, and the barman was kept busy pouring pints of lager.

They kept looking over at us, probably because Bel was the only woman in the bar. One of the pool players, awaiting his turn, came over and drew out a chair. He didn't look at us, but returned to the seat after he'd played. This time he gave us the benefit of his winning grin.

'I don't know why I bother,' he said. 'He beats the pants off me every time.'

I watched the other pool player potting his third ball in a row. 'He does seem pretty handy.'

'He's lethal. Look at him covering that pocket.' He got up to play, but was quickly back in his seat. 'On holiday?'

'Sort of.'

'It's all right, I don't mind tourists. I'm a carpenter. I work for this other guy who sculpts lamps and stuff from bits of old wood. The only people who buy them are tourists.'

'Maybe we'll look in,' I said. 'Where's his shop?'

'He doesn't have a shop. He's got a workshop, but he sells

the stuff through shops in the town. Souvenir shops, fancy goods.'

'We'll look out for them,' Bel said. 'Meantime, could you do me a favour?'

He licked his lips and looked keen. Bel leaned across the table towards him. They looked very cosy, and his friends were beginning to exchange comments and laughter.

'We were told there's a sort of religious commune near here.'

He looked from Bel to me. I tried to look meek, harmless, touristy, but he seemed to see something more. He got to his feet slowly and walked to the pool table. He didn't come back.

We drove into town next morning and bought a map of our own. It was newer than the hotel's map, but still didn't help. We sat poring over it in a coffee shop. The other customers were all tourists, their spirits dampened by another cool, wet day. The rain was as fine as a spraymist, blowing almost horizontally across the town. Bel bought a bottle of Talisker to take back to Max.

An old van puttered past the cafe window where we were sitting. It was an antiquated Volkswagen bus, most of its body green but the passenger door blue. It squeezed into a parking place across the street and the driver cut the engine. He got out, as did his passenger. The driver pulled open the sliding side-door, and three more passengers emerged. They all seemed to be holding scraps of paper, shopping lists maybe. They pointed in different directions and headed off.

'Stay here,' I said to Bel.

By the time I left the coffee shop, they had disappeared. I crossed to the Volkswagen and walked around it. It was twenty-four years old, two years older than Bel. There was a lot of rust around the wheel arches and doors, and the bodywork was generally battered, but the engine had sounded reliable enough. I looked inside. The thing was taxed for another three months. It would be interesting to see if it passed its MOT this time round. There were some carrier bags and empty cardboard boxes in the back of the bus. The rows of seats had been removed to make more space. There was a dirty rug on the floor and a spare can of petrol.

The passengers had looked like New Agers: pony tails and roll-up cigarettes and torn jeans. They had that loose gait which hid a post-hippy sensibility. The few New Agers I'd come across were a lot tougher than their 1960s ancestors. They were cynical, and rather than escape the system they knew how to use it to their advantage. Aesthetics apart, I had a lot of time for the ones I'd met.

'Something wrong?'

I turned. The driver was standing there, lighting a cigarette from a new packet.

'The way you were looking,' he went on, 'I thought maybe we had a bald tyre or something.'

I smiled. 'No, nothing like that.'

'Maybe you're thinking of buying?'

'That's pretty close to the mark. I used to own one of these, haven't seen one in a while.'

'Where was this?'

'Out in the States.' I hadn't actually owned one, but the New Agers I'd met there had.

The driver nodded. 'There are a lot of them still out there, on the west coast especially.'

'Right,' I said. 'They don't use salt on the roads.'

'That's it. They last longer than this rust-bucket.' He gave the van a playful slap.

'The one I had blew up. I'd twin-carbed it.'

He shook his head. 'That was a mistake. You don't live around here, do you?'

'No, why?'

'You're talking. Not everybody does.'

'You're not a local yourself then?'

'I haven't lived here long.'

He inhaled on his cigarette and examined its tip. He was in his 20s, nearer Bel's age than mine. He had short wavy black hair and a week's growth of beard, and wore liver-coloured Doc Marten boots with stained jeans and a thick woodsman's shirt.

'I'm just visiting,' I said.

'Enjoy the trip.' He nicked his cigarette and put it back in the pack, then got into the van and put some music on. As far as he was concerned, I had already left.

I walked back across to the cafe and got Bel.

'I nearly yelped when I saw him coming out of the shop,' she said. 'I knew you couldn't see him. What did he say?'

'Not much. Come on.'

We got into the Escort and drove back the way the Volkswagen had come in. Once we were out of sight, I pulled over again.

'You think it's them?'

'I get that impression. We'll find out.'

So we waited in the car, until the bus announced itself with its high-turning engine. It could put on good speed, which was a relief. I hadn't had much experience in tailing vehicles, but I knew that out here, with so little traffic on the roads outside the town, I'd have trouble keeping my distance from a crawling VW. The thing didn't have side mirrors, which helped, since the driver probably couldn't see much from his rearview mirror other than the heads of his passengers. Habitations became sparser as we drove, and a sudden heavy shower slowed us down, though the driver didn't seem to worry. At last, the tarmac road ended, we went through a five-barred gate and were driving on a gravel track. I stopped the car.

'What's up?' said Bel.

'If he sees us behind him, he'll know we're headed the same place he is. How many houses do you think are up this road?'

'Probably just the one.'

'Exactly, so we can't really lose him, can we? We'll sit here for a minute, then move at our own pace.'

'What are we going to say when we get there?'

'Nothing, not this visit. We'll just take a look at the place, not get too close.'

I looked in my rearview mirror. Not that I was expecting any other vehicles.

The gate behind us was shut.

I turned in my seat, hardly able to believe the evidence in the mirror.

'What is it, Michael?'

There were figures outside the car. One of them pulled open the passenger door. Bel shrieked. The figure bent down to look at us. He was big, cold-looking and soaked, with a beard that looked like it could deflect blows.

'Keep on going up the trail,' he said, his accent English. 'It's another mile or so.'

'Can we give you a lift?' I offered. But he slammed the door closed. I counted four of them out there, all of them now standing behind the car. If I reversed hard enough, I could scatter them and maybe smash my way back through the gate. But it looked like a quality gate, and since we were where we wanted to be, we might as well go on.

So I moved forward slowly. The men followed at walking pace.

'Michael . . .'

'Just remember our story, Bel, that's all we need to do.'

'But, Michael, they were *waiting* for us.'

'Maybe they always keep a guard on the gate.' I said this without much confidence. The man hadn't asked us what we wanted or whether we'd taken a wrong turn. It was true, we were expected.

Well, they might be expecting us, but I doubted they'd be expecting what I had in the car-boot.

The MP5.

*

The commune sat in a glen with a stream running through it. It reminded me of one of those early American settlers' communities, just before the bad guys rode into town. The houses, little more than cabins, were of wooden construction. There were a few vehicles dotted about, only half of them looking like they were used, the rest in a process of cannibalisation. Solar heating panels sat angled towards a sun that wasn't shining. A large patch of ground had been cleared and cultivated, and some lean black pigs were working on clearing another patch. I saw goats and chickens and about thirty people, some of whom, all women, were helping unload the VW bus. The VW's driver nodded at us as we stopped the car. I got out and looked at him.

'You want to make an offer on it after all?' he said, slapping the van.

An older man emerged from the largest cabin. He gestured for us to follow him indoors.

The cabin's interior was spartan, but no more so than a lot of bachelor flats or hotel rooms. It was furnished with what looked like home-crafted stuff. On one table sat a lamp. I ran my hand over the gnarled wooden base.

'You're the carpenter?' I said, knowing now why we were expected.

The man nodded back. 'Sit down,' he said. He didn't sit on a chair, but lowered himself on to the floor. I did likewise, but Bel selected a chair. There was a large photograph of a beneficent Jeremiah Provost on the wall above the open fireplace. He looked younger than in some of the newspaper photos. There was a tapestry on another wall, and a clock made from a cross-section of tree.

'You've been asking about our community here,' the man said, eschewing introductions.

'Is that a crime?' Bel asked. He turned his gaze to her. His eyes were slightly wider than seemed normal, like he'd witnessed a miracle a long time ago and was still getting used to it. He had a long beard with strands of silver in it. I wondered if length of beard equated to standing within the commune. He had the sort of outdoors tan that lasts all year, and was dressed for work right down to the heavy-duty gloves sticking out of the waistband of his baggy brown cord trousers. His hair was thin and oily, greying all over. He was in his 40s, and looked like he hadn't always been a carpenter.

'No,' he said, 'but we prefer visitors to introduce themselves first.'

'That's easily taken care of,' Bel said. 'I'm Belinda Harrison, this is a friend of mine, Michael Weston. Who are you?'

The man smiled. 'I hear anxiety and a rage in your words, Belinda. They sound like they're controlling you. Their only possible usefulness is when *you* control *them*.'

'I read that sort of thing all the time in women's magazines, Mr . . . ?'

'My name's Richard, usually just Rick.'

'Rick,' I said, my voice all balm and diplomacy, 'you belong to the Disciples of Love, is that right? Because otherwise we're in the wrong place.'

'You're where you want to be, Michael.'

I turned to Bel. 'Just ask him, Belinda.'

She nodded tersely. 'I'm looking for my sister, her name's Jane.'

'Jane Harrison? You think she's here?'

'Yes, I do.'

'What makes you think that?'

'Because when she ran away, I went through her room, and she'd cut pieces from newspapers and magazines, all about the Disciples of Love.'

'One of them,' I added quietly, 'mentioned yours as being the only British branch of the sect.'

'Well, Michael, that's true, though we're about to start a new chapter in the south of England. Do you know London at all?'

'That's where we've come from.'

'My home town,' Rick said. 'We're hoping to buy some land between Beaconsfield and Amersham.'

I nodded. 'I know Beaconsfield. Any chance that Jane might be there, helping set up this new . . . chapter? I take it she's not here or you'd have said.'

'No, we've got nobody here called Jane. It might help if I knew what she looked like.'

Bel took a photograph from her pocket and handed it over. I watched Rick's face intently as he studied it. It was the photo I'd taken from the flat in Upper Norwood, the one showing Scotty Shattuck and his girlfriend.

'That's her,' said Bel, 'about a year ago, maybe a little less.'

Rick kept looking at the photo, then shook his head. 'No, I've never seen this woman.'

'She may have cut her hair shorter since,' Bel pleaded. She was turning into a very good actress.

'Take another look, please,' I urged. He took another look. 'She ran off with her boyfriend, that's him in the photo.'

'I'm sorry, Belinda.' Rick handed the photo back.

'And you're sure she couldn't be helping start off your new branch?'

'They're called chapters, Michael. No, there's no possibility. We haven't bought the land yet, there's another bid on the table. None of our members are down there at present.'

I saw now that in a corner of the room beyond Rick sat a fax machine and telephone.

'The estate agent contacts you by phone?'

Rick nodded. 'Again, I'm sorry. Bel, why does it worry you that Jane has left home? Isn't she allowed to make her own choices?'

Maybe the acting had proved too much for her. Whatever, Bel burst into tears. Rick looked stunned.

'Maybe if you fetch her some water,' I said, putting an arm around her.

'Of course.' Rick stood up and left the room. When I looked at Bel, she gave me a smile and a wink.

I stood up too and went walkabout. I don't know what I was looking for, there being no obvious places of concealment in the room. The fax and handset gave no identifying phone numbers, but the fax did have a memory facility for frequently used numbers. I punched in 1 and the liquid crystal display presented me with the international dialling code for the USA, plus 212 – the state code for Washington – and the first two digits of the phone number proper. So Rick kept in touch with the Disciples' world HQ by fax. The number 2 brought up another Washington number, while 3 was a local number.

Bel was rubbing her eyes and snuffling when Rick returned with the water. He saw me beside the fax machine.

'Funny,' I said, 'I thought the whole purpose here was to cut yourselves off from the world.'

'Not at all, Michael. How much do you know about the Disciples of Love?'

I shrugged. 'Just what Belinda's told me.'

'And that information *she* gleaned from magazines who are more interested in telling stories than telling the truth. We don't seduce young people into our ranks and then brainwash them. If people want to move on, if they're not happy here, then they move on. It's all right with us. We're just sad to see them go. The way you've been skulking around, you'd think we were guerrillas or kidnappers. We're just trying to live a simple life.'

I nodded thoughtfully. 'I thought I read something about some MP who had to . . .'

Rick was laughing. 'Oh, yes, that. What was the woman's name?' I shrugged again. 'She was convinced, despite everything her daughter told her, that the daughter was being held prisoner. None of our missions is a prison, Michael. Does this look like a cell?'

I conceded it didn't. I was also beginning to concede that

Rick had never laid eyes on Scotty Shattuck in his life. He'd looked closely at the photograph, and had shown not the slightest sign of recognition. Meaning this whole trip had been a waste of time.

'Prendergast,' said Rick, 'that was the woman's name. You know, I wouldn't be surprised if she's done irreparable harm to her daughter. And from what *I've* read, the daughter is now a prisoner in her home. She can't go out without some minder going with her. So who's the villain of the piece?' Lecture over, he turned to Bel. 'Feeling a little better?'

'Yes, thanks.'

'Good. You've had a long trip from London, I'm sorry it's not been helpful to you. Can I show you around? If Jane is interested in us, it may be that she'll find her way here eventually. I can't promise to contact you if she does . . . that would have to be *her* decision. But at least maybe I can reassure you that we won't have her in a ball and chain.'

'We'd like that.'

He led us outside. He stood very erect when he walked, and his arms moved slowly at his sides. I reckoned he'd been meditating this morning, either that or taking drugs. Outside, the VW driver was resting his hand on the boot of our Escort. I sought his face for some sign that he'd opened it, but I'd locked the boot myself, and he didn't look as handy with a picklock as Bel.

'I'm just going to give Belinda and Michael the tour,' Rick told him. 'Is anyone earthing up the potatoes?'

Understanding, the driver went off to find a spade.

Our tour didn't take long. Rick explained that Jeremiah Provost believed in balance between wilderness and civilisation, so a lot of the land had been left uncultivated. He took us into the woods to show us how they harvested trees for fuel and materials, but did not disturb trees which had fallen of their own volition.

'Why not?'

'Because they nourish the soil and become a place where other things can grow.'

I could see Bel had had enough of this. She might start forgetting soon that she was supposed to have a sister, whereabouts unknown.

'We'd better be getting back,' I said. Rick walked us to the car and shook my hand.

'Belinda's lucky to have a friend like you,' he said.

'I think she knows that.'

Bel was in the passenger seat before Rick could walk round the car. She waved, but didn't smile or roll down her window. Rick touched his palm to her window, then lifted it away and retreated a couple of steps.

'He gave me the heebie-jeebies,' Bel said as we drove back down the track.

'He seemed okay to me.'

'Maybe you're easily led.'

'Maybe I am.'

We didn't see any sign of the welcoming committee on the track, but when we reached the gate someone had left it open for us. I pushed the car hard towards Oban, wondering what the hell to do next.

15

Hoffer didn't see Kline again, which was good news for Kline. Hoffer was nursing the biggest headache since the US budget deficit. He'd tried going to a doctor, but the system in London was a joke. The one doctor who'd managed to give him an appointment had then suggested a change of diet and some paracetamol.

'Are you kidding?' roared Hoffer. 'We've *banned* those things in the States!'

But he couldn't find Tylenol or codeine, so settled for aspirin, which irritated his gut and put him in a worse mood than ever. He'd asked the doctor about a brain scan – after all, he was paying for the consultation, so might as well get his money's worth – and the doctor had actually *laughed*. It was obvious nobody ever sued the doctors in Britain. You went to a doctor in the States, they practically wheeled you from the waiting room to the surgery and back, just so you didn't trip over the carpet and start yelling for your lawyer.

'You're lucky I don't have my fucking gun with me,' Hoffer had told the doctor. Even then, the doctor had thought he was joking.

So he wasn't in the best of moods for his visit to Draper Productions, but when Draper found out who he was, the guy started jumping up and down. He said he'd read about Hoffer. He said Hoffer was practically the best-known private eye in the world, and had anyone done a profile of him?

'You mean for TV?'

'I mean for TV.'

'Well, I've, uh, I'm doing a TV spot, but only as guest on

some talk show.' It had been confirmed that morning, Hoffer standing in for a flu-ridden comedian.

'I'm thinking bigger than that, Leo, believe me.'

So then they'd had to go talk it through over lunch at some restaurant where the description of each dish in the menu far exceeded in size the actual dish itself. Afterwards, Hoffer had had to visit a burger joint. Joe Draper thought this was really funny. It seemed like today everyone thought Hoffer was their favourite comedian. Draper wanted to come to New York and follow Hoffer around, fly-on-the-wall style.

'You could never show it, Joe. Most of what I do ain't family viewing.'

'We can edit.'

Early on in their relationship, Draper and Hoffer had come to understand one pertinent detail, each about the other. Maybe it was Hoffer's sniffing and blowing his nose and complaining of summer allergies. Maybe it was something else. Draper had been the first to suggest some nose talc, and Hoffer had brought out his Laguiole.

'Nice blade,' Draper said, reaching into his desk drawer for a mirror . . .

So it was a while before Hoffer actually got round to asking about Eleanor Ricks.

'Lainie,' Draper said in the restaurant, 'she was a lion tamer, believe me. I mean, in her professional life. God, this is the best pâté I've ever tasted.'

Hoffer had already finished his *salade langoustine*. He poured himself a glass of the white burgundy and waited.

'She was great, really she was,' Draper went on, buttering bread like he was working in the kitchen. 'Without her, three of my future projects just turned to ashes.' He squashed pâté on to the bread and folded it into his mouth.

'How much would I get paid for this documentary?' asked Hoffer.

'Jesus, we don't talk money yet, Leo. We need to do

costings, then present the package to the money men. *They're* the final arbiters.'

'What was Eleanor working on when she died?'

'The Disciples of Love.'

'I think I saw that movie.'

'It's not a film, it's a cult.' So then it took a while for Draper to talk about that. 'I've got some info in my office, if you want it. I should be selling it, not giving it away. I had two detectives took copies away, on top of the half dozen I'd already handed over. It was worth it though. One of them suggested Molly Prendergast take over from Lainie on the Disciples project.'

'That's the woman she was with when she got shot?'

'The same.'

'What about these two detectives?'

'The man was called Inspector Best.'

'West?' Hoffer suggested. 'His colleague was a woman called Harris?'

'Oh, you know them?'

'It's beginning to feel that way,' said Hoffer. 'Did they ask you what colour clothes Ms Ricks liked to wear?' Draper was nodding.

'Uncanny,' he said.

'It's a gift, my grandmother was a psychic. Joe, I'd appreciate it if you could give me whatever you gave them.'

'Sure, no problem. Now let's talk about you . . .'

After lunch and the post-prandial burger, they went back to Draper's office for the *Disciples of Love?* folder and a final toot. Hoffer gave Draper his business card, but told him not to call until the producer had some figures.

'And remember, Joe, I charge by the hour.'

'So do all the hookers I know. It doesn't mean they're not good people.'

The TV show was a late-afternoon recording to go out the following morning. Hoffer went back to his hotel so he could wash and change. He'd bought some new clothes for the occasion, reckoning he could probably deduct them for tax purposes. He looked at himself in the mirror and felt like a fraud. He looked perfect. The suit was roomy, a dark blue wool affair. Even the trousers were lined, though only down to the knees. These London tailors knew their business. Fuckers knew how to charge, too.

With a white shirt and red paisley tie he reckoned he looked reputable and telegenic. It wasn't always easy to look both. They had a cab coming to pick him up, so all he had to do was wait. The burger wasn't agreeing with him, so he took something for it, then lay on his bed watching TV. His phone rang, and he unhooked the receiver.

'Yep?'

'Mr Hoffer, there's a letter in reception for you.'

'What sort of letter?'

'It's just arrived, delivered by hand.'

'Okay, listen, I'm expecting a cab to the television studio.' He couldn't help it, though he'd already told the receptionist this. 'I'll be leaving in about five minutes, so I'll grab the letter when I'm going out.'

'Yes, sir.'

Hoffer put down the phone fast. His guts were telling him something as he rushed for the bathroom.

Sitting in his cab, he told himself it was the langoustine, had to be. Unless he was getting an ulcer or something; it was that kind of pain, like a cramp. It clamped his insides and squeezed, then let go again. Some colonic problem maybe. No, it was just the food. No matter how lavish a restaurant's decor, its kitchen was still just a kitchen, and shellfish were still shellfish.

He tore open the brown envelope which had been waiting for him at reception. He knew from his name on the front that the letter was from Barney. There was a single typed sheet inside. God help him, the man had done the typing himself, but only two lines mattered: the two addresses in

Yorkshire. The gun dealer called Darrow lived in Barnsley, while the one called Max Harrison lived near Grewelthorpe.

'Grewelthorpe?' Hoffer said out loud, not quite believing the name.

'What's that, guv?'

'It's a town or something,' Hoffer told the driver. 'Grewelthorpe.'

'Never heard of it.'

'It's in North Yorkshire.'

'That explains it then, I've never been north of Rickmansworth. Yorkshire's another country, you see them down here for rugby finals and football matches. Strange people, take my word for it. Do you work on the telly then?'

So far this trip, Hoffer had merited only five short newspaper interviews, one piece in a Sunday 'Lifestyle' supplement, a magazine article which he had to share with some new private eye movie that was coming out, and half a dozen radio segments. But now TV had picked up on him, and he made the production assistant promise he could have a recording to take away with him.

'It won't operate on an American machine,' she warned him.

'So I'll buy a British video recorder.'

'Remember, we're 240 volts.'

'I'll get a fucking adaptor!'

'Only trying to help.'

'I know, I'm sorry, I'm just a bit nervous.'

She then explained as she led him along corridor after corridor that he would be on with three other guests: a fashion designer, a gay football player, and a woman novelist. She smiled at him.

'You represent the show's harder edge.'

'If I ever survive this goddamned route march,' Hoffer complained. Then he had an idea. 'Do you have a library in the building?'

'Sort of, we've got a research unit.'

Hoffer stopped in his tracks, catching his breath. 'Could I ask you a *big* favour?'

'You mean *another* big favour.' The assistant checked her watch and sighed. She'd probably had guests ask her for blow jobs before. Compared to which, Hoffer reasoned, his was not such an unreasonable demand.

'Go on,' she said, 'what is it?'

So Hoffer told her.

The show itself was excruciating, and they all had to sit in chairs which were like something Torquemada would have had prisoners sit on when they went to the john. All of them except the host, naturally. Jimmy Bridger, as the gay soccer player explained to Hoffer in the hospitality lounge, had been an athlete and then a commentator and now was a TV presenter. Hoffer had a few questions for the soccer player, like whether anyone else would go in the post-match bath the same time as him, but he might need an on-screen ally so instead told the guy how lots of macho American football and baseball players were queens, too.

Then they went on to the set. The audience were women who should have had better things to do at four o'clock in the afternoon. Jimmy Bridger was late, so late Hoffer, already uncomfortable, was thinking of switching chairs. Bridger's chair was a vast spongy expanse of curves and edges. It sat empty while the show's producer did a warm-up routine in front of the audience. He told a few gags, made them clap on cue, that sort of stuff. TV was the same the world over, a fucking madhouse. Hard to tell sometimes who the warders were.

Jimmy Bridger looked mad, too. He had a huge wavy hairstyle like an extravagant Dairy Queen cone, and wore a jacket so loud it constituted a public nuisance. He arrived to audience cheers and applause, some of it unprompted. Hoffer knew that the hosts on these shows usually liked to meet the guests beforehand, just to lay ground rules, to check what questions might not be welcome, stuff like that. By arriving so late, Bridger was guilty of either overconfidence or else contempt, which added up to much the same thing. Before the taping began, he shook hands with each guest, apologised again for his tardiness, and gave them a little spiel, but you could see that his main concern was his audience. He just *loved* them. He kissed a few of the grandmothers in the front row. Hoffer hoped they had stretchers standing by for the cardiac seizures.

At last the recording got underway. As Hoffer had hoped he would, Bridger turned to him first.

'So, Mr Hoffer, what's one of New York's toughest private detectives doing here in England?'

Hoffer shifted in his seat, leaning forward towards Bridger. 'Well, sir, I think you're confusing me with this gentleman beside me. See, *I'm* the gay NFL player.'

There was a desperate glance from Bridger to his producer, the producer shaking his head furiously. Then Bridger, recovering well after a slow start off the blocks, started to laugh, taking the audience with him. They were so out of it, they'd've laughed at triple-bypass surgery. The interview went downhill from there. They'd probably edit it down to a couple of minutes by tomorrow.

Afterwards, Hoffer didn't want to bump into Bridger. Well, that was easily arranged. Bridger stuck around the studio, signing autographs and kissing more old ladies. Hoffer moved with speed to the 'green room', as they called their hospitality suite. It was a bare room lined with chairs, a bit like a surgery waiting room. Those still waiting to do their shows were like patients awaiting biopsy results, while Bridger's guests had just been given the all-clear. Hoffer tipped an inch of Scotch down his throat.

'I thought he was going to pee himself,' said the gay footballer of Hoffer's opening gag.

'That audience would have lapped it up,' Hoffer said. 'I

mean, *literally*.' He downed another Scotch before collaring the production assistant.

'Forget the video,' he told her. 'You can spring it on me when I'm on *This is Your Life*. What about the other stuff?'

'I've got Mandy from Research outside.'

'Great, I'll go talk to her.'

'Fine.' And don't bother coming back, her tone said. Hoffer blew her a kiss, then gave her his famous tongue-waggle. She looked suitably unimpressed. This was in danger of turning into an all right day.

Mandy was about nineteen with long blonde hair and a fashionably anorexic figure.

'You could do with a meat transfusion,' Hoffer said. 'What've you got there?'

He snatched the large manila envelope from her and drew out a series of xeroxed map grids.

'I've run over it with green marker,' she said.

Hoffer could see that. Grewelthorpe: marked in green. The hamlets nearest it were Kirkby Malzeard and Mickley. These were to the south and east. To the west, there were only Masham Moor and Hambleton Hill, some reservoirs and stretches of roadless grey. Further south another hamlet caught his eye. It was called Blubberhouses. What was it with these comedy names? More relevantly, the nearest sizeable conurbations to Grewelthorpe were Ripon and Thirsk, the Yorkshire towns where Mark Wesley had made cash withdrawals.

'Any help?' Mandy said.

'Oh, yes, Mandy, these are beautiful, almost as beautiful as you, my pale princess.' He touched a finger to her cheek and stroked her face. She began to look scared. 'Now, I want you to do one more thing for me.'

She swallowed and looked dubious. 'What?'

'Tell Uncle Leo where Yorkshire is.'

It wasn't really necessary to clean the Smith & Wesson, but

Hoffer cleaned it anyway. He knew if he got close enough to the D-Man, it wouldn't matter if the assassin was state-of-the-art armed, Hoffer would stick a bullet in his gut.

With the gun cleaned and oiled, he did some reading. He'd amassed a lot of reading this trip: stuff about haemophilia, and now stuff about the Disciples of Love. He didn't see anything in the Disciples' history that would unduly ruffle the red, white and blue feathers of the CIA or NSC. Yet Kline was over here, so someone somewhere was very worried about *some*thing. He imagined the assassin reading the same notes he was reading. What would he be thinking? What would be his next step? Would he take up the investigation where his victim had left off? That sounded way too risky, especially if the Disciples were the ones who'd set him up in the first place.

But then again, the D-Man had taken a lot of risks so far, and every risk brought him closer to the surface. Hoffer had a name and a description, and now he had Max Harrison. He knew Bob Broome wasn't stupid; he'd make the connection too before long. But Hoffer had a start. The only problem was, it meant driving. There were no rail stations close to his destination, so he'd have to hire a car. He'd booked one for tomorrow morning, and had asked for his bill to be made up. He knew that really he should make a start tonight, but he wasn't driving at night, not when he was heading into the middle of nowhere on the wrong damned side of the road.

He needed a clear head for tomorrow, so confined himself to smoking a joint in his room and watching some TV. Then he took a Librium to help him worm his way into the sleep of the just. After all, no way should he be there on merit.

'Don't be so hard on yourself, Leo,' he muttered. 'You're the good guy. You're the hero, you must be . . . Jimmy Bridger told you so.' He finished the glass of whisky beside his bed and switched off the TV.

On his way to the john, he got a sudden greasy feeling in

his gut, and knew what it was. It wasn't cancer this time, or liquefaction of the bowel. It wasn't something he'd eaten or something he hadn't, a bad glass of tap-water or too much hooch.

It was the simple realisation that another day or two would see this whole thing finished.

The car rental firm had the usual selection of cramped boxes, each with as much soul as a fast-food carton.

'So which is the cheapest?'

'The Fiesta, sir.'

Hoffer tried to haggle over the Fiesta, but the assistant couldn't oblige. There wasn't even the chance of a blank receipt, since the whole system was computerised, so Hoffer couldn't hike his expense sheet. He quickly got the hang of driving on the left: it was easy if you stuck to one-way streets. But getting out of London was more pain than he'd bargained for. Twice he had to get out of his car at traffic lights and ask the driver behind for help, then suffer the drivers behind sounding their horns when the lights changed.

He got lost so often that after punching the steering wheel a few times he just stopped caring. He didn't study roadsigns, he just took whichever route looked good. When he stopped for lunch, he yielded to temptation and asked somebody where he was.

'Rickmansworth.'

So he'd reached his cab driver's northern frontier. Cheered by this, he reneged and bought a map book, finding that he would have to cut across country a bit to get on to the right road. The whole UK road network looked like a kid had taken a line for a walk. There seemed no order, no sense to it. Driving was easy in the States, once you'd negotiated the cities. But here the cities didn't seem to end, they just melted each into the other, with preserved blobs of green in between.

As he moved north, however, he changed his mind a little. There was *some* green land between London and Yorkshire; it was boring green land, but it was definitely green. He relaxed into the driving, and even remembered to ask for petrol and not 'gas'. It was late afternoon before he got past Leeds. He came off the A1 and into Ripon, where he stopped for a break and a mental council of war.

If Max Harrison was like any gun dealer Hoffer knew, then he would have an arsenal like something from Desert Storm. And what did Hoffer have? A .457 and a pocket knife. All he had going for him was the element of surprise. That meant he'd have those few initial moments to size the situation up. If Harrison was toting heavy artillery, it was no contest. Likewise, if the man was not alone, Hoffer would be compelled to hold back. He realised too late that he'd drunk a whole pot of tea while mulling this over. The caffeine started its relentless surge through his bloodstream. He took a downer to balance things out, and regretted it immediately: he'd need to be sharp, not dopey.

So he took an upper as well.

But Max Harrison didn't actually live *in* what there was of Grewelthorpe. He lived somewhere on the outskirts. It was almost dark by the time Hoffer made his approach to the farm. Foresight had warned him to bring a torch, and he stuck it in his pocket after killing the engine. There was no other sign of habitation, and Hoffer had stopped the car half a mile from the house. He was going to walk that final half mile . . . Or was he? If Harrison had already heard or seen him, then why make himself an easy target? Better to arrive wrapped in steel than leave wrapped in a coffin. He turned the ignition back on and drove sedately up the track and into the yard.

He killed the engine and looked around. There was no sign of life. He sounded the horn tentatively, but got no response. Maybe the guy was a real farmer, out somewhere with his favourite sheep or cow. He opened his door and eased himself out. He couldn't hear any animals, not even a dog.

'Hello, anyone home?' he called. Only the wind whistled a reply. Hoffer walked to the house and peered in through a couple of windows. He was looking into a large clean kitchen. He tried the door and it opened. He went inside and called out again.

The house didn't feel empty. There was a television or radio on somewhere. He touched the kettle, but it was cold. He came out of the kitchen into an L-shaped hallway. At the other end of the hall was the front door of the house, obviously not much used. A rug had been pushed against it to stop draughts. Halfway along the hall were stairs up. But the sounds were coming from behind a door in the hall. There were two doors. The first was wide open, leading into an empty dining room. Three chairs sat around a four-cornered table. The second was closed, and must presumably lead to the living room. Hoffer's fingers tightened around the butt of his gun. Harrison couldn't have fled: where was there to go? Just the barns or the fields beyond. But he could be hiding. He touched the door handle, then turned it and let the door fall open.

Max Harrison had been beaten to a pulp.

His face was almost featureless, just a mess of blood and clots and tissue, like red fruit after a kid had been playing with it. Barney had told him Harrison was suffering from face cancer. A sort of cutaway plastic mask lay on the floor, and there was a large blackish hole cut deep into one of Harrison's cheeks. Sure, beat up a dying man, why don't you? Hoffer felt rage inside him, but then Harrison wasn't his problem.

He was seated on a dining chair in the centre of the room. His hands had been tied behind him and around the back of the chair, and his feet had been tied to the chair-legs.

'Hey, you Max Harrison?' Hoffer said.

The room was messy too. There'd been a fight here, or

some serious ransacking, or more probably both. A lot of broken ornaments and glass were lying underfoot. Hoffer went over to the chair to take a pulse. As he touched the body, the head rolled from the shoulders and fell on to the carpet.

'Son of a bitch!' Hoffer roared, half-turning his head to spew up tea and cake and scones. He spat and wiped his mouth with the back of his hand. 'Damn,' he said, 'I paid good money for that meal.' He coughed a couple of times and turned back to the headless corpse. He was no pathologist, but he'd seen a few autopsies during his time on the force. The dead man's throat had been cut through so deeply and thoroughly that practically nothing had been holding it on. Whoever had left Harrison sitting like that had known what would happen when someone finally touched the corpse.

'Nice touch, dude,' Hoffer muttered. He thought of his own knife: it wouldn't do to be caught here by the police. He had some quick thinking to do. He took another look at the corpse, then around the room. He couldn't glean much here, so headed upstairs. Could it have been the D-Man's work? Maybe the gun dealer had double-crossed him in some way, and the D-Man had murdered him.

The first bedroom Hoffer walked into belonged to a man. There were no women's things lying around, no dresses in the wardrobe. But there were a lot of framed photos, mostly of a man Hoffer assumed to be Max Harrison with a girl Hoffer took to be his daughter. There were photos of her as a baby, and all the way up to what looked like her 20s. Not a bad looker either. Fair hair, prominent cheekbones, beautiful eyes.

There were two other bedrooms, one of them obviously a guest room, which didn't stop Hoffer looking around for any signs of weapons. The other belonged to a woman, a young woman judging from the magazines and make-up and a few of the cassette tapes lying around.

So Harrison's daughter lived at home . . .

'Whoa!' Hoffer said, sitting down on the bed. 'Hold on there.' He was thinking of the description he'd been given of 'DC Harris', the D-Man's accomplice. He went back to Harrison's bedroom and picked up the most recent-looking photo. Too close to be coincidence.

'Son of a bitch,' he said quietly.

This changed things. Because if the D-Man had killed Harrison, then he'd also taken the daughter with him. Had he taken her under duress? If so, then she was hostage rather than accomplice, which would make a difference when it came time to confront the assassin.

Harrison's bedroom showed no signs of having been searched, and the daughter's bedroom was tidy too. There were paperback books on a shelf above her bed. Hoffer opened one and found her name written in the corner of the prelim page: Bel Harrison. Bel, short for Belinda. Hoffer spent a little more time in her room, trying to find out more about her. She hadn't taken away many clothes; her drawers and wardrobe were more than half full. As he usually did given access to a woman's bedroom, he lingered over the underwear drawer. You could tell a lot about a woman from her underwear. They should turn it into a police discipline, like psychological profiling. He picked up various items, sniffed their detergent smell, then put them back.

There were no posters on the walls, no clues to any hobbies. Her room gave away less than most. He looked under the bed and even under the carpet, but didn't find any dope. There didn't seem to be any contraceptives around either.

'A clean-living country girl,' he said to himself. 'Except, sweetheart, that your daddy dealt in illegal firearms, and now you're running around with the enemy.'

Downstairs again, he checked the cellar. It contained a few bottles of wine and spirits, plus a deep freeze and some DIY tools and materials. He selected a bottle of Scotch and brought it up to the kitchen. He poured from it, then wiped it clean with a cloth, and he held his glass with a piece of kitchen towel. After he'd had the drink, he went around wiping the doorhandles and all the other surfaces he'd touched with his fingers. Then he switched on his torch and headed for the outbuildings. He found the indoor range straight away. From the length of it, it could be used for both rifles and handguns. He still hadn't found any weapons. There had to be a cache somewhere. If he could find it, he could help himself. He looked for twenty minutes without success, and returned to the kitchen.

He had another drink and sat down at the table. The extravaganza in the living room was not the D-Man's style. The D-Man liked to keep his distance. He'd never killed at close range. And for a skilled shot suddenly to revert to a knife or a razor or whatever had been used . . . No, it hadn't been the D-Man. Which left two questions. Who'd done it? And what was Bel Harrison doing with the D-Man?

There was a telephone in the kitchen, hooked to an answering machine. He played the tape but there were no messages. Several choices presented themselves. He could phone for the police, then wait for them. He could phone them anonymously and then get out. He could get the hell out without telling anyone. Or he could hang around and see if either the killers or the D-Man came back. It stood to reason that the daughter would return some time. Maybe the body would have been found by then. There had to be a mail service, even to this outpost of civilisation. The body was still fairly fresh. Hoffer didn't like to think about Bel Harrison stumbling upon it a few days or even weeks hence.

Then again, did he really want another police force involved? What if they scared off the D-Man?

Hoffer didn't know what to do, so he let another drink decide for him.

Then he drove back towards Ripon, seeking a bed for the night.

16

The first thing I saw after breakfast was Leo Hoffer.

That may sound crazy, but it's true. When I got back to my room to do some final packing, I must have left the TV on. I'd been watching the early-morning news. Now there was a chat show on, and one of the guests was Hoffer. Not that he stole much airtime, a few minutes, but he was omnipresent, coughing offscreen, twitching and interrupting when other guests were speaking. I told Bel to come and see. They'd got round to the question and answer segment. The host was moving around the audience, his mike at the ready.

'That's Jimmy Bridger,' said Bel. 'I watch this sometimes.'

A middle-aged lady was standing up to ask her question. 'Is Mr Hoffer married?' The camera cut to Hoffer, who was wearing an expensive suit but wearing it cheaply. The cloth shone but he didn't.

'No, ma'am,' he said. Then, creasing his face: 'Was that an offer?' Everyone thought this very funny. Someone else asked him if he found his weight a problem. He agreed that it was.

'I've got to put on a few more pounds before I can Sumo wrestle, and you know those last few pounds are the toughest.'

This had them practically rolling in the aisles.

'A question for another of our guests,' said the host, making it plain that he wasn't going to let Hoffer hog proceedings. It looked to me like they must have had a disagreement along the way.

'And this is the man who's chasing you?' Bel commented.

'That's him. My shadow. I sometimes think the only reason he hunts me is so he can appear on shows like this.'

'Why would he do that?'

'His ego for one thing. But also, he's in business, and I'm a good advert for him. As far as I can see, I'm the only advert he's got.'

'He doesn't look like he could catch a cold.'

'That,' I said quietly, 'is why he's so good.'

I sent Bel off to do her packing, and then finished my own. We'd take the car back to Glasgow, I'd buy us train tickets south and let Bel make the connections to take her home. As for me, I'd go back to London. What else could I do? I'd wait it out till Shattuck crept out of the woodwork. I'd waited for victims before.

Bel wasn't happy.

'Does this mean the engagement's off?'

'It's the way it was always going to be.'

She couldn't help but notice a change of tone. 'What's up, Michael?'

'Nothing. Just phone Max and tell him with any luck you'll be back tonight. Tell him you'll call from Glasgow with train times.'

So she made the call. It took Max a few moments to answer. Listening, Bel rolled her eyes, meaning it was the answering machine.

'Hi, Dad, it's me. Stick by the phone when you get in. I'm headed home, probably tonight. I'll call again when I know my arrival time. 'Bye.'

We checked out of the hotel, but Bel wanted to go back into town.

'What for?'

'A few souvenirs. Come on, Michael, this is the last day of my holiday.'

I shook my head, but we went anyway. While she was shopping, I walked by the harbour. A ferry was leaving for

Mull. The island was about six miles away, beyond the smaller isle of Kerrera. The sun was out, and a few boatmen were going about their business, which mostly comprised posing for the tourists' video cameras. There was a hotel near the harbour we'd tried to get into, with a low wall alongside it. I lifted myself on to the wall and just enjoyed the sunshine. Then Bel was in front of me, thrusting a large paper bag into my hands.

'Here,' she said.

'What's this?'

'It's *your* souvenir.'

Inside the bag was a thick Fair Isle sweater.

'Try it on,' she said. 'I can always take it back if it doesn't fit.'

'It looks fine.'

'But try it on!'

I was wearing a jacket and a shirt, so took the jacket off and laid it on the wall, then pulled the sweater over my head and arms. It was a good fit. She ruffled my hair and pecked my cheek.

'Perfect,' I said. 'But you shouldn't have. It must've cost—'

But she was heading off again. 'I just wanted to make sure it was okay. I've got to get something for Dad now.' She gave me a wave and was gone.

I didn't dare take the jumper off again. She'd expect me to wear it for a little while at least. Well, it kept out the breeze, but I had the feeling it made me look less like a local and more like a tourist. I took my sunglasses from my jacket pocket and slipped them on.

A car had drawn up nearby. It rose perceptibly on its axles when its driver got out. I nearly tipped backwards off the wall.

It was Hoffer.

He stretched, showing an expanse of shirt and a belt on its last notch. He also showed me something more: that he didn't have a holster beneath his jacket. He did some neck stretches, saw me, and came walking over.

'It's been a long drive,' he said with a groan.

'Oh, aye?' If he'd just come north, maybe he wouldn't know mock-Scots from the real thing.

He wasn't looking at me anyway. He was taking in the harbour, and talking more to himself than to anyone else. I thought he'd been taking drugs. 'This is some beautiful place,' he said.

'No' bad.'

He looked up at the hotel. 'What about this place, is it no' bad too?' I shrugged and he smiled. 'A canny Scot, huh?' Then he turned away and made to enter the hotel. 'See you around, bud.'

The moment he'd gone, I slid from the wall, grabbed my jacket, and walked away. I didn't know which shop Bel would be in, and had half a mind to go to the car instead and get the MP5. But she was coming out of a fancy goods emporium, so I took her arm and steered her with me.

'Hey, what's up?'

'The TV tec is in town.'

'The fat man?' Her eyes widened.

'Don't look back, just keep walking. We're going to the car and we are getting out of here.'

'He *can't* be here,' she hissed. 'He was in a TV studio only an hour ago.'

'Have you ever heard of videotape? They record these shows, Bel. You think anyone would have the balls to put Hoffer on *live?*'

'What are you going to do?'

I looked at her. 'What do you think I should do?'

'Maybe . . .' she began. Then she shook her head.

'What were you going to say?'

'I was going to say . . .' her cheeks reddened. 'I was going to say, maybe you should take him out.'

I looked at her again. We were at the car now. 'I take it you don't mean I should date him?'

She shook her head. 'Michael, did you hear him on TV this morning? All those questions they asked: was he armed, would he think twice about killing you?'

I unlocked her door and went round to the driver's side. 'I get paid to do jobs. I don't do it for fun.'

'There are other ways to make a living,' she said quietly.

'What? Work behind a desk? That's what they like haemophiliacs to do. That way we're *safe*. To hell with that.'

'Don't you think becoming a hired assassin is a bit extreme, though?'

'Jesus, Bel, you're the one who just said I should bump off Hoffer!'

She smiled. 'I know, but I've changed my mind. I think you should stop. I mean, stop altogether. I think you want to.'

I started the engine. 'Then you don't know me.'

'I think I do.'

I let off the handbrake and started us rolling out of Oban. Maybe it was Hoffer, or Hoffer added to the conversation I'd just had. Whatever, I wasn't being very careful. All I knew was that Hoffer's car was still parked when we passed it.

I spotted them just outside town. To be fair, they weren't trying very hard. They didn't mind me knowing about them. There were two cars, one a smart new Rover and the other an Austin Maestro.

'Don't do anything,' I warned Bel. 'Just keep looking ahead. We're being followed.'

She saw them in her wing mirror. 'One car or two?'

'Both of them, I think.'

'Who are they?'

'I don't recognise any faces. They're clean shaven, the one I can see best is smartly dressed, jacket and tie. I don't think they're the Disciples.'

213

'Police maybe? That could be why the fat man's in town.'

'Why not just arrest us?'

'Do they have any evidence?'

She had a point. 'They could do us for impersonating police officers. That would keep us in the cells till they found something. The police'll always find a way to stitch you up if they need to.'

I accelerated, knowing the Escort couldn't outrun the pursuers. We were heading down the coast, since we'd agreed to take a different route back to Glasgow. When we reached a straight stretch with no other traffic in sight, the Maestro signalled to overtake. The way it pulled past, I knew there was a big engine lurking inside it. There was no need for pretence, so I gave the driver and passenger a good look as they cruised past, trying to place them. Both were young and fair-haired and wearing sunglasses. They pulled in sharply in front of us and hit the brakes, so that we'd have to slow down, or else overtake. The Rover was right behind, making us the meat in the sandwich.

'What are they doing, Michael?'

'I think they want us to stop.' I signalled that I was pulling over, and hit the brakes so fast the Rover's tyres squealed as the driver stopped from ramming us. I couldn't see the road ahead, but shifted down into second and pulled out into the oncoming lane. There was nothing coming, so I tore alongside the Maestro, which was already accelerating. There was a bend approaching, and neither car had the beating of the other. Suddenly a lorry emerged from round the bend, and I braked hard, pulling us back into the left lane, still sandwiched.

'I don't think policemen play these kinds of game,' I told Bel. She was looking pale, gripping the passenger door and the dashboard.

'Then who are they?'

'I'll be sure to ask them.'

The front car was braking again. The driver had put on

his emergency flashers. He was obviously coming to a halt on the carriageway. A stream of traffic had been trapped behind the lorry, so there was no chance of us pulling past the Maestro. The Rover behind was keeping its distance, but I knew once we stopped that would be it. One would reverse and the other edge forward until there was nowhere for us to go.

I stopped the car.

'What's going to happen?' Bel said.

'I'm not sure.'

Traffic heading in the other direction was slowing even further to watch. Whoever our pursuers were, they didn't seem to care about having an audience. A normal person might be relieved, thinking nothing serious was going to happen in front of witnesses. But I saw it another way. If they weren't worried about having an audience, maybe they weren't worried about *anything*.

I slid my hand back between the driver's and passenger's seats. On the floor in the back, wrapped in my old blue raincoat, was the MP5. I don't know what made me switch it from the boot when we were loading the car, but I said a silent thank you to whichever bad angel was watching over me.

'Oh God,' Bel said, seeing the gun. I opened my driver's door and stepped out, leaving raincoat and contents both on the floor beside the pedals. The Maestro had backed up to kiss my front bumper, and the Rover was tucked in nicely behind. Three cars had never been closer on a car transporter or parked on a Paris street. I decided to take the initiative and walked to the car at the back. I reckoned the front car was the workhorse; the person I wanted to speak to would be in the nice car, probably in the back seat. Electric windows whirred downwards at my approach. The windows were tinted, the interior upholstery cream leather. All I could see of the driver was the back of his head, but the man in the back of the car was smiling.

'Hello there,' he said. He was wearing ordinary glasses rather than sunglasses, and had short blond hair. His lips were thin, his face dotted with freckles. He looked like his head hadn't quite grown up yet. He was wearing a suit, and a white shirt whose cuffs were slightly too long for the jacket. The shirt was buttoned to the neck, but he didn't wear a tie.

'Good morning,' I said. 'Is there a problem?'

He acted like there wasn't. 'We'd appreciate a few minutes of your time.'

'Pollsters aren't usually so determined,' I said. I was thinking: *he's American*. Was he working for Hoffer? No, I didn't get that impression at all.

'If you and your friend will get in the car, I'd appreciate it very much.'

'You mean, get in your car?'

I didn't even dent his smile. 'That's what I mean.'

I shrugged. 'What's this all about?'

'It can be explained in five minutes.' He held up a hand, palm spread wide to show fingers and thumb.

'You could have talked to us in town.'

'Please, just get in the car.'

At last another vehicle appeared coming from Oban. It was a Volkswagen estate pulling a caravan. The car had a German licence plate.

'Oh oh,' I said, 'here comes an international incident.'

The bastard just kept on smiling. He didn't seem to mind if he held up the traffic for the rest of the day.

'I'll go fetch my friend,' I said.

As I walked back to the car, a van driver idling past asked what was happening. I just shook my head. I stuck my head into the Ford Escort.

'Bel,' I said, 'I want you to be calm, okay? Here, take the keys. I want you to grab the map book, then get out of the car, unlock the boot, and get our stuff. We're changing cars.'

Then I picked up the raincoat and walked forward towards the Maestro. The driver and passenger were watching in their mirrors. When I started towards them, they opened their doors. I came to the passenger side, away from the oncoming traffic, and showed the passenger my raincoat. He could see the gun barrel.

'You've seen one of these before,' I told him. 'Now tell your partner.'

'He's packing heat,' the passenger said. He was American too.

'We're going to see your boss,' I told him, and motioned with the gun for him to move. They walked in front of me. When we reached the boot of the Escort, I told them to keep walking. The German motorist was out of his car and was talking in broken but heated English with the Rover driver, who didn't look to be answering.

Bel had lifted out our two bags. I took one and she the other, and we walked to the Maestro again and got in. I started the ignition and we roared away, leaving the mess behind. Bel screamed with relief and kissed me on the cheek.

'I nearly wet myself back there!'

'Have you got the Escort keys?' I asked, grinning. She shook them at me.

'Then they'll be stuck there till they either push it off the road or learn the German for "back your caravan up".' I tried to relax my shoulders. I was hunched over the steering-wheel like a racing driver. 'It was a close one though,' I said. 'Twice in one day is too close.'

'You think they were something to do with Hoffer?'

I shook my head. 'Too smooth. They had a sort of government smell about them. There's a kind of smugness you get when you know you've got everything on your side.'

'Then they're to do with Prendergast?'

She'd misunderstood me. 'No, they had American accents.'

'The *American* government?'

I shook my head slowly, trying to clear it. 'Maybe I'm wrong. But they were definitely Americans.'

'More men hired by that girl's father?'

'I really don't know. I think it all ties in with the Disciples of Love.'

She looked startled. 'You're not going back there?'

'No, don't worry.'

'I thought you'd ruled out Rick and his gang.'

Now I nodded. 'Maybe it goes higher, Bel.' I didn't bother explaining what I meant.

We'd no hire car to return, so I decided to hang on to the Maestro. I could drop Bel off in Yorkshire then dump the car somewhere. We kept moving, stopping only to fill up with petrol, buy sandwiches and drinks from the filling-station shops, and try getting through to Max.

'Maybe he's had to go somewhere?' I suggested.

'Maybe. He'd have said, wouldn't he?'

'Short notice. I know I've been in a tight spot once or twice and dragged him away with no notice at all.'

She nodded, but stared at the windscreen. To take her mind off Max, I got her round to talking about the men from that morning, what they could have wanted from us, how they'd known where we were.

'What would you have done,' she asked, 'if one of them had drawn a gun?'

'Taken the drawing from him and torn it up.'

'But seriously.'

'Seriously?' I considered. 'I'd probably have gone along peacefully.'

'Really?'

'It's hard to know, but I think so.'

I assumed it was the answer she wanted to hear.

We reached the farm before dark.

I got a bad feeling about the place straight away, and was glad I had the MP5 with me. As soon as I stopped the car, Bel was out and running. She'd felt something too. I called out for her to wait, but she was already opening the kitchen door.

I left the car idling and followed her, holding the sub-machine gun one-handed. With its stock fully retracted, the thing was just like an oversized pistol. I pushed the safety catch past single-shot and on to three-round burst.

Then I went in.

Bel's scream froze my blood. I wanted to run to her, but knew better than that. There could be many reasons for her screams. I peered into the hall but saw no one. Holding the gun in front of me, I walked forward, brushing the wall all the way. I passed the open door of the dining room and noticed that one of the chairs was missing from around the table. Then I saw the living room, things scattered over the floor, and Bel kneeling in the middle of it all, her hands over her face. Finally I saw Max.

'Christ Almighty.'

His headless torso sat on the missing dining-chair, like some ventriloquist's dummy gone badly wrong. Flies had found the body, and were wandering around the gaping hole which had once been a neck. A false glimmer struck me: maybe it wasn't him. But the build was right, and the clothes seemed right, though everything had been stained dark red. The blood on the skin had dried to a pale crust, so he'd been here a little while. There was a sour smell in the room, which I traced to a pool of vomit on the carpet. A tea-towel from the kitchen was lying next to this pool, covering something the size of a football.

I didn't need to look.

I squeezed Bel's shoulder. 'We can't do any good here. Let's go to the kitchen.'

Somehow I managed to pull her to her feet. I was still

holding on to the gun. I didn't want to let go of it, but I pushed the safety back on.

'No, no, no, no,' Bel was saying. 'No, no, no.' Then she started wailing, her face purple and streaked with tears. I sat her on a chair in the kitchen and went outside.

I'm no tracker. There were tyre marks on the ground, but they could have belonged to Max's car. I took a look around, finding nothing. In the long barn, I flicked the lights on and stood staring at one of the distant human-shaped targets on the range. I switched the MP5 to full auto and started blasting away. It took about fifteen seconds to empty the magazine. Only the legs of the target remained.

Bel was standing at the kitchen door, yelling my name.

'It's okay,' I said, coming out of the barn. 'It's okay.' She put her arms around me and wept again. I held her, kissed her, whispered things to her. And then found myself crying too. Max had been . . . I can't say he'd been like a father; I've only ever had the one father, and he was quite enough. But he'd been a friend, maybe the closest I'd ever had. After the tears I didn't feel anger any more. I felt something worse, a cold creeping knowledge of what had to be done.

Bel blew her nose and said she wanted to walk about a bit, so I went back into the house. They hadn't left many clues. The vomit and the dishtowel were curious, but that was about it. Why cover the head? I couldn't understand it. I went upstairs and looked around. The bedrooms hadn't been touched. They hadn't been burglars.

Of course they hadn't. I knew who they'd been. The Americans. And either Max had talked, or they'd worked it out for themselves anyway, or someone from the Oban Disciples of Love had contacted them. I considered the first of these the least probable: Max wouldn't have talked, not when talking would mean putting Bel in danger. As for working it out for themselves, well, if Hoffer could do it so could they.

Bel still hadn't come back by the time I went downstairs. I walked out into the yard but couldn't hear her.

'Bel?'

There was a noise from the long barn, something being moved around.

'Bel?'

I had to go to the car for a fresh cartridge-box. When I pushed it home, I had thirty-two rounds ready for action. I moved quietly towards the barn.

When I looked in, someone had cleared an area of straw from the concrete floor, revealing a large double trap-door, which now sat open. The trap-door led to a bunker. There were wooden steps down into it, and a bare lightbulb inside. Bel was coming back up the steps. She had a rifle slung over each shoulder, a couple of pistols stuck into the waistband of her denims, and she was carrying an MP5 just like my own.

'Going to do some practice?' I asked her.

'Yes, on live targets.' She had a mad look in her puffy eyes. Her nose was running, and she had to keep wiping it with the back of her hand.

'Fury is the enemy, Bel.'

'Who taught you that?' she sneered. 'Some Zen monk?'

'No,' I said quietly, 'my father . . . and yours.'

She stood facing me, then I saw her shoulders sag.

'Don't worry,' I went on, 'you'll get your revenge. But let's plan it first, okay?' I waited till she'd nodded. 'Besides,' I added, 'you've forgotten something.'

'What?'

'Bullets.'

She saw that this was true, and managed a weak smile. I nodded to let her know she was doing okay.

'You don't need guns just now,' I went on. 'You need your brain. Your brain . . . and your passport.'

'My passport?'

'Just in case,' I said. 'Now go pack yourself some clothes. Are there any more sub-machine guns down there?'

'I'm not sure. Why do you ask?'

'I need some practice, that's all.' I started down the steps until I was surrounded by guns, cocooned in oiled black metal. It was like being in a chapel.

It took us some time to straighten things out. We knew we couldn't call the police, inform the proper authorities, anything like that. I did propose that Bel stay behind, a proposal she angrily rejected. So we did what we had to do. The soil in the field nearest the farmhouse was workable. Even so, it took until dark and beyond to dig the grave. It wasn't a very adequate hole. I knew the reason you dug down six feet was that much short of this and you'd get soil disturbance, the ground above the body rising eventually rather than staying flat. But we'd dug down only three or four feet. We could always rebury him later.

'Sorry, Dad,' Bel said. 'I know you were never much of a Christian, but you probably wanted something better than this.' She looked at me. 'He fought that cancer for years. He was ready for death, but not the way it happened.'

'Come on,' I said, 'let's keep busy.'

It wasn't hard. We had to finish packing and then lock up the house. We couldn't do much about the living room, so just left it. Bel couldn't think of anyone who'd come to the house anyway. Their mail was held by the post office and picked up whenever they were in town.

'It might be a while before we're back,' I warned.

'That's fine.'

I was never far from the MP5. I knew they could come back at any minute. I would be ready for them. I'd considered stocking up from Max's cache, but knew it didn't make any sense. So I locked the cellar again and covered its doors with straw. The house was locked now, a timer controlling the lights. I walked through the yard to the field wall, and found Bel there, standing over the closed grave.

'Time to go, Bel,' I said.

'He hated this place,' she said quietly. I put a hand on her shoulder. She took a deep breath and exhaled. ''Bye, Dad. I'll be home again soon.' Even to my ears, she didn't sound like she meant it.

We got on to the A1 and stopped at the first hotel we found. I didn't suppose either of us would get much sleep, but we were exhausted and dirty and our sweat-stained clothes needed changing. We shared a room, as we'd known we would. Bel took the first bath. I soaped her back and shoulders in silence, then towelled her dry. She went through to the bedroom while I changed the bathwater. I was lying back, eyes closed, when she came back.

'Hurry up, Michael, I need you,' was all she said.

We made love hungrily at first, and then with more tenderness than I'd ever thought possible. She cried a bit, but when I tried to ease away from her she held me tight, not wanting to let me go. The only light drifting into the room came from a lamp outside the hotel. I ran my hands over Bel's back, feeling her vertebrae. For a little while there, my hands didn't feel like the hands of a killer.

We rose early and didn't bother with breakfast.

On the road south, she asked me what we were doing. I told her. She didn't know if it made sense or not, but she wasn't in a state to offer ideas of her own. The traffic into London was like sludge easing into a drain. Bel was wearing a scarf and sunglasses. I knew her eyes were red, like she was suffering hay fever. Hay fever could be the excuse if anyone asked. When we got to London, we left the Maestro in a long-stay car park and got our cases out of the boot.

I left the MP5 in the boot but took my raincoat.

We took a taxi with our luggage to Knightsbridge. 'I'll be about five minutes,' I told the driver when we arrived. Then, to Bel: 'Wait here.'

She watched me go into the bank like she'd never see me again.

Inside the bank there were the usual security procedures before I was led into a small room. The room contained a table and two chairs. There were framed prints on the wall showing Victorian London, and a few brochures to read. These offered further bank services. Eventually, the employee who had led me into the room returned with my safe deposit box. I let him leave again before opening the box.

Inside were a passport, a bundle of cash, and some traveller's cheques, about $25,000 in total. I scooped the lot into my pockets, then took out a pen and piece of paper. Hurriedly I scribbled a note outlining events so far. It wouldn't make sense to anyone outside the case. I folded the note and addressed it to the one man I knew *could* make sense of it: Leo Hoffer at Hoffer Investigations, New York City. Then I placed the letter in the box.

As insurance policies go, it was among the worst and most hastily conceived and executed. But it was all I had.

I thanked the assistant, left the bank, and got back into the taxi.

'Where to now?' the driver asked.

'Heathrow Airport,' I told him. Then I sat back, took Bel's hand, and gave it another squeeze.

17

The problem was, Hoffer couldn't find a room in Ripon, or anywhere else for that matter. So he'd decided to keep driving. Then he'd pulled into a parking area to relieve his bladder, and found three lorries there, their drivers having a break and thinking about sleep. Hoffer got talking to them and one of them broke out a bottle of whisky. After which he'd returned to his car, put the seat back as far as it would go, and fallen asleep.

He slept badly, and woke up with stiffness, headache and raging thirst. He was also freezing, and had certainly caught a cold, if not something more serious. He drove to the nearest service station to chow down and have a wash. Then he got back in the car and started driving again.

The map book was a godsend, without it he wouldn't have stood a chance in hell of finding Oban. He parked by the dockside, got out feeling like shit, asked a local about accommodation, then went into the hotel, where they didn't have any rooms left but the bar was open and boasted an open fire.

Hoffer sat beside it with a large malt and wondered how he'd find the Disciples of Love. He asked the barman, but the barman said he'd never heard of them.

'Well, they live here, a whole posse of them.'

But the barman stuck to his story. So, revived by the drink, Hoffer went walkabout. He found a shopkeeper who did business with the Disciples and drew him a map on an empty brown-paper bag. Hoffer got so far, but then found his way barred by a padlocked gate. He looked around him, then fired off a couple of shots at the padlock, busting it open. He was damned if he was going to walk any further.

He'd been annoyed by a sudden realisation that he'd missed his TV appearance. And it looked like everyone in Oban had missed it too, judging by the lack of interest in him.

'Fucking backwoods,' he complained, driving up the track.

After nearly a mile, he came upon habitation, a series of shanty-town shacks more suited to animals than people. There were people about. They stopped what they were doing and stared at him as he drew up. When he got out, they kept on staring. A big bearded man came out of one of the shacks.

'Who are you?' he said.

'Name's Hoffer, sir, Leo Hoffer. I was wondering if I might have a word. I'm looking for a couple, man and woman, they might have been here recently.'

'There's been nobody here.'

Hoffer looked around him. 'This place was started by an American, wasn't it?' The man nodded. 'Only, we Americans have a reputation for hospitality to strangers. I'm not seeing much of that here.'

'How did you get past the gate?'

'Huh? The thing was standing wide open. I mean, it had a chain and all, but it was just hanging there.'

The man told an underling to go check. The underling nodded and jumped into an old hippy van.

'There's nothing here for you,' the man told Hoffer.

'Hey, maybe I want an application form. This looks like my kind of living.'

'I don't think so.'

'You don't?' Hoffer rubbed his chin. It felt raspy. He needed a shave and a soak. 'You know, I could make a habit of this, dropping in on you, asking the same question.'

'You'd get the same answer.'

The man turned his back on Hoffer and walked back into the shack. Hoffer considered following him and introducing the man to the holy rite of pistol-whipping. What the hell, there'd be other times. So he got into his car and left. The VW van was beside the gate. Hoffer tooted his horn and waved as he passed. The VW driver was standing there holding the chain, watching Hoffer leave.

Back in town, Hoffer asked at a couple of places about two tourists called Weston and Harrison. He didn't think they'd keep up their police act, not when it wasn't necessary. The names didn't mean anything, but one shop assistant recognised the photograph of Bel Harrison.

'She was in here this morning. She bought a Fair Isle jumper. It was funny, she was so excited. She rushed out of the shop so her husband could try it on.'

Hoffer started. 'What sort of sweater was this?'

The assistant showed him one just like it. She mistook the look of pain on Hoffer's face.

'We've got it in different colours if you'd prefer.'

He was groaning as he left the shop. He'd actually *talked* to the D-Man, and had been too hungover and crashed to know it. But at least one thing was clear: Bel Harrison wasn't under duress. Captives didn't often buy sweaters for their captors.

More crucially, they might still be around, he had to remember that . . . No, who was he fooling? The assassin knew who he was. He'd be out of town by now and putting miles on the clock.

Either that, Hoffer considered, or he'd be hiding somewhere, wondering how best to hit the detective. Hoffer looked around him at all the windows, large and small. He didn't feel very comfortable.

He went back to the lounge bar and ordered another whisky. There was some gossip being passed around, something about a traffic jam. Hoffer snorted into his drink. A traffic jam, around *here*? Three cars had been left stationary in the road while their drivers had a confab, holding up the traffic behind and providing a sideshow for cars heading north towards Oban.

Something about the story started to niggle Hoffer. He walked up to the storyteller and proffered the photo of Bel.

'I've no idea,' the man said. He held a pint in one hand and a cigarette in the other, so that Hoffer had to stand with the photo held out for his inspection. 'One of the cars, the middle one, it had a woman in it right enough. You couldn't see into the car ahent, and I don't remember the one in front.'

'It had two men in it,' piped up another drinker. Hoffer moved on to this man. He was wearing wellingtons, a check cap and green jacket, and his cheeks and nose were red. 'We were stuck behind Bert McAuley's lorry, bloody old thing that it is.'

'The man and woman were in the middle car?' Hoffer prompted.

'Aye, with a posh car ahent, and a car and caravan ahent that. The front car had his flashers on. They'd either had a bit of a knock, or else the front car had broken down.'

'What about the man and woman?'

'What about them?'

'Remember, Hughie,' said a third drinker, 'the man went and spoke to the people in the front car and they got out.'

'I didn't see that,' said Hughie. Hoffer moved on to the third drinker.

'What happened?'

'It was funny. The man and woman got their stuff out of the boot and took it to the other car, then drove off while the driver and passenger were back at the *third* car.'

Everyone looked at everyone else. It was obvious this story would run and run. Nothing so exciting had happened in weeks.

'Where was this?' said Hoffer.

'Just after the Cleigh turn-off.'

228

While Hoffer bought everyone a drink, the third drinker drew a map on the other side of the brown-paper bag.

It didn't take him long to find the car.

It had been pushed none too daintily up on to the verge. Though the Escort was practically brand new, someone had scored a line all down one side. It looked like the kind of scar kids made with a key, coin or knife.

'Temper, temper, guys,' Hoffer said, giving the car a good lookover. He'd bet it was rented, just like his own. There'd be prints on it belonging to the assassin and Bel Harrison. Fingerprints would be worth having, so Hoffer went to look for the nearest phone. He found a campsite a few miles further south. There was an information kiosk, locked up tight for the day, and a telephone booth outside it. He stood in the booth and called Vine Street. He couldn't get through to Broome, but Edmond finally accepted the call.

'Take your time,' said Hoffer, 'this is costing me a fucking fortune and I'm doing you a favour!'

'What favour?'

'I've got a car near here with the D-Man's prints all over it, plus his girlfriend's.'

Edmond took a bit more interest. 'Where are you?'

'I'm in the Scottish Highlands, south of a place called Oban on the A816.'

'Where's the car?'

'Parked roadside just south of a place called Cleigh.' He spelt the word for Edmond.

'I'll get on to the local constabulary.'

'They probably know about the car already. It's been abandoned after the D-Man got into trouble. There could be a lot of other people's prints on it, but some of them will definitely be his.'

'Wait a minute, what sort of trouble?'

'Money's running out, be seeing you.'

229

Hoffer put down the phone. There was a standpipe nearby, and a girl was filling a plastic jerry-can with water. He went over to her.

'On holiday with your folks?' She nodded. 'I'm looking for a friend, honey. He arrived earlier today towing a caravan.'

'The caravans are over there.' She pointed him in the direction.

'Thanks,' he said. 'Can I carry that for you?'

'My parents wouldn't like it. You're a stranger.'

Hoffer smiled. 'Take care, honey-pie.'

He watched her go. She had to work hard to keep the jerry-can off the ground. She'd be about eleven or twelve, he guessed. He knew twelve-year-olds in New York more grown up than he hoped she'd ever need to be. He liked kids on principle, the principle being that a day would come when he'd be old and they'd be in their prime. He might need their help then. He wouldn't be able to smack them in the head or pull his knife on them. You had to have respect for the future, otherwise it might kick away your stick and punch your dentures down your throat.

It took him a couple of questions to hit lucky. Another caravaner told him the Germans weren't here just now, they'd gone into town. But their caravan was here, and they'd be back. When they'd arrived the man had still been outraged, and had told his story about the traffic jam he'd been stuck in.

'I think I'll wait for them,' Hoffer said. Then the caravaner said his wife and children were out walking and was Hoffer by any chance American? The family had gone to Florida last year and loved it, Disney and the beaches and everything. This year they were on a tighter budget, with the recession and everything and him losing his job. He asked if Hoffer wanted a beer. Hoffer reckoned he could bear to listen to a few stories about Florida, so long as the price was right.

'Sure,' he said, 'why not?'

Then the man said something that warmed Hoffer's heart. 'You know,' he started, handing over a can, 'I can't help thinking your face looks familiar. Have you ever been on TV?'

The Germans weren't late. They were a couple in late middle age, showing signs of having earned well and saved well over their lives. They wore pension fund clothes and drove a pension fund car. When Hoffer told them what he wanted, they unlocked their caravan and took him inside. There wasn't much room, but Hoffer managed to look comfortable as he wedged his legs under the table and sat down.

They were bemused by his questions at first. The woman said she just wanted to forget all about it, but her husband had drunk a beer or two and got back in the mood pretty quickly. His English wasn't great, but it was better than Hoffer's delicatessen German. Hoffer eventually focused in on the back car of the three.

'The driver,' said the German, 'large man, not very happy. He would not speak to me a word just. There is some resentment here still, but I do not excuse.'

'Uh, right,' said Hoffer, 'absolutely. Was there a passenger?'

'On the back chair, yes. He talked to the other driver—'

'You mean the driver of the middle car?'

The German nodded. '—and then the other driver went away, but the man on the back chair would not talk with me. He was smile, smile all the time.'

'Smiling,' Hoffer said.

'This is how I say. And I am telling him what is the problem here? But he is smile only.'

'Smiling,' his wife corrected.

'Can you describe this man, sir?'

'Um . . . he wore a suit, shirt, but no tie I don't think. He was not large like the other men. Glasses he wore, round ones, and his hair it was white.'

'Blonde,' his wife said. 'White is for old people.'

'What happened?' Hoffer asked. The couple probably hadn't noticed how his attitude had changed.

'It was very confusing. The people from the middle car drove away in the front car. The people from the front car talked to the men in the third car. Then three men pushed the second car out of the way.'

'The blond man stayed in his car?'

'Oh, yes, in his car he stayed. Then all together they drove off, no apology to me.' The man's cheeks had reddened furiously. He was beginning to drift back into his mother tongue. His wife stroked his arm, calming him.

'You've been very helpful,' Hoffer said.

'Something to drink?' asked the woman.

'*Nein, danke*,' said Hoffer. He might have had no training in the language, but it was surprising what you could pick up from a few war films and sandwich bars. He unwedged himself from beneath the table and said his farewells, then got back into his car and lit a cigarette. Kline had confronted the D-Man, and the D-Man had escaped, which either made Kline very stupid or the assassin very clever. No one had been shot, that was the really surprising thing. It warmed Hoffer's heart. If the D-Man was not a close-range performer, then all Hoffer had to do was get close enough to him. The further away he stayed, the more danger he was in. But then again, the closer he got, the more chance there was that he'd come slap bang up against Kline and his commandos.

And he'd already seen what *they* would do at close range. They'd saw your fucking head off and leave it for a surprise.

'What kind of shit am I getting into?' he asked himself, starting his car up and heading towards the south.

Part Three

18

We flew into Boston. I always try to do that, avoid JFK. The place is more like a cattle market than an airport, and they do more checks there than anywhere else. We flew as Michael Weston and Belinda Harrison, since our real passports were the only ones we had. I knew we'd taken a calculated risk. Airlines keep computer records, and anyone can access computer data. That was another reason for flying into Boston: it was a long way from our ultimate destination.

At the airport, I found us a hotel room in town, and we took a taxi. Bel was still disoriented from the flight. It was tough on a beginner, flying backwards through time. We hadn't touched any alcohol on the flight; alcohol stopped you retuning yourself. We watched the films and ate our meals and took any soft drink we were offered. Bel was like a child at first, insisting on a window seat and peering out at the clouds. She made me tell her some things about the USA. She'd never been there before, and only had a passport at all because Max and she had taken a couple of foreign holidays. He never took her with him on business trips.

'His wasn't a very honourable profession, was it?' she said suddenly, causing me to look up from my newspaper. I thought of a lot of answers I could give her, the standard one being something about guns never killing anyone, it was only people who did that.

'More honourable than mine,' I said instead. Then I went back to my reading. Bel was coping in her own way. We'd talked about Max, of course, edging around the actual discovery of his mutilated corpse. Bel had gone through a few transitions, from hysterical to introspective, hyperactive to catatonic. Now she was putting on a good act of being herself. It *was* an act though. When we were together in private, she was different. I tried not to show how worried I was. If I needed her to be anything this trip, I needed her reliable.

It was a good flight. There were a couple of babies on board, but they were up at the bulk-head and didn't cry much anyway. Some children nearer us went through a bored stage, but their parents and the aircrew were always prepared with new games, toys, and drinks.

It would have been a good time for me to do some thinking, but in the event I didn't think too much about what we were doing. I had a very vague plan, and maybe if I thought it through too hard it would begin to look mad or full of holes. So instead I read old news, and did some crosswords, showing Bel how you worked out the answers from cryptic clues. That part was easy: the flight, getting past customs and immigration (tourists didn't even need proper visas these days), finding a hotel . . . it was all easy.

But by the time we reached the hotel, just off Boston Common, I realised I was mentally exhausted. I needed rest and relaxation, if only for a few hours. So I closed the curtains and undressed. Bel had slept a little on the plane, and wanted to go out exploring. I didn't argue with her.

She woke me up a couple of hours later and told me how she'd walked around part of the Common, and seen where they used to make some TV series, and then walked up and down some beautiful cobbled streets, and seen inside a gold-domed building, and wandered into the Italian part of town . . .

'You must walk fast,' I said, heading for the shower. She followed me into the bathroom. I hadn't heard half of it. I'd given her fifty dollars and she'd used some of it to buy herself a meal and some coffee.

'I had a hot dog and some Boston baked beans.'

'Yum yum.'

She deflated only slowly. When I came back from the shower she was flicking channels on the remote TV, finding episodes of *Star Trek* and other old reruns, plus the usual talk shows and sports, and the cable shopping and Christ channels.

'Can you turn the volume down?'

'Sure.' She seemed to enjoy the shows just as much without the sound. 'There are a lot of adverts, aren't there? I mean, they even put them between the end of the programme and the closing credits.'

I looked at her and tried out a sympathetic smile, but she was back watching TV again. I knew what she needed; she needed a period of calm, reflective mourning. The problem was, we couldn't afford that luxury. We had to keep moving.

I was making a phone call. Somewhere in Texas, I got an answering machine. I decided to leave a message.

'Spike, it's Mike West. I'm here on a brief trip. This is just to warn you I have another shopping list. I'll be there in a couple of days, all being well.' I didn't leave a contact number.

'Spike?' Bel said.

'That's his name.'

She went back to her TV stupor. A little later she fell asleep, lying on the bed, her head propped up on the pillows. The remote was still in her hand.

I felt a little better, though my nose was stuffy. I went out and walked around. My brain told me it was the middle of the night, but in Boston it was mid-evening. I found a bar with the usual shamrocks on the wall and draught Guinness. Everyone was watching a baseball game on the large-screen TV. There was a newspaper folded on the bar, so I read that and sipped my drink. Drive-by shootings had gone out of fashion; either that or become so prolific they weren't news any more. News so often *was* fashion.

Car-jackings were still news, but it had to be a particularly nice model of car to make a story.

Gun stories were everywhere. People were trying to ban them, and the National Rifle Association was giving back as good as it got. Only now even the President was pro-legislation to curb gun ownership, and a few states had made it an offence for minors to carry handguns. I had to read that sentence twice. In some cities, it turned out, one in five kids took a gun to school with them, along with their books and lunch-box. I closed the paper and finished my drink.

I knew what Spike would say: Welcome to gun heaven.

The barman was asking me if I wanted another, and I did want another. He took a fresh glass from the chiller and poured lager into it, only here it was called beer, and dark beer – proper beer – existed only sparsely, usually in trendy bars near colleges. I couldn't remember how easy it was to buy beer in Boston. I didn't know whether off-licences existed and were licensed to sell at night. Legislation differed from state to state, along with rates of tax and just about everything else. There were no off-licences, for example, they were called package stores and were government run. At least, that seemed right when I thought it. But my brain was shutting down transmissions for the night. I was trying to think about anything but Bel. In seeing her grief, I was face to face with a victim. I'd killed so many people . . . I'd always been able to think of them without humanising them. But they were drifting around me now like ghosts.

I drank my drink and left. There was a beer advert pinned to the door of the bar as I opened it. It read, 'This is as good as it gets'.

I thought about that on the way back to the hotel.

Next morning we went to the Amtrak Station and took a train to New York. Bel got her window seat and became a child again. She was actually well prepared for some aspects of 'the American experience', since back in the UK she watched so much American TV. She knew what 'sidewalk' and 'jay-walking' meant. She knew a taxi was a 'cab', and that chips were 'fries' while crisps were 'chips'. She even knew what Amtrak was, and squeezed my arm as, nearing the end of the trip, she started to catch glimpses of the Manhattan skyline behind the dowdier skyline of the endless suburbs. Upstate New York had just been countryside, and she could see countryside anywhere. She couldn't always see Manhattan.

Our hotel in Boston was part of a chain, and I'd already reserved a room at their Manhattan sister. We queued for a boneshaker yellow cab and tried not to let it damage our internal organs. The hotel was on 7th and 42nd Street. Outside, spare-change hustlers were being told where to get off by merchants trying to sell cheap trinkets, scarves and umbrellas. The sun was hazy overhead. More men shuffled around or stood in doorways, oblivious to the traffic and pedestrians speeding past. I practically had to push Bel through the hotel door.

The reception area was like a war zone. A coach party had just arrived and were checking in, while another consignment of tourists attempted to check out. The two groups had converged, one telling the other useful tips and places of interest. We took our luggage through to the restaurant.

'Two coffees, please,' I told the waitress.

'You want coffee?'

'Please.'

'Anything with that?'

'Just milk for me,' said Bel. The waitress looked at her.

'Nothing to eat, thanks,' I told her. She moved off.

'Remember,' I said to Bel, 'we're only here the one night, so don't start going tourist on me. If you want to see around, fine, I'll do my bit of business and we can go sightseeing

239

together. What do you fancy: museums, galleries, shopping, a show, the World Trade Center?'

'I want to take a horse and carriage around Central Park.'

So we took a ride around Central Park.

But first, there was my business. My safe deposit box was held in discreet but well-protected premises on Park Avenue South, just north of Union Square. I telephoned beforehand and told them I'd be coming. Bel insisted that we walk it, either that or take the subway. We did both, walking a few blocks and then catching a train.

At Liddle Trusts & Investments, we had to press a door buzzer, which brought a security guard to the door. I told him who I was and we were ushered inside, where my passport was checked, my identity confirmed, and we were led into a chamber not unlike the one in Knightsbridge. Bel had to wait here, while the assistant and I went to the vault. It took two keys, his and mine, to open my safe. He pulled out the drawer and handed it to me. I carried it back through to the chamber and placed it on the table.

'What's inside?' Bel asked.

The drawer had a hinged top flap, which I lifted. I pulled out a large wad of dollar bills, fifties and twenties. Bel took the money and whistled softly. I next lifted out a folded money-belt.

'Here,' I said, 'start putting the money into this.'

'Yes, sir. What else have you got?'

'Just these.'

The box was empty, and I held in my hand a bunch of fake American documents. There was a passport, social security card, medical card, various state gun and driving licences, and a few other items of ID. Bel looked at them.

'Michael West,' she said.

'From now on, that's who I am, but don't worry about it, you won't have any trouble.' I smiled. 'My friends still call me Michael.'

She packed some cash into the belt. 'No guns or anything? I was expecting at the very least a pistol.'

'Later,' I said.

'How much later?'

I looked at her. 'Not much.'

'Good.'

I sat down beside her. I could see that Manhattan's charms had failed to take her mind off the fact of Max's murder. I took her hands in mine.

'Bel, why don't you stay here?'

'You think I'd be safer?'

'You could do some sightseeing, have a bit of a break. You've been through a lot.'

Her face reddened. 'How dare you say that! Somebody killed my father, and I want to look them in the face. Don't think you can leave me behind, Michael, because you can't. And if you try it, I'll scream your name from the chimney-pots, so help me.'

'Bel,' I said, 'they don't have chimney-pots here.'

She didn't grace this remark with a reply.

We took a cab back towards Central Park. The driver reckoned we could find a horse and carriage near Columbus Circle. Bel had bought a tiny foldaway map of the island. She kept looking at it, then at the real streets, her finger pointing to where we were on the map.

'It's all so crammed in, isn't it?'

This was before she saw Central Park.

The park was looking at its best. There were joggers, and nannies pushing prams, and people walking their dogs, and throwing frisbees or baseballs at one another, and arranging impromptu games of baseball and volleyball, and eating hot dogs while they sat on benches in the sunshine. She asked me if I'd ever walked all the way round the park.

'No, and I doubt anyone else has. Further north, the park hits Harlem.'

'Not so safe?'

'Not quite.'

Our coach-driver had asked if we wanted a blanket or anything, but we didn't need one. Our horse didn't scare easily, which was a blessing, considering the number of cars and cabs crossing town through the park. Bel squeezed my hand.

'Tell me something, Michael.'

'What sort of thing?'

'Something about yourself.'

'That sounds like a line from a film.'

'Well, this is like living in one. Go on, tell me.'

So I started talking, and there was something about the sound the horse's hooves made on the road, something hypnotic. It kept me talking, made me open up. Bel didn't interrupt once.

I was born near an Army camp in England. My father was an Army officer, though he never rose as far as he would have liked. We moved around a lot. Like a lot of forces kids, I made friends quickly, only to lose them again when either they or I moved. We'd write for a little while, then stop. There was always a lot to do on the camps – films, shows, sports and games, clubs you could join – but this just set us apart from all the other children who didn't live on or near the camp. I used to bruise easily, but didn't think anything of it. Sometimes if I bumped myself, there'd be swelling for a few weeks, and some pain. But I never told anyone. My father used to talk about how soldiers were taught to go 'through the pain barrier', and I used to imagine myself pushing against it, like it was a sheet of rubber, until I forced my way through. Sometimes it would take a few plasters before a cut knee or elbow would heal. My mother just thought I picked off the scabs, but I never did. My father had to take me to the doctor once when I bit the tip off my tongue and it wouldn't stop bleeding.

Then one day I had to have a dental extraction. The dentist plugged the cavity afterwards, but I just kept on bleeding, not profusely, just steadily. The dentist tried putting some sour stuff on my gums, then tried an adrenaline plug, and finally gave me an injection. When that didn't work – I was on my fourth or fifth visit by now – he referred me to a specialist, whose tests confirmed that I was a mild haemophiliac. At first this gave me a certain stature within my peer group, but soon they stopped playing with me. I became an onlooker merely. I read up on haemophilia. I was lucky in two respects: for one thing, I was a mild sufferer; for another, I'd been born late enough in the century for them to have made strides in the treatment of the disease. Factor VIII replacement has only been around since the early 1970s, before that you were treated with cryo. Acute sufferers have a much harder time than me. They can bleed internally, into joints, the abdomen, even the brain. I don't have those problems. If I'm going for an operation or for dental treatment, they can give me an injection of a clotting agent, and everything's fine. It's a strange sort of disease, where women can be carriers but not sufferers. About one man in 5,000 in the UK is a haemophiliac, that's 9,000 of us. Not so long ago, nobody bothered testing blood donors for HIV. That led to over 1,200 haemophiliacs being treated with a lethal product. Over 1,200 of us, men and boys, now HIV positive and doomed.

A similar thing happened in France. They gave contaminated clotting factors to children, then tried to hush it up. I was in such a rage when that happened, such a black rage. I almost went out and picked off those responsible . . . only who was responsible? It was human error, no matter how sickening. That's one reason I won't do a hit in a Third World country, not unless the money is very good. I'm afraid I might be injured and treated with contaminated Factor VIII. I have dreams about it sometimes. There are rigorous checks these days, but does every country check, does every country screen and purify? I'm not sure. I can never be sure.

I carry my works with me everywhere, of course, my syringes and powdered clotting factor and purified water. I'm supposed to visit a Haemophilia Centre when I need a doctor or dentist, and for a yearly check-up. The blood products we haemophiliacs use can contain all sorts of contaminants, leading to liver damage, hepatitis, cirrhosis ... Then there's the bleeding, which can lead to severe arthritis. (Imagine an assassin with arthritis.) Between five and ten percent of us develop inhibitors, antibodies which stop the Factor VIII from working. Like I say, it's a strange disease. We can't have intramuscular injections or take aspirin. But things are always getting better. There's DDAVP, a synthetic product which boosts Factor VIII levels, and now there's even properly synthetic Factor VIII, recombinant Factor VIII they call it. It's like 8SM and Monoclate P, but created in the lab, not from blood. No contaminants, that's the hope.

Meanwhile, there *is* a cure for haemophilia: liver transplant. Only at present it's more dangerous than the disease itself. There will come a cure; it'll come by way of genetic research. They'll simply negate the affected chromosome.

As you can tell, haemophilia has had a massive impact on my life. It started as soon as the disease was diagnosed. My parents blamed themselves. There was no family history of the disease, but in about a third of cases there never is; there's just a sudden spontaneous mutation in the father's sperm. That's how it was with me. My parents, especially my mother, treated me like a china wedding present, as though I could only be brought out on special occasions. No more rough games with the other boys – she made sure the other parents knew all about haemophilia. My father spent more time away from me, at the shooting range. So I followed him there and asked him to teach me. A pistol first, and later a rifle. To stop me bruising my shoulder, he had my mother make a little cushion to wedge behind the stock. I still use that cushion.

My mother was opposed to the whole enterprise, but could never stand up to my father. It was a couple of years before I could beat him. I don't know whether his eyes were getting worse, or his aim less steady, or it was just that I was getting better. When I finally left home, I left it as a marksman.

I'd always been clever at school, and ended up at a university, but I didn't last long. After that there were dead-end jobs, jobs which gave me a lot of time to myself. I worked in a library, then in a couple of bookshops, and eventually got a great job working with kayak rentals in the Lake District. Only that fell through when my employers discovered I was a haemophiliac. They said the job was too risky, I'd become a liability.

Was it any wonder I couldn't hold down a job? The only place I wanted to be was on the range. I joined gun clubs and shot competitively. I even went hunting on a few occasions, looking for a new challenge. Then I met a disarming man called Holly MacIntyre. He swore this was his real name. Friends of his called him 'Mad Dog' MacIntyre. He was huge and bull-headed with cropped hair silvering above the ears. His eyes were bulbous and red-rimmed, like he spent too long in chlorinated swimming pools. He was always ready for aggro, and sometimes initiated it for its own sake. He reminded me of a rugby league forward.

Holly had known my father, and he'd seen me shoot a few times. He was by this time long out of the armed forces and working in what he called a 'security capacity' for a number of countries, though he couldn't name them. In fact, he was a mercenary, leader of a gang of about a dozen men who could be bought, who would go anywhere in the world and train any rag-tag rabble for a price. Mad Dog was on the lookout for fresh blood.

I told him he couldn't have mine, and explained why.

'Is that all that's stopping you?' he said. 'Christ, you could still be useful to me.'

I asked him how.

'Sniper, my boy. Sniper. Put you up a tree and leave you there. You'd be nice and cosy, no cuts or bruises, nobody'd know you were there. All you'd do is pick 'em off as they came into sight.'

'Pick off who?'

'The fucking enemy, of course.'

'And who would they be?'

He leaned close to me and hissed whisky. 'Whoever you like!'

I turned down his offer, but not before he'd introduced me to a few people who were later to prove useful. See, at this time I was a military groupie. I liked to hang around with squaddies and old soldiers, with anyone who shared my background and belief system. I knew which pubs and clubs to go to, which gyms. I knew where some weekend shoot was going to be. These shoots, they weren't paintball or grouse or a few hoary old foxes. They were held in secret, far away from humanity, where you could make a big noise and nobody'd hear you. I used to take bets. They'd place a coin upright on the bonnet of a car, and there'd be someone in the car with his hand by the bonnet-release. At a given signal, I'd have to hit the coin before the bonnet sprang open.

Everyone loved me. But I knew I was turning into a sideshow. Worse than that, I was becoming a freak. So I did something about it. I made myself a life plan. It didn't happen overnight; I read books and went travelling. I knew three things: I was bored, I was poorer than I wanted to be, and I had a skill.

I started small, shooting a few rats I bought from a pet shop. That wasn't very satisfactory: I'd nothing against the rats, and nothing to gain from shooting them. I found I

246

actually liked them better than I liked most of the people around me. I don't like people really, I'm just very good at pretending. I did some hunting in the USA, and that was better than shooting rats. Then one night in New York, I picked off a junkie from my darkened hotel room. They were standing in an alley six floors below me. I reasoned that they didn't have long to live anyway, the life expectancy of a junkie on the New York streets being slightly less than that of your average rat. From then on, it got easier.

I went back to see Mad Dog, only he was somewhere in Africa, and this time he didn't come back. But I knew other people I could talk to, other people who knew what I needed to know. It was six months before I got my first contract. They were expecting me to hit the victim on the head and bury him in Epping Forest. Instead, I took him out from four hundred yards and created an immediate news story. My employers decided this was okay, too. I was paid, and my name was passed along. I knew I wouldn't be working for the Salvation Army. But then I wasn't killing any nuns and priests either. It was only after a few hits that I decided anyone was fair game. It isn't up to the executioner to pronounce guilt or innocence. He just makes sure the instruments are humane.

I noticed that Bel was sitting like a block of stone beside me.

'Sorry,' I said. 'But I'm not telling you anything you didn't already know.'

'Michael, you've spoken for so long, and yet you've said almost nothing.'

'What?'

'Can we go get something to drink?'

'Sure.'

I told the driver to take us back now. We passed another carriage on the way. There were some Japanese tourists in the back. While the drivers exchanged bored looks, the Japanese videoed us, waving and grinning as they did. We looked like a couple weary of their life together, and reeling from yet another spat.

'You know,' Bel said, 'you've never asked me about myself. That's strange. When I've gone out with men before, they've always ended up asking me about myself. How old are you, Michael?'

'My passports say thirty-five.' We were lying in bed together. We hadn't made love, our bodies weren't even touching. The silent TV was playing.

'And you've never been married, never had a steady girlfriend?'

'There've been a few.'

'How many?'

'I don't know.'

'A few hundred? A few dozen?'

'Just a *few*. Christ, Bel.' I threw off the cover and stood up. The air conditioning was whirring away, blowing cool air over me.

'Look,' I said, 'I'm not . . . I never said I was much good at this . . . this sort of thing.'

'Do you hear me complaining?'

'Okay, I'll ask you something about yourself.'

She smiled sadly. Her eyebrows were beautiful. Her lips were beautiful. 'Don't bother,' she said. 'Ask me some other time when I'm not expecting it.'

Then she sat up and started watching TV, disappearing back into herself.

The next morning we flew to New Mexico.

I wasn't going to buy a car in New York. Nobody buys a car second hand in New York if they can help it. The cars are rustier than elsewhere, with more miles on the clock (even if they show *less* miles) and steeper price tags. You either buy on the west coast or you buy in New Mexico, Texas, somewhere like that. We bought in Albuquerque.

Bel was right: the blond man and his team might have no trouble picking up our trail again. From flight and hotel information, they could trace us as far as New York. But Michael West, not Michael Weston, had paid for the flights to Albuquerque, and the name on his companion's ticket was Rachel Davis. I was taking all these precautions when all the blond smiler from Oban had to do was head directly to the Olympic Peninsula and wait for us there. That was okay; I just didn't want him intercepting me. This way, I might get at least one good shot in first.

We didn't linger in Albuquerque. My New Mexico ID and a bundle of cash bought us a fast car. It was a Trans-Am, just right for the trip ahead. I'd picked up a few small ads and car ads magazines from the first newsagent's in town, and we sat in a diner while I scoured them. I ringed half a dozen and went to the pay-phone. The first number I called, the owner was at work and his wife said I'd have to see the car when he was around. I hit the jackpot with the second number. I was talking to a drawling mechanic called Sanch who was mad about 'shit-kickers' (his term for fast cars) and was selling this Trans-Am because he wanted to buy a beautiful old Firebird with a paint job 'to die for, man'.

He was so keen to sell, he picked us up outside the diner in a pickup truck and took us back to his three-storey house along a dirt road in what seemed a nice middle-class neighbourhood.

'I fix all the neighbourhood cars, man, they bring them all to me.'

It looked like half the neighbourhood cars were parked right outside Sanch's house, mostly in bits. He kept his best models in the garage, including another, highly-tuned Trans-Am. I'd rather have had this one, but the one he was selling sounded sweet too. I looked at the engine, and we took it for a spin. It was white, and the interior was a bit grotty, plus it was missing quarter of a fender. The engine was clean though, and it had a hi-fi. He brought the price down another $1,000 for cash and I asked if I could use his bathroom.

While Bel enjoyed a cold beer and the collection of nude calendars in Sanch's kitchen, I unzipped my money belt and took out the notes. Back in the kitchen, Sanch had already filled in the relevant details on his ownership papers.

'Hey,' he said, handing me a beer, 'I meant to ask you, what you gonna use the car for?'

'Just some driving.'

'That's the way to see America.'

'Yes, it is,' I said, handing over the money. He examined it, but didn't count it.

'Looks about right. Here, I got something for you.' It took him a little while to find what he was looking for. It was a Rand-McNally Road Atlas, its covers missing, corners curled and oily. But the pages were all there. 'I got about half a dozen of these things laying around. After all, you don't want to get lost between here and there.'

I thanked him, finished the beer, and put my part of the ownership document in my pocket.

Then we drove to Lubbock.

It served as a nice introduction to American driving. Long straight roads, the occasional shack planted in the middle of nowhere, and sudden towns which disappeared into the dust you left behind. The car was behaving, and, lacking a TV, Bel was communing with the radio. She liked the preachers best, but the abrasive phone-in hosts weren't far behind. One redneck was praising the gun.

'Guns made America, and guns will *save* America!'

'You're loon-crazy, my friend,' said the DJ, switching to another call.

Albuquerque is only about 250 miles from Lubbock. We could do it inside a day easy, but we weren't in any particular rush. When we stopped at a place called Clovis and I still got an answering machine in Lubbock, we decided to check into a motel. The place we chose was choice indeed, twenty dollars a night and decorated in 1950s orange. Orange linoleum, orange lampshades, orange bedspread. We looked to be the only guests, and the man in the office could have given Norman Bates some tips. He rang up our fee on an ancient till and said he was sorry about the swimming pool. What he meant was, the swimming pool wasn't finished yet. It was a large circular concrete construction, waiting to be lined. It was unshaded and sat right next to the road. I couldn't see many holidaymakers using it. There was a hot wind blowing, but the motel boasted an ice machine and another machine dispensing cold cola.

'The TV hasn't got cable!' Bel complained, already a seasoned traveller in the west. Along the route we'd been offered water beds and king-size beds and adult channels and HBO, all from noticeboards outside roadside motels. Bel wasn't too enamoured of our bargain room, but I was a lot more sanguine. After all, the owner hadn't made us fill in a registration card and hadn't taken down the number of our licence plate. There would be no record that we'd ever stayed here.

'Let's go do the sights,' I said.

We cruised up and down the main and only road. A lot of the shops had shut down, their windows boarded up. There were two undistinguished bars, another motel the other end of town with a red neon sign claiming No Vacancies, though there were also no signs of life, a couple of petrol stations and a diner. We ate in the diner.

There was a back room, noisy from a party going on there. It was a fireman's birthday, and his colleagues, their wives and girlfriends were singing to him. Our waitress smiled as she came to take our order.

'I'll have the ham and eggs,' Bel said. 'The eggs over easy.' She smiled at me. 'And coffee.'

I had the chicken dinner. There was so much of it, Bel had to help me out. Since there was no phone in our room, I tried Lubbock again from the diner, and again got the answering machine. After the meal, we stopped at the petrol station and bought chocolate, some cheap cola, and a four-pack of beer. I had a look around and saw that the station sold cool-boxes too. I bought the biggest one on the shelf. The woman behind the till wiped the dust off with a cloth.

'Fill that with ice for you?'

'Please.'

Then I added another four-pack to our bill.

Next morning we filled the cool-box with ice, beer and cola, and had breakfast at the diner. The same waitress was still on duty.

'Good party?' Bel asked.

'Those guys,' clucked the waitress. 'Practically had to hose them down to get them out of here.'

It was ten o'clock and already hot when we headed out of town. One thing Sanch hadn't told us about the Trans-Am, its air conditioning wasn't a hundred percent. In the end, I turned it off and we drove with the windows down. At another service station, Bel bought some tapes, so we didn't have to put up with the radio any more. The drivers on these long two-lane stretches of Texas were kind to a fault. If you went to overtake someone, the car in front would glide into the emergency lane so you could pass without going into the other carriageway. Even lorries did it, and expected you to do the same for them. Not that many people passed us. We cruised at between 70 and 80 and I kept an eye open for radar cops. Every time we passed a car or lorry, Bel would wave to it from her window.

This was the most relaxation I'd had in ages. I'd driven part of the way across the USA before, and had enjoyed it then too. As Bel said, you became your favourite film star in your own road movie. More importantly from our point of view, no one could trace your route.

Lubbock, birthplace of Buddy Holly, was a prairie sprawl with a museum dedicated to ranching. The museum boasted a large collection of types of barbed wire, plus a rifle display that took the breath away. That was all I could tell you about Lubbock. The last time I'd been here, I had failed to find a centre to the place, but that's not so surprising in American cities. Last time, I stayed in a run-down motel near the Buddy Holly statue. But after last night, I reckoned Bel would object, so we found a new-looking hotel just off the highway and registered there.

American hotels and motels used to ask for your ID, but these days all they did was ask you to fill in a registration card. So it was easy to give fake names, fake car details and fake licence. Bel liked the room: it had Home Box Office on cable, plus in-house pay-movies. It also had a king-size bed and a telephone. I called the number one last time, then decided to head out there anyway.

'So do I get to know now?' Bel said as we got back into the Trans-Am.

'What?'

'Who you've been trying to call.'

'A guy called Jackson. Spike Jackson. You'll like him.'

Spike lived not far from Texas Tech and the Ranching Heritage Centre. He'd taken me there on my previous visit. There was a dual carriageway, with single-storey shops along one side, and a couple of lanes off. Up one of these lanes, at the end of the line, was Spike's place. I hoped he wasn't out of the country on business. I knew he did most of his business from home.

We came off the dual carriageway and drove alongside the shops. Bel spotted a western-wear emporium, and wanted us to stop. I dropped her off and said I'd be back in five minutes, whatever happened. She disappeared through the shop door.

There were a couple of cars parked outside the two-storey house, but that didn't mean anything. Like all 'good old boys', Spike usually had a few cars hanging around. He owned at least two working cars, and sometimes bought another dud, which he'd tinker with for a while before towing it to the junk yard. I revved the Trans-Am a couple of times to let him know he had a visitor. I didn't want him nervous.

But there was no sign of life as I walked up the steps to the front door. There was a screened-in porch either side of the door, with chairs and a table and a swing-bench. Spike hadn't had the maid in recently; there were pizza boxes and beer cans everywhere. I rang the bell again, and heard someone hurtling towards the door. It flew open, and a teenage girl stood there. Before I had a chance to say anything, she waved for me to follow her, and rushed back indoors again.

'I'm about three thou off the high score!' she called. I followed her upstairs and into a bedroom. It looked like a radio shack. There were electronics everywhere. Sprawling across a makeshift table (an old door laid flat with packing-cases for legs) was a computer system.

The girl could have been anywhere between fifteen and eighteen. She was thin and leggy, her black denims like a second skin. She'd tied her thick red hair carelessly behind her head, and wore a black T-shirt advertising some rock band. She was back in front of the computer, using the joystick to fire a killing beam at alien crustaceans. Two speakers had been wired to the computer, enhancing the sound effects.

'Who are you anyway?' she asked.

'I'm a friend of Spike's.'

'Spike's not here.'

'When will he be back?' As the screen went blank and a fresh scenario came up, she took time to wipe her hands on her denims and look at me.

'What are you, Australian?'

'English.'

'Yeah? Cool.'

I was tempted to pull the plug on her game, but you could

never tell with teenagers. She might draw a gun on me. I had to attract her attention somehow.

'Spike never used to like them so young.'

'Huh?'

'His girlfriends.'

She smirked. 'Not!' She had dimples and a faceful of freckles, a pale face which seldom saw the sunshine outside. The curtains in her room were drawn closed. She'd stuck photos on them; film stars mostly. 'I'm not Spike's girlfriend.' She rolled her eyes at the thought. 'Jee-zuss!'

I sat down on her unmade bed. 'Who are you then?'

'I shouldn't have let you in, should I? I mean, you could be any-fucking-body, right? You could be a rapist, or even worse a cop.'

'I'd have to be an English cop, wouldn't I?'

'Not. I *know* who you are. Spike's told me about you.'

'Who am I then?'

'He calls you "Wild West".'

I smiled. This was true. She was looking at me again. 'Am I right?'

'Yes, you're right. I need to see Spike.'

'Well, he's not here. Look at that, eight million seven hundred thou.'

'The high score?'

'You bet.'

'I'm a great believer in quitting while you're ahead.'

'Uh-uh, bud.' She shook her head. 'I'm headed all the way to annihilation.'

'Where is Spike?'

'You're getting boring, man. He's on a shoot.'

'A shoot?'

'Down towards Post. It's an hour's drive.'

'Can you give me directions?'

'Sure, head south-east out of town—'

'On a piece of paper?'

She smirked again. 'I'm an American teenager, we don't *write*.'

'I'm going to pull the plug on your little game.'

'Do that and you'll be sorry.' There was no humour in her voice, but I'd run out of patience. I found a four-way adaptor on the floor and picked it up, my hand clenched around the first cable.

'Okay, man, you win.' She hit a button on the keyboard and the screen froze. 'This thing's got a sixty-second pause.' She looked for paper, found a paperback novel, tore the back cover from it, and drew a map on the blank side. She threw the map at me and jumped back into her seat.

'Thanks for the hospitality,' I said.

'How hospitable would you be if your parents kicked you out?'

She was asking me to ask her something. My only weapon was to walk away, and that's what I did.

Back at the store, Bel had bought a pair of boots for herself. They had shiny metal tips and ornate red stitching on black leather. She'd bought a new pair of denims to go with them. She almost looked like a native, which was no bad thing. Maybe that was the reason she'd bought the stuff. Or maybe she was just trying to shed her old clothes, her English clothes. Clothes from a home she no longer wanted.

I handed her the map as we drove off. She looked at the drawing, then at what it was written on.

'"Mainframe bandits",' she read, '"are on the loose in hyperspace, and only you can stop them, playing the role of Kurt Kobalt, Innerspace Investigator, with your beautiful but deadly assistant Ingress".' She looked at me. 'Is that us, do you think?'

'Not.'

19

It wasn't that easy to find the shoot.

The map wasn't wrong in itself, but some of the roads were little more than dirt tracks, and we doubted we were ever going to end up anywhere. As a result, we lost our bottle once or twice and headed back to the main road, only to find we'd been on the right road all the time.

At last we came to a lonely spot, a wilderness of hillocks and valleys. There was no habitation for miles, yet cars and vans had gathered here. Men and women were standing around guzzling from cans. That worried me straight off: guns and alcohol – the worst marriage.

As soon as we stepped out of the car we could smell it: the air was thick with cordite. We couldn't tell if there was smoke or not, we'd kicked up so much dust along the track. I was glad I'd bought the Trans-Am and not some anonymous Japanese car. These were Trans-Am people. There were a couple more parked nearby, along with Corvette Stingrays and Mustangs and a couple of Le Barons.

Somebody yelled 'The line is hot!' and there was a sudden deafening fusillade from behind the nearest rise. Instinctively, Bel ducked, raising a knowing smile from the beer-drinkers. The sound of firing continued for fifteen seconds, then died. There were whoops and sounds of applause. A man came up to us, beer can in hand.

'It's six bucks each, buddy.' I was handing over the money when I heard an unmistakable voice.

'You old dawg, what in the hell are you doing here?' It was Spike Jackson. He had a baseball cap on his head, turned so the shield was to the back. He took it off and ran a hand through his hair. He had thick wavy brown hair swept back to display a high prominent forehead. He wore steel-rimmed glasses, sneakers and old denims, and a T-shirt with the sleeves ripped off, showing rounded muscular shoulders and thick upper arms. He stopped suddenly, arched his back to the sky and threw open his arms.

'This is gun heaven, man! I died and went to gun heaven. Didn't I always used to tell you that, Wild West? That's what this country is, man.'

His audience voiced their agreement. Now he came up to us and, arms still open wide, closed them around me in a hug that lifted me off the ground.

'Wild West, man, how in the hell are you doing?' He let me down and gave Bel a smile, touching his crotch for luck, then turned back to me. 'You old *dawg*, you! Come on, let's go where the action is.' He went to a stack of beer cans and pulled off a few, tossing one to me, but opening Bel's and handing it to her with a bow from the waist.

'Name's Spike Jackson, ma'am, and this one's for you.'

Bel took the beer but didn't say anything. Spike led us around to where, as he'd put it, the action was. In another clearing people milled around examining the damage the latest fusillade had done to a couple of wrecked cars, a lean-to shack, and an array of crates and bottles and cans. Fresh targets were being set up by sweating volunteers.

I knew what this was, of course. Spike had taken me to a Texan shoot before. Forty or fifty enthusiasts would gather together and fire off a range of weapons. You could spectate, or you could participate. A couple of arms dealers, who supplied much of the arsenal, would then take orders. I could see the dealers. They were short and dumpy and wearing holsters under drenched armpits. The day was fiercely hot, and I half wished I'd bought a stetson; or at the very least a baseball cap.

Spike never *officially* organised these shoots, because he wasn't officially a gun dealer. He worked the black market, and got a lot of his stuff from Army bases throughout Texas. He bought from overseas too, though. He just didn't do any of this legally.

'Look at this,' he told me. He had led us to where today's arms were displayed, spread on sheets of plastic on the ground. It looked like an arsenal captured from the Iraqis. Spike had picked up a Browning anti-aircraft gun. It showed off his bronzed arm muscles. 'Something for the lady,' he said, laughing.

I laughed back, and Bel gave me a disgusted look.

'We got your M16s, your AK-47s and 74s.' Spike pointed out the most interesting items. 'Look here, we even got something from Finland or Sharkland or someplace, a Varmint.'

'Valmet,' I corrected. 'The M62.'

'Whatever. We got armour-piercing ammo you wouldn't believe, man. Look here, the M39B. Use it in a handgun, it'll go through a bullet-proof vest. Get 'em while you can. Black Talon bullet here, you ever hear of it?'

'It expands on impact,' Bel said coolly, 'and has these sharp little edges.'

Spike opened his eyes and mouth wide. 'Lookee here, we got us an expert! It's the quiet ones you have to watch out for!' Then he went back to his inventory. 'It's all cute stuff, and believe me we got *everything*.'

'So what would you suggest?'

Spike stopped his spiel and looked at me. He was wavering, but it was an impersonation of a drunk rather than an effect of drink. His blue eyes were clear.

'Well now, depends what you need it for.'

'We need a variety of things. A sniper rifle, a couple of pistols, and maybe an assault rifle, something serious.'

Spike nodded thoughtfully, then counted off on his fingers. 'Sniper rifle for long range, pistol for close range, and assault rifle for taking on the Seventh Cavalry.'

'You might not be far off.'

He finished his beer and crushed the can, throwing it on to the ground. 'What's this "we" shit, man?'

I nodded in Bel's direction. Spike stared at me, working out if I was serious, then he shook his head.

'Maybe we better discuss this,' he said.

I knew he wouldn't want to discuss anything out in the open. Texas had lax gun laws, but that didn't mean illegal dealers were encouraged. After the Waco siege, even Texans had started to ask questions about the amount of guns around.

We followed Spike's pick-up truck. Bel said she wanted to drive, so she drove the Trans-Am. I didn't mind her driving at all; two drivers would make the trip north all the faster. Back at his house, Spike yelled up the stairs that he was home, then went into the kitchen and brought out half a dozen refrigerated beers. We made ourselves comfortable on the porch. Bel said she needed the bathroom, and Spike told her where it was. We didn't see her for a while after that.

Spike drank his first beer in silence.

'So who is she?' he said at last.

'A friend.'

'What's her problem?'

'She's in mourning.'

'Mm-hm.' He opened the second beer and wiped sweat from his brow with his forearm. 'So, what's the story, Wild West?'

I shook my head, and he shrugged.

'That's up to you, of course, but if you're looking to buy so much hardware, people are going to be wondering.'

'That's not my problem. My problems start if you can't get the stuff.'

'Man, I can get anything. I just want to be right in my mind about why *you* want it.'

'What is this, new legislation? You have to have a clear conscience after each sale?'

He smiled and shook his head. 'Things are crazy though.

We've got doctors telling us guns kill more teenagers than every known disease combined. We've got Clinton, man, the most anti-gun president we've ever *known*. That fucker got the Brady Bill through! We've got the NRA fighting its battle, but not always winning any more. I don't always agree with the NRA, man, you know that. It simply isn't right that minors can carry handguns, no way. But now some states are banning assault weapons, they're limiting how many guns you can buy . . . Forty deaths a day, man, forty a day. I know it's mostly gangs fighting each other, but it's a lot of blood.'

'Maybe you're just getting old, Spike. Either that or Democrat.'

'Wash your mouth, boy! No, I'll tell you what it is, it's ever since Jazz came to stay. Her real name's Jasmine, but she likes Jazz. There are kids she hangs around with, they carry guns, a boy in her class got himself shot. There was a shoot-out at some zoo someplace. She tells me all this, and I just . . .' He shrugged his shoulders and finished beer number two.

'Who is she?' I asked.

'Jazz? She's my niece, man, my sister's kid. Her mom and dad split up, and neither of them was ready to take her with them. Hell, I don't blame my sister, she's just mixed up just now, you know. So I said I'd let Jazz stay here for a while, see if I couldn't give her a less crazy environment, something stable, you know.'

I think I nodded.

'She's a great kid, man, clever too. She's got a computer up in her room, she can do *any*thing with that pile of junk. She's some kind of genius, I guess.'

'Can you get me an assault rifle?' I said, smashing into his reverie.

'Hell, yes, just so long as you don't want an ownership licence. Know why they started licensing automatics?' He'd told me before, but I didn't say. 'To stop Dillinger, man, and

261

gangsters like him. They reckoned you could stop those guys by getting the Bureau of Alcohol, Tobacco and Firearms to run background checks. Man, they can hardly check the baseball scores.'

Spike had drunk more than I'd thought. He could ramble on all night, trying to justify his existence and that of the other people around him, trying to make sense of his world. I knew the only place his world made sense was out on the gun range.

'You're staying tonight, right?'

'We've got a hotel.'

'Aw, you could stay here.'

'Thanks, but it's already bought and paid for.' I shrugged my shoulders.

'That's too bad.'

'We can talk more in the morning. How long will it take to get the stuff?'

'I can have it for you tomorrow, I guess. Cash, right?'

'Right.'

'We're talking big numbers here.'

'Let me worry about the money.'

'That's cool.' He looked around. 'Where's your woman?'

'She's not my woman.'

'Oh? Whose is she then?'

'Her own.'

'A ballbreaker?'

'That's not what I said.'

'It's what I hear in your voice. She must've got lost or something.'

We went inside. Bel wasn't lost, she was in Jazz's room, seated at the computer and playing a new game while Jazz gave instructions over her shoulder.

'Time to go, Bel.'

'Five more minutes, Michael.'

Jazz glowered at me. 'If you don't obey him, Bel, he might pull the plug.'

'He'll get a kick in the balls if he does,' Bel said quietly, bringing a spume of laughter from Jazz. Spike mouthed a word at me.

The word was ballbreaker.

We lay in bed naked, damp from our shower, and watched TV. Then Bel did something that surprised me. She turned the TV off and put down the remote.

'Jazz,' she said.

'What about her?'

She turned on her side to face me. 'She's got an incredible computer.'

'Yes?' I started stroking her spine.

'Maybe we could . . . *use* it in some way.'

'How?' I was interested now.

'Keep stroking,' she instructed. 'I don't know how exactly, but you can do things with computers these days, can't you? They're not just for games or glorified typewriting.'

'It's a thought. We'll put it to her.'

'Michael, tell me something. You love guns, don't you?'

'Yes.'

'Why?'

'I don't know. Maybe I can control them.'

'Or control other people with them.'

I shrugged. 'Maybe I should go on one of these chat shows and talk it out of my system.'

She smiled for a moment. 'I hated what was happening out there on that range. Those people were *having fun*. How can it be fun?'

I shrugged again.

'Michael, do you think you love them more than you've ever loved a woman?'

By 'them' she meant guns of course. I thought for a second. 'I wouldn't say that exactly.' She'd turned on to her back, trapping my arm beneath her. Our faces were close.

'Prove it,' she said.

This time when we made love she didn't cry, not on the outside. But there was a rage inside her, and she bucked, punching and clawing at me. Then she stopped suddenly.

'What is it?' I asked after a moment.

'We're going to kill them, aren't we?' Her voice was strangely calm. 'Promise me we're going to kill them.'

Kill them? Jesus, we didn't even know who *they* were.

'Promise,' I whispered. She wanted me to say it louder.

I said it louder.

Spike had invited us round for lunch, which meant barbecued steaks in his 'yard'. The yard was in fact a very long narrow garden, nearly all of it grass, with a wire pen at the bottom where Wilma lived.

'It's a pig,' Bel said when introduced. She was wearing her new denims and cowboy boots with a fresh white T-shirt.

'That's no pig,' said Spike, 'that's a *hawg*. Anyone I don't like, Wilma eats those suckers alive.' He was wearing a plastic cooking-apron and waving a wooden spoon, which he occasionally stuck in his mouth. Then he'd go and stir the barbecue sauce again and add another dash of Tabasco.

Spike's living room was no advert for the bachelor life. There were photos and magazine cuttings covering most of the walls, and you couldn't see the carpet for old engine parts, sports trophies, discarded clothes and memorabilia. Spike collected service-station signs, especially ones made of metal. He also seemed to be going in for full-sized cardboard replicas of his sporting heroes. There was a black basketball player I'd never heard of leaning against one wall, and a baseball pitcher behind the sofa.

'When he's watching a game,' Jazz confided, 'he actually talks to it like it was the real person.' Then she shook her head and went back to her room.

Muffled in black cotton cloth on the sofa were several items for me to look at. Spike, his lips coated orange with sauce, came back in and waved his spoon. 'Gimme a minute and I'll be with you. Bel's gone upstairs with Jazz.'

When he left, I unwrapped the first gun. It was the sniper rifle, a Remington 700 'Varmint'. It wasn't the military version which Max had offered me, but the commercial version, which meant it was beautifully polished and didn't have a pre-fitted telescopic sight. I'd used one before, last time I'd been in Lubbock. Maybe it was the same gun. It was manufactured in Ilion, New York State, and I knew it was an accurate weapon. It wasn't the greatest sniper gun around, but it would do. The sight was a Redfield. I checked that it was compatible with the mounting plate. Then I opened the second package.

These were the handguns, one pistol and one revolver. The revolver was a Smith & Wesson 547, with the four-inch rather than three-inch barrel. I'd never had much time for revolvers, though I knew Americans loved them, more for what they represented perhaps – the past – than for their modern-day ability.

The pistol felt better. It was another Smith & Wesson, a 559 semi-automatic, steel-framed and heavier than the revolver. It took fourteen rounds of parabellum ammo, but wouldn't accept a silencer. Not that I thought I'd need a silencer, though the option would have been welcome.

I was opening the third package when Spike came in.

'Wait till you see,' he said.

I'd been expecting an M16, but this was a lot shorter, almost a foot shorter in fact. It didn't weigh much more than double the pistol, and I picked it up one-handed.

'It's a Colt Commando,' Spike said. 'It's close to the M16, but the barrel's half the length. The stock's adjustable, see, and there's a flash hider if you want it. It'll take anything from a twenty- to a thirty-round mag. Elite forces use them, man, so you know you're talking quality.'

'Spare me the sales pitch, Spike. It won't take sights.'

He grinned. 'That don't matter, see.'

'Why not?'

'Because they're shit long-range. They don't have the muzzle velocity of an M16. You need the muzzle flash, too, because this thing makes a noise like a Gatling gun. But for close-up action, you can't beat it. Tuck it into your shoulder with the stock retracted and you can fire one-handed, just like Big Arnie!'

'I like that it's compact.'

'Man, you can put it in an overnight bag, nobody's going to know. Shit, the steaks!'

He ran out of the room. I tucked the guns away again and checked what ammo he was giving me. I knew I was going to take everything except the revolver. Bel had shown some interest in being armed, but I wasn't about to encourage her. Whatever the NRA says, if you've got a gun, you're more likely to get shot than if you haven't.

I went upstairs and found Bel and Jazz busy on the computer.

'Go away!' Jazz screamed. So I went away.

Downstairs in the garden I opened another tin of Old Milwaukee. 'So how much?' I said. Spike turned another steak and basted it.

'Oh, well now, let me see . . .'

Which meant he already knew the exact figure he was going to ask. He started pretending to tot up numbers. Then he went into the kitchen and brought out a tub of potato salad Jazz had made earlier.

'She's a sweet little thing really,' Spike said. 'I know you didn't hit it off with her yesterday, she told me last night. She always sits and talks with me at night. Of course, then she hits me for a twenty and takes off till dawn.' He laughed. 'Only kidding. She's usually back home by two.'

'That's all right then.'

'Bel seems nice.'

'I know you didn't hit it off with her yesterday.'

'*Touché*, brother. You know me, I'm called Spike 'cause

266

I'm spikey. You say the two of you aren't doing the devil's business?'

'I don't recall saying that.'

Spike smiled, then worked on the steaks again. 'I get the feeling . . . Man, I'm sorry, you know me, I don't pry or anything. But I get the feeling you're in deep shit.'

'I am.'

He nodded to himself. 'And are you going to get out of it all right?'

'I hope so.'

'Wild West, you shouldn't be taking a civilian along.'

'Bel's not a civilian, Spike. Her father was a casualty.'

'I guess that makes it her war too,' he admitted. 'Only, she don't look the type. But then, neither do you.'

'I've become the type.'

'Yeah, I can see that, partner, but I see something else too. I see you're tired of it. That's dangerous.'

'After this trip, I'm thinking of packing it in.'

'That may not be soon enough, Wild West.'

'Just tell me how much I owe for the guns.'

'Well, what do you want?'

'Everything except the revolver.'

He basted the steaks afresh. 'Need any help?'

I knew what he was offering, he was offering himself. He didn't look at me.

'I appreciate it, Spike, but I don't think so. Now, how much do I owe you?'

'Tell you what, come back and see me when it's over. I'll take the guns off you if you've still got them, and I'll relieve you of that car of yours.'

'The Trans-Am?'

'That's the deal.'

'What if I don't come back?'

'You wouldn't do that to me, man.' He stuck his free hand out, and I shook it. 'Only, I don't want no fresh dents in it, okay?'

267

'Immaculate,' I said. Then: 'Do you know anyone who fixes air conditioning?'

Spike called a friend, who could look at the Trans-Am that same day. The guy turned up with a friend, and they took the car with them. Spike had already called upstairs three times that the food was ready. It was more than ready by the time Jazz and Bel came downstairs. They looked shiny-faced and excited about something. Bel had her hand on Jazz's shoulder. Jazz was looking younger and prettier than yesterday. Bel had certainly done something to her.

Spike and I were halfway through our steaks.

'Outstanding potato salad,' he told his niece.

'Thanks, Unc.'

Jazz opened beers for Bel and her. They toasted one another.

'Okay, give,' said Spike.

'Wait and see,' said Bel. 'The printer could be busy for some time.'

After which all they wanted to talk about was the food, the car, and the drive which lay ahead. I tried giving Bel my long hard stare, but it didn't so much as nick her. We feasted on meat and beer, and then Jazz announced that there was something she wanted to show me. Bel came too, Spike staying behind to scrape the plates into Wilma's pen.

Upstairs in Jazz's room, paper had spewed from her printer. She started gathering it up, while Bel explained.

'This machine's fantastic, Michael. We got into an information network and asked for stuff about the Disciples. Where was it we went, Jazz?'

'Library of Congress to start with.'

'Yes, Jazz's computer talked to the one in the Library of Congress. Then we went to Seattle. What was the name of that place?'

'The U-Dub,' said Jazz.

'Short for the University of Washington. We talked to

their information system, and to one at a newspaper, and lots of other places. It only took *minutes* . . . and see what we got.'

Jazz proudly handed me the pile of printed sheets. There were newspaper reports about the Disciples of Love, a whole bibliography of source material. I should have looked more impressed, but I knew none of this could tell me anything fresh.

'This is the guy,' Jazz said, tapping one sheet. It was a piece by a reporter called Sam T. Clancy.

'He's been looking into the Disciples,' Bel explained. 'And now he's disappeared.'

'Gone into hiding,' Jazz corrected. There was a story about this too. After a near-miss hit and run followed by a near-fatal malfunction of his car's braking system, Sam T. Clancy had gone to ground. His newspaper, the *Post-Intelligencer*, had made it front-page news. Being a newspaper, they'd also printed a photo of the journalist. I couldn't see that exactly helping him go to ground.

'I don't see where this gets us,' I said.

'Come on,' said Bel. 'Someone sets you up, someone gets rid of a reporter in England, now they try to bump off a reporter in Seattle. We need to find this Clancy and talk to him, see what he knows.'

'Do you know the north-west, Bel? The coastline, the islands, the wilderness, the mountains? What do we do, climb to the top of Mount Rainier and yell for him to come see us?'

'Jesus,' said Jazz, 'talk about no spine.'

'Look, I appreciate—'

'No forward planning,' Jazz went on. 'Think artillery's the answer to everything.'

Bel just stood there, lips slightly parted like a ventriloquist.

'Big macho guy, kick down a few doors, fire a few rounds, and suddenly everything becomes clear. *Wrong!*'

'Look, Jazz . . .' But she pushed past me out of the room

269

and took the stairs three at a time. Bel was pouting now, her arms folded.

'She worked hard to get that information. She worked fast and well.'

'I know, Bel.'

'And how hard can it really be to find this reporter? Think about it, Michael. He's a *reporter*. If we turn ourselves into a story, he'll come to *us*.'

I had to admit, she had a point.

We got the car back in A-1 shape. The air conditioning worked. It had been a minor repair, no more. The mechanic had also retuned the car. It purred when I turned the ignition. And all for a hundred dollars cash. We celebrated with a trip to the Ranching Heritage Centre. Bel thought the whole thing was a bore, a distraction: the reconstructed plantation houses and windmills, the steam locomotive, the indoor exhibits.

Me, I went and paid my respects to the Winchesters.

We took Spike and Jazz out for a meal that night, but I didn't drink. There'd be a hard day's drive tomorrow, which was no place for a hangover. But I did have a shot of Jack Daniels to finish the meal, just to placate Spike. After all, I had several thousand dollars' worth of guns in the boot of the Trans-Am, and he hadn't even asked for a down payment.

I didn't ask him again about the chance that I wouldn't make it back. I didn't want to think about it.

Back at the hotel, Bel flaked out on the bed. I went for a walk, and ended up at the Buddy Holly statue. He held his guitar the way a marching man would hold his rifle. Well, almost. I'd settled up for our room, explaining that we'd be leaving at dawn and wouldn't require breakfast. I was glad now we'd booked into somewhere comfortable and clean, if utterly soulless. I didn't know how things would go from here on in.

I went to bed at 11.30, but didn't sleep. I lay there for an hour, ticking off the minutes and assuring myself that Bel was fast asleep. Then I got out of bed and went to the bathroom, where I'd left my clothes. We'd packed before dinner, and I picked my bags up on the way out of the room. I'd thought of leaving a note, but couldn't find the right words. Bel would know what was happening. She'd go to Spike's place. I'd phone her there in the evening.

Out in the car park, the streets were silent. I laid my bags on the ground and searched my pockets for the keys to the Trans-Am. I'd left them back in the room. I said a silent curse and hauled my bags back upstairs. We had a room key each, and I'd left mine at reception. Now I had to pick it up again and take the elevator to the third floor.

I left my bags in the corridor and let myself in. The keys had to be lying on the table next to the television, but I couldn't see them or feel them. Bel's breathing was still deep and regular.

'Looking for these?' a voice said.

I turned around. She was still lying with her head beneath the cover, but one arm was raised and she was waving the keys at me.

'I was just putting some stuff in the car,' I said.

'It can wait.'

'I couldn't sleep.'

'Liar. You were creeping off without me.' She pushed the keys back under her pillow. 'I'd've hated you forever if you'd done it. That's why I couldn't let you do it.'

'You'd be a lot safer here.'

'So would you.'

'Bel, it's not. . .'

'I *know* what it is, Michael.' She sat up in bed, drawing her knees up in front of her. 'And it's okay, I accept it. But I need to see those bastards blasted off the planet. I need to be there.'

I stood for a moment in the dark, trying to understand.

271

Then I brought my bags back in from the corridor and got undressed again.

I woke again at five. Bel woke up too. She didn't complain or say anything more about last night. She just got up and showered, then got dressed.

Before she dressed, she gave me a hug, her eyes squeezed tightly shut.

We stayed that way for a long time.

20

Robert Walkins had a house overlooking Chesapeake Bay, between Washington DC and Baltimore and not too far from Annapolis. It was finished in clapboard which had been given a recent coat of brilliant white paint. The picket fence around the house was white too. You couldn't see much of the place from the road. You had to get out of the car and walk around to what should be the back of the house. In fact, the back of the house was what looked on to the road. The *front* of the house, naturally enough, looked on to the bay. The downstairs seemed to be mostly workshop, garage, play room. A flight of stairs led up to a columned balcony, and that's where the front door was. The Stars and Stripes was fluttering from one of the columns. Hoffer blew his nose again before knocking on the door.

While he waited, he turned and looked out across the long narrow lawn which was broken only by a few mature trees as it swept down to the edge of the bay. He knew erosion was a problem for a lot of these waterfront homes. Each year the Bay crept a little closer to your door. There was some wood lying around, either driftwood or part of some scheme to ward off nature's encroachment. And past it, stretching out on to the Bay, was a plain wooden deck. The day was fine and Hoffer had to squint against the water's reflections as he peered towards the deck.

There was someone there, sitting on a chair with their feet up on a circular wooden table. They lifted a glass to their lips, then placed the glass down on a smaller table next to the chair. From this distance, Hoffer couldn't be sure, but he reckoned it had to be Walkins.

As he walked back down the stairs, he didn't know whether to be relieved or not. He didn't like sitting in Walkins's house. The place gave him the creeps, what with there being no photos of the daughter anywhere, and all those photos and paintings of the wife. So he should feel better, more comfortable, talking to Walkins in the fresh air. Only, he wasn't the outdoors type. He'd sat on Walkins's deck for a few hours one time, the salt wind whipping across him, and afterwards his skin had stung for days and his lungs had tried rejecting the smoke he sucked into them.

He crossed the lawn, slipping his jacket off and slinging it across one shoulder. He was nervous too. Well, meeting your sugar daddy face to face. It was bound to make you nervous.

'Sit down,' Walkins said, eschewing greetings. 'Drink?'

There was a bottle of J&B on the table, along with a bucket of ice and a spare glass. But Hoffer shook his head. He gave a half-yawn, trying to unblock his ears. The flight had done for him again. Goddamned flying.

'How was England?' Walkins asked.

'Like it had just lost the war.'

'We took vacations there occasionally. I liked the people.'

There wasn't much to say to this, so Hoffer stayed quiet. He noticed that Walkins was looking old these days. Maybe it was just that he looked bored: bored of doing nothing all day but waiting for Leo Hoffer to call with news.

'Is he here?' Walkins asked.

'Yeah, he's here.' Hoffer was lighting a cigarette. Walkins didn't mind him smoking out here, so long as he took the stubs home with him. Hoffer never did figure it; the whole of Chesapeake Bay for an ashtray, and he had to take his goddamned stubs home with him.

'How do you know?'

'I'm paid to know, sir.' Hoffer tried to get comfortable on the chair. The thick wooden slats didn't make things easy. 'I've got contacts: airlines, travel companies, the airports . . .'

'Yes?'

'They flew into Boston. That part was easy. The woman was travelling under her real name, Belinda Harrison. There probably wasn't time or opportunity enough for them to arrange a fake passport for her.'

'And him?' Walkins was nothing if not singleminded.

'Her travelling companion was called Michael Weston. That's the third name he's used so far this time. I've got a contact in the FBI, I've got him keeping eyes and ears open. If they get into bother, we'll hear about it.'

'Good.'

'Meantime, I've sent one of my team up to Boston to check hotels, car rental, that sort of thing.'

Hoffer was on auto-pilot. It gave him a chance to check out Walkins while he filled him in. Walkins had steel-grey hair and deep grooved lines in his face. He was a handsome man, ageing well despite his tragedies. But his eyes were filled to the brim with liquid, the pupils not quite fixed on the world outside. He took another drink of Scotch, but really the whisky was drinking *him*.

'This is a damned big country, Hoffer,' Walkins said at last. He sounded like he was boasting.

'Yes, sir,' Hoffer replied.

'A man could hide forever in a country this size.'

'Not if someone wants him found.'

'You believe that?'

'Yes, sir, I do.'

Walkins stared at him, so Hoffer daren't blink. He felt his eyes getting as watery as Walkins's. At last the old man pulled himself to his feet and walked to the rail at the end of the deck, leaning on it as he spoke.

'What now?'

'I've got a few leads,' Hoffer said, half-believing himself as he spoke.

275

'A few leads,' Walkins repeated, as though exhausted.

'You might be able to help, sir.'

'Oh? How?'

'Well, I presume you still have friends in positions of seniority?'

'What if I have?'

'Maybe one of them could play with a name. The name's Don Kline. He was in London, and interested in the D-Man. He told me he was agency, but I'm not sure he was. That's K-l-i-n-e.'

'I can ask around.'

The state Walkins was in, Hoffer doubted he'd recollect the name half an hour after Hoffer had driven away. He wrote it on the back of one of his cards and walked to the table, where he weighed it down with the lid from the ice bucket. Walkins was watching from the corner of his eye. He nodded towards Hoffer as Hoffer went back to his seat. Then he turned from the rail to face the detective, and took a good deep breath. Ah, at last, thought Hoffer: the floor-show.

'I want that bastard dead,' said Walkins, 'do you hear? I want his ass as cold as a mountaintop, and I want it delivered to me here.' The voice was growing louder, trembling with anger. Walkins started to move towards Hoffer. 'And I don't want a quick death either, it's got to be slow . . . slow like cancer, and burning like a fire inside. Do you understand?'

'Loud and clear.' It struck Hoffer, not for the first time, but now with absolute conviction, that Robert Walkins was howl-at-the-moon mad. There were white flecks at the edges of the old man's lips, and his face was all tics and wriggling demons.

'You've got it, sir,' Hoffer said, trying to calm things down. He was in the employ of a lunatic, but a lunatic who paid the bills and the rent. Besides, rich lunatics were never crazy . . . they were *eccentric*. Hoffer tried to remember that.

Finally, Walkins seemed to grow tired. He nodded a few times, reached out a hand and patted Hoffer's shoulder.

'Good, son, that's good.' Then he went and sat down again, poured himself another whisky, and dropped some ice into the glass. He sat back, sipped, and exhaled.

'Now,' he said, 'how will you do it?'

It took Hoffer a minute to answer. He was still trying to imagine himself as the Good Son.

21

No sightseeing now, just concentrated travel. North on Interstate 27 to Amarillo, then the 287. We were going to be travelling west back in time, from Mountain to Pacific. But we were heading nowhere but north to begin with. It was over 500 miles from Lubbock to Denver. We skirted the peaks to the west of Denver and crossed into Wyoming just south of Cheyenne.

'Tell me again,' said Bel. 'Why aren't we flying?'

'Air travel's easy to check if you're someone with the clout of a government agency. Also, it's easy for them to have airports covered, or car rental facilities at airports. This way, we're sort of sneaking up on them.'

She nodded, but didn't look convinced. I could have added that I needed time to think, time to plan, time this drive would give me. The thing was, I didn't know what we'd do in Seattle. I hadn't a clear plan of attack. I was praying something would come to me between here and there.

We'd covered over 600 miles by early evening. I'd been thinking about a lot of things. One of them was that it was crazy to arrive at our destination wiped out. Just off the interchange we found a motel. Or it found us. We just cruised into the first forecourt of many on the road and booked ourselves a room.

Standing up and walking were strange. My whole body tingled. In my head I was still in the car, still driving. I'd been on automatic for the past hour or so. My left arm was sunburnt from leaning on the driver-side sill. Bel had done her share of the driving too, seeming to understand the car better than I did, at least at first. We had our differences

278

about choice of music and choice of stops along the route, but otherwise hadn't said much really. Oh, at first we chattered away, but then we ran out of things to say. She bought a trashy novel in a service area and read that for a while, before tipping it out of the window on to the verge.

'I can't concentrate,' she explained. 'Every time I think I'm managing to block it out, I see it again . . . I see Max.'

She didn't have to say any more.

At the motel, we each took a bath. We phoned out and had a restaurant deliver ribs and apple pie. We stared at the TV. We drank Coke with lots of ice. And we slept. The beds were too soft, so I swapped mine for the floor. When I woke up in the night, Bel was lying beside me. I listened to her breathing and to the vibration of the traffic outside. Our room held a pale orange glow, like when my parents had left the landing light on and my bedroom door ajar. To keep away the monsters.

How come the monsters would only come at night? What were they, stupid?

In the morning, we ate at another diner. 'The coffee gets better out west,' I promised. But Bel took a proffered refill anyway.

We took I-80 west across the continental divide. This was high country, and there were tourists around, slowing us down sometimes. They travelled in state of the art vehicles which were like motor caravans only the length of a bus. And behind they usually towed the family car. They probably saw themselves as descendants of the pioneers, but they were just vacationers. It was hard not to get into conversation with them at stops along the route. But if we did, there were endless questions about Europe. One woman even insisted on capturing us on video. We tried to look lovey and huggy for the seeing-eye. It wasn't easy.

'Maybe drugs would help,' Bel suggested.

'Not in the long run. They'd keep us driving, but they

only mask the symptoms, they don't cure them. We'd end up hospital cases.'

'You've been there before?'

I nodded and she smiled. 'I keep forgetting how much more *worldly* than me you are, Michael.'

'Come on, let's see if we can fill up the cool box.'

We stopped outside Ogden on I-84. Another motel room, another long soak, another diner.

Bel rested her head on the table top. 'Remind me,' she said, 'which state are we in?'

'Utah, I think. But not for much longer. It'll be Idaho soon.' The waitress took our order.

'Are you all right?' she asked Bel.

'I'm fine, thanks, just tired.'

The waitress moved off. 'She thinks you're on drugs,' I told Bel.

'Only adrenaline.'

'This isn't the best way to see the country. Actually, that's a lie. This is the *only* way to see America. We'll do it properly one day, if you'd like to.'

'I'd love to, Michael.' She rested her head on the table again. 'Say, in a decade or two.'

'I once spent a week in a car going across the country. I slept in that car.'

'You must have felt like shit.'

I smiled at the memory. 'I felt very, very alive.'

'Well, I feel half-alive at best, but that's better than nothing.' She took a long drink of iced water. 'You know, if I hadn't gone off with you, I mean to London and Scotland . . .'

'I know,' I said.

'Christ, Michael, I'd be dead now.' There were tears in her eyes. She looked away, staring out of the window, and put her hand to her mouth. The hand was trembling. When I made to touch her, she jumped up from the table and ran outside.

I ran out to join her. Our diner was a truck stop. There was a vast tarmac parking area, with only a couple of trucks at its farthest edge. Stadium-style lights shone down on us from the lot's four corners. Our waitress was peering out of the diner window.

Bel was walking in a rough circle, eyes to the ground, and she was wailing. She flapped her arms to keep me away, so I took a few steps back and crouched down on the ground. The tarmac was warm to the touch. I sat there with my legs out in front of me, watching the exorcism with little pleasure.

She was saying things, sometimes yelling them. Curses, swear-words, imprecations. Finally she got to her father's name. When it came out, it was stretched to breaking point, like she was tearing it out of her system. She repeated it over and over, then had a coughing fit. The coughing became a dry retch, and she fell over on to her hands and knees. A huge lorry was pulling into the car park, air-brakes wheezing. The headlights picked out the figure of a crazy woman. The driver made sure to park at a good distance.

Eventually, when Bel was taking deep uneven breaths, I got up and walked over to her and crouched down again to put my arm around her.

'Buy you a coffee?' I said.

Next morning we crossed into Idaho. The state licence plates all had 'Famous Potatoes' written on them.

'Potatoes?' Bel said.

'Potatoes. These are a proud people.'

We were about 800 miles from Seattle. I thought we should get as close as we could then stop for another night, so we'd arrive fresh in the city. Bel wanted to push on. The road really had become her drug. She could hardly relax when we stopped. Even in the motel she fidgeted as she watched TV, her knees pumping. Her diet now comprised hamburgers and milk shakes. Her skin and hair had lost some vitality, and her eyes were dark. All my fault, I kept telling myself. She'd seemed better since last night though, a bit more together. Her voice was hoarse from shouting, and her eyes were red-rimmed. But I didn't think she was going to fall apart again. She seemed more confident, tougher . . . and she was ready to rock.

'No,' I told her, 'we'll stop somewhere, pamper ourselves, take a little time off.'

Problem was, where did you pamper yourself in the wasteland between Salt Lake City and Seattle? A detour to Portland wouldn't make sense. The answer started as a sort of joke. We decided to stop at a place called Pasco, for no other reasons than that it was a decent size and Bel's mother's maiden name had been Pascoe. But on the road into town, alongside all the other cheap anonymous motels, there was a Love Motel, with heart-shaped waterbeds, champagne, chocolates, adult movies . . . Our room was like a department store Santa's Grotto, done in red velvet and satin. There were black sheets on the bed and a single plastic rose on the pillow.

'It's like being inside a nosebleed,' Bel said, collapsing on to the bed. When it floated beneath her, she managed a laugh, her first in a while. But after a bottle of something that had never been within five hundred kilometres of Champagne, everything looked better. And lying on the bed, as Bel pointed out, was a bit like still being in the car. We didn't watch much of the porn flick, but we did take a bath together. It was a spa-bath, and Bel turned the jets up all the way. We started making love in the bath, but ended on the waterbed. We ended up so damp, I thought the bed had sprung a leak. I'd not known Bel so passionate, holding me hard against her like she was drowning. It was the kind of sex you have before dying or going off to war. Maybe we were about to do both.

We fell asleep without any dinner, woke up late and went to an all-night store where we bought provisions. We sat on the floor of our room and ate burger buns stuffed with slices of smoked ham, washed down with Coke. Then we made love again and drowsed till morning. We still had over 200 miles to go, and decisions to make along the way, such as whether it would be safer to stay in a motel out of town or a big hotel in the centre. It made sense to have a central base, but it also made sense not to get caught.

Snow-tipped Mount Rainier was visible in the distance as we took I-90 into the heart of Seattle.

There were things I wanted to tell Bel. I wanted to tell her why I hadn't cried over Max's death. I wanted to tell her why I didn't do what she had done out on that parking lot. I wanted to tell her about bottling things up until you were ready for them. When I met Kline again, the bottle would smash wide open. But somehow I didn't find the words. Besides, I couldn't see how they would help.

It was another hot dry day, and the traffic was slow, but no one seemed to mind too much. They were just happy to be here and not in some other more congested city. The placement and layout of Seattle are quite unique. From the east, we crossed on to Mercer Island and off it again on to the narrow stretch of land which housed the city itself, squeezed between Lake Washington and Puget Sound. We came off the Interstate into the heart of the downtown grid system, Avenues running north to south, Streets east to west. Last time I'd been here, I'd taken a cab from Sea Tac, which took you through a seemingly unending hinterland of sleazy motels, bars, and strip joints advertising '49 Beautiful Women ... and One Ugly One'. This was a much better route. There were a few prominent hotels, all outposts of known chains catering mostly to business travellers. The first one we tried had a vacancy, so we took it. It was a relief to garage the car and take our bags up, knowing we now had a base. We'd decided to stay central, since it would cut down travelling time. We checked in as Mr and Mrs West, since we'd bought pawnstore rings. Bel flicked through the city information pack while I made a phone call.

I spoke to someone on the news desk.

'Can I speak to Sam Clancy, please.'

'He's on a sabbatical.'

'That's not what I've read. Look, can you get a message to him?'

There was a pause. 'It's possible.'

'My name's Mike West and I'm staying in a hotel downtown. I'd like Sam to contact me. It looks like we've been following a similar line of inquiry, only I've been working in Scotland, near Oban.' I waited while he took down the details. 'That's O-b-a-n. Tell him Oban, he'll understand.'

'Are you a journalist?'

'In a way, yes.' I gave him our room number and the telephone number of the hotel. 'When can I expect him to get this message?'

'He calls in sometimes, but there's no routine. Could take a few days.'

'Sooner would be better. All I'm doing here is pacing the floor.'

He said he'd do what he could, and I put the phone down. Bel was still studying the information pack.

'I'll tell you what you do in Seattle,' I said. 'You go up the Space Needle on a clear day, you visit Pike Place Market any day, and you wander around Pioneer Square.'

'Michael, when you were here before . . . was it business?'

'Strictly pleasure,' I said.

'What sort of pleasure?' She wasn't looking at me as she spoke.

'Whale-watching,' I said. Now she looked at me.

'Whale-watching?'

'I took a boat up to Vancouver Island and went whale-watching.'

She laughed and shook her head.

'What's wrong with that?'

'Nothing, it's just ... I don't know. I mean, you're so *normal* in a lot of ways.'

'You mean for a hired killer?'

She had stopped laughing now. 'Yes, I suppose I do.'

'I'm still a killer, Bel. It's what I do best.'

'I know. But after this is over ...'

'We'll see.'

The phone rang, and I picked it up. It was Sam Clancy.

'That was quick,' I said.

'I have to be careful, Mr West. The desk downstairs tells me you only checked in twenty minutes ago.'

'That's right.'

'You're not losing any time.'

'I don't think either of us can afford to.'

'So tell me your story.'

He didn't sound far away at all. He had a soft cultivated accent, which just failed to hide something more nasal and demanding, a New York childhood perhaps. I told him my story, missing out a few details such as my profession and my true involvement in the whole thing. I said I was a journalist, investigating the murder of one of my colleagues. I told him about Max's death, and how the gun dealer's daughter was with me in Seattle. I told him about the Americans we'd met on the road out of Oban, just after a visit to the Disciples of Love. I probably talked for twenty or thirty minutes, and he didn't interrupt me once.

'So what's your story?' I said.

'I think you already know most of it. There have been two attempts on my life, neither of them taken very seriously by the police. They couldn't find any evidence that someone had tampered with my car brakes, but I found a mechanic who showed me how it could be done without leaving any trace. Never buy an Oldsmobile, Mike. Anyway, since Seattle's finest weren't going to do anything about it, I thought I would. Then the paper ran my story, and that merely confirmed for the police that I was seeking publicity, nothing more.'

'You think the Disciples were responsible?'

'Well, I asked my ex-wife and it wasn't her. That doesn't leave too many enemies. Jesus, it's not like I wrote *The Satanic Verses* or anything, all I was doing was asking questions.'

'About funding?'

'That's right.'

'What did you find?'

'I'm still finding. It's just not so easy when I have to walk everywhere with my head in a blanket.'

'I could help you.'

'I've got people helping me.'

'At your newspaper?'

'No names, Mike. I still don't know that I can trust you.'

'Could we meet? I want to talk about the Disciples.'

'I don't know . . . Do you have any proof you could give me? I mean proof of anything you've said, of who you are?'

I thought about this. The answer was, no. 'I think you'd find the murdered man's daughter proof enough, Sam.'

He sighed. 'Is she there with you?'

'She's right here.'

'Put her on.'

I passed the phone to Bel. 'He needs convincing we're genuine.'

'Mr Clancy?' said Bel. 'You've got to help us. If you saw what they did to my father. I mean, they didn't just kill him, that wasn't enough for them. I want them caught . . . whatever it takes. With you or without you, we're going after them.' She handed me the receiver.

'All right,' said Clancy, 'let's have dinner.'

'Where?'

'There's a little Mexican place near Green Lake. Do you know where that is?'

'I can find it.' He gave me the name and address of the

restaurant. We agreed eight o'clock, and the call ended there.

'Sounds promising,' I told Bel, giving her a kiss. 'Is there a street map in that pile of stuff?'

'Only a downtown one.'

'Then let's go do some shopping.'

It's very hard to get lost in American cities, so long as you stick to the grid system. You'll nearly always find the right road, though you may then have trouble finding the right building, since there doesn't always seem to be much sense to the way street numbers run.

That evening, we got on to Aurora and followed it for miles. I don't think Bel had ever seen a street so long, and when we came off at Green Lake, Aurora still had a long way to run. Green Lake was busy with joggers and walkers, skateboarders and roller-skaters, and people just enjoying the air.

We'd had a good afternoon, walking the streets, sitting in coffee shops, making new friends. As I'd promised Bel, the coffee here was definitely a class above the stuff they doled out in diners. She'd already had three cups of Starbuck's, and the caffeine was showing. Every café we sat in, when people heard our accents they wanted to talk to us. So we learned a bit more about the city. Ballard was the district where the descendants of the Norsemen lived. The streets east of the Kingdome were to be avoided. The Mariners were having another lousy season, and were now owned by Nintendo. We'd missed the annual Folklife Festival. There was a drought. A couple of local micro-breweries were producing excellent dark beers ... Some of this I already knew, but some of it was new to me, and I appreciated all the information I could get. Jeremiah Provost, after all, was on home ground. It was important to know as much about the city as he did. That way, we'd be less likely to fall into any traps.

So far, Seattle had looked distinctly free from traps. I showed Bel Pike Place Market, pointed out the bicycle cops in Pioneer Square, and steered her around the street people and panhandlers milling around the streets near the waterfront. The pawnshops were doing good business in Seattle. They had guns and guitars in their windows, but I didn't stop to look. I wasn't carrying a gun with me, but when we headed off for dinner with Sam Clancy, I hid the pistol under the Trans-Am's front seat.

The car was sounding ropey. It needed another tune, oil change, and maybe a new exhaust. Probably it also needed a complete rest. We'd pushed it hard, and it had served us well, but we needed it healthy for a while longer.

We'd overestimated the weight of traffic and were early at the restaurant, so we parked the car and walked back down to the lake. Bel pulled off her cowboy boots to walk barefoot on the grass. She looked okay, not tired or stressed out. She was keen for something to happen, for some showdown to arrive, but she managed not to look too impatient.

By the time we got back to the restaurant she declared herself ready for a drink. There was still no sign of Clancy, but a table had been reserved in the name of West, so we took it. It was laid out for three diners. The waiter asked if we wanted a margarita while we waited. Bel nodded that we did.

'Large or small?'

'Large,' she stated, before ploughing through the menu. 'What's the difference between all these things?' she asked me. 'Tacos, burritos, fajitas, tortillas . . . ?'

'Ask the waiter.'

But instead she took her very large margarita from him and ran her finger around the rim.

'It's salt,' I said.

'I knew that.' Having wiped a portion of the rim clean, she sipped, considered, then took another sip.

There was a man at the front of the restaurant. He'd been

studying the takeaway menu when we'd come in, and he was still studying it. I got up from the table and walked over to him.

'Why don't you join us?' I said.

He tried to look puzzled, then gave up and smiled. 'Have you known all the time?'

'More or less.'

I led him to the table. Sam Clancy was tall and thin with a cadaverous face and sunken eyes. He was in his late 20s or early 30s, with thinning brown hair combed across his forehead. From his voice, I'd imagined he'd be older. He took Bel's hand before sitting down. The waiter arrived, and Clancy nodded towards her drink.

'Looks good,' he said. The waiter nodded and moved off. 'So, I guess I wouldn't make a career working undercover, huh? Do you want some introductory conversation, or shall we get down to work?'

'Let's consider ourselves introduced,' said Bel.

'Right. So, you want to know what I know. Well, here goes. Jeremiah Provost takes a bit of a back seat these days as far as the day-to-day running of the Disciples is concerned. You know a bit about his background?'

'Rich family,' I said, 'bad college professor.'

'That's not a bad precis. Also completely mad. He's been in and out of expensive clinics. No sign that he does heavy drugs or booze, so there has to be some other reason, like pure mental instability.'

'So if he's in the back seat,' asked Bel, 'who's behind the wheel?'

'On the business side, a man called Nathan. I don't even know if that's his first or second name, he's just called Nathan. You know a couple of reporters got hit on by the Disciples? That was Nathan. He didn't like them, so he whacked them.'

'He's a bit handy then?' I said.

'He's a tough mother. Then there's Alisha, she's an earth

mother type with just a streak of junta. She runs the people, makes them do what needs to be done.'

'And this is all out on the Olympic Peninsula?'

Clancy nodded. 'The most beautiful spot on the continent. But Provost isn't there much. He's taken on a Howard Hughes existence in a brand new house up on Queen Anne Hill. Terrific view on to downtown, a few thousand square feet and a swimming pool. Rumour has it Kiefer Sutherland wanted to rent the place when he was here filming *The Vanishing*. Anyway, that's where Provost spends his time, surrounded by phones and fax machines and computers, so he can keep in touch with his minions overseas.'

'There was a fax machine in Oban,' I recalled, 'it had at least two Washington State numbers on its memory.'

'Olympic Peninsula and Queen Anne,' Clancy stated with authority.

'Have you ever spoken to Provost?' Bel asked him.

'I've tried, but he's ringed with steel.'

'But who runs the show really, him or his lieutenants?'

'Now that's a good question.'

Clancy broke off so we could order. Bel took his advice when her turn came, and we ordered another round of drinks to go with the meal. Some tortilla chips and dips had been placed on the table, so we munched as we spoke.

'The men who killed my father,' said Bel, 'if they were the same men who stopped us on the road out of Oban, then they were Americans.'

'They didn't look like cult members though,' I told Clancy. 'They seemed more like government types.'

'Which brings me to my research,' Clancy said, beginning to enjoy himself. 'You know that the Disciples suddenly took off late in 1985? I mean, they started buying land and real estate. Which means Provost had money to spend. Where did it come from? Nobody knows. Did a bunch of rich relatives suddenly and conveniently die? No. Did he win some state lottery? No. A lucky week at Vegas? Uh-uh. It's been driving people nuts, wondering where that money suddenly came from.'

'You've found out?' Bel asked.

'Not exactly, not yet. But I think I was getting close.' So maybe Eleanor Ricks had been getting close too. 'I do know this.' Clancy made a melodramatic point, glancing around the restaurant then leaning forward across the table. I wondered if he could always differentiate between gossip and fact. 'Provost went to Washington DC. Please, don't ask how I know this. I have sources to protect and my . . . uh, techniques weren't always strictly legit. He was in DC for a meeting with some lawyers and other fat cats. But while he was there he had a couple of visitors, two men called Elyot and Kline. They visited him on more than one occasion. This was in January 1986, a few months after Provost started spending.

'Now, I think I've tracked down who Elyot and Kline were and are. There's an agent called Richard Elyot works for the CIA. And at the NSC there used to be a cat called Kline.'

'Used to be?'

'He resigned officially in 1986. Since then he's been on the fringes, only his name's not on the books any longer. Nobody knows why he resigned, whether he was forced out or what. I'm going to describe Kline to you.'

He did. I nodded halfway through and continued nodding. 'Sounds familiar,' I conceded.

'The guy in the rear car, right?' Clancy surmised.

'Right,' I confirmed. 'What about Elyot?'

'Elyot's posted in some overseas embassy just now, not a very prestigious one. He's been getting shitty assignments for about the past five years. I even hear that he was in the US consulate in Scotland for a couple of months.'

'Interesting.'

'It's *all* interesting,' said Bel, finishing her second margarita. 'But where does it get us?'

'The Disciples,' Clancy said, 'are somehow connected to

291

the CIA and the NSC. How come? What could they possibly have in common?'

'And whatever it is,' I added, 'does it add up to Provost being in their pay?'

'Absolutely,' said Clancy, sitting back.

'I wouldn't mind a word with Jeremiah Provost.'

Clancy laughed. 'Get in line, fella.'

'Michael has ways,' Bel said quietly, staring at me.

'Oh, yeah?' Clancy was interested.

'But his techniques,' she went on, 'aren't *ever* strictly legit.'

Clancy looked more interested. 'Bel,' I said, 'it's been a long day.'

'A long day's journey,' she agreed.

'Maybe we should get the bill?'

She didn't say no. I asked Clancy how he wanted to play it. He shrugged, so I made a couple of suggestions. We agreed he'd meet us at our hotel in the morning. I settled the bill with cash. On the back of the check there was a little form asking for comments. We'd seen them before in diners. Bel had filled one of them in. She'd put, 'Service overfriendly, food big but tasteless, have a nice day.' This time she got a pen from Clancy and wrote: 'I love tequila.'

At the bottom she drew a little heart, broken into halves.

22

We met Clancy next morning in the hotel lobby. His first words were, 'I made a few calls to England. Nobody I spoke to has heard of you.'

'Michael does magazine work,' Bel said. 'Let's go get some coffee.' We ordered three *caffè lattes* at a nearby coffee shop and sat at a table inside, even though the proprietor assured us we'd be better off sitting at one of the sidewalk tables. We had a view across the street to the Seattle Art Museum. Clancy just called it 'Sam'.

'There's a porno theatre one block down,' he said. 'It used to advertise Sam exhibitions on its awning. Only in Seattle, friends.'

He told us that Seattle's main industries were Boeing, fish processing and Microsoft, and that things at Boeing were extremely shaky just now. 'We used to be world leaders in grunge music. You know what that is? Torn jeans, drug habits and sneers.'

'Didn't Keith Richards patent that?'

Clancy laughed and looked at his watch. I knew he didn't altogether trust us yet, and I didn't like it that he'd been asking about us in London. Word there could get to anyone. 'Come on,' he said, 'time to rock 'n' roll.'

We took the Trans-Am to a mechanic Clancy knew near the U-Dub. 'He's a Christian mechanic,' Clancy said. 'Every job he does comes with a blessing and a guarantee from above.'

The man was young, stocky and bearded. He reminded me of the Amish. He said the car would take a day or so, and meantime we could have a VW Rabbit. It was a small brown

293

car, perfect for the trip we were about to make. There was a plastic litterbag hanging from the dashboard. It had Uncle Sam's hat on one side, and the Pledge of Allegiance on the other. I took my bag from the Trans-Am and locked it in the boot of the Rabbit. Nobody asked what was in it, and I wouldn't have answered if they had.

Bel sat in the back of the car, and I let Clancy drive. We drove south on Aurora into Queen Anne Hill. This was a prime residential area, mostly bungalow-style housing. A precious few lots sat on the very edge of the hill, looking down on to the city. This was where Jeremiah Provost had his house.

It was big, even by the standards of the area, and it was on an incline so steep it made you giddy.

'I wouldn't fancy walking back from the shops,' Bel said.

Clancy looked at her. 'Walk? Nobody walks, Bel. Nobody ever walks.'

We parked across the road from Provost's house. Even with the handbrake on and the car left in gear, I wasn't sure I trusted the Rabbit not to start careering downhill. We all wore sunglasses, and as further disguise Clancy was wearing a red baseball cap. There was a sheen of nervous sweat on his face. We knew we were taking a big risk coming here. But the time had come to take risks. We were parked outside a house with its own turret. We couldn't see much of Provost's house though. Steps led up through a bristling garden to a white concrete wall, showing no windows or doors.

'There's only one entrance,' said Clancy, 'round the side of the house. There are French windows leading on to the pool and patio, so I suppose that makes it two entrances really.'

'And two exits,' I added. 'Where are the security cameras?'

He looked at me, perhaps wondering how I knew. 'Just as you round the corner.'

'Is there an infra-red trip?'

'I don't know, could be.'

'It's just that on the surface, there looks like there's no security at all. So I take it what security there is is high-tech.'

'Sure, plus the muscle-man on the door.'

'Just the one?'

'Hey, Provost's a religious nut, not a Middle East guerrilla.'

'What about at night? He's got approach lights?'

'Yeah, if a hedgehog so much as inspects the lawn, the place lights up like the Fourth of July.' Clancy was still looking at me. 'You're asking all the right questions, only I'm not sure they're questions a reporter would think to ask.'

'I'm not your everyday reporter,' I said. 'He spends most of his time in there?'

'Yeah. There's a house out on Hood Canal belongs to Nathan. That's hot real estate too. Sometimes Provost goes there for the weekend. He doesn't do much, digs clams, picks oysters at low tide. Mr Microsoft has a compound a few houses down.'

'How much do you know about Nathan?'

'Not much. I got a name and a face.'

'When did he join the Disciples?'

'I don't know. The problem is, only having one of his names, I can't even begin to do a trace back.'

'He handles the business, does that mean the money?'

'Yeah, there's an accountant too, but Nathan does the day to day balance sheet. Thing is, there's very little on the profit side. Very little income compared to the outgoings.'

'Maybe we should talk to Nathan rather than Provost.'

'He's no easier to get to, Mike. And he wears this look like he's just waiting to break someone's face open. These cults, they're always suspicious. I mean, someone comes sniffing around them for a story, chances are it isn't going to be a panegyric.'

I looked out at Provost's house. 'Can we see it from another angle?'

'Yeah, if you walk downhill and take a left. But frankly, you won't see much more than you can from here. More concrete and the top of a window, that's about it. It's a smart design, completely open but totally private. He doesn't even have a fence, but he could be filming hard-core in his pool and none of the neighbours would know.'

'Some of these cult leaders like to initiate new recruits,' said Bel, who'd done her reading.

Clancy shrugged. 'I don't know if Provost shafts the women in the cult. I mean, with a name like Disciples of Love, and starting off where it did and how it did, it's got to be a good bet. But he's never gone public on humping politics.'

'That sounds like a quote from one of your own stories.'

He grinned. 'It is, only the paper spiked it as defamatory.'

'Okay,' I said, 'I've seen enough. Let's go buy what we need.'

The shop we wanted was on Aurora, way north of Green Lake. It was called Ed's Guns and Sporting Goods and was run by a man named Archie with a trace of a Scots accent. I knew pretty much what we needed: camouflage jackets, overtrousers, boots, a couple of tents, a small stove and pot, plates, mugs and cutlery, binoculars, and a couple of rucksacks to put everything in.

The binoculars he showed me were small but powerful. 'Bird watchers love them,' he said, like this was a recommendation.

I handed them back. 'Got anything with a night vision facility?'

'You're talking major expense.'

'So let me talk.'

He went off to find a night-scope. Bel was picking out thick socks to go with her boots. 'We want to look like tourists, right?'

'Right.'

'Then we'd probably have too much gear, all of it brand new.'

'Right again.'

'So I want some new sunglasses.' I nodded and she went to choose some. Meantime I picked out a compass, and studied a few of the available knives. The survival knives looked good. There was one with a hollow handle, inside which were fishing-line, hooks and a needle, a tiny compass, stuff like that. Another was so versatile you could turn it from knife into axe or shovel or even a torch. It was big too. I reckoned it was big enough to scare most people.

'I'll take that,' I said, pointing it out to Archie, who had come back with a plain cardboard box. He was licking his lips, excited at the total sale but nervous about the ease with which we were spending money. Maybe he thought we were going to pull a gun or even one of his own combat knives on him. Instead I pulled out a wad of cash and waved it in his face. He nodded and relaxed a little.

I checked the night-scope. It was perfect. I could use it like a telescope or, with a couple of adjustments, fit it to my sniping rifle.

'How discreet are you, Archie?' I asked.

'That depends.'

'Well, I want to buy all this, and I want to pay cash. But I've a job I'd like to do. Do you have a workshop back there?' He nodded. 'Could I borrow it for, say, fifteen minutes?'

He shrugged. 'You buy that lot, you can bunk in the back for all I care.'

'That won't be necessary.'

Bel was asking Archie about maps when I left the shop. She'd slid a survival knife into the top of her right boot to see how it felt. Clancy stared at the knife for a moment, then followed me out. Clancy wasn't a country boy or a born-again backwoodsman. Seattle still had something of the frontier town about it, but he was strictly *latte* and art museum. He told us the only times he'd been out to the Olympic Peninsula had been to visit the hot springs resort. He'd driven past the Disciples' compound, but only on day trips, and he'd hardly budged from the car.

But a lot of the Olympic Peninsula was wilderness, mountains and first-growth temperate rainforest. I knew there was no such thing as being underprepared. Clancy stood watching as I unlocked the boot and lifted out my bag.

'Come on, Mike, who the fuck are you, man? You're security, right? I mean, a secret agent or something. Reporters I know, they wouldn't have the expenses to claim for that hotel you're staying in, never mind leaving the room empty for a night. Even if they *could* claim it, they'd stay someplace ratty and cream the cash. And they'd never *ever* have so much cash on them. Strictly plastic, and a receipt every time you spend.'

I locked the boot. 'So I'm not a journalist. All you have to know is, if you stick around I'll give you a story. This is better for you, Sam. See, I don't represent any competition. It's your exclusive.'

He was shaking his head. 'I'm not going.'

'Sam, we don't need you any more. You want to stay here, fine. Maybe it'll take us an hour or two longer to find the compound. But we'll find it. I'm not going to beg you to come with us.'

'I could blow you wide open, man. All it would take is a call to Provost.'

I smiled. 'We're not your enemies, Sam. Why would you do that?'

He thought about this. 'I wouldn't do it. Forget I said it.' He followed me into the shop. Bel was trying on a red and black check lumberjacket. Archie gestured for me to follow him. Sam was still on my tail. We entered a back room full of equipment and work benches. There was even a metal-turning lathe. And there were bits and pieces from gun-cleaning kits. I put the bag down on a bench and unzipped it.

'I just want to know,' Sam was saying. 'See, people have been trying to kill me, and I can't afford not to be choosy about my friends. Someone comes up to me with a chickenshit story about being a journalist, and it turns out he's not, then I've got to wonder what he really is.'

The words died in his throat as he saw the Varmint being unwrapped, then the pistol and finally the Colt Commando.

'Sweet Lord Jesus,' he said quietly. I started seeing if I could fit the night-scope to the Varmint.

'Sam,' I said, not looking up, 'you're safe with us.'

'I hear that.'

'I'm a friend of Bel's. I was a friend of her father's. He sold me guns from time to time. I saw what those bastards did to him, and I intend finding out just why they did it. That's the whole story, except for one thing.' Now I looked at him. 'I don't care what it takes.'

His mouth was suddenly dry. There was an open can of beer on the bench, and he took a swig from it.

'Why don't you go get us a pack of those things from the grocery?' I suggested. 'Think things out while you're there. If you want out, we'll get your camera from the car and you can catch a cab back into town.' I made to hand him some money.

'I don't need your money, Mike. I can stretch to a few beers.'

'Okay then.'

And he was gone. Archie put his head round the door.

'Sorry to interrupt, but that lady out there is going to put you in the poorhouse.'

'We'll be the best dressed paupers there.'

He laughed. This was turning into a more interesting day

299

than usual for him. He looked at what I was doing. 'Nice gun. Give you some help there?'

'I might just need it. The receiver and the sight-mounting are all wrong.'

'Well, let me take a look. No extra charge.'

'It's all yours, Archie.'

It took us a little while, but Archie had a few bits and pieces in the back, and one of them seemed to be what we needed. It made the gun look like something from *Man from UNCLE*, but it seemed okay.

'I never ask customers what they're planning to shoot,' said Archie.

'Maybe an animal or two,' I said.

'Yeah, maybe, but that other gun you've got there, that's strictly terror.'

I grinned. 'I hope so, Archie. I really do.'

When we went back out front, there were no new customers and Clancy hadn't come back.

'Where's the nearest place to buy beer?' I asked.

'There's a grocery on the corner,' Archie answered. I nodded to myself. It looked like Clancy had just walked away.

'Better start adding this lot up, Archie.'

'And then maybe I better close for the day for restocking.' He got to work on his calculator.

Bel was back in her ordinary clothes. She hadn't worn anything on her feet but the cowboy boots since she'd bought them. 'Where's Sam?' she said.

'I think we're on our own.'

'He didn't even say goodbye. Will he tell anyone?'

'I doubt it.'

'What did you say to him?'

'I admitted I wasn't a reporter.'

'Did he see the guns?' I nodded. 'No wonder he ran. They have that effect on me, too.'

Archie had paused in his addition so he could fill a few carrier bags with goods already totted up.

'Just put them straight in the rucksacks, Archie, we'll sort them out later.'

I added another torch to the total.

'Listen,' he said, 'I know you may not need it, but I'm giving you a first aid kit and some mosquito repellent. Plus all my cash customers receive a ten percent discount.'

'Thanks.' I turned back to Bel.

'So we're going on our own?' she said.

'I suppose so. I think we can find the ferry terminal, don't you?'

'We can also save some money.'

'How's that?'

'We don't need two tents now, and one big sleeping bag would do us.'

'You've got a point.' But just then the door opened and Clancy staggered in. I thought he was hurt, and moved forward, but he was only staggering under the weight of the shopping bags he carried.

'A few provisions for the trip,' he said, putting down the bags. 'Beer, potato chips, tinned chilli, tuna, franks, and beans.' He put his hand into one bag. 'Look, I even packed the tin opener.'

We all laughed except Archie, who was too busy on his calculator. When he'd finished, it was his turn to laugh. I counted out the money, and Clancy snatched the receipt.

'If you can't claim, maybe I can.'

'Then you can pay for the boat tickets,' I said, hoisting a rucksack on to my shoulder.

'It's a deal.'

The ferry was busy with families heading off on holidays.

'Where are they all going?' I asked Clancy.

'The same place as us,' he said. 'The Olympic Peninsula's popular this time of year.'

'I thought it was wilderness.'

'Mostly it is. The folks you see here probably won't get more than a couple of hundred yards from their vehicles all the time they're away. There's a highway circuits the Peninsula, but almost no roads at all in the National Park itself. Here, I brought a map.'

It was the map the National Park Service handed out to visitors. As Clancy had said, there were almost no roads inside the park, just a lot of trails and a few unpaved tracks. The one good road I could see led to the summit of Hurricane Ridge. We were headed west of there, to Lake Crescent. Clancy pointed it out on the map. Outside the National Park boundaries, the rest of the peninsula was considered National Forest. The National Park ended just north of Lake Crescent.

'See, what Provost did, he took over a house that was already there. They're very cautious about new building inside the park, but there's nothing they can do about homes that were there before the area was designated a National Park. He didn't have too much trouble getting permission to add a few log cabins of the same style. He even had the timber treated so it looked weathered.'

'I bet he's kind to dumb animals too.'

We were part of a slow-moving stream coming off the ferry. There were backpackers trying to hitch a ride with anyone who'd take them. Bel smiled at them and shrugged her shoulders. Everybody took the same road out of Bremerton along the southern shore of Hood Canal. There were no stopping places, other than pulling into someone's drive, so Clancy just pointed out Nathan's house to us as we passed. It had a low front hedge, a large neatly cut lawn, and was itself low and rectangular, almost like a scale model rather than a real house, such was its perfection. Beyond it we could see the canal itself, in reality an inlet carved into the land like a reverse J. We kept along Hood Canal for a long time, then headed west towards Port Angeles.

'From what I've heard,' said Clancy, 'as well as what I've seen today, I think our first priority should be to find a campsite.'

He was right. Fairholm was the closest campsite to the Disciples' headquarters, but by the time we got there it was already full. We retraced our route and called in at Lake Crescent Lodge, but it was fully booked. So then we'd to head north towards the coast where, at Lyre River, we found a campground with spaces. It was less than a mile from the Strait of Juan de Fuca, beyond which lay Vancouver Island, Canadian soil. The air was incredible, intoxicating and vibrant. You felt nobody'd ever breathed it before. It wasn't city air, that was for sure.

Clancy had been telling us that there was bad feeling in the Pacific north west about logging. A lot of loggers were losing their jobs, a lot of logging towns were going broke. They'd asked if they could go into the National Forest and 'tidy up' fallen trees, but this request had been rejected. There were other forests they couldn't touch because of a protected species of owl. They were getting desperate.

'One man's paradise . . .' I said.

At the campground, there was a box full of envelopes. We put our fee in the envelope and pushed it through the posting slot. Then we stuck our receipt in a little display case on a post next to our own little site.

'Isn't this cosy?' I said. Bel looked dubious. She'd been sleeping in too many real beds recently to relish a night under the stars. It was about fifteen miles from here to the Disciples' HQ, so we pitched our tents. Or rather, Clancy and I pitched the tents while Bel walked by the river and chatted to a few other campers. Then, happy with the state of our accommodations, we got back in the car and headed off. We were on the wrong side of Lake Crescent, as we soon found. No road went all the way around the lake. The main road went round the south, and to the north it was half unpaved road and half trail. We were the trail end, which meant we

303

couldn't take the car anywhere near the Disciples without going all the way around the lake and heading in towards them from the west along the unpaved road. We took the car to the trail-head past Piedmont and got out to think. It looked like it was about a three-mile walk. Driving around the lake might save a mile of walking.

'Well,' I said, 'we might as well get our money's worth from all this gear we've brought.'

So we got ourselves made up to look like hikers, Clancy carrying the only rucksack we'd need, and I locked the car.

'You're not carrying heat?' he inquired.

'You've been watching too many gangster flicks.'

'But are you or aren't you?'

'No.'

'Good.'

We walked for about half a mile, till Bel suddenly stopped. I asked what was wrong. She was looking all around her.

'This,' she said, 'is the most beautiful place I've ever been. Listen: nothing. Look, not a soul around.'

She'd barely got these words out when a party of three walkers emerged on the trail ahead of us. They nodded a greeting as they passed. They hadn't spoilt things at all for Bel. She looked the way I'd seen girls in my youth when they were stoned at parties. She was an unfocused, all-encompassing smile.

'It's the lack of toxins in the atmosphere,' Clancy explained. 'If your system isn't used to it, weird things start to happen.'

We walked on, and she caught us up. Clancy had the map.

'There's a picnic area at North Shore,' he said, 'but we'll see the cabins before that. They're between this trail and the one leading up Pyramid Mountain.'

We came upon them sooner than expected. It was a bit like the set-up at Oban, but a lot less obtrusive. No signs or fences or barriers, except that the very existence of the cabins, here where there should be nothing, was a barrier in itself. I couldn't see the Disciples getting many casual visitors.

'So what do we do now?' Bel said.

'We keep walking,' I told her. 'We're just out for a hike. We'll soon be at North Shore. We'll have our picnic and we'll talk. Just now, we're walking.'

But from the corner of my eye I was taking in the cabins, the small vegetable plot, the boat on its trailer. I couldn't see any signs of life, and no cars, no pick-ups or vans. No smoke, but then the cabins didn't have chimneys, with the exception of what I took to be the original structure, slightly larger than the others. Instead, there were solar panels on the roofs, and a couple more on the ground. There was plenty of tree and bush cover around the cabins, and no sign of any pets. I wasn't even sure you were allowed to keep pets inside the park.

There were boats out on Lake Crescent. They looked like they'd come from Lake Crescent Lodge. I could see fathers wrestling with the oars while spouses caught the antics on video and the children rocked the boat further to discomfit 'pop'. We sat down at the picnic site and gazed out over the lake.

'It is beautiful,' said Bel.

'Almost as pretty as a baseball game,' Clancy agreed. Bel ignored him.

'So that was it?' I said.

'That was it.'

'I was expecting more.'

'The Disciples are small-time, Mike. I could show you a dozen cults bigger than them in the US, including the cult of the Sainted Elvis. They're not big, they're just rich and obsessed with their privacy.'

Bel turned away from the view. She had been bitten already, and sprayed more gunk on her bare arms. I'd bought a dark blue baseball cap at Archie's, and was now glad of it. The sun beat down with a sizzling intensity. Clancy opened the cooler and handed out beers.

'So now we go and knock at their door,' said Bel, 'ask them what the hell they were doing murdering my father?'

'Maybe not straight away,' I cautioned.

'But I thought that was the whole point?'

'The point is to play safe. Sam, have you ever heard of anyone leaving the Disciples?'

He shook his head and sucked foam from the can. 'That was my first line of inquiry. If you'd been a real reporter, it's about the first thing you'd've asked me. I was desperate to find someone with inside info, but I never found a soul.'

'Ever talk to any existing members?'

'Oh, yes, lots of times. I'd strike up conversations with them when they went into Port Angeles for supplies. I have to tell you, those were very one-sided conversations. Hamlet's soliloquies were shorter than mine. I got snippets, nothing more.'

Bel was sorting out the food. We had ham, crackers, cold sausage and potato chips.

'Bel,' I said, 'how's your acting?'

'I think I played a policewoman pretty well.'

'How about playing a very stupid person?'

She shrugged. 'It'd be a challenge. What sort of stupid person did you have in mind?'

'One who's on vacation and has gone for a walk on her own. And she comes across these cabins and thinks they must be a restaurant or something, maybe a ranger station or some souvenir shops.'

Clancy was looking at me. 'You're crazy.'

Bel opened a packet of chips. 'Are you saying, Michael, that I'd be going in there on my own?'

'That's what I'm saying.'

'Why?'

'I think they'd suspect you less if you were on your own.'

'Yes, but why do I need to go there at all?'

'Reconnaissance. I want you to learn as much as you can about the lay-out, memorise it. Are there locks on the doors and windows? Are there any alarms or other security precautions that you can see? Any skylights, loopholes, chinks in the armour?'

'You're thinking of paying a night-time visit?'

I smiled at her and nodded. She wasn't fazed at all by my intention. She just ate some crisps and thought about it.

'I'd have to go into the cabins,' she said at last.

I shook my head. 'Just the one, the main cabin. That's the one I want to know about.'

'You're both crazy,' Clancy said, gripping his beer with both hands.

Bel finished her crisps and stood up, wiping her hands on her legs. 'I need a pee,' she said. 'I'll see you back at the trail-head.'

'We'll be waiting.'

I watched her walk away. I'd promised Max she wouldn't be in any danger. I'd been breaking that promise time and time again.

'She's got guts,' Clancy admitted.

I nodded but didn't say anything. Clancy couldn't get a word out of me the rest of the makeshift meal.

We walked back along the trail quite slowly, nodding to people who passed us. Again, we didn't look at the cabins as we passed within a hundred yards of them. They were built on a fairly serious slope. Slopes and night-walking did not make good companions. But if I stuck to the path by the lake, there'd be more chance of being spotted. I had a lot on my mind as we walked the rest of the route. We sat in the car for a while. Clancy switched the radio on and retuned it, and I got out and walked about a bit.

It was over an hour before we saw Bel. She was hurrying towards us, her cheeks flushed with what I took to be success. When she gave me a grinning thumbs-up, I hugged her, lifting her off the ground. Then we got back into the

Rabbit and on the way back to the campsite she told us all about it.

Not that there was a whole lot to tell. She'd found a young woman first of all, who'd turned out to have studied in England for several years. So she'd wanted to ask Bel all about how England was these days, and then Bel had asked to use the toilet, and only then had she asked the woman what this place was exactly. At which she got the story and even a brief tour. Because she and the woman appeared to be friends, no one else batted an eye at first. Then a man came up and asked who she was, and after that everything was distinctly cooler. She'd lingered over a cup of herbal tea the woman had prepared, but then had been asked politely but firmly by the man if she would leave.

She hadn't gotten to see the inside of the old cabin, just its outside. But there were no alarm boxes, and none of the windows she'd seen had boasted anything other than the most superficial locks. There was more, and at the end of it I felt like hugging her again. Instead we celebrated back at the campsite with a meal cooked on our stove: franks and beans, washed down with black coffee. Clancy had bought a pack of filters and some real ground coffee. It smelt great and tasted good. The insects by this time were out in force, hungry for a late supper before bed.

'Oh, one other thing,' Bel said. 'In a couple of days, Provost himself is visiting the HQ.'

'Really?' I looked at Clancy. 'Any significance?'

He shrugged. 'It's rare these days, but not exactly unknown.'

'It'll mean his house in Seattle is empty,' I mused.

'Yeah, as empty as a high-security bank.'

I smiled. 'I get your drift.'

Later, Clancy hinted at taking Bel into Port Angeles to check out the night life. They could drop me off first, then pick me up again on the way back. But Bel made a face. She just wanted to crawl into her sleeping bag with a torch, another beer, and her latest cheap paperback. I was pleased she didn't want to go with Clancy. I sat outside with him for a while longer. He asked if I wanted him to drive me to Piedmont, but I shook my head.

'I'll do this one alone.'

When it was properly dark, I was ready.

23

I drove back to Piedmont and parked a little way from the trail-head. I was wearing a camouflage jacket and dark green combat trousers, plus hiking boots. I had the night-scope with me. If anyone stopped me, my excuse would be that I was out looking for nocturnal animals, maybe the rare Roosevelt Elk.

Firearms weren't allowed in the park, but I had the 559 with me too, fully loaded. I reckoned that, laws or not, the Disciples would have an armoury.

There was half a moon, appearing now and then from behind slow-moving clouds. The cloud cover wasn't thick, so there was a welcome glow, and as my eyes got used to the night, I found I could pick my way forwards without falling arse over tit.

I hadn't done much of this sort of thing before, though of course I'd recced my hits. There was silence in the camp. Bel hadn't heard any radios or seen any TV aerials. It looked like the Disciples were early-to-bed early-to-rise types, which suited me fine. Maybe they were busy making love under their patchwork quilts.

The old original cabin faced the newer ones, so I would be at my most vulnerable if entering by the front. I looked in through the rear and side windows, but couldn't see anyone. The windows were locked though, and I'd no tools with me. I knew Bel could have used her skill here, but no way was I going to bring her with me. In the silence, the sound of breaking glass would be like a foghorn. So I went around to the front of the cabin. Then I saw the torch. I saw the beam first, scanning the ground. Someone had left one of the other cabins. If I moved, I'd be heard, so I stood still, my face averted, hoping I'd blend in with the cabin walls. If they shone the torch right at me, of course, they'd see me instantly. I held my breath and waited.

Someone cleared his throat. Then I heard water pouring on to the ground. He'd come outside to urinate. Yes, I'd seen a compost heap over where he was standing; no doubt he was peeing on to that. I could hear the blood rushing in my ears, my heart thumping. Then the man turned and retraced his steps. I heard a cabin door close, though I hadn't heard it open.

Quickly, I went to the front door of the old cabin and turned the handle. It wasn't locked. I slipped inside and closed the door again slowly. I didn't want to use my torch. It would be too obvious. Anyone stepping out to the compost heap would see its glow reflected in the windows.

As far as I could make out, I was standing in an office. There were two desks, and another table with office machines on it. I saw the outlines of computers and file-boxes, what looked like a photocopier, and several large filing-cabinets. I went to these and tried a drawer. It too was unlocked. I knew I really needed some light, so took the handkerchief from my pocket and wrapped it over the torch. Now when I switched the torch on, there was a faint illumination, just enough to read by. I started working my way through the papers in the first cabinet.

Though the night was cool, there was sweat on my back and my brow. The third drawer down was full of details about cult members. I checked out Nathan and Alisha. Alisha had joined in early '86, having come west from Raleigh NC. Nathan had joined later the same year. His file gave scant details of any life before joining the Disciples, which was unusual. I knew which high school Alisha had attended, when she was born and where, what she had studied at college. All I really knew about Nathan after reading his file was that Nathan was his first name.

His second name was Kline.

It couldn't just be coincidence. I tucked his file back in place and closed the cabinet. I tried a few other drawers, but didn't turn up much. There was certainly nothing about the finances of the cult, other than the daily outgoings. The only way Provost could be financing the set-up was if he had a mountain of cash back in his Queen Anne house. I also found no evidence of conspiracy to murder, though any such documents were unlikely to be kept here. Nathan's house on Hood Canal would be an infinitely better bet, and suddenly I was keen to return there and take a closer look.

But I had other things to do first. Beyond the front office there was a narrow hallway with doors leading off. More offices, by the look of things. I tried a door, opened it, and looked in. Yes, if the front desks were manned by underlings, then these two offices most probably belonged to Nathan and Alisha. One of them might even be Provost's. There were no clues to the owner of either office, and the desk drawers and filing-cabinets were locked. It wasn't very trusting, was it? It told me something about the Disciples. So open on the surface – witness the unlocked front door – yet with secrets which had to be kept locked up. I decided against forcing any of the locks. I didn't want them to know how close I was.

Out in the hall again, I noticed a staircase. It was right at the end of the hall, and led up into the roof-space. I hadn't thought about the roof-space. There were no windows up there, so I hadn't considered it used. Yet here was a stair leading up.

I'd climbed three steps when I saw the figure standing at the top.

'Who the hell are you?' he said.

But I was already running. He took the stairs quickly, but not quickly enough. I was out of the front door and running. I didn't think he would follow, but he did. He must have been wearing shoes, or the forest floor would have cut his feet open in seconds.

I didn't have any plan other than flight, but of course my pursuer knew the woods better than I did. He hadn't yelled out for help, so it was one-on-one. What's more, I had a gun and a knife. I was feeling a little more confident when he appeared suddenly in front of me. I went for the knife, but he slammed a fist into my face and a foot into my leg. I knew he was trying for the kneecap, which told me he'd been trained. But he landed high, numbing my thigh but not paralysing me. He was quick, no doubt about that. But now I had the gun in my hand. He snatched at it, his hand snaking out of the dark, and twisted my wrist until it nearly broke. I let the gun fall and went for the knife with my left hand. This gave him all the time in the world to land another punch and kick. The punch caught me on the side of the head, and the dark suddenly became fifty shades of stunning blue. His kick was Kung-Fu style and just missed my heart. It had enough power to throw me back through the trees. I kept my balance, God knows how. I knew I had to get the damned knife into play.

The moon appeared, lighting his bare torso. It was criss-crossed with cuts from branches, but that wasn't going to slow him down. There was a snarl on his face as he launched himself at me, hurling himself forward, arms outstretched. He knew all about close-quarters combat, knew I couldn't use the knife once he got me in a hug.

I dived sideways, falling as I did. I heard him grunt as he missed me. There was a cracking sound. I got to my feet as quick as I could. He wouldn't miss a sitting target. But when I looked, he was standing very still, his arms hanging by his sides. Then I saw why. There was a low branch sticking out through his back. He'd speared himself on a hemlock.

'Thank Christ for that,' I said. Then I switched on the torch and found my pistol, sticking it back into my trousers. I considered burying the body, but knew it wouldn't be easy.

At least leaving him here, any coroner might be persuaded of a bizarre accident. It certainly didn't look like murder. I shone the torch into his face, and saw the resemblance to his brother immediately.

'Hello, Nathan,' I said.

I was shaking as I drove back to the campsite. I hadn't been so close to death before. I'd never seen that much fresh blood close up. I'd seen Max of course, but Max's corpse hadn't been warm. The picture of Nathan Kline would stay with me long after my victims' had faded. I didn't think liquor and a holiday would ever wipe out Nathan's staring face.

Clancy and Bel were still awake, awaiting my return. When they saw me, they knew something had gone badly wrong. One side of my face was swollen, bruising nicely. My chest hurt, and I was still limping from the kick to my thigh. My hair was tangled with sweat, and my clothes were smeared with earth.

'I need to get to a hospital,' I said.

'There might be something at Port Angeles.'

'This is sort of specialised,' I said.

'Michael's got haemophilia,' Bel explained.

'It'll have to be Seattle or Tacoma,' Clancy decided.

So we packed everything up by torchlight. Or rather, they did while I stayed in the car. A couple of campers complained about the noise, until Bel explained that we had an emergency and had to get someone to hospital. I'd been hoping she wouldn't say anything. Now we had campers out looking at me like I was a zoo exhibit. I kept my head bowed so they wouldn't see the bruises. I knew most of the campers would be gone by morning, when Nathan's body would be found. But the police could find them elsewhere in the park and ask them about tonight. And now they'd be able to tell all about a man with his head hidden from them, a sudden need to break camp in the middle of the night.

Things, I thought, had taken a very bad turn.

We got out of there and Bel apologised.

'I just didn't think,' she said.

'That's okay.'

Clancy was driving. There were no ferries that he knew of, not this late, so we headed south on 101 and picked up I-5 through Tacoma to Seattle. There was a hospital not too far from our hotel. We had to go through the usual American bureaucracy, details taken, disclaimers and waivers signed, and of course they wanted to know how they'd get paid, before a doctor took a look at me. He wasn't a haemophilia specialist, his first few questions were all about what had happened.

'A fight outside a bar,' I told him.

'You're not supposed to get into fights.'

'That's what I told the guy who hit me.'

Eventually he gave me a dubious all-clear, but told me to come see a specialist in the morning. I paid cash back at the desk and Clancy drove us back to the hotel.

The night staff didn't say anything when Bel asked for the room key. Maybe they'd seen wasted-looking people before, turning up in the wee small hours wearing hiking outfits.

We broke into a bottle of tequila Bel had bought, and I put some ice into a towel for my bruises.

'I still don't get it,' said Clancy. 'You say his name's Nathan *Kline?*'

'That's what it said on his file.'

'You think he's some relation of Kline's?'

'There were facial similarities.'

He shook his head. 'Jesus,' he said.

'And whatever he was, he wasn't my idea of a "disciple of love". He knew unarmed combat like I know rifles. I'm lucky we were fighting at night. In daylight he'd have killed me.'

'So what does that make him?'

'Ex-military, something like that. Maybe CIA or NSC. All I know is that it makes him dead.'

Bel was staring at me, so I turned to her.

'I don't feel great about it, Bel, but this time it was him or me. And I didn't kill him, a tree-branch did. But I *would* have killed him. And he'd have killed me.'

'I know,' she said quietly. 'I'm glad he's dead.' Then she went back to her drink.

Clancy didn't go home. He slept in a chair, while Bel and I took the beds. We talked some more, and finally settled down to sleep as the sun was rising. I probably slept for an hour, maybe a little more. Then I went into the bathroom, closed the door and turned on the light. I looked like I'd been in an accident with a timber-lorry. My chest and thigh were purple with shades of mauve and black. My eye had closed up a little as the flesh below it swelled. It was tender to the touch, but at least I hadn't lost any teeth.

I didn't think I was going to die. Haemophiliacs rarely die these days, not if they look after themselves. But I'd go back to the hospital anyway and have a proper check done.

I went down to the lobby and out into the fresh air of a new day. Only in my head it was still the middle of the night and I was out in the woods, being taken apart by a crazed jungle-fighter. I tried not to limp as I walked. I'd changed into some clean clothes. There were a few early risers about, driving to work, or shuffling through the streets examining garbage. I headed for the waterfront to do some thinking.

I didn't doubt that Nathan was Kline's brother, which tied the Disciples of Love very closely to the NSC. But a question niggled: did anyone at the Disciples know Nathan's real identity? And come to think of it, what was so important that Nathan would go undercover for nearly eight years to protect it? They might have discovered his body by now. They might be contacting the police. If they *didn't* contact the police, that would be a sign of the whole cult's complicity. I knew I had to go back to the peninsula to be sure.

I also wanted to investigate Nathan's house on Hood

Canal. If I wanted to do it, I'd have to do it fast, before Kline got to hear of his brother's all-too-suspicious demise.

'Great day for it,' a woman told me as she pushed a supermarket shopping-trolley over the train lines. A train had just crept past, holding up the few cars. It carried wood, thousands of planks coming south from Canada. We'd both watched it roll inexorably past.

'Great day for it,' she said again, waving to me as she moved away.

We went out for breakfast and ate huge blueberry muffins, washed down with strong coffee. I told Clancy and Bel I wanted to go back to the peninsula.

'You're out of your mind,' Clancy said.

We'd listened to the early-morning radio news, and there'd been nothing about Nathan's death. And only a few minutes ago, Clancy had phoned a colleague at the newsdesk and asked if any reports had come in of 'anything' happening in the park. The colleague's reply had been negative.

'First,' Bel said, 'you're going to go back to that hospital. I don't want you keeling over on me, Michael.'

'And we need to change cars,' Clancy added. He had a point. It would be a lot safer heading back to the peninsula in a new car. The campers had seen me sitting in a VW Rabbit, which was a world away from a Trans-Am. 'Look,' he said. 'Why don't I drop the two of you off at the hospital, go fetch the Trans-Am and pick you up again afterwards?'

'Sounds good to me,' said Bel.

So that was agreed. We checked that the car was ready and that my hospital appointment was confirmed. I checked we'd left nothing in the Rabbit before we left the hotel.

The car worried me. All it needed was for one camper to remember the licence plate and reel it off to the police, and they would track it instantly by computer to the repair shop, where the owner knew Clancy. And once they knew about Clancy, that would be the end of it.

I had to trust to luck that no one would remember the plate. And I hated trusting to anything other than myself.

Bel and I sat in the hospital for a while. She remarked how bright and new it seemed, how well equipped. She was just making conversation, that was all.

'Wait till you see what they charge,' I told her, 'then you won't be surprised.'

We were getting through the money. I didn't like to think about how I'd go about earning some more.

'I wish I'd been there when you killed him,' Bel said quietly.

'I didn't kill him,' I reminded her. 'And for God's sake, why would you want to be there?'

She turned to me and smiled a humourless smile.

I saw the doctor and everything seemed to be all right. He insisted on a few blood tests, since he wanted to be 'on the safe side', even though I objected I'd be flying back to England in a few days.

After all of which, I parted with some cash. The person behind the desk pointed out that they couldn't know yet how much everything would cost, since the blood tests were done at an independent lab, so they'd bill me later. I gave my fake address again, the same one I'd given the previous night, and walked out of the hospital knowing I'd saved a few dollars at least.

Then we waited for Clancy. We waited a long time. At last we gave up and took a cab back to the hotel.

The receptionist remembered something as Bel and I stood waiting for the elevator.

'Oh, Mr West? Did your friends get in touch?'

'Sorry?'

'There were a couple of calls for you yesterday evening. I said you were out.'

'Did they leave a name?'

'I'm sorry, sir, they just said you were expecting them to call.'

Well, in a way this was true. I walked back to the desk.

'We'll be checking out,' I said.

She looked surprised. 'Nothing wrong, I hope?'

'I've got to go back to England. You can see I've been in an accident . . .'

'Well, I wasn't going to say anything, but—'

'And the medical costs here are too high. We're just going up to our room to pack. Could you make up our bill?'

'Yes, of course.'

The elevator had arrived. I followed Bel into it. She waited till the doors had closed before she asked what was wrong.

'Everything,' I said. 'Someone knows we're here. It had to happen, we're just lucky we got this warning.'

We packed quickly. I kept the Colt Commando near the top of my bag, and put the pistol in my waistband. If you see someone in the US with his shirt hanging outside his trousers, think gun.

I paid our bill and the receptionist hoped she'd see us again. I wasn't laying bets on it as I went outside and found a cab. Only when he'd pulled up to the hotel door did I signal for Bel to come out. We loaded our bags into the boot, as well as a carrier bag belonging to Clancy. Inside it were a camera, film, and a small cassette recorder.

'Sea Tac?' our driver asked. But I gave him the address of the car repair shop instead.

We passed close by the hospital and stuck to the main route. But the road ahead was cordoned off, and a police officer was waving traffic on to other streets.

'Musta been an accident,' the driver said.

'Can you pull over?' I asked him. He did. 'Wait here, I'll only be a minute.' I told Bel to stay put. I think she knew what was going through my mind. She bit her lip but nodded.

I walked back towards the cordon. There were sightseers

319

standing beside it. A car was standing at traffic lights, officials milling around it. An ambulance was there, but mostly I saw people who looked like detectives. Some of them were taking photographs.

The stalled car was our white Trans-Am. There were splashes of blood on the windshield. A sightseer asked what was going on. A veteran at the scene was eager to supply details.

'A drive-by shooting. Probably pushers, it's getting as bad here as LA. Guy's dead. They sprayed him all over the inside of the car. Looks like strawberries in a liquidiser, the cops told me.'

'Strawberries, huh?'

I walked away with deadened feet. Bel didn't need to ask. I told the driver there was a change of destination. He took us out on to Aurora until we found a cheap motel with a red-neon vacancy.

It reminded me of the first motel we'd stayed in after buying the Trans-Am: gaudy colours and infrequent maid-service. I went out to the ice machine while Bel unwrapped the 'sanitised' plastic tumblers she'd found in the bathroom.

We drank tequila. Bel finished her second one before collapsing on the bed in tears. I stood at the window and looked out through the slats in the blind. I'd specified a room round the back of the motel, not sure how much safer this made things. My view through the window was of the parking area, strewn with litter, and behind it a narrow street with junkyard housing, hardly meriting the description 'bungalows'.

'What do we do now?' she said.

'Same as we would have done,' I replied. 'Only now we know they're close to us. Forewarned is forearmed.'

'Yes, and cleanliness is next to godliness. It doesn't *mean* anything, Michael.'

'Bel.' I went to the bed and pulled her up, hugging her

close. I ran my hands down her hair. I kissed her wet cheeks. I didn't know how long we'd be safe in this motel. A couple of days maybe, but it could be less. There were dozens, maybe hundreds of motels on Aurora. But I was sure Kline or his men would search each one. The quicker we went to work the better.

'Stay here,' I said. 'Switch the TV on. They've got HBO.'

'I don't want HBO! I want this to end!'

'Bel, it's ending, believe me.' I just didn't trust myself to script the finale.

I did something not many people do on Aurora. I walked. There wasn't much in the way of pavement, and the drivers looked at me like I was roadkill. I didn't have far to walk though. Our motel hadn't been entirely chosen at random. It happened to be close to half a dozen used-car lots. I walked into the first one and browsed. There were some serious cars here, highly-polished numbers from the 50s and early-60s, all chrome and fin and leather. But I wanted something a lot more prosaic. Most important of all, I wanted local plates. We needed to merge with the scenery.

'Hi, can I help you?'

He was exactly what you'd expect: ill-chosen clothes and a grinning cigar. He walked with splayed feet and was shaped like a rugby ball: all stomach, tapering off top and bottom. I asked about a couple of the cars, and said I might be back. I also told him I'd be paying cash.

The next lot I tried was full of dodgems, not a roadworthy car in the place. They had a good mechanic though. He'd done a few tricks to make the cars look and sound nice. You had to study the trick twice or even three times to see how he'd done it. The Americans have a love affair with their cars, as a result of which there are a million products on the market for the home mechanic. You can pour gunk into your car which will temporarily stop an oil leak, or make the engine sound smoother, or stop the thing sounding like a

321

cancer patient. They weren't even remission, these cures. They were quack.

The next place along had some nice newer models. There was a Volvo I liked the look of, and an older Mercedes. A Ford Mustang was an expensive option I toyed with for a couple of minutes, but then I saw the VW Camper. I knew it was by no means perfect. It wouldn't outrun a bicycle, was slow on hills, and was noisy. In its favour, we could get out of town and sleep in it instead. The guy was asking $4,000 for it, but when we had trouble sliding open the side door, he came down to three and a half. I studied the engine. It had been twin-carbed, and not by an expert. I told him I didn't want anything twin-carbed.

'Brings the life span and the resale down.'

I walked away from the vehicle, then turned and looked at it again, ready to banish it from my thoughts.

'Oh, did I mention I'd be paying cash?'

He came down to three and told me he was cutting his throat.

'Just don't splash blood on the hubcaps,' I said. I shouldn't have: it made me flash back to the Trans-Am and Sam Clancy's death.

We settled the paperwork and I drove out of the lot. The steering felt slack, but not too slack to be fatal. The indicators weren't working either, so I didn't make many friends crossing the traffic into the motel. I parked right outside our room. Bel was standing at the door, hugging herself, bouncing on her toes. I didn't imagine the sight of the VW had got her so excited.

'He's alive!' she said. I got her inside and shut the door. 'What?'

'He's okay, he's not dead. It was on the TV news.'

I sat down on the bed. 'Clancy?' I said. She nodded, biting back tears. We watched the TV together in silence, holding hands. It took a while till we got another news bulletin. There was a reporter at the hospital.

'That's the same hospital I went to.'

The reporter said that the driver of the vehicle, Sam Clancy, a local journalist who had been in hiding after what he claimed at the time were attempts on his life, had been shot four or five times, once in the head, once in the neck, and at least twice in the shoulder. He was in a stable condition, but was still unconscious. Police were at his bedside and were on armed guard outside his room.

'I'll be damned,' I said.

There was an interview with a senior police officer. They asked him about the previous attempts on Sam Clancy's life, but the cop had nothing to say at this juncture. Then they spoke to Sam's editor and to a colleague. It could have been the man I spoke with the first time I phoned the paper. And finally they showed pictures of the Trans-Am and the repair shop.

'Shit.'

So they would have talked to the owner, who would tell them that it wasn't Sam Clancy's car, no sir, it belonged to a couple of English friends of his ... Which would set the police wondering: where were those friends now? And if they were *really* clever, or really lucky, they'd connect Sam and his friends with the late-night disappearance of three people, one of them injured, from a campground near where a man had died.

Bel saw it all too, of course, and she squeezed my hand all the tighter.

'We've got to move,' she said. 'Before this starts falling around our heads.'

I nodded slowly, and she smiled at me. 'He's alive, Michael. He's alive.' We hugged one another, then I pulled her off the bed. 'Come on, places to go, people to see.'

'By the way,' she said, 'what were you doing in that rattle-wagon?'

That rattle-wagon took us back over to Bremerton and into

the Olympic Peninsula. The gearbox had a habit of springing back into neutral, but apart from that there were no problems. The van didn't have air conditioning of course, or a radio. But Bel lolled in the back and opened all the little cupboards and took the cover off the sink, and seemed to like it well enough in the end.

It was true there wasn't anywhere to park on the road along Hood Canal. I suppose they'd done it on purpose so tourists wouldn't stop and gawp at the nice houses. However, you couldn't always see the house from the driveway, and vice versa, so I stopped in a driveway across the road from Nathan's house and a couple of houses down. Effectively, I was blocking the access, but the only people likely to complain were the occupants of the house, and they might never know. Clancy had pointed out that a lot of the homes here were used only at weekends and vacation time. I went round the back of the VW and propped open the engine, so we could claim mechanical trouble if anyone asked us. I'd tell them we were waiting for the triple-A.

We seemed to sit in the van for a long time. We hadn't brought anything with us, nothing to eat or drink or read. Bel found a pack of cards in the glove compartment, but there were only thirty-three of them. She found a few other bits and pieces too. A soiled dollar bill, a cushion-cover, the whistle from a steam-kettle, an unused stick of Wrigley's, and a bicycle pump.

'If we had a boot,' she said, 'we could have a car-boot sale.'

'Hey, come and look at this.' She came forward and peered through the windscreen. A car was coming out of Nathan's drive. It hadn't been there earlier when we'd passed, so must have been parked in the garage. It was smart, long at the front and squat at the back. I guessed it to be a Buick sedan. We'd seen enough cars on the road to make us expert.

'It's a Lincoln,' Bel said.

'Is it?'

As it passed our drive, I caught a glimpse of the figure in the back. All I could make out was platinum hair and a suit, but by this time that was enough.

'You want to break into the house?' Bel asked.

I'd been thinking this over, and now I shook my head. 'The house is just a meeting place. I don't think we'd find anything there.'

'So what now?'

'Now,' I said, 'we follow Kline. Here, you drive.'

'What?' We started to change places.

'He doesn't know you,' I said. 'At least, he hasn't met you. If we're going to tail him, it better be you in the front seat and me in the back.'

'He saw me when I got out of the car that time outside Oban.'

'He didn't see much more than the back of your head. Besides, you weren't wearing sunglasses then.'

Bel squeezed into the driver's seat. 'He's probably halfway to Seattle by now.'

'Doesn't matter,' I said. 'I think I know where he's headed.'

The problem was the ferry, or it could have been. But we stayed in the van, sitting in the back, pretending to play cards with our incomplete pack.

'Snap,' Bel said. We didn't look up much from the table, just in case Kline happened to stroll past and glance in. To the outside world, we must have appeared as engrossed as any poker fiends. We needn't have worried. Kline's sedan was in a different line, and about eight vehicles ahead of us. He stayed in his car, while his driver went for a smoke on-deck. I saw the driver very briefly, and recognised him as the same man who'd been driving for Kline that day in Oban.

We followed them off the boat, but lost them on the steep streets up near the Seattle Centre. It didn't matter. I directed

Bel up into Queen Anne and then over to the big houses off Bigelow. The second street we tried was the right one.

'How's the handbrake?' Bel asked as she parked roadside.

'I haven't needed it yet,' I answered.

Jeremiah Provost's house boasted a cellar garage with a slope running down to it from the pavement. This was where Kline's car was parked, its nose almost touching the garage's closed door. Bel had taken us a bit further down the hill, which was fine. We couldn't afford to be obvious; it was still daylight. But I decided to take one risk anyway.

'Stay here,' I said.

'That's what you always say.'

'This time I mean it.' I left the van and stuck my hands in my pockets, whistling like a regular Joe on his way home from work. I climbed back up the hill and passed Kline's car. Bel had been right, it was a Lincoln. I didn't suppose the licence would help me, but I memorised it anyway. I passed the path which led around to the side of the house. I looked up and down the street, but there was no one about, no one to see me dive into the shrubbery and begin crawling my way around to the front door. Clancy had mentioned night-lights, but this was still daytime. I was hoping the system would only work at night.

I could hear voices, and slowed my pace accordingly. I could hear Kline's voice, then another man's. It seemed, amazingly, that they were holding a conversation – and a heated one at that – on Provost's doorstep. I could hear snatches. Kline kept his voice low, the other voice was the angry one.

'I told you not to come back here! You never did listen, did you?' This was the other voice talking.

Then I found myself nose to a prickly bush, and looking through its foliage across a postage stamp lawn to the open front door. A man stood in the doorway, looking down on to where Kline and his driver stood. The driver had his hands behind his back. Kline stood with hands in pockets, head bowed. He started to make a speech I couldn't hear. Above the three men, I could see a lamp high on the wall of the house. It was pointing in my direction and it was on. I must have triggered a beam. I prayed they wouldn't look up and see it. There was no point worrying anyway.

So instead I concentrated on Jeremiah Provost.

It was my first sight of him, and he was impressive in a mad professor sort of way. He looked like he'd gained weight since the most recent newspaper photos. His beard was longer and greyer, his frizzy hair swept back and out from his forehead, like he had electricity searing through him. He was wearing denims and a T-shirt and an old cardigan. There was a strand of thick round beads around his neck, and he touched them as he spoke. His stance made it clear he had no intention of letting Kline over the threshold.

That was the most puzzling thing of all.

Kline's speech over, Provost looked to the sky for guidance. 'Look,' he said, his voice an educated drawl, 'just stay the fuck away, okay? Is that too much to ask?'

More undertones from Kline.

'I *know* he's dead,' Provost snarled. He meant Nathan. Nathan's gory end still hadn't been on any news I'd seen. No doubt Kline and his men had been busy covering it up. Provost was still talking. 'As yet,' he said, 'we don't know anything other than that he *is* dead. What're you saying?'

I almost whistled: Provost didn't know the connection between Kline and Nathan. I even felt a moment's pity for Kline, who had just lost a brother. Then I smiled to myself.

The light overhead was still on. I wondered what kind of timer it had. And I thanked God it wasn't wired into any alarm. There was a camera, but it was aimed at the path, just in front of the main door. Kline was shuffling his feet. He said a few more words, then turned to go.

'Yeah,' said Provost, 'and don't forget to take your fucking gorilla with you.' I could see the gorilla clench his fists behind his back. Oh boy, he wanted to swipe Provost. But all he did was give him the surreptitious finger instead.

I waited till they'd gone and Provost had closed and locked his door, then worked my way around the rest of the perimeter towards where the shrubbery ended just before the swimming pool. 'Swimming pool' was actually stretching things; it was more an outsized bath. The French windows were open, curtains wafting through them. There was a big white open-plan living area, and a dumpy woman standing in the middle of the floor. She was stroking Provost's hair and kissing his neck, whispering to him. I squinted against the glare from the sinking sun. On the other side of the house, I could hear Kline's car pull back on to the street and drive off. The woman had long lifeless hair and was wearing a floaty kaftan which caught the breeze from the French windows. I guessed she might be Alisha. She stepped back from Provost, who was rubbing his hands over his face, a man carrying the weight of the world. He started flapping his arms, shouting something, near to frenzy or madness or something.

'What's on your mind, Jerry?' I said to myself, hoping he might yell out an answer.

But instead the woman hiked the kaftan over her head and let it fall to the floor. She was naked underneath. It wasn't a bad move. Provost stopped fretting and started looking. There was a lot to look at, including a wondrously large pair of breasts. He walked forward to meet her, and she took his head and rested it against her. He seemed like a child then, as she spoke quietly to him and stroked his hair and soothed him. When he broke away from her long enough to start taking off his own clothes, I back-pedalled through the shrubbery and on to the street.

My knees and elbows were black with earth, and with my bruised face I knew anyone seeing me now would have little hesitation calling the cops. So I fairly jogged back to the VW and got in.

'I saw them leave,' said Bel. 'When you didn't come back straight away, I thought—'

I stopped her panic with a kiss. What do you know, it worked, just as it had with Provost. In fact, she took another kiss and then another, this time with eyes closed.

I told her what I'd found out, but she couldn't make much out of it.

'Things seem to be getting more confused all the time.'

She had a point. It took us a while to find a road down on to Aurora, where we found ourselves part of the evening rush-hour. There was a drive-in burger bar, so we stopped there for dinner. The burgers were huge and delicious. Then Bel dropped her bombshell.

'I want to see Sam.'

24

New York, New York. Hoffer was back in his element.

He loved all of it, from Brooklyn and Queens to downtown Manhattan. He *belonged* here, along with all the other movers and shakers, the trick operators and cowboys and scammers. New York made sense to him, he knew its rules, knew when to play and how to play. Other cities, other countries: fuck 'em.

He stood outside the splatter gallery and felt so euphoric, he almost climbed the stairs to his office. Then he crossed to the diner and phoned his secretary instead.

'Moira baby, I'm down here if anybody wants me.'

'Sure. Constantine's here.'

'Send him down in five minutes.'

'Okay. Did you bring me a souvenir?'

'Hah?'

'A souvenir,' she persisted. 'I wanted something royal.' She sounded petulant.

'Give me a break,' Hoffer told her, putting down the phone. He didn't recognise any of the waitresses. The one who came to his table told him it was vacation time, everyone waiting tables this week was relief.

'And do you *give* relief as well, honey?' Hoffer said, grinning. She stopped chewing her gum and gave him a look. You couldn't have called the look 'interested'. 'Just coffee,' Hoffer said, dismissing her.

He glanced at his watch. Five minutes gave him time for one quick coffee. He didn't intend staying here, not with Constantine. That fuck always had an appetite, and never

330

seemed to have money enough of his own with which to satisfy it.

Constantine was one of Hoffer's three employees. He'd just come back from Boston, and Hoffer wanted the lowdown. Meantime, he drank his coffee and stared out of the window. The street was noisy with cabs and drunks and what looked like a few tourists. Someone who looked like a prospective buyer even walked into the splatter gallery. That had to be a first. Then he saw Constantine come out of the building. The guy was young, mid-20s. He was always sharply dressed. Hoffer reckoned he had a side job. He sure as hell didn't buy all those clothes on what Hoffer paid him. Constantine was a shrewd guy, despite his years. He'd grown up on the street, or not far from it, and had a good way with words. He usually got people to talk.

Hoffer was at the diner door waiting for him. He put an arm round Constantine's shoulder and led him away from the diner.

'Let's walk, get some air.'

'I was gonna have some cheesecake,' Constantine complained.

'Sure, kid, later. First, tell me about Boston.'

What was there to tell? Armed with the information that the D-Man and Harrison had touched down there, all Constantine had done was find their hotel.

'They only stayed one night,' he told his employer. 'Staff hardly saw them. Crashed out, I'd guess.'

Hoffer was only half-listening. Between his friend in the FBI and Robert Walkins's contacts, he'd been able to find out a little about Don Kline. This past day or so, he'd found himself thinking more about Kline than about the D-Man. After all, the D-Man had never had the bad grace to disturb Hoffer at breakfast.

Kline was ex-NSC. Nobody seemed to know why he'd resigned; at least, nobody was telling. This niggled Hoffer, because now he couldn't be sure who was paying Kline.

Somebody had to be paying him. That trip to the UK must have cost something, plus he had men to feed. Kline was beginning to worry Hoffer more than the D-Man himself was. Maybe he was just nervous that Kline might track the D-Man down before he did. Maybe there was more to it than that . . .

'What's that you said?' Hoffer said suddenly.

'The sister hotel,' Constantine repeated. 'That's where they headed after Boston. They booked from their hotel.'

'Sister hotel where?'

'Here,' Constantine said, opening his arms wide. 'That's what I've been telling you. Here in Manhattan.'

'Where in Manhattan?'

'The corner of 42nd and 7th.'

Hoffer was already waving down a cab.

The hotel was a typical tourist place, lacking style but clean enough to suffice. They'd booked in as Weston, and again they'd stayed just the one night. Hoffer handed a twenty to the desk clerk, as agreed.

'Any idea how they spent their time?'

'Sir,' said the desk clerk, pocketing the money, 'to be honest, I don't remember them at all.'

'You don't, huh?' The clerk shook his head.

'Well, thanks for your time. Rate you charge, I'd've been cheaper renting a hooker.' Hoffer turned away and found himself face to face with Constantine. 'I don't like it,' he said.

'What?'

'The fact that the D-Man's been *here*. This is my fucking town!' Then he stuffed his hands into his pockets and charged out of the hotel, nearly toppling two elderly tourists in his wake. Constantine followed him into the street. Hoffer turned so suddenly, the two almost collided.

'Right,' he said, 'look at flights, trains, coaches, car rental, the lot. Leave nothing out. Names to check: Weston, West, and Wesley, pre-names Michael or Mark. And remember

332

there'll be a female companion.' Hoffer turned away again and faced the traffic. He wasn't seeing it.

'What was he doing here?' he asked. 'What did he come here for? He must've had someone to see, maybe something stashed away.'

'You don't think he's still here, chief?'

'What am İ, fucking Sitting Bull? Don't *ever* call me "chief", understand?'

'Sure.' Constantine swallowed. He'd never seen his boss like this. Come to that, he'd seldom seen his boss *period*. But the guy paid, always on time and always the amount owing, and you had to respect that. Money: it was practically the only thing, excepting the Giants, his mother, and the pairing of Cary Grant with Katharine Hepburn, that Constantine *did* respect.

'So what're you waiting for?' Hoffer said. 'A gratuity?'

Then he turned away from Constantine and walked away. Constantine watched him go. There was room in his heart for a moment's pity. He wouldn't like to be Leo Hoffer, not for a day, not for a hundred thousand dollars (which was what he reckoned Hoffer earned in a year). There couldn't be many years left inside Hoffer's oversized body, maybe ten at most. Guys his size never lasted; they were like dinosaurs that way, neither species meant to last.

Eventually, Constantine's attention was diverted by a burger bar across the intersection. He dug into his pocket and started counting his change.

Back in his apartment that evening, Hoffer took a shower, then wished he hadn't.

His ears still hadn't recovered from the flight, and he got some water and soap in one of them, making it worse. It was like the wax was moving in there, like it was alive, crackling. Maybe the stuff was evolving or mutating. He stuck a match in, but that hurt, so he let the wax be. Maybe it was more than wax, some infection or something. He took some painkillers and had a hit of his duty free. Then he slumped on his sofa and took a look around him.

The apartment didn't have much to it. No personality or anything like that. It was a place to sleep, to ball sometimes, a place to cook up a meal if he could be bothered. He didn't have hobbies, and he wasn't about to waste his time decorating or anything like that. He never brought friends back here, because he didn't have any friends. There were a few guys he might go to a ball game with or play poker with, but that was always someplace else, not here. They were men he'd known on the force. Actually, these days, he hung out with more old hoods than old cops. A sign of the way his life had gone.

He couldn't remember the last woman he'd brought back here. Why should he? They were always one-night stands, the woman was usually drunk, and so, come to that, was Hoffer. He had plenty to waste his self-pity on. He could sit here all night bawling inside like a baby. Or he could go get ripped at the bar down the street. Instead, he pulled out the file Joe Draper had given him. And he wondered again, what am I doing here when I could be in Seattle? He knew that's where the D-Man would head, maybe not straight away, but eventually. So what was Hoffer doing hanging around New York? He reckoned he had half the answer: he wanted the D-Man to do his thing. Because Hoffer too wanted to know who had set the D-Man up, and why. He wanted to know who else wanted the D-Man as badly as Hoffer himself did. Part of him didn't like the competition. It was like someone was trying to steal his pet mutt.

But there was more to it than that. There was Kline. He still couldn't see where Kline fitted in, but he knew Kline would be on the lookout for him. Since arriving back in the States, he'd been watching for tails, checking for bugs. Kline would be keeping tabs somehow. Hoffer didn't want to look too keen. He'd hit Seattle soon, but on his own terms. And by then maybe Kline and the D-Man would be out in the open. That would be interesting. That would be very interesting.

'Yeah,' he said, nodding to himself. Then he got up and put his jacket back on. All of a sudden he wanted two things: a drink, and not to be alone.

'Simple needs,' he muttered, locking the door behind him.

25

It was time Bel had a disguise.

So we dyed her hair dark and I helped her with a haircut. Her hair had been short to start with, now it made her head look like a hedgehog. Not that I told her this. She quite liked the cut, and ran her hand over her head, enjoying the feel of the bristles. She used an eyelash-brush to dye her eyebrows. Then she started playing with the make-up we'd bought in the supermarket next to the motel.

Bel trimmed my hair. She was good at it, she'd gone on a course once. My own choice of dye wasn't so successful, and left my hair streaky. I didn't bother with the eyebrows.

'How do I look?' said Bel. The truth was, she looked stunning. It was just that she didn't look like Bel any more. Her eyes were heavily made up, black, and incredibly sexy. It was hard to look at them without looking away again quickly. She'd dusted her cheeks and applied cherry lipstick to her mouth. She'd bought some cheap jewellery, and now wore earrings and bangles and a gold chain around her throat.

'You look different.'

'Different is what we want.' She pouted. 'Now, Mikey, do I get to go to the hospital?'

'Just don't try an American accent, all right?'

'You got it, Mikey.'

Actually, to my ears her accent was pretty good. Its only flaw was that it sounded like an actress doing it rather than the real thing. I guessed she'd picked it up from TV and films rather than from our travels.

She seemed confident, so I drove her downtown. Part of

me was hoping she'd walk into Clancy's room and be arrested on the spot. I didn't think she'd tell them anything, but at least she'd be safely locked away. I considered phoning the cops from a callbox and tipping them off, only she'd know who'd done it.

So I dropped her off near the hospital steps and drove the VW around the block. There was a visitors' car park, and since I couldn't find a space anywhere else, I ended up there. The problem was, I couldn't see the hospital entrance, so I got out of the van and walked about, kicking my heels like I was waiting for someone. I wasn't alone. There were a couple of other men doing the same thing, plus a cab driver chewing gum and leaning his arm out of his cab to beat a tattoo with his fingers on the roof.

It was a warm evening, but not sticky. It had been about this time of year that I'd come here whale-watching. I'd been lucky. I'd seen several pods of Orcas. I couldn't remember now why I'd wanted to watch whales, but I was glad I'd done it.

'I hate hospitals.' I turned towards the speaker. It was the cabbie. I walked over towards him. 'I mean, I could wait inside, right? But I prefer to wait in the car. Inside, I could maybe get a coffee, but then there'd be that smell wafting up at me. You know that smell?' He waved his hands beneath his nose. 'That damned doctor smell, things in bottles. That sort of smell.'

'I know what you mean.'

'You need a cigarette?' He offered me one, and for some reason I took it. He decided this had broken sufficient ice for him to get out of the car. Once out, he lit both our cigarettes. He had an ex-boxer's face and a few faded blue tattoos on his arms. He was wearing a short-sleeved shirt with a row of pens in the breast-pocket. 'You ever wonder how many people are dying in there while you're waiting outside, huh? How many are throwing their guts up or haemorrhaging? You get in a fight or what?'

I touched my face. 'Yeah, sort of.'

'Jesus, what did he hit you with, a tyre-iron?'

'Actually, it was his fist.'

The cabbie whistled. 'Big fuck, huh?'

'Huge.'

He flexed his shoulders, wondering if he could have made a better job of my opponent.

'Have you ever boxed?' I asked him.

'Yeah, I used to do some.'

'I thought so.'

'You?'

'I'm a man of peace.'

'Well, in my estimation, everyone's a man of peace until he gets steamed up about something. I had a lot of aggression in my youth. What was I going to do, be a public nuisance or step into a ring? Step into a ring, all that aggression is licensed. It's entertainment.'

'You enjoyed it, huh?'

'I didn't much enjoy getting beat.'

I wasn't listening any more. I was watching the entrance. A few people had just come out of the hospital and were standing on the steps. I recognised Kline first. It took me another moment to recognise Bel.

Kline was looking up and down the street. At first I thought he was looking for me, but in fact they were waiting for a car. One of his men, the passenger from the front car in Oban, spoke into a radio. Bel was staring at the ground. Kline had a hand on her arm.

'Hey, you okay?'

The cigarette had dropped from my mouth. I turned away from the cabbie and walked quickly to the van. I went into the back, opened a cupboard, and brought out the Colt Commando. It was pre-loaded and ready for action. Then I got into the driver's seat and started the van. The cabbie was wide-eyed as I passed him, one hand on my steering-wheel and the other gripping the gun.

338

Kline's car was just arriving. They'd brought Bel down to the kerbside. I speeded up and hit the kerb, bouncing the van on to the pavement. Kline and his men looked surprised, then scared. They dived out of the way as I let rip with a few rounds. Bel didn't need to be told what to do. She opened the passenger door and clambered in.

'Hey, Kline!' I roared. 'We need to talk.'

He was crouching behind the car. 'Fuck you!'

I fired another burst to keep them down, then reversed back on to the road, hit first gear again, and roared forward.

'Get down!' I yelled. I fired a burst up into the air, but they weren't scared any more. The initial shock had worn off and they'd found their pistols. I felt rounds thumping into the side and rear of the van. But they missed the tyres. We took a hard right into another street, ran a red light and took a left. I didn't know where the hell we were, but I knew we were out of range.

'We don't seem to be having much luck with our vehicles,' I said. I was thinking: at the very least now they'd know that I was seriously armed and driving a VW van. They might even have got the licence number. It was only three letters and three numbers, easily memorised. I kept checking in the rearview, but there was no sign of pursuit. I slowed down a bit until I'd got my bearings. Soon we were back on 99 and heading north.

'Don't you want to hear what happened?' Bel said. She was shivering. I wound my window back up, then realised that wasn't why she was shivering.

'So what happened?' I was more than angry with her, I was furious. I'd told her not to go, I'd known it was a stupid idea. Yet I hadn't stopped her. I was furious with myself.

'They must have been in the reception area, only I didn't see them. I asked where I could find Sam Clancy, and the woman on the desk pointed me along a corridor. Only, halfway along they grabbed me. They had a good look at me, and then Kline told me to say something.'

'You tried your American accent?'

'Yes. The bastard hit me. So I started swearing at him, and all he did was smile. Then he told me he knew who I was and he asked me where you were.'

'What did he call me?'

'Weston.'

'Not West?'

'No, Weston. Or maybe West. I don't know. Jesus, I was petrified, Michael.'

'Did you say anything else?'

'I told him I knew he killed my father and I was going to kill him for that.'

'Well then, you've told him pretty much all he needs to know. He can't let either of us live now.'

She bit her lip. 'Thanks for bailing me out.'

I managed to smile at her.

I passed the motel without stopping, turned at a fast food place, and waited for a minute by the roadside. No one was following us.

'Tomorrow we have to move again. For tonight, we sleep in shifts. The other one keeps watch from the window. Okay?'

'Okay.'

As it turned out, I didn't have the heart to wake her. It was all my fault she was here in the first place. What had I been doing taking her to London with me? Of course, if I hadn't taken her with me, they'd probably have killed her when they killed Max. This thought pushed away the guilt. I sat in a chair by the window, and went out to the vending machine occasionally for ice-cold Coke and chocolate bars. I crunched a few caffeine tablets until my heart rate sounded too high. I knew every inch of the parking lot, every scrap of trash blowing across it. The sodium glare hurt my eyes. I wanted to close them, to wash them out. Then I closed them for a second too long.

I slept.

It was morning when I woke up, and not early morning either.

Through the window I saw the maid's cleaning cart. She was looking at me, so I shook my head and she pushed the cart along to the next room, knocked, and then went into it.

My watch said 10.15. I got up from the chair and stretched, shrugging my shoulders free of their stiffness. I needed a shower.

'Bel,' I said. 'Time to wake up.'

She rolled over, exhaled, and then lifted her head from the pillow. Like me she was almost fully dressed.

'What time is it?'

'It's gone ten. Come on, get up. You can take first shower.'

I watched her as she slunk into the bathroom and closed the door. I knew our options now had narrowed considerably. We were no longer the hunters but the hunted. Worst of all, I still didn't know what was going on. I could think of one man who knew: Jeremiah Provost. But Kline would have Provost covered. Kline would have *everything* covered.

I had enough quarters left to buy us a couple of breakfast Cokes. I had a head full of mud and my body felt like it was dragging weights. The vending machine was next to the ice-box in a little connecting alley between the back of the motel and the front. There was a concrete stairwell up to the rooms on the first floor. I'd sat there last night for a while, listening to traffic. Now, as I got the second can from the machine, I heard tyres squeal out front. I looked around the corner and saw a car sitting next to the motel office. A man was getting out of the passenger side, buttoning his jacket as he walked to the office. He wore sunglasses and looked around him. I didn't recognise the man, but he didn't look like a typical resident. He looked official. I ducked back into the alley and flew to our room.

'Got to go!' I called. Bel came out of the bathroom dressed

and rubbing her hair with a towel. 'Got to go,' I said. When she saw me throwing stuff into a bag, she took the hint, threw down the towel, and started packing.

'What's the problem?'

'Bad guys at the office. They could be asking about VW vans.' I took hold of the Smith & Wesson. 'Here,' I told her, 'take this.'

She didn't say anything. It took her a moment to make up her mind, then she snatched the pistol from me. She checked the clip, slapped it home and made sure the safety was on. I didn't have time for a smile.

They say discretion is the better part of valour, but we were anything but discreet leaving the room. We ran to the van, heaving bags into the back. Bel was toting the pistol, and I had the Colt Commando by its carrying handle. I'd taken off the flash-hider. When I'd used the Commando last night, the noise without the hider had been impressive. It had made people duck. So the hider stayed off.

Now we were in the van, I hesitated for a second. What were we supposed to do? Cruise past the car with a nod and a smile? Play hide and seek around the motel? Or leave the van and take to the streets? I certainly didn't want to leave the van, not just yet. So the only thing to do was drive . . . drive, and see what happened. I knew I could tell Bel to split, to run off on her own, or stay holed up in the room. It was me they wanted. But of course they'd want her too. We were a package now; she knew everything I did. Besides, she wouldn't stay behind. It wasn't her style. I turned to her.

'Tell me about yourself.'

'What?'

'You said I should ask you some time when you weren't expecting it.'

'You're crazy, Michael.' But she was grinning. I realised she was probably readier for this than I was. I started the engine.

'It's just, it'd be nice to have known you before we die.'

'We're not going to die.' She raised the pistol. 'I love you, Michael.'

'I love you, too. I always have.'

She flipped the safety off the semi-automatic. 'Just drive,' she said.

I drove.

We took it slow out of our parking bay and around the side of the motel, then speeded up. I saw that the car was still parked. Worse, it had reversed back to block the only ramp into and out of the car park. I brought the van to a stop. The passenger came out of the office and saw us. He pointed us out to the driver, then took a radio from his pocket. With his other hand, he was reaching into his pocket for something else. And when the driver got out of the car, I saw he was holding a machine-gun. I risked a glance over my shoulder, but all I could see were walls.

'Come on, Michael, let's do it.'

'Do what?'

'What do you think?' She pushed open her door, readying to get out. The driver was taking aim against the roof of the car. I opened my door and steadied the Commando.

Then I saw it.

It was a flat-bed pick-up with a cattle bar on the front and searchlights on top of the cab. I don't know where it came from, but I could see where it was going. It mounted the pavement and kept on coming. Hearing the engine roar, the car driver half-turned, saw what was happening, and pushed himself away from his vehicle, just as the cattle bar hit it from behind. The pick-up's back wheels lifted clean off the ground from the force of the collision, but that was nothing compared to the car. It jumped forward and then spun, looking like a wild horse trying to throw off its rider. Its boot crumpled and then flew open, its rear window splintering. Both driver and passenger had hit the ground. Now a shotgun appeared from the pick-up's passenger-side window and blasted two rounds over the heads of the men, shattering the office window. Then the pick-up reversed back down the short ramp and out on to the road, stopping traffic.

'He's waiting for us!' Bel yelled. She was back in the van now, and slammed shut her door. I drove out past the wrecked car, keeping the Commando aimed out of my window in case the two men decided to get up. The pick-up was already moving, so we followed it, stalled cars complaining all around.

'Who is it?' Bel was shouting. 'Who's in the truck?'

I had a grin all over my face. 'Who do you think it is? It's Spike, of course.'

26

The pick-up seemed to know where it was going.

We followed it east on to I-5 and then south through the city till we connected with the I-90 east out of town.

We were headed for the interior.

'Why doesn't he stop?' Bel said.

'I don't know.' I'd flashed my lights a couple of times, but all I'd received in return was a wave from the window. We crossed over Mercer Island, retracing the route we'd taken into Seattle when we'd arrived. Soon we were on a wide road with wilderness either side. This really was frontier country. Few tourists or holidaymakers ventured into the interior. It was hot and dry, and if you didn't like hills and trees there wasn't much in the way of scenery. That this was logging country was reinforced by crudely made roadside signs denouncing government policy, foreign timber imports, owls and environmentalists. Not always in that order.

We came off the Interstate at Snoqualmie. I was wrong about the tourists. A lot of cars had come to see the Snoqualmie Falls. The pick-up signalled into the car park and we followed. The only space left was a dozen cars away from the pick-up. I could hardly turn the ignition off quick enough.

I sprinted back to the pick-up. There was no one in the cab. Then I saw Spike. He was crouched in front of the vehicle, examining the damage to his cattle bar. He stood up and grinned at me, showing gorgeous white teeth.

'You look like hell,' I said.

'I've been driving all night, what's your excuse?'

We met and hugged, and this time it was me who lifted him off the ground.

'Damn it, Spike, I don't know where you came from, but you're an angel straight from heaven.'

'Man, you know where I come from: Lubbock, Texas. And the only angel I ever was a hell's angel. Oo-ee!' He touched the bruise on my face. Then Bel came running up, and there was a hug and a kiss for her.

'Why didn't you stop before now?' she asked.

'I wanted to be sure those chimpanzees weren't on our tails.'

'Are you kidding? Did you see what you did to their car?'

'Oh, but they've got friends. And you folks, looks like you've got enemies.'

'And not many friends,' I conceded.

'But we only needed one.' And Bel pecked Spike's cheek again and squeezed his arm. He blushed, but covered it up by wiping his face with a red bandana. He had dark eyes and greasy hair and three days of beard growth.

'Man,' he said, 'I been living in these clothes.'

'Yeah, we can tell.'

He punched me in the chest. It was a playful punch, but it hit a raw spot. I winced and doubled over.

'Jesus, Wild West, I'm sorry.'

Bel helped me upright and explained, 'Michael got into a fight with one of the bad guys.'

'I see you've got a story to tell me.'

'We have,' I said, now recovered. 'And we've a few questions for you.'

Spike shrugged. 'Let's find a bar in town, somewhere to take the weight off.' He thought of something. 'You didn't swap my Trans-Am for that Nazi shit, did you? The thing's full of bullet holes!'

I thought of an answer. 'Let's get a beer first.'

'Follow me.'

It turned out that Spike knew the Snoqualmie and North Bend area pretty well.

He'd hunted out here, he had old friends here, and he'd once crashed a car here, which put him on crutches for a month.

'Good people,' he said in the bar, 'but some of them can be a bit strange. I don't know, inbreeding or something. You know they filmed *Twin Peaks* here?'

My face remained blank, but Bel looked interested.

'So what made you follow us?' I asked.

Spike took a mouthful of Rainier. 'Figure it out. I knew you were in trouble, Wild West. Jazz told me some of what Bel had told her. I got the kid to tap back into her computer and print me the same stuff she printed for you. I knew then why you were headed for Seattle, and I knew it could get serious. These cults are bad news. I had a friend got mixed up in one. He's still in therapy. And don't forget, I have a Trans-Am riding on this. So I thought maybe I'd tail along.

'I got to tell you, though, it was coincidence I was there this morning, not inspiration or anything. I hit town first thing this morning, and I was cruising up and down Aurora looking for a motel I liked the look of. I have to tell you, I passed yours twice and never even considered it. What's wrong, man, your credit no good in this town or what?' He sniffed and leaned back in his seat. He'd crossed a foot over one leg, showing off scuffed silver-toed shitkicker boots. Very clearly, he was enjoying telling the story. 'Anyway, as I was going up and down I was seeing these cars with suits in them. They didn't look like Aurora types at all. They looked like the worst kind of normal. They were checking all the motels, not looking for rooms, that was obvious. They were asking for someone. I followed one of them into an office and got to hear the description he gave to the clerk: man and woman, English, in a Vee-Dub. Well, apart from the car, that seemed to fit. So I stopped looking for a room and started following. When I saw your Volkswagen, man, I knew I'd done something right.'

'You can say that again,' said Bel.

'The Trans-Am got shot up,' I said. 'That's why we're in the camper.'

'What happened to it?'

'A man called Kline had his men spray it with bullets. A journalist who'd been helping us was driving at the time.'

'Is he . . . ?'

'He's okay, we think. He's in hospital.'

'So those sonsabitches shot up my car, huh?' Spike had a determined look on his face. It was the sort of look he got every time he picked up an assault rifle. 'We've got to total them, man.'

'Not so fast,' I said. 'You haven't heard our story yet. Maybe when you have, you won't be so enthusiastic.'

'Then let's get some more beers in and tell me all about it.'

We got in more beers.

'This guy called Kline,' said Spike, 'I've got to waste him, man. I've never met him, he doesn't know me from shit, and yet I just *know* I've got to waste him. I won't rest easy till I do.'

It wasn't just the beer talking; it was all the drugs he'd been taking on the road, drugs to keep him awake, drugs to push the accelerator harder, and drugs to hold it all together. I could see that in anywhere between five minutes and a couple of hours he was going to come crashing down.

'I need some sleep,' I said. 'My brain's stopped working. I was awake all night. Why don't we head out into the country, find a quiet spot, and recharge a little?'

'Hey,' said Spike, 'I know just the place.'

He led us out of Snoqualmie on the North Bend road, but then turned off and up a forest track. He was kicking up so much dust I thought our engine would die on us, but the VW just kept on going. The track got narrower, then narrower still. At first it had been a logging track, wide enough for a transporter, but now the trees were scraping both sides of the van, and there was grass growing through the gravel. I counted eight miles of this before we emerged into a clearing. So far since coming off the main road we hadn't seen a single signpost, and no signs of habitation: no electricity pylons or phone lines or mailbox or anything.

But here was a big log house, fairly new and with a lawn surrounding it, beyond which lay impenetrable forest. Spike sounded his horn a few times, but no one came out of the house. We went up to the front door together. There was a note taped there, which Spike read out.

'"Dear Friend, If you've travelled this far, then you probably know us, so you also probably won't be surprised that we're not here. We're in Portland for a few days and will be back Thursday or Friday. You're welcome to camp. There's a stream if you know where to find it. Love and peace, Marnie and Paul."'

'Friends of mine,' Spike said. There were potted plants all around the outside of the house, and he tapped a few playfully with his toe. 'We go back a long way.'

'This is fine,' I said. 'We've got tents in the van, and the van itself is good for sleeping in.' He was bending down, lifting the plants and looking at them, sniffing them. 'We even have a stove . . .' My voice died away as he turned a small plant pot upside down and eased the earth and shrub out on to the palm of his hand. There, embedded in the soil and the thin white roots of the plant, was a house-key. Spike winked at me.

'Friends know where to find the key.'

Inside, the house was fantastic, almost too bright for my liking. Sun streamed through huge louvred windows in the roof. There was unpainted pine everywhere. The walls and furniture were made of it, and the ceiling was panelled with pine tongue-and-groove. There was one large living room, complete with a central stove. Then there were doors off to bedrooms, bathrooms and a kitchen.

'The bathroom has a whirlpool spa,' Spike informed us. He flopped on a white sofa. 'Man, this is the life.'

I didn't want to sit down. I didn't want to touch anything for fear of contaminating it. I was amazed to see that when Spike got up again he hadn't left black smudges on the white material.

Bel had examined the place like a sceptical would-be buyer. She picked up a wastepaper basket and showed it to me.

'They've cleaned the inside of it,' she said. And so they had.

'Hey,' said Spike, 'you want trash, you come back to my place. This is perfect for our purpose.'

'And what is our purpose?' I asked.

'Follow me and find out.'

He led us back down to the pick-up. I noticed it had a rifle rack behind the bench-seat, but the rack was empty. Spike had opened the door of the cab so we could see in. It wasn't a pretty sight. The ashtray was brim-full, with cigarette ends lying on the floor where they'd been stubbed out. There was enough lettuce and tomato to make a family a salad. I guessed Spike had been fuelled by service-station subs. There were empty cans and dirty socks and a begrimed T-shirt and maps and cassettes lying everywhere.

'Nice,' I said, 'we'll take it.'

Spike just smiled and swept everything off the bench-seat on to the floor.

'Put some carpet down there and it'll all look spick and span.'

He was still smiling as he unhooked a couple of catches underneath the seat. Then he pulled at the bench-seat, sliding out the actual part you sat on. He pulled the whole thing out and stood it against the pick-up.

'Well, well,' I said.

There was a lot of storage space underneath the seat. Spike had filled the space with a lethal array of arms.

'I think I thought of everything,' he said.

Bel stuck in a hand and pulled out a cartridge belt. It was full of very long brass cartridges. She held it up like it was a python which had wrapped itself around her wrist.

'Heavy artillery,' I said.

'The time for tiptoeing through the tulips is long past,' Spike said, pulling out what looked like an Ingram, maybe a Cobray. Beneath it I could see some M16s. My mind boggled at what else he might have in there. 'No dynamite,' he said ruefully. 'Otherwise I couldn't have taken a chance on ramming that asshole. But I've some *plastique* if you're in the mood.' He put his face close to mine. It was a good-looking face, typically American in being well-fed but still hungry. He was wearing one of his sleeveless black T-shirts with black denims. 'Gun heaven, Wild West, pure gun heaven.'

I hesitated for all of five seconds.

'Let's do it.'

We slept the rest of the daylight away. I emerged to find Spike dressed only in fresh T-shirt and shorts, chopping onions in the kitchen. He'd found a marijuana plant in the main bedroom and pinched off a few leaves. The aromas in the kitchen weren't just cooking herbs. He held up the chopping-knife for me to see. It was a rubber-handled combat knife with a fat nine-inch blade, the last three inches of which were saw-toothed.

'Chops vegetables great, Wild West.'

'I'll take your word for it.' I looked in the fridge and pulled out a carton of orange juice. I was a lot more comfortable about the place. The condemned man tends to worry less about the state of his cell. I shook the carton and drank from it.

'Oh, man, cooties!' Spike complained. 'Glasses are in the cupboard over the sink.'

So I poured the rest of the juice into a glass, filling it to the brim. I'd drunk half the juice when Bel came in, wearing a long trucker's T-shirt and not much else that I could see. She'd bought the shirt at a service station. It showed a chrome-fronted truck blowing out smoke like steam from a cartoon bull's nose. There was a Confederate flag in the background and the legend 'Ain't No Chicken!'

Spike was trying not to look at her legs as she stood in front of the fridge, bending from the waist to see what there was.

'Any juice?'

'Here.' I handed her my glass. 'We're on cootie-sharing terms,' I told Spike.

'Cosy,' he said, still chopping. He scooped the onion into a pan and added oil. Bel went to watch. 'Uncle Spike's Texas-Style Chilli,' he revealed. 'So long as I can find all the ingredients.' He opened a tin of tomatoes and poured the lot in, along with half a tube of puree. Then he added chilli powder and some other herbs, and finished with a drained tin of red kidney beans.

'Can't find any meat, but what the hell. How hot do you like it?' He offered Bel a spoonful of the juice. She thought it was hot enough already.

'Chicken,' he said to her.

'Well, Spike, why don't you pour some into another pan, that can be my pan? Then you two boys can add as much fire as you like to your share. I'll just sit and watch you tough it out when it comes time to eat.' She patted his back. 'It's food, remember, not an arm-wrestling contest.'

Spike waited a few moments, then howled with laughter.

'Bel, you've got more balls than half the guys I know. Move down to Texas and marry me.' He got down on one knee and grabbed her hand. 'I'm proposing right now, proposing to the woman of my dreams.'

She pushed him away with her bare toe and he sat back on the floor, arms behind him.

'The Good Lord spare me from rejection!'

'Sorry, Spike. Maybe one day when you're older.'

'Come on,' I said, leading her through to the living area. There was a breakfast bar between it and the kitchen. We flopped on to the sofa while Spike sang a few bars of some country song, then decided to whistle it instead.

'Bel,' I said quietly, 'I want you to stay here while Spike and I—'

She leapt back up. 'No way, José! I come this far and now you want to dump me?'

'Sit down, please.'

She sat down. 'Listen, before you try any other speeches or tactics, Michael, I know why you said what you said, and I appreciate it. It shows you care. But you couldn't stop me coming with you if you put a gun to my head, not even one of those M16s. If you leave me here, I'll wave down a car, cosh the driver, and come after you. And I *won't* be in a good mood.'

'Bel, I only want to—'

'I know you do, sweetheart.' She stood up, then bent over me and planted a kiss on my forehead. Then she went over to the hi-fi and searched for something suitable.

Well, I thought, that went pretty much as predicted. I'd tried, which didn't mean I could now progress with a clear conscience. What I'd been about to tell Bel was that if she came along, she'd only be a liability. She might get in the way, or she might cause us to make a critical misjudgement. I knew if I was wounded and there was heavy fire, Spike would leave me . . . and he'd be right. But would either of us leave Bel under the same circumstances? Spike had already confided that he didn't want Bel along.

'I'm not being sexist, man, but this won't be any party for a lady. Nobody's going to be eating sausage-on-a-stick and drinking Californian white. There won't be nice dresses and urbane conversation. It's going to be expletives and explosives, and that's pretty much all. What if she freezes? What if she chokes, man? What then?'

I hadn't an answer for him. It was a question, really, that had to be put to Bel.

Bel put Springsteen on the hi-fi, which met with a roar of approval from the chef. It was early Bruce, and even I knew the record. We sang along where we could, and Spike even sang along where he couldn't. Bel disappeared back into the bedroom and reappeared wearing jeans and boots. Spike had worked up a sweat in the kitchen, and guzzled from a bottle of red wine. He saw me looking at him.

'Hey,' he said, 'not a touch after this, okay?'

'That's okay,' I said, 'we're not going out there tonight.'

'Why not, Wild West?'

'Lots of reasons. They're almost certainly expecting us, we're not ready, we're still all a bit zonked or a bit hyper. Lots of reasons.'

'Not ready? Man, how ready can we be?'

'Readier than this. We want to be fully rested. Tomorrow is better.'

'What? Tomorrow at dawn?'

'Tomorrow night.'

'Why wait, man?'

'Because Jeremiah Provost's supposed to be visiting HQ tomorrow.'

Bel sat down beside me. 'You think he still will?'

'I don't know, maybe.' Spike had come out of the kitchen. He handed round glasses and poured wine into them from the bottle he'd been swigging from.

'It's safe, Wild West, no cooties on me.'

'He means germs,' I told Bel.

'I knew that,' she said coolly.

'Spike,' I said, 'we need this extra time. You've still got to show us how to use that arsenal you've provided.'

'Yeah,' he conceded, 'that's true. I was just itching to do it tonight.'

'Relax, calm down. Take a slow drink and we'll eat a lazy meal. Tomorrow we'll fire off some guns, check their action.'

Bel shook her head. 'If we're going to the peninsula tomorrow night, surely it makes more sense to try out the guns tonight, when conditions are the same?'

Spike whistled through his teeth. 'That is a *good* point.'

'I do have my good points,' Bel said, accepting more wine.

Twenty minutes later, we sat down to the meatless chilli. We ate it with rice and nothing else. It was fine, but Spike kept complaining about how tame it was and splashing pepper sauce over his. His forehead was all perspiration as we talked.

'That Commando is pretty good,' I said. 'Kicks a bit.'

'You're using it one-handed, of course it kicks. Wait'll you try the Ingram, that thing is like somebody's standing there jostling your arm all the time. We are *not* talking pinpoint accuracy, but it's a nine-point-five on the mayhem scale.' He scooped up another spoonful of beans. 'Have you tried the Varmint yet?'

'Haven't needed to.'

'Been one of those weeks, huh? Well, here's my plan. I'll fire an Ingram up into the air and flush them out, then spray the fuckers, while you sit up a tree and pick off the clever ones who're hiding in the cabins. How does that sound?'

'Lousy,' I said, reading Bel's mind. Me, I didn't think it was such a bad plan.

But Bel threw her spoon into her bowl. 'You could be shooting innocent people. We don't know that they're *all* involved. So far as the cult goes, we don't know that *any* of them are involved.'

'That's true, Spike,' I said quickly. I didn't want to give him a chance to say something that would really get Bel angry. 'From what I heard and saw of Provost's conversation with Kline, they're not exactly buddies. Kline couldn't have been treated worse if he'd been selling Bibles in hell.'

'Hell's full of Bible salesmen,' Spike said, and I smiled a wide smile at his joke. Bel was still stony-faced, but he had one weapon to throw at her.

'Bel,' he said, lobbing it without looking, 'now don't get me wrong, but I don't want you along tomorrow night.'

'Tough,' she said. Spike looked to me for support, but I was busy trying to get the last few beans on to my spoon.

'See,' he went on, 'Wild West and me, we've been there before in our different ways. Never as a team exactly, but we know the situation and we know the ground.'

'No,' she said to him, '*you* don't, *I* do. I've been out there, I've been in the fucking compound! And you expect me to sit here knitting you scarves for winter while you go scurrying off to play your little game? No way.'

'Bel,' he said, 'I know you *know* about guns, but can you actually use one?'

There was a silent stare between them. Bel was first to speak. 'You son of a bitch.' She turned it back into four words, where for most Americans it was one. Not sumbitch but son of a bitch. Then she stood up, left the table, and went outside.

I followed, curious to see what she'd do. What she did was find a switch on the wall outside. I suppose she'd noticed it before. Bright white light filled the clearing. I thought I caught a glimpse of a young deer melting back into the woods. There were lamps at ground level and up in the trees. It was like watching a stage-set. Spike joined me on the porch, handing me my wine glass. Bel got into the pick-up and started its engine.

'What's she up to?' he said.

'I think I've got an idea.'

She drove the pick-up to the far edge of the clearing and parked it. Then she started looking around her. I took the

356

empty wine bottle from Spike and headed down the stairs. By the time I reached her, she'd found a couple of large stones and an empty Coke can. I handed her the wine bottle. She smiled and placed it on the bonnet of the pick-up. Then she reached into the cab and emerged with some weapons.

Spike had come down the stairs too. Even he knew what was going on. Bel walked back towards the house and turned to face the pick-up. It was standing side-on to her, the targets all in a row along its bonnet. She chose a handgun first. Expertly she checked and reloaded the clip, then held it out one-handed, closed her left eye, and let off three shots. She hit the can and two of the stones, sending them sliding across the bonnet. I replaced the stones and the can, by which time she'd got to know the small service-style revolver. Three more shots from that, all finding their target.

Spike started clapping, spilling wine from his glass. 'Okay,' he said, 'another good point. Message received.'

But she wasn't about to take that. She got the Varmint from the camper and loaded it, then fired off six elegant shots, each one on target. She hadn't nicked the pick-up's paintwork. For her final shot, she smashed the wine bottle to pieces.

Spike was clapping and whistling again. She turned to face him.

'I can shoot,' she said. 'I just don't like it. And I especially don't like it when innocent people get hurt.'

'Okay,' said Spike, arms open in conciliation. 'Give us another plan.'

'I've got a plan for you,' I said. 'It's in the form of a question. How do you sort out the good guys from the bad?'

They both shook their heads, so I supplied the answer.

'You see who runs away. Now come on, the next drink is on the house.'

But we had coffee instead of wine, and we sat on the ground outside while Spike spread out his wares. He laid everything out on a couple of old blankets.

'You ever see that film,' he said, 'where all the guns are laid out on the bed, and De Niro's buying? Man, I can't wait to see their faces when we turn up toting this little package.' Spike's grin was halogen-white.

I thought I saw Bel shiver, but then it was getting late. I felt a little shivery myself.

27

And still there were decisions.

For instance, should we check Provost's house, see if he really had gone to Lake Crescent?

Should we visit the house on Hood Canal first? That way, we might take out possible reinforcements. We didn't want to lay siege to the cabins only to have a vanload of newly-summoned heat creep up on us from behind.

Should we take the pick-up, the V-Dub, or both? They'd be looking out for the camper, but then they'd also be on the lookout for a crazy pick-up driver with dents in his cattle-bar.

One thing we knew: it was too dangerous to cross on to the peninsula by ferry. They'd almost certainly be watching Bremerton. In fact, there weren't nearly enough roads into the Olympic Peninsula for my liking. For an area measuring roughly ninety miles by sixty, it boasted only two routes into it. There was just the one main road, the 101, circling the perimeter of the National Park and National Forest. Using as few as maybe half a dozen men, they'd have advance warning of any approach we might make.

There were other possibilities, but they were time-consuming. One had us take a boat to Victoria, British Columbia, and then another boat back from there to Port Angeles. The two crossings would take a total of several hours, and as Spike pointed out, Kline would already have considered this. If he was agency or government, he'd have an order put out for all sailings to be watched.

'What you're saying,' said Bel, 'is that there's no way in there without them knowing about it?'

Spike nodded, but I had an idea. It was just about my craziest notion yet, but my partners went for it. After that, things started slotting into place.

Since the authorities weren't on the lookout for Spike, we rented a car in his name in North Bend. It was a bland family model, and Spike decried the loss of his beloved stick-shift. But it gave us the confidence to head back into Seattle. We stopped at Ed's Guns and Sporting Goods. I asked Archie if anyone had been asking questions. He shook his head.

'What're you looking for this time, son?'

'Balaclavas and warpaint,' I informed him.

It was when I said this that it all hit home, the sheer madness of it all. I was way out of my league; I was playing a different game altogether. I should have been scared shitless, and I was. I could hardly stop my hands shaking – not exactly a good sign in a professional sniper. My heart was thumping and I kept thinking I was going to be sick. But at the same time it was like being a little drunk, and Bel and Spike felt the same. We kept grinning at each other and collapsing into fits of nervous giggling. I burst out laughing in Archie's shop. He gave me a look, and smiled like he got the joke.

'There's no joke,' I told him. And there wasn't. There was just the euphoria of fear. I was pushing myself towards the confrontation as though each step had to be taken in thicker and deeper mud. It was the slowest day of my life. For all the activity and movement, it was slower than all the days I'd spent in hotel rooms, waiting for my hit to arrive in town, all the days I'd sat by windows, working out firing angles and distances. Archie seemed disappointed at the size of the sale.

'I see your friend's going to be all right.'

'What?'

He smiled. 'Don't worry, I won't tell anybody. They had a photo of him on TV. I recognised him straight off.'

'What's the latest?'

'He's awake. The police are talking to him. So far it's as one-sided as staging *The Price is Right* in a convent.'

I nodded, relieved. 'Archie,' I said, 'could you go to the hospital, say you're a friend of his?'

'You want me to go see him?'

'If you give your name and address, I think he'll agree to see you.'

'Well, hell, what am I supposed to say?'

'Tell him we're fine. Tell him today's the day. It might help cheer him up.'

He screwed shut one eye. 'Does this make me an accessory?'

'What's the crime?'

'Well . . .' He scratched his head. 'I can't close up the shop till six.'

'This evening would be fine. It'd be perfect.'

I tried handing him a twenty for his trouble, but he wouldn't take it.

'Be careful out there,' he told me.

'I will, Archie, I will.'

'I hate this car,' said Spike. 'This is the most boring car I've ever sat in in my life. Period.'

We were parked at the top of the hill, a hundred yards from Provost's house. We'd been sitting watching for a while, Spike drumming his fingers on the steering-wheel.

'I say we switch to my plan.' Spike's plan was simple. He'd walk up to Provost's front door and ring the bell.

'Just like the Avon lady,' he said.

The plan depended on two things: the fact that Provost, Kline and the others didn't know Spike, and that Spike could manufacture some bullshit excuse as to why he was ringing the bell in the first place.

We took a vote: it was two to one in favour. I was the lone dissenter. So Spike got out of the car and jogged his way down the hill.

'What's wrong?' Bel asked.

'I can't help feeling we're playing our joker a bit early.' She didn't get it, so I explained. 'Spike's our secret weapon. If they rumble him, we're back to square one.'

She smiled. 'Aren't you mixing your card games and your board games?'

I gave her a sour look, like I'd just bitten on something hard and was checking my molars for damage. Then I watched through the windscreen for Spike's return.

It wasn't long before he came jogging back up the hill again. He cast a look back to see if anyone was watching him, then got into the car and turned the ignition.

'The place is empty,' he said. 'I took a look around, nothing. They've got curtains over the windows, but even then I could tell nobody was home.'

'Then he's gone to the peninsula,' said Bel.

'Looks like. Either that or he's off to Costco for his month's groceries.'

This was it then. We were headed out to confront Provost and Kline. I felt weary, and leaned my head against the back of the seat, happy to let Spike do the driving. He turned on the radio and found a rock station. Springsteen: Born in the USA. Spike turned the volume up all the way and sang his heart out to the distorted song.

We already knew we were taking the long route to the peninsula, south through Tacoma and then north again.

'Spike,' I said, 'we really appreciate you helping us.'

'Man, I'm not helping you, I'm on *vacation*.'

'How's it been so far?'

'More fun than EPCOT, I'll tell you that.'

'I'm not sure that's a recommendation.'

He was grinning with his near-perfect teeth. 'It is, believe me. We should all go to EPCOT when this is over.'

'Who knows?' I said quietly. We drove into Port Angeles

and then out again in the direction of Pioneer Memorial Museum.

We stopped on the southern edge of town, not far from the Park Headquarters. Then we put my plan into action.

Bel managed to get the attention of two park wardens who'd just driven their car out of Park HQ. She brought them over to our car, where Spike and I smiled and nodded a greeting.

'What's the problem here?' the first of them asked pleasantly.

'This,' said Spike, pointing the Ingram at the man's chest. The man, to give him credit, saw the problem immediately. It wasn't our problem, it was *his*. We took him and his partner in the Chrysler, while Bel drove the Park Service car. A little further out of town, we pulled off the road on to a track in the woods and stripped the wardens of their clothes.

'Jesus, why did you have to pick on Laurel and Hardy?' Spike complained to Bel. He was having trouble getting his uniform on, while mine fell off me like washing on a clothes-horse. We'd already tried swapping, but it had been worse.

We tied the wardens up thoroughly, and left one of them lying in the front of the Chrysler, the other in the back. We transferred our stuff to their car, and Bel got into the back, lying down across the seat and covering herself with a tartan travel-rug.

'National Park Service,' said Spike, getting into the driving seat. 'Here to serve and protect the wildlife.' He laughed. 'We'll show them what a wild life really means.'

Then he reversed all the way back on to the road. We took the 101 west. Five miles out of town, the road forked, but we kept heading west on 112. Just after the branch-off, we saw them.

There was a 4×4 parked by the side of the road, and two men standing beside it. They were as obvious a lookout as we could have hoped for. We debated stopping and confronting them – Spike said it would be a test of our disguises if nothing else. But I prevailed, and we drove past. If we'd put them out of action, their absence might be spotted. And we needed time to set things up. So we left them there, knowing that if they were summoned to the Disciples' HQ, it would still take them half an hour to get there. I didn't think we'd need more than half an hour. The way Spike saw it, if we went along with *his* plan we wouldn't need more than five minutes.

If you've ever seen the napalm attack in *Apocalypse Now*, you'll get some idea of the scale he was thinking on.

I crouched in the woods and watched the world through my night-vision scope. Strange things were happening in the Disciples' compound.

Or rather, *nothing* was happening.

And that was strange.

It wasn't that everyone had retired for the night. I got the feeling that most of the cabins were devoid of life. Spike and Bel had gone on a recce and come back with the news that they couldn't see any vehicles anywhere. Well, I could see one: Kline's Lincoln. It was squeezed in between two cabins, supposedly out of sight. But I couldn't see any other cars.

Only one explanation made sense: someone had sent the Disciples away. Now why would they do that? Obviously, because they weren't wanted. It meant one thing to me: the Disciples didn't know what was going on, and Kline and his men didn't *want* them to know what was going on.

I was concentrating not on the original cabin, the one where I'd been disturbed by Nathan, but on the smaller cabin next to it. This was where the light was burning. It looked like an oil-lamp or something powered by gas, and gave off a halo of yellow light. The pow-wow was taking place in this cabin. I was waiting for the braves to emerge.

Meanwhile I scanned the rest of the compound. It was pitch black, but to my right eye the world was a red filter with a black cross-sight. It was still and quiet. Sound carried a long way out here, and I actually heard a distant rattle as the cabin door opened.

I moved the scope back to the cabin and watched as a man appeared in the doorway. He was one of Kline's men, and he was smoking a cigarette. Other men filtered out on to the porch and lit up. Provost must be a non-smoker. They'd been in a room with him, and were now desperate. There were six of them. Three I thought I recognised from Oban, and three I didn't. Provost and Kline must still be in the cabin. The door opened again and someone stepped out.

A woman.

I recognised her by her shape. She was Alisha, Provost's lieutenant and lover. She accepted a cigarette and stood talking to the men.

They spoke in undertones, but even so I could hear the noise they made, even if I couldn't hear the words. The men were wearing suits. There would be handguns under the suits, but they were more prepared than that. Two of them had rested their M16s against the wall of the cabin while they smoked. They kept looking into the distance, mostly towards me. But from where they were, I knew they couldn't see anything. All they could see was movement, and the only things moving were the branches of the trees as the breeze passed over them.

I waited, but Kline and Provost didn't come out. Nor did they pass in front of the window. I adjusted the scope a fraction, and felt better. The scope was attached to the Varmint, and the Varmint was loaded with its full five rounds. I didn't have any padding against my shoulder. I didn't mind if I bruised. Bruising seemed the least of my problems.

I heard movement behind me.

'Well?' Spike whispered.

'I count six men so far. I haven't seen Provost or Kline, but there's one woman. So that's a total of nine.'

'And seven of those we can take out straight away,' Spike said.

'I'd like Kline alive . . . at least until he's talked to me.'

'Then we'd better get a car battery and a couple of electrodes. I mean, he's not going to talk for the fun of it.'

He had a point. Bel had moved more quietly than Spike. She was the other side of me. All three of us were wearing balaclavas and face-paint: green and black. Just in case they had a lighting system rigged up somewhere. So far, they were relying on darkness. But they could always change tactics and light the forest up. If they lit us up, of course, they also lit themselves up. And we'd be camouflaged. We were wearing green and black jackets and green trousers. We certainly looked the part, even if we didn't feel it. Spike was in his element, but the markings on Bel's face only hid the fact that she had lost all colour. Even her lips were bloodless.

As for me, I'd lost the shakes, but I still wanted to play it cautious. This was all new. I wasn't a mercenary, though I'd hung with them. I wasn't Action Man or GI Joe. I wasn't Spike.

'What about all the regular hippies?' he asked.

'They've shipped out.'

'That's perfect. That's beautiful.' He fixed his eyes on me. 'I got them here, man,' he whispered. He was holding four short, fat cylinders.

'So you keep saying.'

'When are we going to do it?'

I looked to Bel, who nodded. 'We're doing it now,' I said.

'Well, all right then,' said Spike, disappearing back into the gloom.

Bel and I stared at one another for a while. I wanted to kiss her, and I think she knew it. But she just smiled and nodded again, then squeezed my shoulder and started creeping away in the opposite direction from Spike.

It was my play now. I rested the Varmint's stock against

my shoulder again and took a look. I knew I had to give Spike and Bel a minute or two. The guards had finished their cigarettes. They were kicking their heels. I liked the way they were lined up on the porch like targets on some fairground rifle-stall. I heard the static crash of a radio, and saw one of them lift a walkie-talkie out of his pocket. I was glad now that we hadn't hit the men at the checkpoint. It would have meant a welcoming committee.

But then at least a welcoming committee would have prompted action.

I counted up to thirty. Then I did it again.

When I reached twenty-nine for the second time, I started firing. I'm no speed-shooter, remember, but I knew I had to knock down as many of these guards as I could. I wasn't concentrating on any clever shots, I just aimed to hit the targets anywhere I could.

I'd fired off two shots before they located me. That's the problem with shooting at night with no flash-hider. They saw the second blast of fire from my barrel. Not that it helped them, not at this distance. They were still firing at shadows, and I was picking them off. Two bodies had gone down when the first of Spike's flares landed in the compound. To get it so near the cabin, he must've crept up suicidally close. He chucked a couple more flares. They burnt orangey-pink and let off a lot of smoke. I fired off the final three shots from my clip before the smoke got too bad. They'd tried retreating back into the cabin, but were being ordered to spread out across the compound.

Which was just what we'd expected. That's why Spike was way over one side of the compound and Bel, armed with two handguns, was over the other. The guards were firing now, spraying automatic rounds. From somewhere, I heard the unmistakable sound of Spike's Ingram firing back. I took off the night-sight, put down the Varmint, picked up my Colt Commando, and waded in.

The compound was all smoke and circus lights now, but

the breeze was dispersing the smoke as rapidly as it formed. I decided to frighten whoever was left in the cabin, so let off a few rounds at it. The walls were thin wood planks over wood studding. In films, walls like that could stop bullets, but not in real life. I drilled into the walls until I could see light coming out through them. Then someone turned the lamp out. I'd been firing high, guessing anyone scared would be ducking or lying flat. I hoped I hadn't hit anyone I didn't want hit. Then I realised something.

I realised I was the only target the guards had. A bullet from a handgun flew past my head. I squatted down and let off a burst with the Colt. I hit the gunman three times across his chest, sending him flying backwards into the dirt. I could hear Bel now, firing in quick bursts the way she'd been taught. One-two-three, one-two-three, like dance steps. And Spike, Spike was back on the range in Texas, wasting bullets but making plenty of noise. They must've thought there was an army coming at them. And it was working, the guards were firing but retreating at the same time. If you fire a gun while you're moving, forget about accuracy. I held my ground and fired another burst from the Colt. It was fitted with a thirty-round clip. I had a few more clips in my pocket.

Then the cabin window shattered and someone started firing through it. I heard a dull thwump and realised they were firing grenades. I dived sideways, thudded into the ground, and started moving. The explosion was way behind me and over to one side, but it still lifted me off the ground. I felt the earth swell beneath my chest, like the planet was taking a deep breath, and the blast kicked my legs up into the air.

I lay flat facing the cabin and started firing, only to have the magazine die on me. It took a few seconds to reload, by which time another thwump had signalled a fresh grenade. I crawled again. The blast was a lot closer this time. It closed off my eardrums and rattled my head. I rolled and kept rolling, bits of earth and tree-bark raining down on me.

There was nothing but a mute hissing in my ears, and somewhere behind it the distant firing of guns.

I tried to shake my head clear, and realised something had hit me. A rock or something. My left arm felt numb from the impact. I bit my fingers, trying to force some sensation back into them. Then got on to my feet and started firing again. There were bodies in front of me, three of them. They were lifeless. Two I had hit on the porch, and another hit since then, I couldn't say by whom.

Then I saw another figure darting through shadow. I put the night-sight to my eye and made out Spike. He knew I could see him, and gave an OK sign with thumb and forefinger. Not that he could see me, but he gave it anyway. I fired another spray towards the cabin. There were no more thwumps, which meant that Kline only had the two grenades. Now I could hear a woman shrieking, and hear two men shouting. I checked over to my right with the night-sight, but there was no sign of Bel.

Then the cabin door flew open, and Alisha came stumbling out.

'Don't shoot!' she yelled. 'I'm not armed or anything!' She was wailing, and holding her arm. It looked like she'd been winged.

'Everybody else out of the cabin!' I called. My voice sounded firm enough, from what I could hear of it. 'Out of the cabin *now*!'

Spike had come forward and was yelling Bel's name. There was no answer.

'Go find her,' I ordered, trying to keep the panic out of my voice. I took a slow-burn flare out of my pocket, stuck it in the ground, and lit it, moving away immediately. Spike was moving towards the side of the cabin. A man appeared at the cabin door. It was Jeremiah Provost. He had his hands up. Now that the flare was lighting up the scene, I saw he had blood on his white shirt. But it was a smear, nothing more, and I guessed it to be not his blood but Alisha's.

'Lie on the ground, Alisha,' I ordered. 'Why don't you join her, Provost?'

'Who are you?' He wasn't moving. 'What do you want?'

There was a sudden pistol shot, and Spike slumped to the ground. I moved towards him, then realised my mistake. I half-turned in time to see Alisha drawing a gun from beneath her. I shot her in the head with the Colt. One shot was all it took.

Then I turned again, and saw Kline stepping over Spike's body. He had his pistol pointed at my head. I ducked down, firing as I did so. His body fell forwards and landed on the ground. From behind him stepped Bel. Wisps of smoke were rising from the barrel of her pistol. The back of his head was matted with blood where she'd hit him.

She collapsed to her hands and knees and threw up on the ground.

'Are there any of them left, Bel?'

She managed to shake her head. I turned the Colt to Provost. He'd come down the cabin steps and was kneeling over Alisha.

'Why?' he said, repeating the word over and over again. I left him there and checked the cabin. It was empty. The back window Kline had climbed out of stood wide open. Smells of forest and cordite were mixed in the air. I walked back out, and found Bel sitting on the ground next to Spike. She was stroking his forehead.

'He's alive,' she said. 'Should we move him?'

'We may have to.'

I took a look. There was warm sticky blood all over his chest. He'd taken a clean hit in the front and out the back. If he'd been a little further away, the bullet might have stuck or burst open inside him. I didn't know whether he'd live.

'You got a stretcher here?' I said to Provost. He looked up at me with tears in his eyes, and mouthed the word 'Why?'

'I'll tell you why. Because she had a gun. Why did she have a gun? Because she wasn't a Disciple of Love, she was working for Kline, the way Nathan was. Did you know Nathan was Kline's brother? Did you know he was Nathan *Kline*? No?' Provost shook his head. 'It's in the files in your own office. How come your beloved Alisha didn't tell you? Work it out for yourself, but first tell me if you've got a first aid kit and a fucking stretcher!'

He stared at me. 'No stretcher,' he said. 'There's first aid stuff in the office.'

I turned to Bel. 'Go fetch it.' Spike was breathing in short painful gasps, but he was breathing. I went over to him again. His eyes were closed in concentration. He was concentrating on sticking around.

'Spike,' I said, 'remember, you can't afford to die. I suppose I better tell you the truth, Spike. There aren't *any* guns in heaven.'

He almost smiled, but he was concentrating too hard.

I went back to Provost and stood over him.

'Time to talk,' I said.

'Talk? We could have talked without *this*.'

'Not my choice, Provost, Kline's choice. Your man's choice.'

'My man?' He spoke like his mouth was full of bile. 'Kline wasn't my man.'

'Then who was he?'

'He used to work for the NSC. Have you heard of them?'

'A bit.'

'They retired him after an accident. *I* was the accident.'

'I don't understand.'

'You will.' He stood up. 'You really think Alisha was working for Kline?'

'It doesn't mean she didn't love you.'

He glowered at me. 'Don't patronise me, Mr West. Kline told me about you. He said you were coming after me. He failed to specify why.'

'Questions, that's all.'

He turned away from me and sat on the cabin steps,

holding his head in his hands. 'Fire away,' he said without looking up.

Fire away? I hardly knew where to begin. Bel had returned with the first aid kit and was starting to staunch Spike's bleeding. I walked over to the steps and stood in front of Provost. I'd taken Sam Clancy's recording walkman from my pocket, and switched it on.

'A woman was killed in London,' I said. 'Her name was Eleanor Ricks. She was a journalist, investigating the Disciples of Love.'

'I don't know anything about it.'

'You didn't sanction her killing?'

'No.'

'Then Kline acted alone.'

Now he looked up at me. '*You* killed her?'

'Yes.'

'Then answer me a question. Why would Kline need to pay someone to do the job when he had his own hired army?'

It was a good question. So good, in fact, that I didn't have an answer . . .

'I don't know,' I said. 'You tell me.'

Provost smiled. 'I can't tell you. I can only tell you what Kline told me. He doesn't *know* why you've been snooping around. He didn't order any assassination, and he, too, was wondering who did. When you started asking questions, you became a threat.'

'He's had journalists killed, hasn't he? He had Sam Clancy shot.'

'Kline didn't have much of a conscience, if that's what you're saying.'

'But what was he trying to protect? Why was he shielding you?'

'Money, Mr West, what else? Oh, I don't mean I was paying him. I mean *he* paid *me*, and he's been paying for that mistake ever since.' He glanced down at Kline's body. 'He paid most dearly tonight.'

'I still don't get it.'

'Kline worked for a part of the NSC involved with funding the Nicaraguan Contras. This was back in the mid-80s. He managed to wheedle ten million dollars out of . . . I don't know, the Sultan of somewhere, some Middle Eastern country. At this time, I had a little money. Elderly relatives kept dying. I got bored attending so many funerals. I liked to keep my money my own business, so I held an account in Switzerland.'

'Go on.'

'It was quite a coup for Kline, getting so much money for the Contras, but he didn't exactly know what to do with it. Someone at the NSC, I'm not saying it was Colonel Oliver North, suggested holding it in a bank account until it could be disposed of as intended.'

'A Swiss bank account?'

'The NSC held just such an account. Only the gods of fate and irony stepped in. Kline copied the details of the account down wrongly. I can't recall now exactly why I decided to check the state of my account, but I telephoned Switzerland one Thursday morning their time, and was told the exact amount I had on deposit. It seemed larger than I remembered, about ten million larger. I asked my account manager how much notice I had to make of a large withdrawal.'

Provost stopped there.

'You took out the whole ten mil?'

'No, in the end I merely transferred it to a new account.'

'Christ.'

'It was Kline's mistake. He was sent to reason with me – no matter how discreet Swiss banks are, the NSC has ways of tracking people down. We came to a compromise. I handed back half the money. The other half I kept.'

'And he went along with that?'

'He didn't have much choice.'

'He could have killed you.'

Provost smiled. 'The NSC weren't mentioned in my will, Mr West. He still wouldn't have gotten the money. Besides which, his superiors were furious with him. They couldn't possibly sanction something so messy.'

'So they booted him out?'

'No, they booted him into the shadows. His remit was to make sure no one ever got to learn about the whole thing.'

'And that meant stopping reporters from snooping too deeply?'

'Exactly.'

'Which is why Eleanor Ricks had to be stopped.'

He shook his head. 'I've already told you, Kline denied it. And he went on denying it.'

'Then it doesn't make sense.'

'Maybe someone else hired your services.'

'Yes, but I've . . .'

He saw what I was thinking. 'You've come all this way and killed all these people, and you're no further forward?'

I nodded. My mind was reeling. I'd got most of my hearing back, but it didn't matter, I could hardly take any of it in.

'Two digits, that's what did it,' Provost was saying. 'Kline wasn't much of a typist. He transposed two of the digits on the account number. And in doing so, the NSC paid for the Disciples of Love. *That*, Mr West, is why they had to keep it quiet. They'd funded a religious cult, and the interest on their money is still funding it.'

'Where's the proof?'

'Oh, I have proof.'

'Where?' I wasn't sure I believed him, not completely. There had to be something more. He looked to be having trouble with his memory, so I tickled his chin with the Colt.

'Remember what I do for a living, Provost.'

'How can I forget? There are papers in my wall safe, and copies with my lawyer.'

374

Maybe it was the word 'lawyer' that did it. I almost felt something click in my head.

'You're going to open your safe for me.'

'It's not here, it's in my home in Seattle.'

'Fine, we'll go there.'

'I want to stay here. The combination's easy to find. I can never remember it myself, so I keep it written on a pad beside the telephone. It's marked as an Australian telephone number.'

I knew I had to see it for myself. I had to hold some proof of his story in my hands. Even then, it wouldn't be enough. I'd come through all this, and dragged Bel and Spike with me, and still there was no answer, not that Provost could provide.

A shot rang out. I spun round with the Colt. The guard had crawled from where Spike must have left him. There was blood all down his front. I didn't make things much worse by snuffing out what life he had left. I'd robbed him of a few minutes, that was all.

But when I turned back to Provost, I saw that he'd taken a shot to the heart. The guard had been aiming at him, not me. Suicide orders from Kline, no doubt. I eased the body on to the ground. Bel barely glanced up from her work. She'd patched Spike up as best she could.

'He's still losing blood,' she said. After feeling for Provost's pulse and finding none, I walked over to her. Then I saw the car between the cabins. Its rear windscreen had been shattered, but when I went to look, it had its tyres intact. I felt in Kline's pockets and drew out the keys, then reversed the car into the clearing.

With Bel's help we got Spike into the back of the car. He groaned and winced a little, so I repeated my warning to him about gun heaven. Then we got in the car and drove off.

'What are we going to do?' Bel asked.

'Get Spike to hospital.'

'But after that? I heard what that man said back there. He was telling us we'd come all this way for nothing. He was saying all those people died . . . and my father died . . . for *nothing*.'

I looked at her. She was crying. 'Maybe he was lying. Maybe . . . I don't know.'

We passed a car on the road, hurtling towards Crescent Lake. It was the lookout. They didn't even give us a second glance. I took a detour back to where we'd left the wardens. They seemed terrified to see us. I pulled them out of the Chrysler and left them propped back to back on the ground.

'You take Spike to hospital,' I said.

'Where are you going?'

'Provost's house.'

She looked at me. 'Do you think you'll find what you're looking for?'

'I don't know what I'm looking for, Bel. Look after Spike, eh?' Then I kissed her and got into the Chrysler.

On the road back into Seattle, I managed to put America out of my mind. Instead, I thought back to London, right to the start of this whole thing and to Scotty Shattuck. Why hadn't I hung around until he'd turned up again? He was the key to the whole thing. My impatience had led me the wrong direction. I'd been going wrong ever since.

Maybe I was still going wrong, but I kept on driving.

28

I was prepared to kick down Provost's door.

But it wasn't necessary. The door was unlocked. I eased the Smith & Wesson 559 out of my waistband and crept into the house. Someone had been there before me. The place had been turned over in what looked like robbery, except that nothing obvious was missing. The TV, video and hi-fi were still there, as was some women's jewellery scattered over the floor in the master bedroom. It had to be Alisha's jewellery. I didn't feel too guilty about killing her. She'd have killed me. But seeing the jewellery, plus her clothes, plus smelling her perfume . . . I had to rest for a moment and control my breathing.

And that's when he found me.

I felt the cold muzzle of the gun against the back of my neck. It froze my whole body for a moment.

'Toss the gun over there.'

I did as I was told, and then was frisked from behind.

'Walk into the living room.'

I did so. I recognised the voice. I knew who was behind me.

'Now turn around.'

I turned around and was face to face with Leo Hoffer.

'Sit down,' he said. 'Take the weight off. You look like you've had a heavy night.'

'It's been heavy.' I sat down on the sofa, but I rested on its edge, ready to spring up if I got the chance.

'Get comfortable,' he said. 'Go on, sit right back.'

I sat right back. The sofa was like marshmallow. I knew it

was almost as good as restraints. I wasn't going anywhere in a hurry.

'Yeah, it's a bitch, isn't it?' Hoffer was saying. 'I sat in it earlier on while I was figuring out what to do. Took me five fucking minutes to get out of it. It's a regular Venus fly-trap. So, Mr Wesley-Weston-West, what're you doing here?'

'The same as you probably.'

'Well, I hope you've got some tools with you, because that safe isn't budging.'

He was pointing in the direction of the far wall. He'd taken down a large seascape painting to reveal a small wall safe. Even from here I could see he'd had a go at it. The wall all around it was scraped and gouged, and the metal surface of the safe was scratched and dented.

'I can open it,' I said.

'That's good. Because I want to stick your head in it then push my pistol up your ass.'

'That's class, Hoffer.'

'I'll tell you what class is, class is leading me on this fucking chase halfway across the world and back. That's so classy I'm going to blow you away.'

I felt tired suddenly. I mean, dog-tired. There was no steam left in me, no fight. I rubbed at my forehead.

'I want a drink,' I said.

'Provost hasn't got a damned drop in the house.' He reached into his jacket and pulled out a half bottle. 'That's why I had to go fetch this.' He tossed the bottle on to the couch beside me. It was Jim Beam, a couple of inches missing from the top. I unscrewed the cap and took a good deep gulp. Afterwards, I didn't feel quite so tired.

'How did you find me?'

He came close enough to me to take back the bottle, then retreated again. He took a slug, keeping his eyes and his Smith & Wesson 459 on me. He didn't bother recapping the bottle, but left it on the mantelpiece.

'Don't forget,' I said, 'your prints are on that.'

'And yours,' he said. 'I'll wipe it before I go. You look like you're ready for another shot already.'

But I shook my head. 'Any more and I'll fall asleep, no offence.'

He smiled. 'None taken. But I don't want you asleep. I've never killed a man while he's sleeping. In fact, I've never killed anyone, period, not even in anger, never mind anyone defenceless. I'm not like you, man. I don't kill the innocents. You fucked up big when you hit Walkins's daughter.'

'I know.'

'Yeah, and I bet you still lose sleep over it. I bet you lose sleep over all of them, man, all your victims. Well, I'm going to enjoy killing *you*.'

'Killing isn't as easy as you might think. Maybe you should hide me away till your client can come and help. I'm sure he wouldn't mind firing off a round or two.'

'You're probably right, but then he hasn't worked for that privilege the way I have. How did I find you? I didn't. *You* found *me*. I was waiting outside to see who turned up. I was expecting Provost or Kline.'

'You know Kline?'

'I've met him.'

'He's dead.'

'I'm pleased to hear it. He was about as evil a fuck as has ever given me indigestion. I hate indigestion at breakfast, it stays with me the rest of the day. Heartburn, you know.'

I nodded. 'Provost's dead, too.'

'You've been busy. So what the fuck was it all about?'

I shrugged. 'Listen,' I said, 'I want to thank you for something.'

He narrowed his eyes. 'What?'

'Covering up Max's head the way you did. His daughter found him.'

'Well, those sick fucks left the head teetering on the body.'

'I know, and thanks.'

'Is she still around?'

'She's . . . she's still around.'

'Don't worry,' he said, 'I've got no grudge with her.'

'Yes, I know.'

'This is you and me, Mikey, the way it was always supposed to be. Oh hey, your folks say hello.'

It was like a blow to the head. 'What?'

'I had this Army guy check haemophilia cases. It was a short list, and one of the names was Michael Weston. I found your mom and dad. They say hello. That's why I was so long getting here. Sidetracked, you might say. But I know a lot about you now, and that's nice, seeing how we're not going to be able to get acquainted the normal way.' He saw something like disbelief on my face. 'Your father's called John, he's retired now but he's still Army through and through. Your mother's called Alexis. They live in Stockport.' He smiled. 'Am I getting warm?'

'Fuck it, Hoffer, just kill me.'

'What's in the safe, Mike? Get me interested.'

'Huh?'

'You came here for whatever's in that safe. I want to know what it is.'

'Proof,' I said. 'This whole shitty deal is down to Kline and a bloody typing error.'

I had his interest now, which was good. It kept me from being killed. I told him the story, taking my time. I decided I didn't want to die. I didn't want anyone else to die. Not today, maybe not ever.

'That sounds,' Hoffer said, finishing the hooch, 'like a crock of twenty-carat gold-plated shit.'

'There are papers in the safe.'

'And you can open it?' I nodded. 'Go on then.'

He followed me to the telephone. There were a lot of scribbles on the message-pad, a lot of numbers and letters. I found what I wanted and tore the top sheet off, taking it with me to the wall-safe.

'Bullshit,' Hoffer sneered disbelievingly as I read from the sheet and started turning the dial. I pulled on the handle and opened the safe slowly.

I looked inside, knowing if he wanted to see, he'd have to come right up behind my back. I could feel him behind me. He was close, but was he close enough? If I swung at him, would I connect with anything other than air? Then I saw what was in the safe. There were papers there, and a tidy bundle of banknotes. But there was also a snub-nose revolver, a beautiful little 38. I took my decision, but took it too late. The butt of a gun connected with the back of my head, and my legs collapsed from under me.

I woke up cramped, like I'd been sleeping in a car. I blinked open my eyes and remembered where I was. I looked around. The pain behind my eyes was agony. I wondered if Hoffer had been in there and done some DIY surgery while I'd been out. Maybe a spot of trepanning.

I was in a bright white bathroom with a sunken whirlpool bath and gold taps. I was over by the sink, sitting on the cold tiled floor with my arms behind me. My arms were stiff. I looked round and saw that they were handcuffed round a couple of copper water pipes beneath the sink. My feet had been tied together with a man's brown leather belt.

Most disconcerting of all, Hoffer was sitting on the toilet not three feet away.

He had his trousers on though. And he'd put the toilet lid down so he'd be more comfortable. He had my money belt slung over one shoulder, and he was leafing through some documents.

'Well, Mike,' he said, 'looks like you were right, huh? Some fucking business, handed five mil by the government. Thank you very much and shalom. Jesus.' He patted his jacket pocket. 'Yet the scumbag only kept five thou in his safe. Still, it'll buy a few lunches. And thanks for your donation.' He tossed the money-belt towards me. 'I've left you the traveller's cheques. I don't want to get into any forgery shit. Not that they accept traveller's cheques where you're headed.'

I rattled the handcuffs.

'Good, aren't they? New York PD issue. Before they went over to plastic or whatever shit they use now. Look, I'll leave the key over here, okay?' He put it on the floor beside him. 'There you go. It'll give you something to do while you're dying. Of course, you may already be dying, huh? I whacked you pretty good. There could be some internal haemorrhaging going on. See, I know about haemophilia, I did some reading. Man, they're *this* close to a cure, huh? Genetics and stuff. Fuck all those liberals trying to stop laboratory experiments. Mike, we need *more* of those lab animals with holes drilled in their scrotums and wires running through them like they're circuit-boards or something.'

'Circuit-boards don't have wires, Leo. At least, not many.'

'Ooh, pardon me, professor.' He laughed and rubbed his nose. I knew he'd done some drugs since I'd last been conscious, but I couldn't tell what. He was feeling pretty good though, I could see that. Good enough to let me live? Well, he hadn't killed me yet. He stood up and opened the medicine-cabinet.

'All this organic shit,' he muttered, picking out bottles and rattling them. He half-turned towards me. 'I get fucking earache when I fly. And it's all your fault I've been doing so much flying of late.'

'My heart bleeds.'

Now he grinned. 'You can say that again. So Kline set you up, huh?'

'Provost says he didn't.'

'Well, somebody did. As soon as I heard you'd been asking the producer and the lawyer what clothes Eleanor Ricks usually wore, I knew the road you were going.'

'Then you're cleverer than me.'

'Whoever paid you knew what she'd be wearing, didn't they?'

'Yes.'

'Well, Mike, that kind of narrows things down, doesn't it?'

It struck me, the problem was I hadn't let myself narrow it down enough. Too late now, way too late . . .

'So,' I said, 'you know I'm a haemo. And you're right, a simple knock on the head might just do it.'

'But I know something that'd do it a lot better.' He stood up and came over, crouching in front of me. He had something in his hand. When he unfolded it, I saw a short fat blade. It was a damned pocket-knife.

'Beautiful, isn't it? Look, there's a serpent running down its back. That's the trademark. Talk about Pittsburgh steel, man, *this* is a piece of steel.'

'What are you going to do?'

'You know what I'm going to do, D-Man. I'm going to demolish you. The death of a thousand cuts. Well, maybe just a dozen or so.'

I started to wriggle then, pulling at the pipes, trying to wrench them away from the wall. Kicking out with my tied-together legs. He just crouched there and grinned. His pupils were pinpoints of darkness. He swiped and the first cut caught me across the cheek. There was nothing for a second, then a slow sizzling sensation which kept on intensifying. I felt the blood begin to run down my face. His second slice got my upper arm, and a short jab opened my chest. I was still wrestling to get free, but it was useless. He hit my legs next, more or less cutting and stabbing at will. He wasn't frenzied. He was quite calm, quite controlled. I stopped struggling, hard though it was.

'Leo, this isn't any way to settle it.'

'It's the perfect way to settle it.'

'Christ, shoot me, but don't do *this*.'

'I'm already doing it. Slice and dice. And . . . *voilà*!' He stood back to admire his work, wiping the blade on some toilet roll. I couldn't count the number of cuts on my body.

There were over a dozen. They all hurt, but none was actually going to bleed me dry, not on its own. But all together . . . well, all together I was in deep shit. My shirt was already soaked in blood, and there was a smear of red beneath me on the tiles.

'Leo,' I said. Something in my voice made him look at me. 'Please don't do this.'

'The magic word,' Leo Hoffer said. Then he walked out of the bathroom.

'Leo! Leo!'

But he was gone. I knew that. I heard the front door close quietly. Then I saw the handcuff key. I stretched my feet towards it, but was a good ten to twelve inches shy. I slid down on to the floor, nearly taking my arms out of their sockets, and tried again, but I was still an inch or two away from it. I lay there, exhausted, pain flooding over me. Haemophiliacs don't bleed faster than other people, we just don't stop once we've started. I was a mild case, but even so there was only so much clotting my body could do for me. Leo must've known that. He knew so much about me.

'You son of a bitch!'

I sat up again and twisted the chain linking my cuffs. Every chain had its weakest link, but I wasn't going to find it, not like this. I looked up. Resting on the sink were a toothbrush and tube of toothpaste, and a small bar of soap, like something you'd lift from your hotel room. Soap: maybe I could grease my wrists and slip off the handcuffs. Except that there was no give at all in the cuffs. I've always had skinny wrists, much skinnier than my hands. No way this side of the grave was I going to be able to slip my hands out, soap or no soap.

I sat back against the wall and tried to think. I thought of a lot of things, all of them brilliant, and in the movies one of them would have worked. But this was a bathroom floor in Seattle, and all I was doing here was dying.

Then the front door opened.

'Hey!' I yelled. 'In here!'

Who did I expect to see? Bel, of course. I'd half expected she'd follow me here, once she'd got Spike to the hospital.

'In here!' I yelled again.

'I know where you are, dummy,' said Hoffer. He stood in the doorway, hands on hips. He was a big bastard, but not as big as he looked on TV. He gave me a good look, like I was a drunk cluttering up the hall of his apartment building. He was deciding whether to kick me or throw me a dime.

He threw me the dime.

Rather, he stepped on the key with the tip of his shoe and slid it closer to me.

'Hey,' he said, 'what's life without a bit of fun? Now I want you to do me a favour.'

'What?'

He was fumbling in his pocket, and eventually drew out a small camera. 'Look dead for me.'

'What?'

'Play dead. It's got to convince Walkins, so make it good. The blood looks right, but I need a slumped head, splayed legs, you know the sort of thing I mean.'

I stared at him. Was he playing with me? Hard to tell. His eyes were dark, mostly unfocused. He looked like he could burst into song or tears. He looked a bit confused.

I let my head slump against my chest. He fired off a few shots from different angles, and even clambered up on to the toilet seat to take one. The noise of the camera-motor winding on the film seemed almost laughably incongruous. Here I was bleeding like a pig while someone took snuff photos from a toilet seat.

'That's a wrap,' he said at last. 'Hey, did I tell you? Joe Draper's going to make a documentary of my life. Maybe we'll talk about my charity work, huh?'

'You're all heart, Leo.'

'Yeah, yeah.'

He turned to walk away, but then thought of something. He kept his back to me as he spoke.

'You going to come gunning for me, Mikey?'

'No,' I said, not sure if I meant it. 'I'm finished with that.' I found to my surprise that I did mean it. He glanced over his shoulder and seemed satisfied.

'Well,' he said, 'I've done some thinking about that, too. See, I could break your hand up a bit, take the fingers out of the sockets, smash the wrist. But the body has a way of repairing itself.'

'I swear, Leo, I'm not—'

'So instead of that, just in case, I'm putting contracts out on your parents. If I buy it, they buy it too.'

'There's no need for that.'

'And your friend Bel, too, same deal. My little insurance policy. It's not exactly all-claims, but it'll have to do.'

He made to walk away.

'Hoffer,' I said. He stopped. 'Same question: are you going to come gunning for me?'

'Not if you stay dead. Get a fucking day job, Mike. Stack shelves or something. Sell burgers. I'm going to tell Walkins I stiffed you. I'm hoping he'll go for it. I'm losing my best client, but this ought to help.' He patted his pocket again, where the money was. 'I may tell a few other people too.'

I smiled. 'You mean the media.'

'I've got a living to make, Mike. With you dead, I need all the publicity I can get.'

'Go ahead, Hoffer, shout it from the rooftops.'

'I'm going.'

And he went. I got the key, but even so it was hell unlocking the cuffs. How did Houdini do it? Maybe if you could dislocate your wrist or something . . . Eventually I got them off and staggered out of the bathroom, only to fall to my knees in the hallway. I was crawling towards the door when it opened again, very slowly. I saw first one foot, then the other. The feet were dressed in shitkicker cowboy boots.

'Michael!' Bel screamed. 'What happened?'

She took my head in her hands.

'Got a Band-Aid?' I asked.

29

Hoffer went back to New York with nine and a half grand in his pocket and Provost's papers in his case.

He didn't know if he'd ever do anything with those papers. They were worth something, no doubt about that. But they were dangerous too. You only had to look at the D-Man to see that.

The press were going to town on the Seattle story. Shoot-out at the home of the Disciples of Love. Hoffer could see there was a lot the authorities weren't saying. Even so, it didn't take long for the majority of the bodies to be identified as serving and ex-employees of the security services. The explanation seemed to be that Kline, an embittered ex-employee, had somehow persuaded some serving staff to work for him, and the whole lot of them were involved in some dubious way with the Disciples of Love. Sure, and the tooth fairy lives on West 53rd.

Nobody was mentioning the ten mil or the Middle East.

Hoffer didn't go to the office for a couple of days, and when he did he thought better of it after half a flight of stairs. After all, heights gave him earache. So he retreated instead to the diner across the street. The place was full of bums nursing neverending cups of coffee. They'd discovered the secret of life, and they were tired of it. A couple of them nodded at Hoffer as he went in, like he was back where he belonged.

Donna the waitress was there, and she nodded a greeting to him too, like he'd been there every day without fail. She brought him coffee and the phone, and he called up to his secretary.

'I'm down here, Moira.'

'Now there's a surprise.'

'Bring me the latest updates and paperwork, messages, mail, all that shit. We'll deal with it here, okay?' He put down the phone and ordered ham and eggs, the eggs scrambled. Outside, New York was doing its New York thing, busy with energy and excess and people just trying to get by if they couldn't get ahead.

'More coffee?'

'Thanks, Donna.'

She'd been serving him for a year, best part of, and still she never showed interest, never asked how he was doing or what he'd been doing. He'd bet she didn't even remember his name. He was just a customer who sometimes made a local call and tipped her well for the service. That was it. That was all he was.

Jesus, it was going to be hard getting by without the D-Man.

The parents, he should never have talked to the parents. They'd made the guy too real, too human. They'd stripped away all the cunning and the menace and had confronted him with photos of a gangly awkward youth with skinny arms and a lopsided grin. Photos on the beach, in the park, waving from the driving seat of Pop's car.

He should never have gone. He hadn't explained what he was doing there. He'd mumbled some explanation about their son maybe being witness to a crime, but now nobody could find him. They didn't seem to care, so long as he wasn't hurt.

No, he wasn't hurt, not much. But he'd done some damage in Washington State.

Hoffer knew the parents weren't the only reason, but they were an excusable one. He didn't really know why he hadn't killed the D-Man. Maybe he didn't want another death on his hands. He'd told Michael Weston he'd never killed anyone. That wasn't strictly true.

389

Hoffer had been killing himself for years.

The papers, of course, did not connect the D-Man to any of the stuff about Kline and Provost. Hoffer could have done that for them, but he chose not to. Instead he was biding his time. He was waiting for a lull in the news, when empty pages and screen time were screaming out to be filled. That was the time for him to step forward with his story and maybe even his photos, all about tracking down the D-Man and killing him. There was no body to show, of course, so Hoffer must've disposed of it in some way.

He'd think of something.

Meantime, he fed on the newspapers, on fresh twists about a man admitted to a local hospital with a gunshot wound. Of a mystery woman who dumped him there. Then there was Provost's luxury Seattle townhouse. How to explain the blood on the bathroom floor or the pair of metal handcuffs hanging around a water pipe?

'Better than the movies,' he said to himself, just as Donna arrived with his food.

'You say something?'

'Yeah,' said Hoffer, 'I said would you go to the movies with me some night?'

'In your dreams, sweetheart,' she said, 'in your dreams.'

Part Four

30

Not only did Spike walk out of that hospital having said nothing about how he came by his injuries, not only did he find that his bills had been taken care of, but he tracked down the authority holding on to the Trans-Am and managed to wheedle it out of them. He sent me a photo by the usual route. It showed Jazz and him leaning against the car. Scrawled over the photo were the words 'A little piece of heaven'.

Me, I claimed I was a tourist attacked by assailants who were after my traveller's cheques. Nobody really cared, they were too busy keeping an eye on the affair out on the Olympic Peninsula. Everyone had a theory. They were all far-fetched and they were all more feasible than the truth. Well, all except the one published in the *Weekly World News*.

A package arrived one day at Sam Clancy's hospital bed. It contained his walkman with a tape already inserted and ready to play. I didn't know what Sam would do with Jeremiah Provost's confession. It wasn't really my concern, not any more.

As soon as we could, Bel and I got out of the USA. Back in London, we spent a night in a hotel, then she headed back to Yorkshire. She had a lot of stuff to clear up. She wondered if I knew anyone who'd buy half a ton of unwanted weaponry.

Oh, I could think of a few people.

It was a drizzly London morning when I turned up at the offices of Crispin, Darnforth, Jessup. I shook rain out of my hair as I walked up the stairs. I knocked on the door before entering, and smiled as I approached the secretary's desk.

'Mr Johns, please.' She frowned and removed her spectacles.

'Is he expecting you?'

'I'm not sure.' She waited for me to say more, but I just stood there smiling and dripping water on to the pastel pink carpet.

'I'm afraid he can't see anyone without an appointment. He's very busy today.'

'He'll see me.' I could see my smile was beginning to irritate her. She stuck her glasses back on, pushing them up her nose.

'What name shall I give?'

'None.'

She picked up her phone and punched a number. 'Mr Johns, there's a Mr Nunn here. No, he's being very mysterious.' She looked at me. 'Well, he doesn't *look* like he's selling anything.' I shook my head in confirmation. 'Yes, sir.' She put her hand over the mouthpiece. 'If you'd like to make an appointment . . .'

I snatched the receiver from her and spoke into it.

'You know who I am. I came here before as a policeman.'

Then I slammed the receiver back into its cradle and waited, while the secretary gave me a look like I'd just tried to jump her. Johns opened the door of his office and stood there.

'Ah yes,' he said, 'do come in, won't you?'

I walked into his office and looked around. There was nobody else in there. It was just going to be the two of us.

'Take a seat, please,' he said. Then he sat down across the desk from me and put his hands together, as if in prayer. 'Yes,' he said. 'I remember you. As you say, you came here as a policeman. That, I take it, means you're not a policeman now.'

'I wasn't one then either.' It took me a little while to sit down. The bandages and plasters were tight across my body. Beneath them, the healing wounds were itching like hell.

394

Johns was nodding, as though I'd merely confirmed something. I wanted to damage his shiny face, the wealthy confidence in his eyes. He wasn't afraid of me. He'd seen worse than me before, if only in his dreams.

'I'm afraid I'm a bit in the dark,' he said.

'That makes two of us. Tell me about Mrs Ricks's death.'

'What? Again?'

'No, this time I want the truth. You weren't surprised she died, were you?'

'No.'

'Why was that?'

He pouted, his lips touching the tips of his fingers. Then he sat back in his chair, touching its sides with his arms. 'You killed her?' he said.

'Yes.' I didn't mind him knowing, not now. If he was going to be honest with me, he'd expect me to be honest too. In fact, he'd demand it.

'I see,' he said. 'In that case, I've something for you.' He stood up and went to his safe. It was a free-standing model, dark green with a brass maker's plate, like you see the bank robbers dynamite in old cowboy films. He unlocked it with a key and turned the handle. When he looked round at me, I was pointing a pistol straight at him. It didn't faze him, though last night it had fazed Scotty Shattuck when I'd relieved him of it.

'There's no need for that,' Johns said quietly. He opened the safe wide so I could see inside it. It was packed full of papers and large manila envelopes. He lifted the top envelope out and handed it to me. It didn't have a name or anything on it, and felt flimsy in my hand. I gestured for him to return to his chair, then sat myself down. I put the gun on the desktop and tore open the envelope. There were two typed sheets inside, written as a letter. The signature at the bottom read Eleanor Ricks.

I started to read.

'If you're reading this, you've done well, and you're

sitting in Geoffrey's office. Maybe you've got a gun trained on him. Maybe you intend him some harm as vengeance for what you've been through. Please, believe me when I say he doesn't know anything. I'm leaving this with him as proof of that. If you're here, you probably intend him some harm. I wouldn't like anything to happen to Geoffrey, so please read this before you do anything.

'Another reason, I suppose, is that I feel this tremendous need to get it all down, to tell someone . . . even if it has to be you. Indeed, I can think of no better figure for my confessor.

'Actually, I say Geoffrey doesn't know anything, but by now he probably knows quite a lot. I didn't tell him anything, but he's not stupid, and I needed his help, so he knows a little.

'For example, I asked him to call the police at a certain time, some minutes before I would be walking out of the hotel with Molly Prendergast. That will be the hardest thing to do, walk out of there knowing you're waiting for me. I know that when I walk out of that hotel, dressed in the colours you're expecting, I'll be trembling. But I'd rather know why I'm afraid, and know something's going to stop me being scared and angry and in pain. Rather that than the slow, internal death.

'All the same, I'll be shaking. I hope I make it out of the door. I hope I make an easy target for you. Please, I hope I didn't linger. I found out several months ago that my condition is terminal. I didn't tell anyone. I didn't want that. But I felt this flow of frustration within me, anger that there would be so many projects left unfinished . . . including this one, my present one.

'I got the idea from Scotty Shattuck. Or, rather, thinking of Scotty, I came up with the idea. If you're reading this, you've probably spoken with Scotty.'

I paused and looked up at Geoffrey Johns. He was staring out of the window. Oh, I'd spoken with Scotty. I'd done a lot more than that, too. But he was alive, and it's amazing what they can do in hospitals these days, isn't it? I started reading again.

'Scotty helped me. I knew him from assignments in the Falklands, when he was a soldier, and later in ex-Yugoslavia, when he was a mercenary. I knew I could never commit suicide, not self-assisted suicide. My will to live, you see, is strong. It's the pain I can't stand. I asked Scotty if he thought he could kill someone for money. He rambled on in his usual way, then he mentioned you. An assassin. A good one, not cheap, but a very public success. And I got the idea. Because if my assassination was spectacular and public enough, then other journalists, the media, the police, maybe even Interpol or some other international group . . . they *all* might start asking who would want me killed. And that would lead them to investigate the Disciples of Love. Maybe then they'd uncover the cult's secret, whatever it is. I *know* there's something there. I weep to think I'll never know what it is . . . unless there's a heaven.

'I'm giving this to Geoffrey with instructions to keep it safe, just in case you ever come calling on him. I wonder if you will? I mean, I'm timing things just right. The police will be contacted a few minutes before I walk out on to the steps. There's a station not far from the hotel, but I'm not sure of the protocol. Maybe the police will have to be issued with firearms, delaying their arrival. Maybe they'll suspect a hoax and not turn up at all. You may be caught, or you may escape. If you're caught, the story becomes even bigger, with more media attention. If you escape, maybe you'll be driven to wonder why and how the police were tipped off. And by whom.

'God, you could end up doing my work for me, couldn't you? It's horrible not knowing how any of this has turned out. I've planned and arranged the whole thing, and I'm the only person who won't be around to see what comes of it. I want headlines, not an obituary. I hope I got them.

'I'm telling Geoffrey to tell the police there's an assassin in the apartment block across the street from the hotel. That's where you'll be, though I know I can't possibly stipulate anything like that in my instructions to you. I've had to be careful with those, so you won't suspect me straight away. I keep thinking of the wrong turnings the media could take. Maybe they'll suspect Freddy, or an enemy from my past. I wasn't exactly kind to the Bosnian Serbs, or to the mercenaries, come to that. Not that Scotty knows that; he's never read my piece. He says he never reads. I know that, for money, he'd probably kill me himself, but I prefer the thought of your anonymity. I want a stranger to kill me, and I want somebody more competent than Scotty.

'Forgive my typing. I'm getting a bit shaky. There are tablets I can take, but they deaden everything, and with so little time left, I want life, not a numb, hazy delusion of well-being. I see everything so vividly. A single blade of grass has more beauty than any painting, but any painting can make me weep.

'I hope my timing is right. I'm afraid the police may arrive too early and scare you off. I must wind my watch. These days, I often let it run down. But I'm determined that on my last day, everything will run the way *I* want it to run. I'll be in charge. I wonder if I have the power to stop you killing afterwards? I mean, maybe you'll be so shaken up that you'll retire. That would be good. I'd be saving lives and sacrificing none. Tell Geoffrey I'll miss him. Bless him, he always loved me.'

There was a signature, nothing more.

I looked up at the solicitor.

'She left two envelopes,' he confirmed. 'The first one was to be opened the day she . . . died. I opened it at the time stated, and it said to call the police anonymously and tell them a murder was taking place outside the Craigmead Hotel. I'd to put the other envelope in the safe until someone came for it.' There were tears in Johns's eyes. 'I phoned the police, but then I phoned the Craigmead and had Eleanor paged. They paged her, but she never came to the desk. She just walked outside, ignoring the call, and was shot.'

'She set the whole thing up herself,' I said. I'd known as much since last night, when Shattuck had admitted it. He'd known who was hiring me, but not that she was her own target. When he heard the news, he fled. Up until last night, he'd thought I killed the wrong person. But I'd put him right on that.

Who'd known what Eleanor Ricks would wear that day? No one but herself.

Geoffrey Johns was blowing his nose. Then he got up and walked over to a cupboard, where he found a bottle of whisky and two glasses. He stood with his back to me, pouring.

'She said I'd know you when you came ... I'd know to give you the envelope. Tell me, please, why did she do it?'

By the time he turned round again, I'd already left the room. I took her confession with me. I didn't owe Johns anything. The only debts I owed were to the dead.

The village was one of those Hollywood-style affairs, by which I mean it was so quintessentially English that you suspected it had to be fake.

Certainly the people seemed fake, like actors playing their given roles, be it bumpkin or squire or commuter. Everyone in the hotel bar was called George or Gerry or Arthur, a few of them wore cravats, and they drank from pewter tankards. The bar had wooden beams painted black. They looked like plastic, but weren't.

Bel loved it. Our room was all Laura Ashley, picked from a brochure or magazine feature and copied exactly. The bed was a new brass four-poster with a flower-print canopy. The walls boasted hand-painted wallpaper, so the manageress told us. It's just as well she mentioned it, for you'd never have guessed otherwise. It looked like wallpaper, and very plain wallpaper at that. It wasn't even signed.

I had to smile when the first thing Bel did in the room was switch on the TV. She lay on the bed with the remote, picking complimentary grapes out of a bowl and popping them into her mouth.

'Look at that,' she said.

She'd found the CNN news. Two East European nation-states were on a war footing.

'Looks like my phone call didn't do much good,' I said.

I was on my best behaviour throughout. I didn't complain. I was compliant, agreeing with everything Bel said. I've said before, I'm very good at looking like I fit in, like I'm normal, just like you are, standing at your bar with your tankard, or walking your dog around the golf course, or choosing yourself a new sweater or shirt. I can do all those things and show nothing but contentment.

It's an act, that's all.

Hoffer's a good actor too. He believes his role. He's all method. I get the feeling we'll meet up again, whether we like it or not. We're not two sides of the same coin; we're the *same* side of the same coin.

Not that Bel suspects any of this. She thinks it's all over. She thinks we came here for a lovers' weekend, a break from the past. From this day on, we'd be starting anew, putting the horror behind us. At lunch and dinner, I held her hand across the table and exerted the gentlest pressure. The light in her eyes was pure and radiant, almost unbearable in intensity. I kept swallowing back words, images, sentiments. I kept true to myself in the realm of thought.

We walked around the village. There wasn't much to it. Narrow streets, sloping up from the main thoroughfare on both sides. A train station, shops, five pubs, the one hotel, a churchyard with rose bushes all around it. Nobody poor seemed to live here. Bel didn't know that when I stopped to admire a particular house, I had an ulterior motive.

It was a large detached property with a low front wall and a well-tended garden. There was a gravel driveway, and a Volvo estate parked by the front entrance.

Bel squeezed my arm. 'Is this the sort of place you want to live?'

I thought about it. I wanted a penthouse in Manhattan, so I could look down on an entire city, like holding it in my open hand.

'Maybe,' I said.

There was a nameplate by the garden gate, but I deflected Bel's attention by pointing to some trees across the road. Maybe she wouldn't have noticed the name anyway, not that Ricks is *such* a common name.

They were Eleanor Ricks's parents.

This was where she'd been born. Just over forty years ago. I'd read that much in the papers. Her parents had been eloquent after her murder. They weren't in favour of the death penalty, even for terrorists. That was big of them.

Bel and I made love that night under our canopy. The room was costing £85 a day, including Full English Breakfast. My reserves were pretty low. Soon, I'd have to raid my Swiss account. Bel had posed the question of jobs. She thought she could get work as a secretary or something. And maybe I could . . . well, there'd be something I could do.

Sell burgers maybe, or stack supermarket shelves, like Hoffer had suggested.

We made love, as I say, and she went to sleep. I got dressed again and went down the stairs. The bar was still busy with Saturday night spenders, but nobody saw me as I passed into the night.

I walked through the village. Even at night it was picturesque, all hanging baskets and tile roofs, distant hills and low stone walls.

The walls around the cemetery were high though. The Real England had no place for death. Even so, I was coming here to pay my respects. The gate was unlocked, so I pushed it open. The wrought iron swung open in silence.

It didn't take me long to find what I was looking for. There were still fresh flowers on Eleanor Ricks's grave. I stood there for a while, shuffling my feet, hands deep in my pockets. I wasn't really thinking anything. After about five minutes, I left the cemetery again.

Her parents' place was just up the hill.

Acknowledgements

I'd like to thank The Haemophilia Society, and especially Alan Weir, for help with details of some aspects of haemophilia. Those who require more information should write to: The Haemophilia Society, 123 Westminster Bridge Road, London SE1 7HR. Thanks also to David in Edinburgh, Andrew Puckett, and my wife Miranda for helping with research.

Gerald Hammond was knowledgeable as ever about firearms, and I should also thank the Estacado Gun Club for taking me along on a shoot. In fact, so many people in the USA helped with this book that it would take a sizeable supplement to list them all. So a general thank you must suffice. But special honours must go to Becky Hughes and David Martin in Seattle, Jay Schulman in Arlington, Mass., and Tresa Hughes in New York, for putting up with me, Miranda and our son Jack for so long.

The Chandler-Fulbright Award made it possible for me to spend so much time (and money) in the United States. I owe a debt to the estate of Raymond Chandler and to the staff of the Fulbright Commission in London, especially Catherine Boyle.

The real unsung heroes of this book are probably Elliott Abrams and Fawn Hall. For those who don't know who they are, a two-part essay by Theodore Draper in the *New York Review of Books* serves as a good introduction, though you've really got to go to Draper's book *A Very Thin Line: The Iran-Contra Affairs* or to the full Congressional Hearings to get the bigger picture. I quote from part one of the essay, published in the edition of 27 May 1993:

Unfortunately, Abrams didn't know how to set up a secret account in which to deposit the expected $10 million from Brunei [with which to fund the Contras]. He went to Alan Fiers of the CIA and Oliver North of the NSC staff for tutoring, and chose to follow North's advice. North gave him an index card with the number of a secret Swiss account, which North controlled; North's secretary, Fawn Hall, accidentally transposed two digits in typing out the number on another card; Abrams gave the erroneous information to the Brunei foreign minister; and $10 million went into the account of a stranger from whom it took months to get it back.

available from

THE ORION PUBLISHING GROUP

☐ **Black & Blue** £5.99
IAN RANKIN
0 75280 948 2

☐ **The Black Book** £5.99
IAN RANKIN
1 85797 413 1

☐ **Bleeding Hearts** £5.99
IAN RANKIN
0 75284 332 X

☐ **Dead Souls** £5.99
IAN RANKIN
0 75282 684 0

☐ **The Hanging Garden** £5.99
IAN RANKIN
0 75281 711 6

☐ **Hide & Seek** £5.99
IAN RANKIN
0 75280 941 5

☐ **Knots & Crosses** £5.99
IAN RANKIN
0 75280 942 3

☐ **Let It Bleed** £5.99
IAN RANKIN
0 75280 401 4

☐ **Mortal Causes** £5.99
IAN RANKIN
1 85797 863 3

☐ **Set in Darkness** £5.99
IAN RANKIN
0 75283 708 7

☐ **Strip Jack** £5.99
IAN RANKIN
0 75280 956 3

☐ **Tooth & Nail** £5.99
(previously published as *Wolfman*)
IAN RANKIN
0 75280 940 7

☐ **Witch Hunt** £5.99
IAN RANKIN (writing as Jack
Harvey)
0 75284 289 7

All Orion/Phoenix titles are available at your local bookshop or from the following address:

Mail Order Department
Littlehampton Book Services
FREEPOST BR535
Worthing, West Sussex, BN13 3BR
telephone 01903 828503, *facsimile* 01903 828802
e-mail MailOrders@lbsltd.co.uk
(Please ensure that you include full postal address details)

Payment can be made either by credit/debit card (Visa, Mastercard, Access and Switch accepted) or by sending a £ Sterling cheque or postal order made payable to *Littlehampton Book Services*.
DO NOT SEND CASH OR CURRENCY.

Please add the following to cover postage and packing

UK and BFPO:
£1.50 for the first book, and 50p for each additional book to a maximum of £3.50

Overseas and Eire:
£2.50 for the first book plus £1.00 for the second book and 50p for each additional book ordered

BLOCK CAPITALS PLEASE

name of cardholder ....

address of cardholder ....

delivery address
(if different from cardholder)

postcode ....   *postcode* ....

☐ I enclose my remittance for £........................

☐ please debit my Mastercard/Visa/Access/Switch (delete as appropriate)

card number ☐☐☐☐☐☐☐☐☐☐☐☐☐☐☐☐☐☐

expiry date ☐☐☐☐   Switch issue no. ☐☐

signature ....

prices and availability are subject to change without notice

H 6195

6-36 Colosseum AD